ENEMIES OF DOVES

SHANESSA GLUHM

Relax. Read. Repeat.

ENEMIES OF DOVES
By Shanessa Gluhm
Published by TouchPoint Press
Brookland, AR 72417
www.touchpointpress.com

ISBN-13: 978-1-946920-91-1

Editor: Kimberly Coghlan
Cover Design: Dimitar Stanchev

Visit the author's Facebook page at
Facebook.com/authorshanessagluhm

First Edition

Printed in the United States of America.

For my grandma, Rosie Brannan, a first reader and editor of this book. I love you.

And for my Pops, Floyd Brannan. If there is a way to get a bootleg copy of this in heaven, I know you will find it. I miss you.

CHAPTER 1

Carthage, Texas, 1932

Joel woke up to a white world: white walls, white sheets, a white pitcher of water, and a stranger wearing white. White like Mama's favorite flowers, white like the coat Daddy wore to work, white like the doves that…

No, don't think about doves. Don't think about doves ever again.

The white was better than his last memory: black. Ravenous black. It had swallowed everything.

Harsh light speared into the room, painting sharp rectangles on the linoleum floor. Joel blinked involuntarily. The lady in the white uniform noticed. "He's awake!" she called. "Mrs. Fitchett, he's awake!"

Mama and Daddy charged in, talking at the same time, asking the same questions.

"I'm okay," Joel said.

Mama's hands hovered a few seconds before settling on his arm. "I'm sorry we weren't here. I told your daddy we shouldn't both leave but—"

"Are you in pain, son?" Daddy rarely let Mama finish a sentence.

"My stomach hurts." Joel didn't recognize the sound of his own voice, so small and croaky.

"Nurse! Bring this boy something for the pain," Daddy yelled.

"A magnesia tablet." Mama put her freezing hand on his forehead. "He might have a fever too."

The nurse let out a noisy breath. She didn't bother with his temperature, but the two bone-white pills she handed Joel appeased his parents, got them quiet at least. Joel raised his head, sweat-soaked hair sticking to his forehead. Or was it blood? He touched the bandage covering his face and winced. The details of the night before seeped into his mind. He could think of nothing that wasn't contaminated by this memory.

The pills tasted like chalk and made his throat burn. "Can I have some water?" Before anyone responded, two taps at the door drew their attention away from him, away from that perfect pitcher of water.

Mama rubbed her forehead. "Can't we go ten minutes without a knock on the damn door?" Joel knew Mama must be upset to use a word like that. Nancy Fitchett taught Sunday School and had taken soap to Joel's mouth for less.

"Oh, for god's sake!" Daddy threw up his hands. "He just woke up. Give us a minute with our boy."

Two figures stepped through the door. A cigarette hung immobile in the mouth of the stubby police officer in front. "I understand, Mr. Fitchett, but the more time that goes by, the more victims forget. It's vital we speak now."

Forget? Joel knew better. He couldn't forget, not till heaven anyway, and at twelve, heaven was a long wait.

The other officer stepped from the shadows. Like Dick Tracy, he wore a black suit and fedora instead of a uniform. He looked at Joel like he already knew the truth or could figure it out in the same effortless way Detective Tracy did in the comics. "Truth is," —he reached into the hallway and pulled Clancy into the room — "we can't get any information from this one. We hope your other boy will be more cooperative."

Joel's head sank into the pillow. So, Clancy hadn't told. Even now, he only wanted to protect his little brother. Poor kid looked scared out of his skin.

"You all right, Joel?" Clancy's voice shook.

"Don't you worry about me, Clancy. I'm as right as rain, good as gold."

"Nice as nectarines," Clancy said. They often played this game, but Joel couldn't think of another simile, so he offered a smile instead. It hurt like hell, but he wanted to assure Clancy he was okay. Joel was only a year and a half older, but the gap felt wider. Joel had always been mature for his age; everybody said so.

"I have nothing to say, sir," Joel told Dick Tracy. His voice was still high pitched, but he tried to make it boom like Daddy's. Tom Fitchett had a way of making people listen when he talked.

"And why's that?" The tiny officer lit his cigarette.

"I don't remember what happened." The bed gave a muffled creak as he adjusted his position.

The detective looked at his partner. "Get Clancy out of here, will you? And the folks too."

"We won't leave." Daddy pushed his shoulders back.

"Have it your way. Look here, Joel; we know who did this to you."

The words made Joel forget his stinging face and terrible thirst. He watched a cockroach scuttle into a floor crack. Did they know? No one was around for miles. He was bluffing.

"Then go arrest the bastard," his father said. "Don't waste time traumatizing injured and frightened boys."

Had Joel heard Daddy right? Had he demanded these important men, *lawmen*, stop traumatizing his boys? Something he did for sport? How strange to have Daddy in his corner for once.

"You may reconsider your statement when you learn who hurt the boy."

"Impossible!" Daddy slammed his hand on Joel's tray and knocked over the pitcher of water. Mama grabbed a towel and sopped it up. Even in crisis, her instinct to clean up Daddy's messes took over. "Who did this?!" Daddy yelled.

Joel cringed, but at least this time his father's fury flew at somebody else. Joel took a few deep breaths. Maybe if he stayed calm, everyone else would calm down too.

"It was him." The officer stuck his finger in Clancy's face.

Mama clutched him tightly, her arms a shield against the accusation.

The detective knelt in front of Clancy. "You did this. The only question I have is why?"

The room spun again. Joel looked for an anchor, but the patterns on the linoleum played leapfrog, and the walls closed in. His parent's gasps faded into the white surrounding him, and once again, the world went black.

CHAPTER 2

Gib Lewis Unit, 1991

Garrison wiped beads of sweat on the sleeve of his new suit. Why had he chosen it on a day as hot and as nerve-inducing as today? To look like he was more than a nobody college kid? He regretted it, just as he regretted applying for a contact visit. This would be easier behind a glass partition. But how could he gain a man's trust without shaking his hand? And he *had* to gain his trust. There was no other way.

"Right this way," the guard said. "Fitchett's waiting. He's nicer than he looks but still the meanest sonofabitch in here." A final gate slammed behind Garrison, a buzzer sounded, and the door to the visitation room slid open.

The odors of sweat and metal greeted him first, followed by the cloying fragrance of musk body spritz. The room was packed with tables, the tables packed with visitors. So many voices, so many faces, but it was all white noise and blurred features. Only Joel Fitchett came into focus.

Garrison concentrated on Joel's shaved head and massive biceps. Anything to avoid the scar.

"Hello, Mr. Fitchett." He extended his hand. "I'm Garrison Stark."

"I know who you are. Did you deposit the cash?"

"Yes, two hundred dollars."

"All right. Sit." Joel's voice sounded different than Garrison imagined it. It wasn't gruff or threatening, just normal. Too normal for a killer.

Garrison followed Joel's lead and sat. So much for shaking hands.

Joel looked up at the guard. "That will be all for now, Jeeves."

"I'll be on the wall, Mr. Stark," the guard told Garrison. He patted his gun. "Call if you need to, *when* you need to."

4

Garrison cleared his throat. "If you don't mind me asking, why do you need money in here?"

"For the canteen."

"The what?"

Joel sighed. "Think prison 7-Eleven."

"Oh yeah?" Garrison imagined prisoners sitting in a cell, doing push-ups, and carving into walls, never shopping. "What do you buy?"

Pulling out a pack of Camels, Joel motioned for a guard. "Well, I sure as hell don't spend it on ramen noodles and stamps." Smoke was a trigger for Garrison's asthma, but he would hold his breath. Two hundred dollars and a nagging cough weren't too steep a price for this opportunity.

Joel relaxed in his chair. "So, Gary, is that what brings you here? Curious about the fascinating world of the prison economy?"

Garrison winced. No one had called him Gary since his mom died last fall. "It's Garrison, actually. May I call you Joel?"

"Say what you came for, *Garrison*. Your letter said you aren't a reporter and your reasons for the visit are personal. I've nearly died from curiosity."

A cloud of smoke encircled Garrison. He fanned it away. "I'm here about Clancy."

"Clancy?" Joel shot up like the back of his seat caught fire. "What do you know about Clancy?"

"Not much." Garrison choked back a cough. "That's why I'm here."

"Why do you care about my brother?" Joel took another drag and slumped further down in his seat.

Garrison scraped his hand through his hair. "I think Clancy Fitchett is my grandfather."

Joel burst out laughing.

"I don't understand what's funny."

"Lighten up, college boy. Your grandma, what's her name?"

"Maiden name was Dorothy Ellison."

Joel tapped the table. "Don't ring a bell. Sorry you came for nothing, but hey, thanks for the money."

"Everyone called her Dolly." Garrison raised an old photo of his grandmother.

Joel barely glanced up. "Dolly Ellison... Dolly Ellison. Still nothing."

Garrison lowered the picture. "I didn't figure you would remember, but I'm sure Clancy will."

"Clancy and I, we shared a lot back then. I'd remember if he had a kid."

"He might not have known. My mom was born in 1942. Clancy joined the war that year. It was one of the few facts about him I found in public records. That, and his marriage to a woman named Lorraine in 1946."

The mention of her name changed the shape of Joel's face. Garrison couldn't tell if he wanted to smile, cry, scream, or reach across the table and kill him. The scar camouflaged emotion.

"I don't remember a Dorothy Ellison or no Dolly Ellison either. So, if that's why you came, you can scat."

Garrison planted his feet. "Do you talk to Clancy?"

"You betcha, Gary. We meet weekly for lattes. Discuss our illegitimate children and the like."

"I meant, maybe you got a Christmas card? A deposit into your account? Anything? I've looked but can't find any information on them, not even a phone number. It's difficult being a ghost nowadays, but they've managed it."

"Sounds like they don't wanna be found."

"I don't care what they want. Clancy owes me an explanation, one my mom never got. Everybody deserves to understand where they came from; everyone deserves a family." Garrison regretted saying that. It sounded like a line from an after-school special. Worse, it sounded vulnerable, but he *was* vulnerable. The seed planted that snowy February evening when Grandma Dolly let her secret slip had grown into an obsession. He realized she wasn't herself anymore. Outlandish stories were the norm now. But what if this claim about Clancy were true?

"You kids today don't understand life." Veins in Joel's neck throbbed. "Think it owes you something; think you deserve this and that. Makes me sick. Here's a lesson they won't teach you at that fancy college of yours. Life ain't a fair boss. It don't always hand you the paycheck you earned."

"Looks like it did you." Garrison's foot jittered across the floor. "My search for Clancy might have come up short, but I know about you."

Joel smirked, "Such as?"

"I know who you killed."

Joel leaned back, resting his hands behind his head. "Who doesn't?"

"This is the third prison you've been in. You're always looking for a fight, and they are easy to find in a place like this. You've settled down the past five years. No more fights, less trouble with the guards. I assume that's due more to the lack of agility than desire, but it doesn't matter. Good behavior or not, you aren't getting out."

"Sounds like you've got me figured out. Did the crime, doing the time. Thanks again for stopping by."

"What about the scar?" Garrison stared at the diagonal line across Joel's face. "Was life fair when it dished that out?" He hadn't planned on bringing up the scar, but Garrison didn't regret asking. Joel Fitchett needed the cockiness knocked out of him.

Joel surged out of his seat and around the table. While Garrison's heart ricocheted against his ribcage, the rest of his body froze. He felt his chair tip back and then Joel's hands tight around his neck. Pressure built in Garrison's head; every vein bloated. He kicked his legs, dug his fingernails into Joel's arms, but his grasp was unrelenting. He felt like he was dying, drowning on this cold, concrete floor.

It took the strength of two guards to break Joel's python grip. Garrison backed up, gasping for air. He had been wrong about the lack of agility. For a seventy-one-year-old, Joel surprisingly still had enough strength, speed, and anger.

"Hit the road, kid," a guard said as a crowd gathered.

"And don't cha come back no more," Joel sang, fighting the guards like a fish caught on a line.

Garrison turned to leave, but this was not the end. Finding Clancy was his last chance. Joel could sing his warning all he wanted, but Garrison would be back.

CHAPTER 3

Longview, Texas, 1941

Clancy Fitchett had plenty to worry about. Mr. Rogers threatened to fire him again. He owed money to Crawl, and Crawl had friends. The kind of friends Clancy should fear. Besides that, it was the first of the month. Rent was due. Then there was the girl. There was always a girl, wasn't there? And girls caused more trouble than work or money ever did. "Marry me," she'd said. Said it like she was asking him to the movie or a dance. It was a ridiculous request, even if her daddy's job was moving them across the country. It had only been a few weeks. Clancy liked her well enough to miss her when she left—but not enough to marry her.

He tipped his head back, warming his face in the glorious sun. He was his own man, and today belonged to him. Sure, it was Sunday. That meant dinner with Daddy. He'd try to make it tonight; he would. He'd already missed church. "Sorry Mama," he said to the sky. "I'll go next week." He hadn't promised her he'd go *every* week.

Clancy tapped his coke bottle against the porch railing, and the lid popped off. Nothing like that burn in the back of his throat that only a first sip brought. People worried too much. What was there to fuss over on a day this warm? With a Coca-Cola this cold? After a wintery two weeks, he welcomed a warm Sunday in November. Berry red and honeydew gold leaves periodically dropped from the oak tree shading the yard. Clancy watched them dance in the morning light that seemed to make everything clearer and brighter.

No, nothing could spoil today. He had a carton of Coca-Colas, a pack of smokes, and a Cornell Woolrich thriller. This wasn't the first time Mr. Rogers threatened to sack him. He hadn't done it yet; he wouldn't do it now. And money was just money. There was always a way to get more. He'd been late paying

Crawl before and still had full use of both his kneecaps. And so what if they missed rent once? He and Joel did so much work on Daddy's other rentals, they'd surely earned a free month. Not like the old man needed the money, no matter what he claimed. His dental practice thrived and always had. Daddy had only given his family hell over every dime because he wanted to hoard it for himself. Greedy ole codger. And the gal, she'd be just fine. She was date bait here and would be in Oklahoma or Ohio or wherever her daddy was taking her. See, nothing to worry about.

Clancy's mood and stomach fell when he spotted a pair of doves a few feet in front of him. He reached his toes down to stop the swing. "Get out of here, both of you." The doves lifted their heads to look at him then pecked the dead grass. Mocking him. He picked up a rock and rubbed its smooth surface. "Get out of here," he said again. When the doves didn't move, Clancy chucked the rock right between them. That did the trick. He grabbed another, just in case.

Clancy started the swing again, tried to recapture the peace he'd lost, but the fall leaves were washed out by the sun's intense, harsh light, and the sharp edges of the rock he gripped cut into his hand. He took another sip from his bottle, but it was already warm. Two doves and a flat Coca-Cola. Maybe it was going to be a bad day after all.

***

Joel never minded his Sunday drive, but today's was different. It wasn't dinner with his daddy he dreaded; it was the stop before that made him sweat. He promised he was done with this. Crawl was dangerous. If Clancy continued to place bets, that was on him. Yet, Joel could tell by the late night phone calls that Clancy owed him more than usual this time. This was serious. Too serious to ignore.

How did anybody lose as much as Clancy did? If it wasn't cards, it was picking the wrong boxer or baseball team. Why did he continue something he was so bad at? Maybe it was an addiction, like Crawl's amphetamine habit. It didn't matter. It would end today.

Joel needed a shower the minute he crossed the border to Louisiana. If the humidity didn't drown him, his own sweat would. The Pelican State bordered Texas, but it seemed like an entirely new world. The black-trunked trees grew taller, darkening twisted roads. Alligators and insects swarmed the deep swamps, equally eager to make a meal out of him. The people were a different breed too.

All the talk about voodoo and swamp monsters gave Joel the creeps. But God willing, this would be his last trip here. God and Crawl willing.

Crawl lived in a small, neglected house, but it came with privacy and a lakefront view. The scummy lake proved convenient for Crawl. Both for pulling fish out and pushing bodies in. That was the local legend anyhow. But Joel suspected a search under that floating algae would sooner reveal decaying bodies than swamp monsters.

The ground to Crawl's door sank beneath Joel's feet like wet sponges. Wind chimes clanged against a crooked horseshoe nailed over the porch steps. A similar one hovered above the door. Joel stopped short of knocking, fear twisting in his gut. Why couldn't Clancy have found someone else to make bets with? Someone with a regular job, regular home, regular name?

The warped door scraped open before he knocked. Joel recognized the man who answered. He had a look hard to forget. The missing eye and leathery skin weren't as memorable as his Herculean build. He was a character who belonged in an Old Testament story—or at the top of a beanstalk.

"Hello." Joel swayed on his feet. "Crawl around?"

"Who's asking?"

"Joel Fitchett. I'm here about my brother, Clancy."

The man's expression softened. "Say no more. I remember you now. Come in and take a seat."

Joel sank into a springless couch and sniffed the air. The smell wasn't unpleasant, but he couldn't place it. He glanced around. What a strange feeling to be the most normal one in a room. Several men had extravagant tattoos, and others had scars worse than Joel's. One was missing an arm. What about Crawl drew in misfits?

Joel heard a whistle and turned around.

"Only conceited boys turn when someone whistles." A woman spoke with a cigarette between her crooked and rotting teeth. Joel always noticed teeth, the price of being a dentist's son. "But don't worry, sweetheart," she said. "I don't mind a big head or a big anything else."

Joel's face burned as the room erupted in laughter. Somehow, he still managed to be the main attraction in this sideshow.

"Leave him alone, Doris." The giant of a man had returned. "Crawl said come on back."

The smell grew stronger the closer they got to Crawl. A strange mix of garlic, lemons, and a just-blown-out match. Joel spotted another horseshoe above Crawl's door.

Crawl rose and greeted Joel. "Look what the cat drug in." Crawl's steel blue eyes were red-rimmed, and he wore a few days growth of a beard. Rumor had it, Crawl rarely slept. But that didn't make him some god like people claimed. It more than likely meant he was a man with a lot to lose sleep over. "What brings you here?" Crawl spoke deliberately, his enunciation of each syllable impeccable.

Joel wiped his forehead with a handkerchief. He pointed at the chair on the other side of Crawl's desk. "Mind if I sit?"

"Not at all. Cyril, crack open a window. Let the fresh air in." Crawl sat behind his desk. "I hope you don't mind, but my friend, Cyril, is joining us."

Joel fell into the chair. If he minded the one-eyed giant's presence, he wasn't going to say so.

A Joe DiMaggio poster hung behind Crawl. Besides the horseshoes, it was the only decoration in the house. "Baseball fan?" Joel asked.

Crawl smiled, unearthing a single dimple. "I'm a follower of all sports."

Joel slumped back in his chair. What a stupid question. Of course Crawl followed sports; it was how he made his living. Sports and cocaine, or so Joel had been told.

"I'm a fan of Joan Crawford and fishing," Crawl explained. "Not much else."

"And money," Cyril said.

"That too." Crawl stretched a pack of Pall Malls towards Joel.

"No, thanks."

Crawl shrugged. "More for me."

"Are the horseshoes for good luck? With the bets?"

Crawl lit his cigarette. "Keeps the witches out."

"Witches?"

"Yes, witches. Something funny, Fitchett?"

Joel squirmed in his chair. "No. I noticed several of them and was curious."

"We can never be too careful, can we?"

This wasn't going well. Small talk with Crawl was useless. He needed to get to the point. "I'm here to pay Clancy's debt."

Crawl flicked ash into the tray in front of him. "Where is that precious brother of yours?"

"Home, I guess."

"So he passed the buck to you again? Can't say I'm surprised."

"He doesn't even know I'm here."

"No fooling?" Crawl set his cigarette down and used a rubber band from his desk to pull his blonde hair back. "I don't guess I'll ever understand brotherly love, but whatever pays the bills, right? I believe his tally is one-hundred-fifty."

It was roughly three weeks' pay but less than Joel expected. He set two bills on the desk.

"You knew you'd get paid today, didn't you, boss?" Cyril asked.

"Well, my palms were itching." Crawl scribbled into a black ledger. "Put that in the safe." He turned his attention to Joel. "Feel free to go on now."

Joel kept his wallet on the table. "I was hoping to make a gentleman's agreement."

"I wasn't aware men who weren't gentlemen could make such an agreement." Crawl resumed with his cigarette. "I'm speaking of myself, of course."

"How much would it take for you to end all your dealings with my brother?"

Crawl raised his eyebrows. "Is it me you take issue with or gambling?"

"Gambling." Joel wasn't surprised at how easy lying came anymore.

"I hate to break it to you, but plenty of others would be glad to take Clancy's barely-earned money. So, this agreement you desire won't iron out what troubles you."

Joel opened his wallet. "How much?"

"Didn't you listen to anything I said?"

"How much?" Joel asked louder.

"More than you got, pal."

"Five hundred?"

"I wish I could, but—"

"A thousand." It was all Joel had. A savings he'd been building his whole life. He held the ten bills between his sweaty fingers.

Crawl snapped his pencil in two. "I was happy to see you, but now you're getting under my skin." He stood and leaned over Joel. "I know I've got a bad rap around these parts. Folks say I lose my temper, and I sometimes do. But only when I'm not paid or not heard. Clancy doesn't pay; you don't hear. So, hang it up already. Take that money and buy liquor or a lady. Something to take the edge off."

Joel hooked his feet around the chair legs. "I'm not leaving." He braced himself for a punch, but a crash of thunder granted him a reprieve.

Crawl turned and pushed the window shut. "Cyril!" he yelled. "Close the windows and check the sills for acorns."

Cyril peeked his head into the room. "Acorns, boss?"

Crawl pointed to the one by his window. "Yes, dammit! Acorns. I've told you it's the only way to keep lightning out. And Cyril"— Crawl's voice calmed —" find something to keep this one out while you're at it."

Cyril lifted Joel and pulled him towards the door.

"I don't understand. One thousand dollars. It's more than Clancy makes in a year."

Crawl raised his hand, signaling for Cyril to stop. "That's what separates folks like me from folks like you. You're looking at *right now*. I consider tomorrow. I think about Clancy's lifetime and how much more I can get than what you've brought today."

Joel's pulse slammed into his neck. "I'll tell Clancy you said that. I'll make sure he never comes back to see you!"

Crawl laughed so hard he choked. "He'll come back," he finally managed. "He'll always come back because you see, Clancy's not a bad man—just has a weakness for bad men. Men like us."

Joel recoiled. "Like us? I'm nothing like you."

"But you are. I have a gift, some say."

"A gift of ripping off desperate people?"

"Nah, not that gift. A different one. A gift for seeing inside people; it's somewhat magic. It's part of how I can heal."

"Heal?"

Crawl stepped forward till they were nose to nose. Joel felt the hot breath of Cyril down his neck as wind chimes clanged relentlessly outside. The rain was louder now. Joel wanted to back away, at least look away, but he couldn't let his fear show. Crawl fed on fear.

"I see inside you, Joel Fitchett." Crawl made no move to separate from Joel as he spoke. "You try to be good, but you aren't. Good men wouldn't do the things you've done. Wouldn't shore up so many secrets. You are doing an all right job of pushing the wicked down, but you can't forever. It will rise. Rise quicker than a thermostat in July."

Joel pressed his elbows into his side, making himself small. Had Crawl seen something? Cyril's fingers dug deeper into his skin. The room seemed charged. As Joel lost his footing, a bright flash of lightning outside caught his eye. It steadied him somehow. Brought back reason. Crawl saw nothing, knew nothing. He was like one of those ten-cent palm readers whose vague fortunes could apply to anybody. Joel wasn't bad. He did something bad. Once. That was all.

He shook his arm free. "You're delusional." Cyril grabbed him again and mumbled something, but Joel only heard a barrage of thunder.

"That's close." Crawl looked outside. "You checked the windowsills?"

"Gordy's taking care of it."

Something still wasn't right. Joel's skin tingled, and the hair on his arms rose. Cyril must have noticed it too because he let go of Joel's arm and hit the ground, covering his ears. A blazing light flashed outside. Gold and purple sparks erupted from a nearby tree, and its branches exploded in every direction. The thunder was almost simultaneous, a crack so loud, Joel shrieked in pain.

"Boom!" Crawl echoed, hands triumphant in the air. "Look at you two, cowering and crying. Don't you understand that lightning recharges the earth?" If Crawl was tired before, it didn't show now. His eyes became wide and bright.

"Kills folks too." Cyril stood, rubbing his ears.

Joel stared out the window where the tree once stood. "It just missed us."

Crawl picked up the acorn and smiled. "Bye now," he said without turning back to Joel.

***

"He's not coming, Daddy. He would have been here by now." Joel checked his watch. Forty-five long minutes had passed since he'd arrived in Carthage. He'd already talked about the sports scores he'd brushed up on, the weather, and cars. He couldn't keep this up much longer, especially when he needed to get home and talk to Clancy.

"You know, it wouldn't kill you to drive your brother here now and then. His truck isn't as reliable as yours. And fuel isn't cheap. What's so damn hard about driving him here?"

Joel shifted in his seat. What was *so damn hard* was Clancy was never around. Joel had offered and more than once. But he choked the words back. No need to start a fight or hurt any feelings. "I'll ask him next time. He wasn't home tonight."

"Oh." Daddy rearranged his silverware. "Well, he's been busy. Told me he's been cleaning the shop with Earl on weekends, helping with the books too."

"Is that so?" Joel didn't know which was worse, Clancy's lies or Daddy's trust in someone who had done so little to earn it. Tom Fitchett had dispensed his wrath on both boys growing up, but Clancy was on a pedestal now.

For the next ten minutes, the only sounds were the fire's crackle and the clink of Daddy's beer bottle against the table each time he slammed it down. Joel was relieved when his father went for another beer and returned with the stew.

"How are things at the office?" Joel slurped his first bite. It was still hot, but he didn't care. As soon as it was gone, he could be too.

"Been better. Fired that gal I hired as a secretary." Daddy downed his second drink. "Caught her stealing."

"Did you report it?"

"Nah, it wasn't much. A couple hundred. She's not a bad girl, just a girl down on her luck."

Joel shoveled more thick stew into his mouth. Hard to believe this same man beat Clancy with a belt for stealing a piece of bubble gum when he was five. Maybe he'd relaxed in his old age. Or maybe he was sleeping with the secretary. That seemed more likely. He'd had a hard enough time staying faithful when Mama was alive.

"Say, Joel, have you given any thought to what we talked about?"

Joel stiffened. He thought he'd wrapped up this conversation last week, but Daddy must have been too drunk to remember. "I'm happy where I am. I wouldn't make a good dentist."

"Someone has to take over the practice when I'm gone. I'd pay for the schooling, train you. It's good money."

Joel pushed the stew around and avoided his father's eyes. "I appreciate the offer, but I'm doing what I love. You taught me how to fix cars."

"As a hobby, not a job. Now look, I won't keep asking. You are the oldest, and you did the best in school; that's why you get first choice. But this offer doesn't stand forever. I'll give you one more week to decide before I offer it to Clancy."

Considering they had to bribe Clancy to even finish high school, Joel knew his daddy would either sell his business or it would die with him. Joel felt no guilt. He didn't take pride in much, but he was good at what he did.

"How will you ever support a family if you are content to work for someone else?"

Joel crossed his arms over his chest. They both knew Joel would never have a family, not as long as he had the scar. While Daddy droned on, Joel allowed his mind to wander. What would his life be like without the scar? It had never occurred to him before, but with the right money and the right doctor, there must be a way to get rid of it. Surgery maybe? He was only twenty-one; there was plenty of time to change his life. And maybe it was good Crawl hadn't taken his money. Because those one hundred-dollar bills might make it all possible.

CHAPTER 4

Woodville, Texas, 1991

It was with little expectation that Garrison sat in front of the microfilm reader at Allan Shivers Library. Clancy wasn't from Woodville, so a mention in the paper seemed unlikely. But he couldn't try to visit Joel again until tomorrow, so he might as well see if he could find anything to make the day something other than a complete waste.

Garrison perked up when he saw the archives dated to the paper's founding in 1928. It was possible a crime would make its way into a nearby county's paper. Wouldn't tell him where Clancy was now, but it interested him.

"Are you finding everything all right, sweetheart?" a librarian whose nametag read Betsy asked. Her hair was poofed, and her face was painted and pulled like a carousel horse.

"I'm good." He tried not to choke on the smell of her hairspray.

Garrison struggled to keep his eyes from crossing as he scanned the pages. He slowed his scrolling when he reached September 23rd but saw no mention of the crime. Just a slew of articles detailing local church functions and sawmill life.

His pulse sped when he noticed an article titled, *Mystery Surrounds Crime in Carthage*, in the September 30th edition. He read it twice. There was nothing earth-shattering, but he wanted to make sure he caught every detail. Only one section stood out.

The boy's brother, present during the crime, refuses to answer questions. Their father, Thomas Fitchett, a well-respected dentist, was questioned. Dr. Fitchett gave his full cooperation and provided an alibi.

It was no surprise they questioned Clancy. He was the only known witness, and his refusal to speak only heightened guilty suspicions. But why Tom? What reason did they have to question the good doctor? Standard procedure? Or something more?

Garrison loaded the next film and scanned through the next few months of papers, but found no further mention of the Fitchetts again. A different story took over the headlines, when the body of a local man was found, buried shallowly in the Carthage soil.

It didn't matter, Garrison told himself. He was here to find Clancy, not to solve any crimes. But he did hope to discover something that would clear Clancy of any involvement that night.

"Find what you are looking for, sugar?" Betsy hovered over his shoulder.

Garrison gathered his things. "Not specifically. Needed information on Clancy Fitchett."

"Is that the boy from Carthage who got..." She took an acrylic nail out of her mouth to scratch it across her face.

"That was Joel, his brother, but information on either would help."

"That's right. Not sure why I always get their names confused. They say Clancy did it. That he slashed his own brother's face. And that it messed Joel up so bad, he grew up to be a murderer." Betsy gave an exaggerated shiver. "Their story is all anyone could talk about when Joel was transferred here in 1983. Same year I got this job."

"Eighty-three," Garrison repeated. He already knew that, but it hadn't occurred to him to search the papers for that year.

"This is a long shot, but have you talked to Joel in prison?" Betsy asked.

"Yes, and he wasn't much help."

"I can imagine not." She twirled her hair. "What makes you interested in them anyhow?"

Garrison gritted his teeth. Betsy was awfully nosey. But then again, he was the one poking around in a stranger's life.

"Oh, I know!" Betsy's increased volume combined with the snap of the air conditioner switching on made Garrison jump. "You must be in that college course at LeTourneau. Your classmate came by early this morning looking for information on that crime. The one with dark hair and a sweet face. I never forget a face, but what was her name? Megan? No, that's not right."

"Umm, I'm not sure what—"

Betsy waved her hand dismissively. "It will come to me. Anyway, you want me to pull those articles from '83 for you?"

"That might help. Thanks." Garrison felt guilty for being so annoyed with her. His stomach rumbled. Hopefully the hunger was to blame. "Excuse my stomach. I skipped breakfast."

"Goodness gracious. It's nearly noon. You need to eat. Go grab lunch, and I'll give Sylvia a call."

"Sylvia?"

"She's the research librarian here. Left early for an appointment. She helped that gal from your class find articles."

"You don't need to do that. I'm okay."

"Well, your stomach disagrees, darling."

Garrison was still hesitant, but the prospect of eating lunch while someone else did his dirty work was too tempting to pass up. "Okay. I'll give my eyes a break and shut up my stomach."

"Go to Pickett House Restaurant. Best fried chicken you ever ate."

"A couple fifty-nine cent tacos will hit the spot for me."

Betsy wrinkled her face. "Taco Bell is not food."

Garrison could argue it had sustained him for the past two years, but he was in a new place. It might be time to broaden his horizons and eat off a plate instead of a wrapper. "All right, which way to Pickett's?"

***

Bright pink lipstick was spread across Betsy's teeth and a smudge of mascara dotted her face when Garrison return. She looked deflated somehow. "Sorry, but I didn't find much. A few articles about Joel transferring here but nothing on Clancy. Sylvia didn't answer."

"That's okay." Garrison faked a smile. Not her fault he had gotten his hopes up over Pickett House's cobbler.

"But I know that gal's name. The one in your class. I found her Student ID in the stacks." Betsy squinted to read it. "Molly Hamilton. Maybe you can talk to her since I couldn't find much." She handed Garrison three sheets of still warm paper and the student ID. "Do you mind giving this back to Molly? When you see her in class?"

Garrison looked at the picture. All he could tell from the tiny image was that Molly was a pale brunette who didn't appear excited to have her photo taken. "Umm, actually—"

"Actually, there she is right now!" Betsy waved as the front door opened. "Back for your ID, sugar? I gave it to your classmate here. He's working the same case as you, so maybe you two can share information."

Molly stepped to the desk. "My classmate?"

"Garrison Stark." He threw out his hand.

Molly hesitated but gave a halfhearted shake.

"Do you have a minute?" Garrison asked.

"Just sixty of them each hour." She switched her bag to her other arm. "I've never seen you before. You must be in the Monday/Wednesday class."

"Uh, yeah, that's right."

"Did Professor Grant give you permission to do the same case as me? He knows how hard I've worked, and I'm not sharing my findings. Did he say I would?"

Betsy bit down on her lip. "I think I'll leave you two be." She headed toward the shelves with a pile of books. "It was nice meeting you, Garrison. If you ever find yourself back around these parts, stop by and say hello. Like I said, I never forget a face."

Before he could thank her, Molly raised her voice. "Professor Grant was adamant that each student would work their own case. What changed?"

Garrison sighed. "Okay, listen. I'm not taking the class. But I *am* interested in the case. We can help each other."

Molly shook her head. "No thanks."

"I'm Clancy's grandson," he blurted out.

"You're lying."

"I'm not. Well, I don't think I am. Please, hear me out. Let me start over."

Molly crossed her arms. "Third time's a charm."

"I've never met Clancy. Never heard of him till a few months ago. My grandmother claims he was my mom's biological father. But I can't be sure until I find him. I visited Joel at Gib but—"

"Wait!" Her eyes widened. "You talked to Joel Fitchett? In person? What did you say for him to agree to meet with you?"

"The truth."

"Did it take you three lies to get to it? Or just two?"

"No lies. Just a fair share of letters."

"I've written more than you. I can guarantee that. So, you sat across the glass and had a conversation with Joel Fitchett?" The excitement in her voice threw him. Had he accidentally said Patrick Swayze?

"I did better than that. Sat across a table from him. No glass, no cuffs."

"Well, now you've got my attention." She leaned against the desk. "Did he tell you anything?"

"No. He might have if I hadn't gone stupid and mentioned his scar."

Molly's mouth fell open. "You didn't. What was his response?"

"Attempted murder."

A laugh escaped Molly before she pushed her lips together.

"It's okay, laugh. I guess assault and battery is sort of funny."

"I can't say I blame him is all. You suck at first impressions."

Garrison shrugged. Couldn't be all that bad. She was still talking to him.

"Did you ask him if he did it?" she asked.

"No."

Molly hit his arm. "You were face to face with Joel Fitchett and didn't ask him the million-dollar question?"

"I was there to find Clancy."

"What a waste."

"I didn't think it was a question of if he did it, just why."

She squeezed a book against her chest like a shield. "You sound like the rest of Longview. I know better, and I'll find the real story."

Well, that was a new one. He wondered what could inspire anyone to believe that Joel Fitchett was innocent. "Tell me about it over dinner."

Molly glanced at her watch, but it hardly seemed long enough to check the time. "Can't. I have to get back to Longview and get to work. I'm the editor for the school paper. You know, the school I actually attend."

"Tomorrow then?"

"We're up against a deadline. I won't have time to eat or much less breathe till Monday."

"Monday's good for me. I'm going to try to visit Joel tomorrow. Maybe I can get more out of him this time."

"Take a deck of cards."

"What?"

"Joel loves cards. I read an article about how they tried to ban playing cards from Gib because so many inmates lost all their toiletries to Joel in poker matches."

"Well, there you go!" Garrison slapped the table. "I love cards. I'll get him playing, get him talking, and will be ready with lots to share on Monday."

Molly lowered her eyebrows. "You smile too much. Like you are hiding something. How do I know you aren't some psycho murderer?"

"Me?!" Garrison laughed. "I'm not the one with the jailhouse crush on Joel Fitchett."

"Crush!" Molly straightened. "If you call trying to vindicate an innocent man a crush, then okay."

"Joel is many things, but I doubt innocent is one of them."

"Well, if you don't want my opinion, you don't want my information either."

"I'll take both," Garrison said. "With a side of pancakes. 8:00 am Monday? There's an IHOP in Longview, right?"

Molly bit her lip.

"Come on. It's not like I'm asking you to meet in the back of my van. If one of us turns out to be a serial killer, at least there will be witnesses."

"I'll think about it. I don't share my information with just anyone. Grandson of Clancy Fitchett or not."

"Perhaps this will sweeten the deal." Garrison dangled the ID in front of her face. Molly reached for it, but he raised it higher. "Not so fast. You don't want breakfast with me, you don't want the ID either."

"You're holding my ID hostage? Really?"

"That ought to show how harmless I am. Wouldn't I have something more valuable for ransom if I was any good at this?"

She stood on her toes and snatched it out of his hands before he could pull it back. "I don't know about that, but I'd expect you to be quicker." She was nearly out the door before she shouted, "See you Monday."

***

Garrison sat on an empty metal stool at the end of a long line of strangers and waited for Joel. No one even seemed to notice him, each so immersed in conversation with the men behind the glass. It was different in here than in the general visiting area: no crying babies, squeaking chairs, or clang of change in a vending machine. But without all the extra noise, it was impossible not to eavesdrop on the father and son to his left. A second appeal, a second mortgage for the lawyer bills, a second round of chemo for a mother who sends her love. The kid behind the glass couldn't be older than Garrison. What had he done to end up here? Not just a prisoner but one who couldn't even be trusted to shake his father's hand? Garrison's heart broke as the father's voice did. He wished the same glass that divided them from the prisoners divided these cold metal stools too.

An alarm sounded on the other side of the glass, and Joel shuffled in. Once he was seated and his hands unchained, he picked up the telephone. Garrison did the same, ready for silence—or an earful.

"You rich or something?"

That, he wasn't prepared for. "Huh?"

"The warden doesn't do any favors. How much did you pay him?"

"Nothing. I told him yesterday was my fault. And it was. I'm sorry."

"Don't apologize. We're both men. You said what you meant, and I meant what I did. End of story."

"Okay." Garrison stopped short of apologizing for apologizing.

"So, are you rich?" Joel asked again. "You got that look. Spoiled white rich kid."

Garrison shifted on the stool. "My parents left me some money. Can live comfortably but not extravagantly." He borrowed the words his financial adviser had used after everything was final. It was a wonder he remembered anything about that time in his life besides the unimaginable pain.

"Trust fund baby."

"Life insurance baby. Car accident last fall." Garrison's voice was sharper than he meant for it to be.

Joel met Garrison's eyes for the first time today. "That's rough. Both my folks are dead too." He laughed. "But I guess you know that. Neither of us would be here if my old man wasn't dead."

Garrison hadn't even been sure if Joel would speak to him today, but now he was casually referencing the crime that landed him here. If there was ever a time to try, it was now. "Why did you kill your father?"

"Next question."

"How old were you when you lost your mom?" It wasn't a pleasant topic, but one they had in common at least.

"Seventeen. Lung cancer." Joel pulled out a cigarette and turned to the guard. "A hand here?"

The guard huffed but lit it anyway.

"I've been trying to go the same way but no luck." Joel waved the cigarette. "I don't want to talk about my folks."

"What about your brother then? Does he smoke too?"

"How the hell should I know? Haven't seen or heard the man's voice in nearly fifty years. He may be dead. It's a waste of my time to talk about a dead man."

Garrison detected veins throbbing in Joel's neck again. "You're right. I didn't come to talk Clancy. I came to talk cards."

"Cards?"

"I heard you played. Another thing we have in common."

"Fascinating. Maybe we were separated at birth."

"I had hoped we might play a few hands today."

Joel tapped the glass. "This might make that difficult."

"Yeah, I didn't count on the warden only agreeing to a no-contact visit. I hoped it would be like how we met yesterday, minus the part where you pinned me to the ground."

Joel smiled. It was quick, but Garrison saw it. "I still might have. Wouldn't be the first time I pinned a man during a game."

"Well, I never took down one of my parents but did my fair share of sulking when I lost."

"What'd y'all play?"

"Everything. Texas Hold 'Em, Black Jack, Seven-Card Stud, Spoons, Hearts, and Loony Rummy mostly."

"Loony Rummy. What the hell is that?"

"It's a more fun, more challenging version of Rummy."

"I'm listening."

Joel was engaged. This was good. Garrison explained the game best he could. Joel set down his cigarette and leaned in, occasionally nodding or quirking an eyebrow.

"Is the count the same as in Rummy?" Joel asked.

"No. Cards below eight count as five; eight and above are ten. Except for aces, which are twenty."

"Twenty?! Just count for one in Rummy."

"Yeah, takes getting used to, but your points are your own, and low score wins. Want me to write down how many runs and sets you need each hand?"

Joel's shoulders lifted in a shrug. "Nah, it sounds lame."

"You sounded interested a few minutes ago."

"I changed my mind." Joel's voice boomed. So much for his pleasant tone, so much for engaging. Good moods didn't stand a chance when they accidentally landed on Joel Fitchett.

"Next time we should play a game, and you can judge for yourself." Garrison knew he was grasping at straws. His plane left Tuesday; there wasn't a next time.

"Well, Gary. I think it's time for you to go home. I have no clue where Clancy is."

"But you can still help. Anything you can share from the past might help me find him."

"And meanwhile, you'll keep depositing your life insurance money in my account?"

"If that's what it takes."

"What do you take me for, kid?"

Garrison's thoughts scrambled. "If you need money, I can help. If you don't, it's fine. We can play cards when you don't want to talk."

"I'm not this underprivileged kid you need to adopt. This is a prison. I appreciate your tenacity. Coming all this way to find what you think you want. But you are asking me to talk about the same people I've spent forty-five years trying to forget."

People. The word echoed louder than the rest. He was talking about Lorraine too. Joel was hiding something. "There has to be a way to change your mind. Something I can get you?"

Joel snorted a dismissive laugh. "I want plenty. But nothing you can get." He jabbed his finger against the glass. "Now, go!"

Garrison hated quitting, but his borrowed half-hour was up. Time to get back to the hotel, order a pizza, and figure his next steps. He had poked Joel's demons again and wouldn't hang around for the show, protective glass or not. He dropped the phone and left without saying goodbye.

CHAPTER 5

Longview, Texas, 1941

Lorraine Applewhite had only been in Longview ten minutes but already hated it. Were there seasons in Texas? She ached at the thought of silent snow falling on the Wyoming Mountains. Despite Santas decorating store windows, it felt like summer here.

She was sick of being in the car, cramped like her childhood Jack-in-the-box. She should be home reading by a popping fire. Except now, this was home. Would it ever sink in?

"Come on, Lori. Give us a smile. You don't want that scowl to freeze on your face."

"My face can't freeze, Daddy. Not when it's seventy degrees."

"Lorraine, that's enough." Her mother turned around. "Let's make the best of this new adventure."

Lorraine slumped in her seat. Ever since she heard the story of Peter Pan, her mother sprinkled the word adventure on any iffy situation like it was magic fairy dust. *The first day of school will be an adventure! I can't wait to hear about your adventures at Girl Scout Camp!* Well, it had lost its effectiveness. Hadn't Peter Pan also said dying would be a great adventure? Obviously not all adventures were good ideas.

A notebook was spread wide on her lap, but she had written nothing worth keeping the whole trip. In fact, she hadn't written anything good in months—too much on her mind. When her emotions got jumbled, her head was a fog.

She was aware of the reasons her parents came. New job, bigger house, oil boom, greener grass and all that, but why did they have to drag her along? She'd be eighteen in less than two weeks; she could have stayed. She was a grown woman, or nearly so. But instead, she had crammed a whole semester of high school into one month. She didn't want to finish school early. She wanted to eat lunch with her friends on the school lawn, walk across the stage at graduation, and summer in Europe with Linda and Bev. Now *that* would have been an adventure. Couldn't her parents see how important senior year was? "Opportunities like this don't come along every day, Lori," her dad liked to say. Well, neither did the Senior Spring Formal.

Lorraine coughed into her handkerchief. "Does the whole town smell this awful?"

"It's a gas station, Lori. Doesn't smell any different from the ones back home."

She kept the handkerchief over the bottom half of her face. "It's worse here."

Her mother's sigh was so heavy, Lorraine felt the seat move in front of her. And her parents said she was dramatic. "Do you need to use the restroom?"

"I can wait."

"Fine, stay in here and sulk."

She intended to. She intended to sulk a lot, actually. *I hate it here*, she scribbled on a blank page of her notebook. There. The first true sentence she'd written in months.

"Whatcha writing there?"

Lorraine slammed the notebook shut and turned toward the man pumping gas.

"Is everyone here so nosy?" Loraine asked.

"We call it friendly."

She held her notebook against her chest. "I'm writing a novel."

"What's it about?"

"A family recovering from the Depression."

"Autobiographical?"

"No. My family was luckier than most." She climbed to her knees and leaned towards the stranger. "Did you know three million aren't working? Three million! And just as many don't even make minimum wage."

"I didn't." His dimples fought to distract her. "But the government is handling that."

"Says you." Lorraine plopped back into her seat. "They *must* do more. This book will raise awareness of that."

"Why not write a newspaper article?"

"People are sick of news. They don't care about what they read in a paper. A novel brings the issue into their living rooms, lets them care for people and understand their struggle."

"Fictional people."

"But real issues," Lorraine spoke over the gurgle of gas through the hose.

He touched her shoulder. "Don't get in a lather. I read solely for entertainment."

Lorraine tried not to notice the definition of his biceps under his too-tight shirt as she pushed his hand away. "It will entertain. Books can do both. Good ones do. Don't suppose you've read Steinbeck or Faulkner?"

"I prefer *As I Lay Dying* to the *Grapes of Wrath,* if that's what you're asking."

Lorraine was impressed. She didn't know many boys back home who read, but he didn't have to be so smug about it. "*As I Lay Dying* isn't even his best," she said. "Did you read *Light in August?*"

"Oh yeah. Dug the characters. All outcasts, all haunted. Good stuff."

"Yes," she agreed. "And it has the most brilliant quotes, doesn't it? 'She was the captain of her soul.' I adore that. I want that." Lorraine felt a twinge of disappointment when she spotted her parents at the cash register. "Faulkner's not my favorite, though. Have you read Fitzgerald?"

"Ah, *Gatsby*. Didn't care one bit for it, old sport. All that talk about green lights and boats tossed in time. Not for me."

Lorraine wanted to disagree, but it was impressive he had even heard of the book. "What about *This Side of Paradise?*"

He shrugged. "Wasn't a fan of that one, either. Now, Hemingway, he can tell a damn story. He has what Fitzgerald is missing—grit."

Lorraine opened the door, barely missing the dingy gas pump. Blood charged through her, and she needed to stand. "First of all, Fitzgerald was a poet. The language is as powerful as the stories he told. Both *Paradise* and *Gatsby* looked at conflicts between social classes and the failure of American dreams. What's not gritty enough about that?"

"Oh, Lori, spare him." Her daddy opened his car door. "We didn't raise her to be a Democrat. I honestly have no idea why she's become obsessed with the plight of the poor."

Lorraine followed the attendant to the front of the car. "What meaningful issues did Hemingway ever write about?"

He wiped the windshield. "Love, war, and loss for starters. Have you even read *A Farewell to Arms?*"

Her father cleared his throat. "Perhaps you two can continue this conversation next time I need my tank filled."

"Of course, sir." The stranger stuffed the towel into his back pocket. "Hope to see you all again." He looked at Lorraine, a smile dangling on the corner of his lips. So obviously flirting and in such a silly looking hat too.

"We may not be back," she said. "I'm sure there are other stations closer to our home."

"Ones with attendants who will gush about Fitzgerald?" he asked.

She gestured toward the overflowing garbage bin. "One that doesn't reek of trash spoiling in the sun."

He opened her door. "I'll take care of that. And I'll be watching for your book."

"You do that."

"Whose name should I look for? On its spine?"

"Lorraine Applewhite," she said over the hum of the motor. "I'll try to keep my sentences short as Hemmingway does so you can understand them."

"Goodbye, Lorraine Applewhite." He studied her with a stare so intense, she felt his eyes on her even after she looked away.

She pulled sunglasses over her eyes. "Goodbye, you."

Though she tried not to, Lorraine kept replaying that stare as they traveled down the road. Why was she obsessing over it? A look was such an insignificant thing, but so was the first raindrop of a summer storm. Too bad she didn't need a scene involving a look like that for her novel. She was sure she could write ten pages on it. Maybe she would, but she'd better put it where it belonged. She shoved the manuscript into her bag and pulled out her diary. For the first time in months, the words came easily.

***

Joel peeled the mask from his face and stared into the mirror. As much as he wanted to see a change, he couldn't. Day five and the scar hadn't lessened, no matter how often he tried to convince himself otherwise. He knew a mask of raw honey and baking soda was a long shot, but how would he know if he didn't try? He could always keep using it, just in case, but it was time to search for other methods too.

Joel jumped at the sound outside. It was only four-thirty. Of all days for Clancy to come home early. He used a hand towel to wipe the last bits of honey off his face and the bathroom sink.

The knock told him it wasn't Clancy. The door wasn't locked. Joel tripped over the end table on the way to the window, his curse louder than the crash. Whoever it was knew someone was home so he might as well open it.

His hand stuck to the doorknob. He'd have to remember to wash off the honey residue before Clancy came home. The petite blond with big curls and bigger green eyes in front of him was not familiar. A new one. Whatever had happened to the last one? "Sorry, he won't be back till five." Joel tried to shut the door, but her hand stopped it.

"Excuse me." She gave the door a push. "I thought they grew gentlemen in the South."

He hadn't meant to be rude, but none of Clancy's girls had ever cared for small talk with him. "I'm sorry."

"I should hope so." She brushed a curl away from her face. "How do you know who I'm here to see anyhow?"

"Just assumed you were here for Clancy."

She crossed her arms. "Well, you're wrong. I'm looking for Joel."

This was a first. He was sure he didn't know her. He would have remembered a face like hers.

She must have picked up on the confusion because she didn't seem so sure of herself anymore. "Do I have the wrong house? Oh, dear, feel free to slam the door on me again if I do."

"No, this is the right house. I'm Joel Fitchett."

She tapped a bright red-painted nail against her matching lips. "How strange. Do you work at the service station on Main?"

Joel nodded.

"This must sound silly, but is there another Joel there?"

"No, ma'am." He looked into the driveway. "Did I work on your car?"

"No. I'm new in town. My family went to the station a few days ago, and a fella filled up our gas. I was rude to him, and it's been eating at me. I've come to apologize."

"Clancy then. You want Clancy."

"Clancy? No, I'm sure the shirt said Joel."

"Two days ago, you said?" It came together then. Clancy had forgotten his uniform that day. Hadn't been the first time and wouldn't be the last. "He wore my shirt that day." Joel extended his hand but remembered the honey and retracted it. "I'm Clancy's brother, Joel Fitchett."

"Lorraine Applewhite." Her voice was weaker. "Or Lori if you prefer. Sorry for the confusion. Appears I've embarrassed myself in front of both of you now."

"Nothing to be embarrassed about." Joel reached to scratch his scar, feeling especially self-conscious. He wanted her to leave, but he couldn't send her away, not after he had been so rude. "Clancy will be home soon. Want to come in?"

"Lorraine glanced around. "It's such a nice day. Should we sit out here?"

Of course she wouldn't come inside with a scar-faced stranger. What a dumb thing to ask. "I have lemonade." Joel shoved his hands into his pockets. "I mean if you want some."

"That sounds delicious." Her lopsided smile was both endearing and terrifying. He couldn't remember the last time a girl this beautiful smiled at him.

He found the lemonade pitcher nearly empty. Clancy must have helped himself again. Joel frantically made another batch, leaving a sticky, sugary mess on the counter. Not to mention the disarray he'd left from preparing dinner. Judging by the mess, it was probably best she hadn't come inside.

He carried two full glasses outside, relieved to see Lorraine hadn't left. "Here you go."

"This smells great. I love the scent of freshly squeezed lemons."

Joel nodded at the seat beside her. "Do you mind?"

She swallowed her first sip. "It's your swing."

"I just meant if you'd rather wait for Clancy alone that's fine."

"Oh, stop." She patted the empty seat. "Sit, I love company."

He was careful not to touch her as he lowered himself onto the swing. Careful not to spill a drop on her perfect orange dress. "You say you are new here?"

"Yes, moved from Wyoming." She said Wyoming with the reverence people usually reserved for discussing heaven or the New York Yankees. "But Daddy's work brought him here."

"Oilfield?"

"How did you guess?"

"It's East Texas. Oil is king. These little towns doubled in size when I was a kid." Joel took his first sip of lemonade. It was too sweet.

"I'm sure this place was swell before oil derricks sprouted every few feet. I don't think I'll ever get used to so many of them or the odor either. It seems like a waste for there to be so much money here while half the country is starving."

"Nothing wrong with working hard and keeping what you earn. It doesn't belong to the government." It was strange hearing his father's words in his own voice.

"Are you implying the rich work harder than others?"

"No, but if you want equal wealth distribution, you're living in the wrong country."

"Maybe so," she said. "But I didn't say to divide it evenly, just that it wouldn't hurt if some of this oil revenue went elsewhere."

Joel had more to say but kept his mouth shut. No good ever came from arguing politics. He set his glass on the ground beside him. "So what do you do for fun?"

Lorraine cocked her head. "Say what you were going to say."

"Huh?"

"It's written all over your face. Come out with it."

Joel rubbed the back of his neck. "It seems hypocritical is all—that you have a problem with oil money when it's what has paid for your life."

"You're right; it has—and done a good job of it. It's my parents' money, and I can't tell them what to do with it. But as much as we have, it's still not enough. Had to move here to get more. Nothing wrong with money, besides that it's worse than whiskey. Once someone has a drink, their thirst is never quenched. It doesn't seem right for some to let food spoil in the pantry while their neighbor starves to death."

"President Roosevelt has done all he can to help people get on their feet, to make sure no one is starving."

"He's done a lot but not enough."

Joel sighed, but didn't argue. There was something to be said for her moxie.

"Why don't you and your brother work in the oil field? Get a piece of the excess?" she asked.

"It's not that the money wouldn't be nice, but I enjoy what I do. Finding a problem with a car and fixing it is satisfying. My daddy and I worked on cars when I was a boy."

"Well, that's something to admire. Doing what you love." She smiled again. Joel wasn't sure if it was the sugar surging through him that made him feel so alive or something else. "And your brother? Does he like what he does? He's a natural."

And there it was. The crash. The reminder that she was here for Clancy, not him. "Yes, he appears to enjoy his job. He's comfortable there and social, so it's a good fit." By comfortable Joel meant lazy. Far too lazy to work for a boss who wasn't best friends with his dad. And Clancy was only social with the customers who wore skirts and lipstick. But she would learn the truth soon enough; they all did.

"Aren't you going to ask what I do?" she asked.

"I assumed college."

"I'm supposed to start next fall. Besides taking it upon himself to move us across the country, Daddy also filled out my applications to Kilgore College and the College of Marshal.l I'm supposed to pick one, but he doesn't know I've applied at others. Ones that will get me far from here. Honestly, I don't even care about school. I'd finish my book faster without wasting time in classes."

"Your book?"

Joel spotted a gleam in her eyes. "Yes, I'm a writer. Well, I want to be one. I'm working on a novel about a couple trying to navigate through the Depression. And the turmoil the lack of money can cause to otherwise happy people. What it can do to a once happy marriage." Despite the tense subject, joy bubbled from her words.

"Sounds interesting."

"I hope so. Are you a reader?"

"Not unless you count comics. But I'll read *your* book."

She turned her body to face him. "You promise?"

"Promise."

She held out her hand to shake, but he kept his glued to his knee. "I'm sorry. I have honey on my hands."

Her laugh was loud and unpolished. "What a scream. I knew I smelt something besides lemons and couldn't place it. But that's it, honey and lemons. Reminds me of being sick as a girl."

"So, I remind you of sickness?"

Lorraine slapped his knee. "No, silly. It's a good memory. When I was sick, Mother made me a delicious honey and lemon tea to coat my throat. Comfort in a glass, it was. Is there honey in the lemonade?"

Joel nodded. As sweet as the drink tasted, it was a believable lie at least.

"How did it get up there?" A muscle in Joel's face twitched as Lorraine brought her hand towards him. He fought his instinct to recoil.

"Messy cook," he said.

She scraped honey from the skin around the scar—a scar no one had been this close to. And her hand stayed, even after she finished. Joel's face warmed, outward evidence of the heat coursing through his veins. Lorraine looked like she wanted to say something. He braced himself for a question about the scar.

"You have the most beautiful eyes," she said. She kept her hand against his skin, but she didn't seem to regard the scar anymore. She looked into his eyes. He needed to say something but what? Hundreds of words knocked around in his head, but he couldn't grab the right ones. "Blue as the Wyoming sky," she added.

"Sky's blue in Texas too."

She removed her hand and looked up. "Still bluer there."

Had he upset her? If he'd kept quiet, would she have kissed him? Probably not, but then again, she had left her hand on his face for an awfully long time.

Joel contemplated what else to say when he spotted a flock of birds circling above them. Lorraine laid her head back. "You ought to get a bird bath. Poor dears must be parched. Mother used to spread birdseed in our backyard in Wyoming, and we saw all sorts of bird species stop by. I don't think there's anything more lovely than a red cardinal on a snowy branch."

Joel wiped his hands across his pants. "I'm not a big bird watcher."

"Huh?" Lorraine sat up. "Sorry, it's hard to hear over the chirping."

"I don't care for birds," he said louder.

"Why not?"

The squawking was louder now, like the sparrows were descending on them. "They spread diseases."

"So do we."

"Have you considered law school? You have an argument ready for anything."

She smiled. "I enjoy discussions. They are a means to understand people, see what makes them tick. All good for my writing."

"So, I'm research?" It had been a while, but this felt like flirting.

"Something like that." Her wink made him aware of the sound of his own heartbeat. It was louder than the sparrow's song.

She drug her foot in the dirt hollow under the swing. "I should go. I've taken too much of your time."

"No, stay," Joel said. "I don't have anything going on." Except for the dinner he was burning.

"Mother and Daddy will wonder where I am."

"Come back tomorrow then?" He caught the eagerness in his voice. "To see Clancy, I mean." The loud rumble of a motor made them both flinch. Joel knew who it was. For someone infamous for being a no-show, Clancy sure had a knack of appearing at all the wrong times.

Lorraine used her hand as a shield against the sun. "Is that him?"

"Yep." Joel helped Lorraine stand, holding on to her hand a little longer than necessary.

Clancy slammed the truck door. "Lorraine Applewhite."

"Clancy, not Joel like my shirt says, Fitchett," Lorraine retorted.

"That's me." Clancy pointed to the name on his chest. "Got the right one on today." He took wide steps up the driveway. "Joel, what are you doing hanging around a gal like this? She's a Democrat—and worse than that, a Fitzgerald fan."

Lorraine laughed at the joke Joel wasn't a part of. She had sat with him for the last half hour, but one sentence from Clancy and she'd forgotten about Joel and her half-finished lemonade.

"I came to see you," Lorraine said. "To apologize for how I acted. I'm not an impolite person. The move has just been tough for me, and well...none of that matters. I'm sorry. I enjoyed our chat more than I let on."

"How did you find my place?" Clancy asked.

"I went back yesterday hoping to find you, but your boss said you were off. So, I asked for your address. Drove by, but no one was here, so I tried again today."

Clancy stepped closer. "No one goes through that for an apology."

"I do."

"So, you didn't come to take me to dinner?"

She raised one eyebrow.

He leaned in. "All right, my treat. What do you say?"

She hesitated, but Joel understood it was all part of a game they were playing. "I suppose it *is* dinner time," Lorraine finally said.

Joel stared at the sidewalk. So much for Lorraine's parents wondering where she was.

She turned towards Joel. "Want to come?"

Clancy stepped behind Lorraine and shook his hands and head back and forth. Joel didn't blame him. He hadn't wanted Clancy showing up when he did either. Three was a crowd, especially on a date.

"I've got a casserole in the oven," Joel said.

"Oh." Lorraine looked at Clancy then back to Joel. "We could stay here. If there's enough for three?"

"He just makes enough for him," Clancy said.

It was a lie but not the worst idea for the future, given how Clancy treated him. All eyes were on Joel. "You two go on. Nice meeting you, Lorraine."

"It was a pleasure. Thanks for the cold drink and warm conversation."

"Anytime," Joel said even though he knew this wouldn't happen again. Clancy helped Lorraine to the truck before sprinting back towards the house. "Need to change?" Joel asked.

"No, I need *some* change." Clancy sniffed his shirt and stretched it to Joel's face. "Why? Do I stink?"

Joel shook his head, even though the shirt reeked of gasoline.

"So, got a couple bucks you can spare? I can pay you back tomorrow."

Like a reflex, Joel reached for his wallet.

"Thanks, Brother. Be home later. Don't wait up."

"See ya." Joel waved in Lorraine's general direction but avoided looking at her. Clancy climbed back in, and just as suddenly as she'd come into his life, she left. Gone in the passenger seat of Clancy's truck, leaving her own car and Joel abandoned in the driveway.

Chapter 6

Texas, 1991

Garrison might as well have had fifty-pound weights hanging from his limbs as he packed. All the planning and nothing to show except a bruised neck and an enormous room-service bill. That and a breakfast meeting with a stranger tomorrow. A stranger who probably had every intention of standing him up.

He needed to call and remind Amber to pick him up Tuesday. They hadn't spoken since his first night here. He didn't want her to know how unsuccessful he'd been, but had to face her sooner or later.

Just the sound of her hopeful hello comforted Garrison. He knew he should marry her and guarantee that comfort always. But were there really guarantees? It was hard to imagine a future knowing how uncertain life was, knowing that control was just an illusion. Still, Amber wouldn't wait forever.

"What did you find out?" Amber asked. "I've tried calling."

"Not much to tell. Not much good anyway." He explained both failed visits and waited for the, "at least you tried speech," but she said nothing.

Just as he assumed they'd lost connection, she finally spoke. "What's your gut saying?"

Garrison knew what Amber wanted to hear. That his gut said come home, but he'd never been good at lying to her. "Joel's hiding something, possibly a lot." Garrison flopped onto the hotel bed. "But he turned on me twice. He won't talk. The newspapers and library were a wash. Time to come home."

"Garrison, you are going about this all wrong."

He spun the cord between his fingers. "How so?"

"I'm from North Carolina, remember? In the South, you don't go to libraries to get to the bottom of something; you go to the next-door neighbors, the hairdressers, the Sunday School teachers."

It hadn't occurred to Garrison to search further than public records and Joel Fitchett for information, but he never expected he'd have to. Where would he even start? "I don't know if I'm up for it."

"Try, Garrison. You're only hours away from the town Clancy grew up in. You'll never be this close again. There's still time before summer semester starts."

And there it was. The ten thousandth mention of summer semester. Amber couldn't fault Garrison for dropping his classes after the accident, but she couldn't hide her disdain when he didn't return in spring. If he couldn't finish school, he wouldn't get a job, and he couldn't marry her. Amber obviously wanted him to get this out of his system and get back on the path they had carved years ago. But whatever the reason for her goodwill and encouragement, there was no reason not to take advantage. No reason except one. "I'm worried about Grandma Dolly," he said. "I called yesterday, and the nurse said she hasn't been lucid since I left."

"She hasn't been lucid in months, Garr." Amber's voice was soft. "I'll check in on her while you're gone. Every day if you want."

"And you'll tell me if she asks for me?"

"Promise. Now call the airline and reschedule your flight. You need to do this. It's important."

It *was* important. He wouldn't have come so far if it wasn't. He could call the rental company about keeping the car a few more weeks. Find an economy room with a microwave and a Walmart where he could pick up several boxes of Hot Pockets and an extra pack of underwear. "I'll call you back and let you know about the flight."

"Praying it comes together. You deserve some good luck."

"Thanks, Amber. I miss you." He wasn't sure he did. She had barely crossed his mind. But that had to be normal with so much to think about.

"I miss you too," she said. "But I love you more."

"Love you too." That one he was sure he meant.

While he waited on hold with the airline, Garrison unfolded the Texas road map. His eyes roamed until he found the tiny dots of Carthage and Longview. Where to start? The place Clancy grew up? Or the town he disappeared from?

He thought again of Molly. If she did show up tomorrow, she probably wouldn't know anything that could lead to Clancy, but maybe it was worth a try. He took his index finger and traced the route to Longview, Texas.

***

Molly was already situated at the corner booth at eight, throwing back her coffee like a runner chugging water at the finish line. Garrison squeezed into the seat across from her. "Good morning."

She rubbed her eyes. "Maybe after one more cup."

"Late night?"

"And early morning."

"Only for us college kids," Garrison said.

"So, you are actually a college student?"

"Ohio State."

"What's your major?" she asked.

"Astronomy & Astrophysics. And no. I'm not sure what I'll do with it. Had dreams of NASA but will settle for teaching other schmucks like myself with similarly unattainable dreams."

"That's an impressive major. I've always struggled in science." Molly flagged the waitress to refill her cup.

"Can I get one too, with cream?" Garrison asked. "And a breakfast platter." He lowered the menu. "Did you order?"

"My body can't break down solids before ten."

Garrison smiled. He'd always been awkward around new people, but Molly was easy to talk to. "And what are you studying? I mean, besides Joel Fitchett."

Her cup only partially hid her smile. "Political Science with a minor in Communication. Next stop law school."

"Ah, a defender of the Joel Fitchetts of the world?"

"Something like that. I wouldn't even be looking at law school if not for my parents. Not that I won't enjoy defending people like Joel, but I'd rather sit across from them for a hard-hitting interview."

"A journalist at heart then? Explains the school paper."

The waitress deposited a cup in front of him. "Food will be out soon, darling."

"Thanks." He reached for the sugar caddy. "What got you interested in this case?"

Molly set down her cup for the first time. "I don't remember why, but it started when I was a girl reading too much Nancy Drew. I must have heard people talk since it happened in Carthage. I got older, researched more, and it doesn't add up. Everyone has an opinion, but nobody bothered with evidence."

Garrison watched the cream swirl in his cup. "Tell me more."

"Dr. Fitchett was murdered behind his practice. Why wouldn't Joel kill him at home? Why risk witnesses?"

"Heat of passion? Or he wanted it to look like a random crime."

"Joel has never admitted guilt," she continued. "Nor has he claimed innocence. Why won't he talk? What's he hiding?"

"Isn't a guilty plea the same as admitting guilt?"

"No, that was his lawyer's call. And his lawyer, don't get me started. I don't even understand how he passed the bar."

"They had the bar exams back then?"

Molly tilted her head to the ceiling and sighed.

"Hey now," Garrison said. "I may not know the bar exam's history, but I bet you didn't know Saturn would float in water."

"Because of the rings?"

"Wow, you do suck at science. Saturn is mostly gas, and gas weighs less than water. The problem would be finding a big enough body of water. It's the second largest planet."

Molly rubbed her forehead. "Anyway, about the exam. They had one, but anyone could sit for it. John Sawyer was obviously better at taking tests than defending a life."

"Maybe he thought Joel did it."

"It doesn't matter!" Molly raised her voice. "A lawyer's job is defending their client. Period. He just had to create doubt. There were a million ways to do that."

"What would you have done to create said doubt?"

Molly slammed her hand on the table like a gavel. "Motive. There wasn't one. Tom Fitchett was well liked. Good reputation as a dentist. No problems with the law. Joel visited regularly."

"Rich?"

"He did all right for himself, yes."

Garrison threw his hands up. "Well, there you go. The oldest motive for murder."

"I believe that would be jealousy. And if Joel wanted his money, why didn't he defend himself? Hard to collect an inheritance when you are sitting in…"

Molly stopped when Garrison's food arrived and let the waitress fill her cup again. No wonder she was so high strung. Garrison offered a strip of bacon. "Sure you aren't hungry?"

She shooed it away. "Joel was a straight arrow. Kept to himself; didn't get into any trouble. Not like...well, never mind."

"Not like who?"

"Well, Clancy."

Garrison stopped mid-bite. "What do you mean?"

"Clancy's the one with the record."

The quietly spoken statement seemed to amplify other sounds in the room. Bacon sizzled, a microwave dinged, and a chair scraped against a floorboard. Garrison lost his appetite. How had he never come across a criminal record? "What was he arrested for?"

"Mostly petty stuff growing up: theft, destruction of property, assault once."

Garrison let that information mingle with the picture of Clancy in his mind. It was hard to reconcile what he wanted versus what was. But everyone made mistakes when they were young. He had—not anything that went on a permanent record, thank God, but still. "Anything from recent years?" Garrison took the first gulp of his coffee. Even with all the cream and sugar, it was too strong and burnt his throat on its way down.

"Not that I've come across. But I can't find zilch about him now. He pretty much fell off the face of the Earth after his father's murder." She stared like she was waiting for him to come to the same realization she had.

"You think Clancy did it?"

She wiped her mouth with a napkin. "The timing seems odd."

Garrison's defenses rose the same way they did anytime someone reminded him his mom wasn't wearing her seat belt when she died. "Of course he had nothing to do with his brother. Joel killed their father. Why would he?" Garrison barely heard himself over the ringing in his ears. "And I'm sure he and Lorraine wanted a fresh start."

"You're probably right," Molly said, but her voice lacked passion. "I have the police reports and newspaper articles at my place. You are welcome to look."

"Anything that might help me find Clancy?" As interesting as the case was, Garrison needed to stay the course. He had his own mystery to solve, and it had little to do with Joel Fitchett's guilt or innocence.

"Nothing I can remember. But I haven't been looking for Clancy. So there might be something I missed."

Garrison picked up his fork again. His heart resumed its regular rhythm. Clancy's rap sheet was minor. Molly may not have information that could help him, but he enjoyed her company. If nothing else, he'd found a new friend. Still, Molly's words planted a seed in his mind. Why had Clancy run away the night of the murder? Not just run away but disappeared? It was suspicious behavior but didn't mean he was involved. What if Joel was innocent and whoever killed Tom was after Clancy? Maybe unraveling Joel's story would help Garrison more than he could foresee. He pushed his plate away. "I'm ready now if you are."

***

The sheer size and elegance of Molly's home surprised Garrison. He didn't expect the plain-dressed and plainspoken Molly to live in a three-story mansion secured by a perimeter fence and covered in crawling ivy. The inside was even more impressive. The high, dark ceiling brushed with silver resembled a starry night. The chandelier hanging from it dripped with crystals that shot refracted light throughout the room. Were those diamonds too? Garrison looked away from the light fixture that could probably pay for an entire semester of college. "Nice place you have here."

"It's my parents' but thanks." Molly tossed her bag onto the couch. "They travel a lot, and my brother lives on campus most of the year, so it's usually just me. But I'm not complaining."

"Are they gone now?" Garrison realized that statement could really creep out a woman who had invited a stranger inside. Luckily, Molly didn't seem fazed.

"Won't be back until August."

Garrison noticed the floors and brass all shined. The air had a higher concentration of Pine Sol and Windex than nitrogen and oxygen. Housekeepers obviously kept Molly company while her folks were away.

Molly tightened the hair tie holding her ponytail. "Ready to start, or do you need a tour?"

"I'm good. Let's get started."

Molly motioned around the circular room. "Sit anywhere. I'll grab my files. Want something to drink? Coffee?"

"Still good." He sat beside Molly's bag. The couch was as hard as a brick. A solid white brick. There is no way a couch this firm and this clean was meant for sitting. He stood and inspected a wall of childhood photos while Molly's boots thudded up the stairs above him. School photos were always so unflattering with their laser light background and stiff, unnatural poses. Yet Garrison's parents had paid for their package each year, creating an unforgiving record of his awful hairstyles and fashion choices. At least they were hidden away in a scrapbook somewhere.

When she returned, Molly was carrying a box half the size she was.

"Let me get that for you."

"I got it." Her voice came from somewhere behind the cardboard. "It's not heavy." She dropped it and threw off the lid. She was right. There wasn't much inside. She pulled out a binder first. "This is the transcript of Joel's trial."

"Umm, I'm sure that's interesting, but I'll start with the police reports."

"Suit yourself." Molly handed him two file folders. He opened the red one labeled "1932" first. There wasn't much to the document. Joel's family had friends over for dinner, and at 7:25, Nancy Fitchett reported that both her boys were missing. Joel had gone looking for his brother around 6:30, and neither had returned. Her husband and one of their dinner guests, Danny Montgomery, eventually ventured out to search. Around 7:45, a call came in from Rover's Diner about two injured boys. Witnesses said Joel stumbled in carrying an unconscious Clancy. Later, both boys refused to discuss what happened. There was nothing else to the report except attached statements from the Fitchetts and Montgomerys.

"Have you talked to these people?"

"What people?"

"The friends over for dinner." Garrison checked the name again. "The Montgomerys."

"Pretty sure they're dead."

"Their daughter may not be."

Molly closed the binder. "Wait. Who?"

"In his statement, Mr. Montgomery mentioned their twelve-year old daughter played with Joel before he went looking for Clancy."

"Oh, her. She was there that night and knows Joel's parents weren't involved, but beyond that, what can she tell us?"

"Maybe she kept in touch with Clancy."

Molly shook her head. "You're reaching. People don't stay friends with kids they knew when they were twelve."

"Some do." Garrison wasn't close to his childhood best friend, but they kept in touch. "And what does it hurt to check?" He grabbed Molly's pen and scribbled, *Find Katie Montgomery* on his arm.

"Umm, would you like a piece of paper?"

"Nah, this works."

"Did you read where they suspected Clancy?" Molly avoided looking at Garrison, focusing instead on shuffling papers around in the box.

"I did, but there's no basis."

"Just that he was a troublemaker."

"Yes, but the statements said the boys got along," Garrison said.

"But all brothers have a degree of trouble between them, don't they?"

"I wouldn't know. Only child."

"Lucky you."

Garrison had once agreed. He liked having his parents' undivided attention and undivided resources when Christmas rolled around. But now that they were gone, he didn't feel so lucky anymore.

The newspaper article from the Carthage paper was almost identical to Woodville's. There was a single follow-up piece attached with no new information. Garrison held it up. "Any others?"

"Afraid not."

"So, the coverage just ended?"

"It was replaced by another local story. People have short attention spans."

Garrison traded the 1932 folder for the 1945 one. He took his time reading the police report. He learned that Tom Fitchett was stabbed outside his practice around eight thirty in the evening. It wasn't unheard of for Dr. Fitchett to see patients after hours, but there was nothing in his appointment book. Could have been an emergency, but there were no used tools or trash suggesting a late-night procedure. The only witnesses were a young couple leaving through the back exit of a party across the alley. It was dark and spitting snow, yet they both saw a young, white male fleeing the scene in a blue Ford pickup. "He had an appalling cut," the woman said of the suspect. "Stretched clear across his face. I'll never forget it as long as I live."

"The description fits Joel," Garrison said.

"So what?"

"You don't think there happen to be two young, white males with the same scar and truck in town that night?"

"No, Perry Mason, I don't. But I also don't believe that everyone tells the truth. They might have had it out for Joel."

"Said they had only moved to Carthage a month before. And Joel hadn't lived there since graduation."

"It was his hometown, though. Someone else could have had a grudge. Plus, do you think anyone who stumbles out the back door of a tavern does it sober?" Molly raised her palms before Garrison could counter. "Look, I didn't bring you here to debate. Just to help you find Clancy."

Garrison said nothing else to Molly, but the more he read, the more convinced he was of Joel's guilt. The police had been to Joel and Clancy's the day before the murder when a neighbor called about an altercation between Joel and his father. What more of a motive did Molly need? And Joel's initials were engraved on the knife. If that wasn't evidence, what was?

Garrison's eyes skipped down a few sentences when he spotted Clancy's name. He and Lorraine were present during the argument with Mr. Fitchett, but everyone refused to give any information. What was with the perpetual silence of Clancy and Joel when questioned by officers? A distrust of the law—or too much to hide? Garrison finished reading the file. Clancy's name didn't appear in it again. "What other color files you got in there, Hamilton?"

Molly handed over an accordion file. "Here are interviews I've done, but there's not much to them. Seems everyone who knew Joel is dead. Therefore, it's mostly hearsay and speculations. Look if you want, but do it expecting disappointment."

"You're an extremely positive person. Has anyone ever told you that?"

Molly looked up from the paperwork to smile. "Never."

The shrill ring of the phone made Garrison jump like it had caught him doing something wrong. Amber's face popped into his mind.

When Molly took the cordless phone into the kitchen, Garrison slid to the floor and reclined against the couch. It was more comfortable to lean against than sit on. He tried to ignore Molly's conversation. She obviously wanted privacy, but her voice boomed.

"But Mom, I have school, I can't just... I know Mom, but Lew is in the dorm and... I understand that, but it would still be my responsibility... Hold on, let me grab a pen."

Garrison thumbed through the accordion. Molly was right. Not much to read. When she came back to the room, her face had fallen. "Everything okay?" he asked.

Molly's exhale caused her bangs to rise and fall. "It's my Grand Pappy. He's sick. Going downhill fast and can't live on his own anymore. Too stubborn for a nursing home, so Mom offered him a room here."

"I'm sorry he's not well. When will your parents be moving him?"

"Are you kidding me? Adele and Doyle Hamilton wouldn't let a sick father spoil summer vacation."

"So, it's up to you to get him here? And take care of him too?"

Molly held up her notepad. "They gave me the name of a home health agency to handle things. This is so typical yet somehow still unbelievable. Are your parents this oblivious to reality?"

Garrison swallowed. He wasn't ready to go there, so he avoided an answer altogether. "Are you close to him? Your grandpa?"

Molly shrugged. "Lew and I spent a week every summer with him. It's not that I don't want him here. I do. I'm shocked he agreed to come. He's always hated Longview. Calls it a shithole, but I guess when push comes to shove, a shithole trumps a nursing home."

"Right, paper covers rock, and shithole sinks nursing home."

Molly fell into the couch. "Sorry, you must think I'm awful. Here you are looking for your grandfather and I'm—"

"Say no more. No judgment. It's a lot to take on. If I can help somehow, lay it on me."

Molly's smile looked forced, but it was better than the scowl she entered the room with. "Did you find anything to help you?"

"Not yet, but this piqued my interest." He held up a paper, blank except for the name Earl Rogers penciled in at the top.

"Oh, him. Earl owned a service station that employed Clancy and Joel. I believe he was a family friend as well. We had scheduled an interview, but he had a heart attack a few days before and was in the Critical Care Ward. He's nearly one hundred anyway."

Adrenaline slammed through Garrison. "We have to talk to him. That might be gold."

"I know. That's why I scheduled it. But did you miss the part where he's one hundred years old and sick? May still be in the hospital."

"You mean you haven't kept up with him? How long ago did this happen?"

"Not that long, a month or so."

Garrison jumped up. "A lot could happen in a month, especially when you are one hundred years old."

"I planned on following up, but I've been...busy. Busy with other leads."

Garrison picked up the thin stack of files. "Obviously."

"Fine, I forgot. Got busy reading the trial transcript trying to find violations of procedure."

"Tomorrow then," Garrison said.

"Tomorrow, I have class. Tomorrow, I need to get a room ready for Pappy. Tomorrow, I pour a glass of wine and sit in front of the TV for the mindless entertainment of *Roseanne*."

"Wrong." Garrison raised the blank page. "Tomorrow we dine on lousy hospital food and see about filling up this paper."

CHAPTER 7

Longview, Texas, 1941

Lorraine emerged from her bedroom, leaving a mountain of dresses on the floor behind her. Two hours getting ready, and she still looked all wrong. But Clancy would be here any minute; he should *already* be here. It had been a week since their dinner together. A week she had spent convincing her parents it didn't matter what Clancy did for a living or how old he was. It was only a date, not a marriage proposal. Lane and Birdie wanted so much for Lorraine, but usually, they wanted to give her exactly what she wanted.

Memories of that dinner danced around Lorraine's brain. In less than two hours, Clancy Fitchett had blown away her preconceived notions about him. He had no shortage of charm, but he was also intelligent, well read, and well informed of current affairs. Her mother would be glad to know he was a perfect gentleman. Not so much as a kiss goodnight, even though she hinted it was perfectly okay to give her one. She wasn't old fashioned. Maybe that would come tonight. They'd only known each other a week, but a kiss already seemed overdue.

"Stop fidgeting, Lori; you're lovely," her mother said.

The clock chimed, announcing Clancy was now fifteen minutes late. Fifteen minutes! What if he was just another cad? How long should she sit here embarrassed before she ran crying into her bedroom?

The bang on the door was louder than a gunshot. "Hasn't he heard of a doorbell?" Her mother still had her hand over her heart. Lorraine checked her stockings for runners and fluffed her curls.

Her parents beat her to the door. "Welcome. I'm Lane Applewhite." Her father sounded sterner than usual. "This is my wife, Birdie."

"Pleased to meet you both." Lorraine tried to peer over her parents to get a look at Clancy, but Mother was wearing her heels. "Sorry I'm late. There was a wait at the florist."

Lorraine pushed passed her parents to find Clancy holding out a bouquet of daffodils.

"And then my heart with pleasure fills and dances with the daffodils," he said, quoting the Wordsworth poem she gushed about over dinner. The yellow flowers were beautiful, the borrowed words even more so, but neither held a candle to Clancy. She'd never seen him in something besides his uniform. The khaki slacks and fitted sweater were certainly improvements.

"These are darling. I'll get them in water."

"Get him a glass too, unless you prefer something harder?" Lane asked.

"Only if by harder you mean an ice-cold Coca-Cola."

Lane slapped Clancy's back. "Now you're cooking with gas. I'm a Coca-Cola man myself."

"We should probably let them go," Birdie said. "Or else you'll keep them all night."

Clancy smiled. "Yeah we better scoot if we want to make Lake Lamond before dark."

Lorraine looked at her dress and shoes, trying to hide her disappointment. "Should I change?"

"Are you kidding? Couldn't look better if you tried."

"I didn't know if this dress was lake-appropriate."

"Looks like as good a dress as any for a picnic. And we won't stay long. Joan Crawford's got a new movie where she plays a writer. Thought you may enjoy it."

"All right." The movie sounded fun, but Lorraine wished she could trade the picnic for an early dinner at a nice restaurant in town. But when Clancy's hand touched the small of her back, she knew she would let him lead her anywhere. Lake Lamond in a yellow dress and red heels was only the beginning.

***

The lake was deserted but still beautiful. The evening light seemed to dip everything in a warm glow. Lorraine couldn't wait to see it when the grass was green and the pavilion alive with activity. She imagined teenage sweethearts waiting for a boat ride, children splashing, and old men fishing for hours.

Lorraine lowered herself onto the quilt Clancy spread out. She tucked her legs to the side and pulled at her dress to cover as much of her legs as possible.

"Need a blanket?" Clancy asked.

"I'm okay."

"Not that I mind the view. Just don't want you to be cold."

"Cold? This isn't cold; it's perfect. I don't do well with heat."

"You are in the wrong place then."

"Tell me about it," she said, even though sitting here with him didn't feel so wrong. "What's for dinner?"

Clancy opened a brown grocery bag. "Sorry, I don't have a picnic basket. Pretty unromantic of me. And I hope you like sandwiches."

She unwrapped one. "Who doesn't like sandwiches?"

"Atta girl."

"Is this why you brought me here? To make sure I'm not some highbrow who won't sit on the dirt or eat sandwiches? Not that I'd blame you for thinking differently. I guess I can be high maintenance. I've never had to do without, but I try not to be a brat. I volunteered a lot back home."

"That's great. Plenty of opportunities here."

"Are there?" Lorraine sat up straighter. "Do you volunteer?"

"I help sometimes when the church has a work day, but honestly, I do sign up for the easiest job. What about you?"

Lorraine had taken a bite of her sandwich in anticipation that his answer would be longer. She chewed and swallowed quickly. "I worked at a soup kitchen on the weekends. And my church did work all over the community."

"Have you found a new church?"

"Not yet. But I see as many around here as I do oil derricks. I was raised Methodist, but I'm not strict with it or anything. I attended a Presbyterian church with a friend for years."

Clancy took a swig of Coca-Cola. "You rebel, you."

"Which church do you attend?"

"Kelly Memorial Methodist—when I go." Clancy wiped his mouth with his sleeve. "But I'd be lying if I said that was every week. That chapel was my second home growing up. I figure once I have a family, I'll become a regular again."

Lorraine's heart beat faster hearing Clancy discuss a future family. She had never even been sure she wanted children, and now, she wanted them to have Clancy Fitchett's smile. She realized they barely knew each other, but her future suddenly felt like a field of dandelions just waiting to be wished upon. "So, family is important to you?"

Clancy's mouth was full, but he gave a reassuring nod.

"Are you close to your father?" she asked.

"Not really. I mean, I don't have a beef with him." He paused. "I don't have a beef with him *anymore*." Clancy reached beyond the quilt and pulled out a handful of dried grass. "Hopefully I'm a better dad than him. Not that he was all bad. He taught me plenty. Taught me to fix things, to add fractions, to work hard. It's just that he was a...well, a hard man."

Lorraine nodded. She wanted to know more; she wanted to know everything, but it would come in time.

Clancy dropped the grass and attempted a smile. "Your folks seem nice."

Lorraine put down the sandwich, knowing she wouldn't get another bite in. "They can be suffocating, but they want what is best for me. They created a wonderful childhood full of love and traditions. Mother is big on traditions, on routines. We go to the movies every Saturday afternoon, and on Tuesday at 8:30, you'll find us gathered around the radio for *The Aldrich Family* show." Lorraine wanted to go on, but she was talking too much again and using her hands too. Mother always scolded her for that. She pushed them underneath her legs to stifle their gestures.

"We had a few of those too," Clancy said. "Mama and I came here for her birthday picnic every year. All the way from Carthage." He pointed across the lake. "We'd sit underneath those trees bowing over the lake and watch the water lap the shore." His eyes searched the area, but she knew he wasn't seeing what she was; he was seeing into the past. "Sometimes it still feels like she's here. Waiting for me."

"She might be. I mean, when you think about it, how could ghosts not exist?"

Clancy shrugged. "Guess I never thought much about it."

Lorraine turned toward him. "You remember the Bible story where Jesus walked on water? Well, when the disciples saw him, they were scared to death. Said they thought he was a ghost. Now if ghosts weren't real, don't you think Jesus would scold them for their belief in witchcraft or something? But he didn't. He said, 'If I were a ghost, would I have flesh and bones?' Why didn't he tell them ghost weren't real?"

Clancy gave a slight laugh. "Fair point, but I don't like the idea of Mama just wondering around the Earth with nothing to do."

"Who says she has nothing to do? Watching out for you must be a full-time job. But you're right; it's surely easier to do from heaven." She picked at the crust of her sandwich. "So, tell me more about those birthday picnics."

"The first time I remember coming here was the year Joel started school. So it was just me and Mama home. Bet that was a good year. Wish I remembered more of it. Wish my mind recalled the good as vividly as the bad." Clancy stopped talking, but Lorraine didn't feel the need to interject. Sometimes silence was the ticket. "One year we didn't get to go," he continued. "She didn't get me from school, and that evening, Joel had a surprise party for her. I went to bed heartbroken. It was her birthday, yet I felt forgotten. Go figure."

"All children are selfish. Basic nature."

"Not Joel. He baked a cake and made decorations. Wouldn't have occurred to me to do something for her birthday. Didn't occur to Daddy to do much for her, ever. Anyway, she woke me up in the middle of the night, and we drove here for a midnight picnic." He paused, and Lorraine saw him wipe away a tear. "The sky was so clear, you'd swear we could see every star in the galaxy." Clancy cleared his throat trying to appear more stoic than he was. She took his hand. He squeezed back but waited till he regained composure to face her. Men were funny when it came to emotions that didn't involve laughing or throwing a punch.

Clancy's eyes suddenly appeared bluer and more magnetic. His gaze was both intoxicating and frightening but impossible to turn away from. To put her head down and deny this moment was not an option.

"My god, you're beautiful," he said. And when he leaned forward, she did the same. Clancy took a firm hold of her neck and pressed his lips against hers. All her senses heightened, yet she couldn't see, smell, touch, taste, or feel anything she had only moments ago. A world beyond Clancy Fitchett didn't exist. It was Clancy who pulled away, spooked by something she hadn't noticed. She turned to see what had stolen him from their private world.

She giggled. "Silly bird. You startled us."

Clancy didn't laugh. His face turned chalky, and sweat dripped from his brow. He kept his eyes glued to the bird as he yanked at the blanket, but it only let out a shrill cry that made Clancy jump again. How odd for him to be afraid of a harmless bird.

"It's a mourning dove," Lorraine explained. "You can tell them apart from other doves by their brown color and the sad cries they make. So, this little fellow was just earning his name."

"What's that? Oh yeah, a mourning dove." His voice sounded relaxed, but his whole body was tense. "He ruined our kiss."

"He didn't ruin it."

"You'll have to give me another try at it, later." Clancy stood and extended his hand.

Despite all the movement, the dove still sat, nestled into the blanket. "How odd." She knelt to examine the bird. "You don't think he's hurt?"

Clancy jerked the quilt harder, and the dove fluttered away. "Seems okay," he said. "Now let's go see about that movie."

***

No matter how he tried, Clancy couldn't stop thinking about that damn dove. It wasn't just the bird—it was what it represented. Something terrible was coming. It looked like that stubborn dove that camped on the windowsill the morning Mama passed. Years before, a white one brushed against his shoulder just before his femur snapped during a football game. And of course, there was the first time—the doves that changed everything. It wasn't just Joel's life ruined that day. Clancy had a scar too, even if no one else noticed it.

Things had been going so well with Lorraine. Clancy tried to continue on with their date as if an omen didn't loom over it. He held Lorraine's hand and waited in line to buy her popcorn. He let her lay her head on his shoulder and pretended to care about the movie's love triangle.

An hour in, the Coca-Colas caught up with him. He was glad for an excuse to walk around. His arm was asleep and his skin still clammy. A smoke in the cool night air would do him good. "I'll be right back," he whispered. "Want something?"

Lorraine shook the empty popcorn box at him.

"You got it."

Clancy tried to take his time, but footsteps pounded behind him. He sped up, but whoever was following did too. He turned around when he reached the lobby, fists clenched. "Spread out, will ya, pal?"

"Easy now. I didn't figure you recognize me in that dark theater, but I must have come into focus here under these house lights."

The Coca-Cola sloshed in Clancy's stomach. First doves, now Crawl. Clancy couldn't decide which was worse. "Oh hey." Clancy shook his hand then stepped back. "Surprised to run into you. Don't they have movie houses in Louisiana?" Clancy didn't even recognize his own forced laughter.

"They do, but Longview has that hot little number sitting next to me in there. You aren't the only one these Texas girls are stuck on."

"I'll let you get back to her then." Clancy stepped away, but Crawl grabbed his shoulder. "Missed seeing you last month."

Clancy swallowed. "You got your money. I'll pay Joel back."

Crawl's gaze was tight and focused. "Start out by staying on top of your accounts with me. You can worry about that hacked up SOB later."

"I won't be late again." Clancy only took a few steps toward the theater before Crawl's words stopped him cold.

"Say hi to Lorraine for me."

"What did you say?"

Crawl smirked. "That's her name, right? Lorraine Applewhite?"

Fear clawed through Clancy, jostling his insides then scratching up his throat. "Leave her alone, please."

"She ought to be wary getting involved with someone like you. Does she know about me?"

"No. It's only a first date. Nothing serious." Clancy felt like he was trying to appease a jealous ex.

Crawl leaned against the wall and fumbled his cigarette package. "By your present manner, I'd guess you were plenty serious about her. As serious as *you* can be anyway."

"You've always got your money and you always will."

"Hope so." Crawl raised an eyebrow. "For Lane and Birdie's sake. How unpleasant would it be to lose their only child over something so silly?" Crawl stuck a cigarette between his teeth. "It's been dandy catching up, but let's get back to our girls and that sensational film."

Clancy barely made it into the bathroom before he threw up. *I told you not to get involved with him.* Joel's admonishment looped in his head. Clancy knew that; he always had. But what else could he have done?

His stomach still wasn't settled, but he forced himself back to Lorraine. Making it to the seat on his wobbly legs felt like a victory.

Lorraine stared at him. "Well...."

"Sorry, I ran into somebody."

"Did they steal my popcorn?"

The popcorn. He'd forgotten about it. "All out," he said. He looked behind him till he spotted Crawl. There was no girl beside him. Crawl raised a hand in greeting, and his white teeth gave an eerie glow in the dark theater.

Clancy couldn't do this. Crawl would always be in his life, but he didn't have to be in Lorraine's. Clancy had to protect her, and there was only one way to do it.

***

Something had gone wrong, but Lorraine couldn't pinpoint what. She folded her hands on her lap. "Did you enjoy the movie?"

Clancy shrugged. "I guess."

The ride home was silent. Plenty of time for Lorraine to replay the whole date over and over in her head. Had she talked about herself too much? Let him kiss her too soon?

"I'm sorry," Clancy finally whispered once he pulled up to her house. Lorraine relaxed, expecting an explanation of what was bothering him. Something unrelated to her. But if that were true, why wouldn't he look at her?

She turned to face him. "What are you sorry for?"

"That this isn't going to work."

The words turned everything upside down and inside out. She could feel the wheels move even though the truck was parked. One by one, the stars disappeared like jacks snatched by children.

"I'm not ready for something serious," he said.

Lorraine clamped her sweater closed. Was he giving her the brush off after saying he wanted a family? What a liar. She needed to yell at him, but the words stuck in her throat. "What happened?" she finally managed.

When Clancy looked at her, his eyes weren't just void of sympathy; they were void of everything. Clancy leaned over her and pushed the truck's door open. "Take care."

The night air hit her like an icy wave. Lorraine looked at him one last time, eyes pleading for him to reconsider, but he stared straight ahead. She slammed the door. It was the only fight she had in her. She ran inside without bothering to see if that had finally gotten his attention.

Chapter 8

Longview, Texas, 1991

Garrison thought about his Grandma Dolly as he walked the wide hallways at the nursing home in Longview. He made eye contact with the residents and smiled. Molly kept her head down. Garrison didn't fault her for it. "Here we are," he said, "Room 214." Molly backed away as he knocked. There was no response, so he stuck his head in. "Knock knock," he said.

A man with sagging skin and mashed potatoes caught in his beard stared at them, a spoon of blue Jell-O suspended in midair.

"Earl Rogers?" Garrison asked.

The man shoveled in the Jell-O. "Yeah."

Garrison pushed Molly in. "I'm Garrison, and this is Molly."

"You kids here to sing Christmas songs or something?"

"I don't think waiting until after Thanksgiving is necessary, but Christmas in May seems wrong," Garrison said.

"May, eh?" He adjusted his sheet to cover his legs. "I wouldn't know. Threw the calendar away a long time ago. I don't need a reminder of how many days waste away right along with me." He took a final bite of what smelt like a tuna salad sandwich. "Had a good life, though, did a lot, saw a lot, but don't do or see nothing now. Except for what's on that TV box up there. *Wheel of Fortune* and *The Price is Right* keeping me company while I wait to die."

Garrison wasn't sure what to expect today, but it appeared only Earl Rogers' body was floundering, not his mind. Garrison noticed the blank walls. No family photos like the ones that lined Grandma Dolly's room. No corkboard full of birthday cards and letters. "Don't you have any family?"

"I did. Was married sixty-three years to the same sweet lady, but we couldn't..." He sighed. "What would it matter anyhow? I'm one hundred damn years old. If I had children, they'd be dead, and my grandkids would be spending their retirement with their own grandchildren. Kids your age are too self-centered to worry about some great great great grandpa."

"Well, we're here," Garrison said.

"Yeah, why is that again?"

"Mind if we sit?"

"Give the lady the comfortable seat." Earl gestured to a pristine, blue chair in the corner. "You can pull up one of those folding chairs from outside. Just make sure one of my jail mates ain't already sitting on it."

Garrison gave Molly another push. She squeezed by Earl's bed, to her assigned seat.

"So young lady, why are you here?" Earl asked again.

Molly tucked her hair behind her ears. Garrison hadn't noticed she'd worn it down until then. It was different. It was nice. "We're here about Clancy Fitchett," she said.

Earl shoved back his tray. "Are you from that damn 60 Seconds show? I don't want to be on any TV program."

"We aren't," she said.

"Are you writing a book about that mess?"

If Earl got any louder, a nurse would kick them out. Garrison needed to say something that would tranquilize the old man. He settled on the truth. "Clancy may be my grandfather, and I need to find him."

"Is that so?" Earl relaxed in his bed. "I don't know where he is."

"Anything you remember about him would be helpful." Molly pulled out her notepad. "Mind if we take notes?"

Earl shook his finger at Garrison. "As long as it ain't gonna be in some magazine or book. I meant what I said about that."

Molly cleared her throat. "In the interest of full disclosure, I'm the editor of the school paper. That's not why we are here, but I *am* writing a paper."

Garrison cringed. Leave it to Molly to rile Earl up again.

"A paper?" Earl's spit flew in every direction. Garrison was glad he was sitting out of the line of fire, but he enjoyed watching Molly wipe her arm discreetly.

"Yes, about Joel. I don't believe he received a fair trial. More than that, I don't think he's guilty," Molly said.

Garrison braced himself for more screaming and spitting, but Earl immediately relaxed. "In that case, I'll answer your questions." He pointed to her notepad. "Quote me."

Molly clicked her pen and shot Garrison an "I told you so" grin.

"I've maintained Joel's innocence for years," Earl said. "No way he killed Tom. He didn't have it in him. Joel was nothing like his brother."

Garrison was sick of the jabs at Clancy. So what if he'd been a troubled kid and Joel a saint? Somewhere along the line, that saint had turned murderer. "Tom was your friend, right?" he asked.

"Speak up, boy," Earl yelled. "The hearing left me when control of my bodily functions did." Seemed convenient he heard Molly just fine, but Garrison repeated his question. Earl gave a half shrug. "Yes, we were friends."

"Did Joel have problems with his dad?" Garrison asked, loudly this time.

"No different from most fathers and sons, I imagine."

"Was he stern?" Garrison asked.

"Hell yes, he was!" Earl slapped the bed rail. "That was how it was in my day. None of this, 'go sit in the corner and reflect on your life' garbage. It was a belt and to bed without supper. Disrespect was not tolerated."

"What about after Joel left home?" Molly asked.

"They got along fine then. Joel handled the upkeep for Tom's rentals. He took care of Tom, and Tom took care of him. Clancy didn't take care of either of them, but everybody still took care of him." Earl slurped his apple juice through a straw. "Not that I should talk. I gave him a job as a favor to Tom, but that boy didn't know a damn thing about life. He was always showing up late or not showing at all. Forgetting his uniform, asking for an advance on his pay and—"

"Gotcha," Garrison interrupted. He had a feeling Earl had plenty of stories about Clancy's work habits, but none of that mattered. "So, he was lazy, irresponsible. He was a kid, big deal."

"Except he was a grown man—or supposed to be. He got mixed up with a damn Louisiana boy who was always in trouble with the law. Kept Joel up at night."

"There had to be underlying problems you weren't aware of between Joel and Tom. Considering the fight they…." Garrison almost gagged at the sudden smell of urine. He hoped it came from the hallway and not Earl. He faked a cough so he could cover his face with his hand.

Molly took advantage of the break in his questioning to reclaim the conversation. "Have you talked to Joel since he's been in prison?"

"I tried several times, but he refused. Guess he assumed I would be angry with him, but I wanted to help get him a decent lawyer. Tried to write him a few times but no response. I should have kept trying, but I was taught to keep my nose out from where it wasn't wanted."

Molly put her hand over his. "You did more than anyone else."

The smell dissipated, but now something else made Garrison queasy. He couldn't listen to this. Easy for them to glorify Joel Fitchett. They hadn't felt his hands wrapped around their throats.

"Have you read the papers since?" Garrison asked incredulously. "Heard about the trouble Joel's caused?" He kept his face to Earl but felt Molly pinning him with her eyes. "He's been in what? Five prisons?"

"Three," Molly corrected.

"How do you reconcile that with the good ole boy you describe?"

"Garrison, that's enough," Molly said.

"Why? He doesn't have any problem sharing stories of Clancy's sins. Why the double standard for Joel?" Garrison replied.

Molly stood, but Earl raised his hand to stop her. "It's all right, doll. He's got a point. But any of us would behave strangely, being in a cage. It changed Joel. All the more reason I shouldn't have given up on him. I've let him down—and Tom too."

Molly scooted her chair even closer to the bed. "Mr. Rogers—"

"Call me Earl."

"Earl, do you have any idea who may have wanted Mr. Fitchett dead? It's not too late to find justice for him—and for Joel too."

"I don't have any evidence to base anything on."

"A gut feeling?" Molly asked.

"I thought it was shady of Clancy to take off. Not that I would expect him to do much, given his history, but to disappear like he did...hard not to wonder why." Molly gave a crisp nod and scribbled on her notepad.

"Satisfied?" Garrison asked.

"Not until I get Joel out of prison," Molly said.

"It's not just the leaving either," Earl continued. "Clancy wasn't right after the war. Quit working, started drinking. Hard to imagine a worse combination."

"Was he violent?" Molly asked.

"On occasion. He'd get this look in his eye, hard to describe it. He did some strange stuff. Guess it was common for boys coming home."

"PTSD?" Garrison asked.

"Huh?"

"Post-Traumatic Stress Disorder."

"Is that what they call it now? My word, they've got to come up with a new name for everything now, don't they? Call it what you want, shell shock, battle fatigue, PTS whatever but yeah, I guess so."

"Seems he went to San Antonio at some point. He and Lorraine were married there. Did you ever hear about that?" Molly asked.

Earl picked at his dried lips. "Nope. All I know is he never came back to Longview, not even that one time Lorraine did."

"When was that?" Molly asked.

"Back in the seventies after her daddy passed. Cleaned the place and took her Mama home with her."

"Clancy didn't come to the funeral?" Garrison asked.

"There wasn't one. There was a viewing, and then they took his body to Montana or Wyoming or wherever they came from. Her mother passed not long after. They auctioned that house and everything in it. I tried to get Mrs. Applewhite's china for the Misses, but that pharmacist on 2nd Street got it. What was that old son of a bitch's name?"

"So, Lorraine only came home once? Was she not close to her family?" Garrison asked, ignoring his question.

"They visited her. Mrs. Applewhite would fly out for months at a time until her husband retired. Then they'd leave for entire summers, a month at Christmas and so on. Never said where they went, but we all knew it was to see her."

If only Garrison could get his hands on those plane ticket records right about now. "What was Lorraine like?"

"A sweet gal. Good family. Not sure what she saw in Clancy, especially knowing she could have been with Joel." He raised an unruly eyebrow. "That boy was in love with her."

"Did he say that?" Molly asked.

"Didn't have to. I worked with him every day. It was clear from listening to him talk. And I have my suspicions they had something going on while Clancy was fighting. They spent an awful lot of time together."

"The plot thickens," Molly said, tapping her chin.

"See," Garrison said. "Even better than the ABC Tuesday line up."

"They were all just kids," Earl said. "Didn't know anything about love."

"They must have learned something along the way. Clancy and Lorraine never divorced," Garrison said smugly.

"Well, we don't know that," Molly said. "Seeing as how there are no records of them at all."

"But if they divorced, we'd have found it, same as death certificates. They're still married, still alive somewhere," Garrison said.

"Unless they changed their names," Molly suggested.

Garrison didn't even want to consider that. A new identity would be a dead end if there ever was one. He didn't need to waste any more time arguing with Molly; he needed to get as much information from Earl as possible. "The night Joel was attacked, the Fitchetts had dinner with the Montgomery family. Did you know them?"

"A little. Mr. Montgomery ran a grocery store in Carthage. Nancy and his wife were close."

"What about their daughter, Katie?"

"Katherine did some housekeeping for us. Married a man who went to our church. Didn't stay long after that. Her husband got transferred someplace cold. North Dakota or somewhere."

Garrison couldn't believe his luck. Not only was Earl still alive, his memory was a marvel. A little more information like this, and Garrison could forgive the digs at Clancy. "Do you remember her husband's name?"

"He was German. I remember that much because it was the worst time to be a German in America—or to marry one. So, his name was German; that's all I can tell you."

"How did Joel get the scar?" Molly asked.

"Hell if I know. The boys will probably take it to the grave."

A nurse who came to take Earl's tray stared at the clock. Molly got the hint and stood. "Visiting hours are over. We should go."

"Mencken!" Earl shouted. "The boy Katherine married. Frank Mencken."

Garrison pantomimed for Molly to write it down, but she already had her pencil tucked behind her ear.

"I'd like to visit again, if that's okay," she said.

"That would be fine, but I don't know anything else that can help with your paper."

"Not for that, just to talk about the weather or watch *Wheel of Fortune*."

The nurse returned with a paper cup full of pills. She set them in front of Earl, but he ignored them, studying Garrison instead. "You're too skinny, and your hair is darker and too damn long." Garrison smiled. What the elderly lacked in hair pigmentation, they usually made up for in candor. "But your eyes and chin, they belonged to Clancy first."

The room shifted. Garrison grabbed Molly's arm to steady himself. He had no idea how much he needed to hear those words until that moment. "Do you have a picture?"

"No. Take my word for it. You *are* kin to him. I don't doubt that. My ears and heart may have failed me, but the peepers still work fine."

"Wish we knew where to look for pictures," Molly said.

"Mugshots?" Earl winked at her.

The tap of the nurse's foot sounded like machine gun fire, but Garrison had one more question. "Do you remember Dorothy Ellison? She's my grandmother. She didn't live around here long, but based on the timeline I worked out, she dated Clancy right before Lorraine."

"I'm sorry. I don't. Lots of girls were in and out of his life. Clancy was a good-looking kid, like you. Wish I remembered her. I'm sure she was a great lady to have a grandson like you. Family must be important for you to go through all this."

"Thanks, but don't forget I'm one fourth Clancy Fitchett too," Garrison said with a laugh.

"Well, nobody's perfect. You kids get along now." Earl flapped his hand toward the door. "Go watch a movie or something. I would say life is too short to worry about the past, but in my case, it's been long enough." He raised the paper cup holding his pills in a mock toast as the nurse shooed them out the door.

***

"Now what?" Molly buckled her seat belt.

"A call to directory assistance. See if we can find the Fitchett's hopefully not so long-lost friend. Speaking of..." He reached across her to pull a napkin out of his glove compartment. "Got a pen?"

Molly pulled four from her purse, all different colors. "Need paper?"

"This is paper." He scribbled *Katherine/Frank Mencken* on the napkin and shoved it into his pocket.

Molly kept her hand extended until she got her pen back. "You sure you still want to find him?" She wiped the pen on her tee shirt like Garrison had contaminated it. "After what Earl said?"

"Can't hurt. Can't be worse than meeting Joel, who literally *did* hurt me."

Molly reclined her seat. "So what movie are we going to?"

"Huh?"

"Oh, come on. It's not the worst idea, is it?"

Garrison meant to decline, but Molly's bright face was a welcome sight after all the dirty looks she'd given him tonight. "Okay, but I pick."

"I changed important plans for you. Your treat, I pick. Pull in here, and I'll get a paper."

Garrison made a sharp turn from the wrong lane into the Circle K parking lot.

"Want anything else? Candy to smuggle in?" she asked.

"As many peach gummy rings as your purse can hold."

A familiar emotion washed over Garrison as soon as he was alone. Guilt. It was one thing to have a research partner but another to take her to the movies. To top it off, he hadn't called Amber in two days. He needed to tonight. He should tell Molly he couldn't go. Make up a last-minute excuse. He was trying to come up with one when she plopped back into the car.

"*Drop Dead Fred.*" She shoved the paper in Garrison's face.

"You are kidding, right?" He tilted his head to read the other choices. "Isn't there a new Seagal movie out?"

"Yes, just about every week. Come on, it looks hilarious. We could use a break."

She had a point. And it's not like she picked some chick flick with a romantic storyline. It was a movie about an adult with an imaginary friend. What harm could come from that?

"All right, all right." Garrison put the car into reverse. "Which way to the theater?"

***

Turns out Molly had been right. They had needed a laugh, and the movie and dinner afterward provided plenty. He hadn't wanted to take her home. Spending time with Molly was even more fun when they weren't talking about anyone with the last name Fitchett.

When he finally sat down to call Amber, the ticket stub in his jeans poked against his leg like a thorn, and the hotel's phone might as well have been cement. The call he'd been looking forward to now seemed like an obligation.

"Garrison?" Amber's voice was croaky. He had forgotten about the time difference.

"Did I wake you?"

"No, well yes, but it's okay."

"I'm sorry. Let's talk tomorrow."

"No, no, I'm good." She yawned. "How are you? Find anything out?"

"Got a few leads. Met a man whose memory I wish I could loan Grandma. How is she?"

"Really good."

"Good?" he asked.

"Well, she's sick again. But Garrison, she remembers."

"Remembers what? You?"

"Yeah. I had to remind her yesterday, and she was in and out, but today she said my name as soon as I walked in. Talked about you, told me cute stories."

"Wait, two good days?" Garrison wasn't sure how to feel—glad Grandma Dolly was remembering or cheated he was missing it. "But what about current things? Does she understand where she is?"

"She does; she even remembers what she had for lunch. We talked about the president today."

"Bush?"

"Yep. She knew it was Bush."

"And she didn't claim to be his lover?"

Amber giggled. "No, nothing like that. She's pretty lucid, Garrison. I've never known her like this."

Garrison felt a pulling sensation in his gut. "I'm coming back."

"You're what? But what about your research? And Clancy?"

"It can wait a few days; Clancy can wait."

Amber squealed into the phone. Garrison pulled it away but not soon enough. He couldn't hear the rest of what she said over the ringing in his ears, but her excitement was obvious.

"I'll call tomorrow and book a flight," he said. "Know any cute blondes who can pick me up from the airport?"

"Just one. And that's all you better know too."

Garrison hung up the phone and turned on the TV. He hadn't even made it past channel six when the phone rang.

"Miss me already?" Garrison asked.

"Um, hello to you too."

Garrison shot up in his bed. "Oh, hey Molly. What's up?"

"I need a favor. I'm sure I've probably called them all in today by making you watch *Drop Dead Fred*, but something came up."

"Maybe I can grant one more wish if you let me pick the next movie." Garrison winced. Why did he say that? It was a step beyond friendly.

"You may want to pick the next three when I tell you what the favor is. Mom called. Pappy has to be out of his apartment next week. I've got to make the drive to Odessa ASAP."

"Odessa?" he asked.

"A barren land about a seven-hour drive away. What it's missing in trees, it makes up for with relatively low humidity. Want to help me?"

"You had me until the word "help." I thought maybe you just wanted me to ride shotgun, eat peach gummies, and sing country music."

"Country? Wasn't that a Red Hot Chili Peppers tape blaring in your car?"

"Well, yeah. But everyone listens to country music on road trips. You have to, I don't know why. Can you imagine how angry you would be after seven hours of Red Hot Chili Peppers?"

"I'd feel the same after seven hours of George Strait myself, but if it's country you want, sure. Just as long as you help me with the heavy lifting. Pappy doesn't have much, but he insists on bringing a few items, so I'll take my brother's pickup. We can leave whenever. I just need to be back Monday to turn in my paper and take one last final exam."

Garrison couldn't think of anything more fun than a road trip with Molly, but he couldn't do that and see Grandma Dolly simultaneously. "I'd like to, Molly. I'm not just saying that, but I made plans to go back home."

"Home? Already?" Her voice was barely audible.

"Not for long, a week tops. My grandma is doing better. I'd put it off, but who knows how long this good spell will last."

"I understand. Do your parents take care of her?"

The realization of how little Molly knew about him caught him off guard. "She's in a home."

"That explains why you were so comfortable today. I'd never been to one before. It really wasn't so bad."

"Most of them aren't. Grandma Dolly's been in this one a year. She couldn't take care of herself any longer. Mom and Dad considered moving her in with them, but it's for the best they didn't. They died last October, car crash."

"What? Oh Garrison, how awful. I'm sorry."

"Thanks."

"No really, I'm sorry. Sorry for that crap I said about my parents. And saying you were lucky to be an only child. I suck."

"It's okay. Didn't offend me. I'm just sorry I can't go with you. Are you sure you can't put it off one more week?"

"Don't feel bad! It's not a big deal. Enjoy your time with your grandma."

And girlfriend, he thought. Now was a perfect time to break the news, but he couldn't bring himself to say it. "So, will you go to Odessa alone?"

"Nah, I'll make Lew go. He won't miss anything besides a weekend of frat parties. Won't be as good company, but the music'll be better."

"I wish I could go, Molly. I'll make it up to you. Take you and your pappy to dinner."

"You bet you will. See you in what? A week?"

"I'm sure I'll talk to you before then." Garrison immediately regretted saying it. He needed to see Amber and not think about Molly, not think about her, and definitely not call her. He loved Amber. He was going to marry Amber. If the accident hadn't happened, they would be planning a wedding. He wouldn't be here now. So much would be different had the accident never happened. But he couldn't think about that. Two women were enough to occupy his mind tonight.

CHAPTER 9

Longview, Texas, 1941

Lorraine woke up to a hazy world. She'd fallen asleep with tears in her eyes; it only made sense she would wake up with them too. But as she lolled in the bathtub, her mother came in and told her that Clancy was waiting downstairs to take them to church. Waiting in a dark blue suit, waiting with all the right words. And just like that, they were back together. Lorraine hoped she hadn't made a mistake. He just got a little scared is all. He didn't seem scared now, laughing with her father in front of the radio, turning back to steal glances at her in the kitchen every few minutes.

Lorraine was icing a cake when the laughing stopped, when the music on the radio stopped. She stepped back into the living room. "Hey, I was listening—"

"Shhhh!" Daddy scolded while Clancy simply held up a finger to silence her. It only took a few seconds of listening to understand why.

"The Japanese have attacked Pearl Harbor, Hawaii by Air," came a voice through the static. "President Roosevelt has just announced. We take you now to Washington."

"Birdie, come listen to this!" Lane called.

"Details are not available. They will be in a few minutes," came another voice. "A Japanese attack on Pearl Harbor would naturally mean war."

Lorraine trembled. She wished Clancy would come take her in his arms, but he was finished stealing glances at her. His attention was on the radio now. He leaned closer to it as his eyes grew darker.

Ten long minutes passed before anyone spoke. "Can we turn it off?" Lorraine's voice shook.

Clancy's head snapped up. "Turning it off won't make it go away. No more than ignoring what was going on in the rest of the world did."

"I know, but they keep saying the same thing over and over." Tears ran down her face, stinging the places where her tears the night before had chafed.

Daddy came to comfort her. Clancy exploded out of his chair and kicked it. "Those yellow bastards!" he yelled.

"Boys will be banging down the door at the recruiting offices in the morning," Daddy said.

Clancy made eye contact with Lane. He didn't say anything; he didn't have to. The look said it all.

Lorraine retreated back into the kitchen and slapped icing onto her cake. But she could still hear the beep from the radio alert—and still see the spark in Clancy's eyes at the mention of signing his life away.

***

Sitting in this cold, gray room, Joel wondered if he'd made a mistake. But a week of trying medical remedies from a library book had been a week wasted. This was his last resort.

He knew it was a risk to travel to Shreveport to meet Dr. Wheat. What if he ran into Crawl? It was a big city, but Joel suspected if Crawl needed a doctor, this would be the one he visited. Dr. Wheat was known for his unorthodox practices; it was why Joel was here. Still, the cascading crystals, paintings of ancient shamans, and the sign that read *Healer Wheat* made Joel nervous. This guy was an actual medical doctor, wasn't he? Now that Joel thought about it, Wheat didn't even sound like a real last name.

"Mr. Fitchett, please follow me." A young nurse appeared in the doorway.

She led Joel to a room in the back of the house. It was simple, not much more than an exam table, a cabinet, and a desk, but it was well lit and clean. The plainness of the room relaxed him.

Dr. Wheat arrived immediately. He was older than Joel expected and had a difficult time walking, even with his cane. His cheeks were hollowed and his eyes cloudy. His haggard appearance and hacking cough made Joel more nervous than the sitting room decorations had. He looked like a man who needed a doctor himself.

"I'm all right," the doctor insisted as the nurse helped him to his desk. "What can I do for you, Mr. Fitchett?"

"I hoped you would prescribe me colloidal silver."

The doctor adjusted his glasses. "Silver's gone out of favor. Haven't you heard of the miracle of antibiotics?" The sarcasm in his tone was evident.

"I have, but they won't help this." Joel turned his face so the doctor could better see the scar. Dr. Wheat ran his finger over it. "I read if silver applied topically can help scarring," Joel added.

"The use of silver goes back before Christ. Our ancestors carried water in silver vessels to keep from contamination. Silver coins dropped in milk will keep it from spoiling. Hippocrates wrote of how it destroyed infections and cured diseases. I've seen shingles, whooping cough, boils, all powerless against it." Joel didn't mind the sermon; he'd heard Dr. Wheat had a chip on his shoulder about penicillin.

"So is the silver still available?"

"For now. But you must be careful. Some sold only has a trace amount of actual silver in it. There are many other methods."

"No." Joel was ready for this answer and also prepared to stand his ground. "I've tried everything. I need silver."

Dr. Wheat made a steeple with his fingers. "I can get you the real stuff, but it *will* cost you."

"I'm okay with the price. If it will work."

The doctor examined the scar again. Joel wished he would stop touching it. "Won't make it disappear. Would have done more good applied at the time of injury. Still, it can destroy the bacteria and aid with the creation of new healthy tissue."

Joel's heart raced. "How long will I have to use it?"

"Hard to say. I'll write you an initial prescription to try. Two weeks' worth."

"And if it's getting better, you'll write another?"

The doctor chuckled. "Yes, but you have to be careful with silver. It can give skin a blue tint if overused."

Of course, it could. Joel didn't get good news unless it dragged bad news behind it. He could trade the scar for blue skin. Sounded great.

"Don't worry, it won't change your color in a few weeks." He reached for his pen. "But I believe we'll see a noticeable difference in the scar in that time."

A noticeable difference. Joel replayed the phrase in his mind as the doctor tore off the prescription. He left the office clutching onto this tiny piece of paper that had the power to change everything.

Joel was so fixated on the prescription he almost didn't see the dead crow beside his truck. Something about the way it was lying, flat on its back, its beak pointed straight to the sky, looked unnatural. Like someone had posed it that way.

It wasn't flattened, and no insects swarmed it. Joel's first thought was Crawl. He spun in circles, but he saw no sign of Crawl or his bonfire red Mercury. He was being paranoid. Sometimes a dead bird was just a dead bird.

There was no way to climb into his seat without stepping on it or moving the carcass, so Joel crawled through the passenger side and drove straight to the druggist.

***

"Awful business about Pearl Harbor, isn't it?" Joel's father asked. "I can barely get into my office in the mornings due to the lines at the recruiting office next door. They're staying open twenty-four hours a day."

Joel didn't want the conversation to go here. He knew his daddy wanted, probably expected, them to enlist. But Joel wasn't going to be guilted into it. Plenty of men were built for pushups and combat—but not him. He didn't want to say so; now was the worst time to admit something like that. He needed to change the subject. "So, what should we bring for Christmas dinner, Daddy?"

"I won't be bringing anything this year," Clancy said.

Daddy lowered his spoon. "You're not boys anymore. I don't owe you a Christmas meal or any meal." Hearing the growl in his father's voice turned Joel into a child again. He wanted to slide down his chair and disappear under the table.

"Don't worry, Daddy, I'll handle the meal," Joel offered.

"Not so fast," Clancy said. "I have a better idea."

Joel wondered why Clancy was so giddy. What was behind his stupid smile?

"And what's that?" Daddy asked.

"I want you both to come to the Applewhite's for Christmas dinner."

"I understand you'd want to spend Christmas with your girlfriend, but I'd rather not inconvenience her family," Daddy said.

"It was their idea," Clancy spoke with his mouth full. "They want to meet you."

"All right." He refolded the napkin in his lap. "Tell them I'll bring a bottle of wine."

Joel stared at his father. He couldn't even convince the old man to come to dinner at their house. But it was fine; Joel would spend Christmas alone. It could be just another day, one with no family duties to perform.

"You'll be there too." Clancy pointed his fork at Joel. Something about the gesture got under Joel's skin. Like he didn't even get a say in his own life. He'd let Clancy call a lot of shots, but this decision would be his.

"No thanks." Joel blew on his slice of apple pie.

"Why not?" Clancy's expression sobered. "You're always avoiding Lorraine. Do you not like her?"

I like her too much. "I don't like crowds. Just don't think I'd be comfortable."

"It's not a crowd, Joel. Just Lorraine and her folks."

"I'll pass."

"All right, here's the thing. The reason I need you both here is because I'm going to ask Lorraine to marry me." He slammed his hands down. "Hot Dog! That's the first time I've said it out loud."

It was only the table Clancy shook, but Joel felt the entire room shift. "What? Marry her? It hasn't even been a month."

"But we've spent every day together." Clancy looked to his father. "When you know you know, right Daddy?"

Joel knew their father would side with him. Where did Clancy think they'd live? Who would pay the bills? But instead of raising his voice, Daddy raised his glass. "When you know, you know," he repeated. "Congratulations, son. May you be as happy as your mother and I were."

Happy? That was news to Joel. When it came to Mama, Daddy was always looking for an infraction. Joel had heard more angry outbursts over uncleaned dishes and misspent dollars than 'I love yous'— that was for sure. Joel tried to lift his glass, but it felt too heavy. He couldn't fake a toast or fake his happiness.

"We are making a toast, son. Raise your glass."

"How about a question instead? Have you bought her a ring?" Joel asked.

Clancy sipped his wine. He never drank unless he was here. You couldn't be around Tom Fitchett without having alcohol poured down your throat.

Joel downed his entire glass waiting for Clancy's answer.

"Well, I haven't bought one yet, but I *am* saving."

"You think Lorraine Applewhite will be satisfied with an IOU? A girl who's never had to ask twice for anything?" The question spilled out of Joel. He was through trying to choose words carefully.

The look on Clancy's face was hard to decipher. Anger at an underhanded insult of Lorraine? The realization Joel was right? Or maybe shock that Joel was calling him out on one of his bullshit ideas.

Clancy looked back at Daddy. "Actually, Pops, this is the part I hoped you could help with."

Joel relaxed in his chair, deciding to give the pie time to sufficiently cool. This here was typical Clancy. Asking their dad for a loan. Their dad! There was no way in this life or any other that Tom Fitchett was loaning anything to anyone. This was the same man who sent his boys hunting for worms rather than spending a quarter on bait. The father who made them reuse bath water and sliced open toothpaste tubes to make sure none was wasted.

Their father didn't say no right away. He wiped his mouth on his napkin and retreated into the bedroom without so much as a word.

Clancy took a bigger drink of his wine. "Okie dokie then. Guess I should have known better."

"Oh well. You can put back a little each month, and in a year, you'll have enough." A year, Joel liked the idea of it. A lot could change in a year. Lorraine probably wouldn't be around, and if she was, at least it would give Joel time to get used to the idea. To get rid of his jealousy—and his scar too.

Clancy's face twisted. "A year? No way. Too much could go wrong."

Joel wondered what Clancy meant but didn't ask. Daddy reentered, clearing his throat the way he did when he wanted everyone's attention. "As you are both aware, I make it a point not to give you boys money. You're grown men—time to learn how to behave as grown men and manage your money as grown men. The way I taught you from both words and example."

Joel stopped listening. He had heard this speech before. So many times. Daddy should realize the reason these lectures came so effortlessly was because it wasn't his first time delivering them.

Joel didn't tune back in until he saw Daddy pull something from his pocket. A ring. Not just any ring—Mama's ring. How strange to see it again, and not on her hand. The diamonds circling the large pearl still had a faint sparkle. It was simple and beautiful, just like Mama. Joel's muscles shook as he put two and two together. No. This was not happening.

"Are you sure? I never meant for you to give me this," Clancy said. But despite the surprised act, he was quick to snatch the ring from their father's hand.

"Nancy would want it this way," Daddy said.

Except that wasn't true. She meant for Joel to give it to his wife. She'd said so. "No," Joel whispered.

"No what?" Clancy asked sharply.

"You can't have it. Mama meant it for me." Joel reached for the ring, but Clancy pulled it back closer to him. Like they were boys fighting over the last Gingerbread Puff.

Clancy closed his fist around the ring and pulled it to his chest. "I don't understand why you have this sense of entitlement when it comes to Mama's things, but it's starting to gripe my soul. Just because you're the oldest doesn't mean she wanted you to have everything."

"She didn't mean for either of you to have it," Daddy said. "She meant to wear it longer than she did. So now it becomes my decision, and I've decided."

Joel thought back to his conversation with Mama. It was in this kitchen, staring at this same vomit yellow wallpaper. She had lost so much weight, she already wore the ring on her middle finger, but it slipped from there as she carried her plate to the sink.

"Looks like I'm outgrowing it." She forced a smile. "Make sure a special girl gets it next, okay?"

While Joel wasn't sure those were her exact words, the sentiment had been obvious to him then and now. He wasn't a greedy man, but someone ought to respect Mama's wishes. "She told me to make sure it went to a special girl."

"Well, it is going to a special girl," Daddy said. "It's nothing personal, Joel. If you were marrying first, I'd have given it to you."

"How can you be sure I won't be? Don't ignore Clancy's record. What happens to Mama's ring when he doesn't make it to the altar?"

"Hey now." Clancy stood. "Don't run your mouth about things you don't understand."

Joel's body seemed to rise on its own accord. "I understand you, Clancy. Lorraine isn't going to last any longer than Dorothy did—or the girl before her. I've always minded my business, but I draw the line at this."

"What line?" Clancy stepped toward him. "This line?" Another step. "Or this one?" This close, Joel smelled Clancy's sour breath. The father who bought cheap, sour wine was apparently generous when it came to giving away other people's things.

Joel shoved Clancy, something he hadn't done since they were boys. It felt good to release some of the rage bottled inside of him. Clancy pushed back harder, and it was the kitchen stove that broke Joel's fall. The crash was jarring, but nothing hurt. He bounced back up, fists clenched.

"Come on," Clancy beckoned, keeping his own hands in front of his face. "Hit me."

"Boys, sit down!" Daddy yelled.

Joel's first swing missed. Clancy was quicker, more experienced, but Joel had plenty of fight left in him.

"Come on." Clancy's pupils flared. "Winner takes the ring."

Joel swung harder. Turning the ring into some prize showed how little it meant to his brother. Clancy dodged the second punch too, but this time, he grabbed Joel's arm and twisted it behind his back. It stung like the Indian burns they'd given each other as boys, but Joel refused to cry out.

Clancy shoved Joel against the wall. He caught himself, but Clancy rushed up behind him. Joel could tell by the foul smell and heavy breaths that Clancy's mouth was open, that he was about to pop off again. Joel couldn't stand to listen to another word. He forced his elbow back and felt it connect with Clancy.

"Son of a..." Clancy was on the floor, shaking his head like a wet dog, splattering blood in all directions. Daddy rushed to his side, but Clancy waved him away. He tried to stand on his own but stumbled again. Seeing Clancy so dazed somewhat satisfied Joel's rage. He left to grab his jacket from the couch.

"Where are you going you little son of a bitch?" Clancy called. "Come back here and face me like a man."

There was so much Joel wanted to say, yet there was nothing left to say. He checked his pocket for the keys and headed for his truck.

***

The glass from Clancy's empty coke bottle shattered on the driveway. Joel realized he'd be the one sweeping it up tomorrow, but breaking it somehow made him feel better. Would Daddy drive Clancy home or would he have to find his own way for once? Joel's rescuing days were over; that, he was certain of.

He checked his face in the bathroom mirror. His chin was scraped up, but the bleeding had stopped. He didn't mind. It might even take a little attention away from the track across his face.

Joel applied the silver and sealed it with a bandage. It would keep it moist and conceal what he was doing if Clancy came home. Confidence surged through Joel with the tingle of his skin. Day three and it was working. Already fixing the scar. Joel collapsed on his pillow. "Heal, heal," he whispered. The closest he had come to a prayer in a long time. Joel wasn't even sure why the words caused tears, but he caught them on his sleeve before they ran down his face. He couldn't afford to let them wash away any silver. He lay on his pillow and wondered if after the scar healed, he could too.

CHAPTER 10

Ohio, 1991

Garrison couldn't figure out why he wasn't happier to be home. Maybe he'd been so immersed in the lives of Clancy and Joel that pushing above water felt strange. Or maybe he was just tired from an already long day.

"Are you nervous or something?" Amber checked her lipstick in the rearview mirror.

"No, why?"

"You've hardly said a word."

She was right. This awkwardness around Amber was the worst. It felt like a first date. A bad one. Honestly, things had been different for a while now. He and Amber had been together almost two years, but they had both changed so much. Lately Garrison wondered if they'd outgrown their relationship.

He quickly dismissed the thought. Amber had seen him through so much. They'd just been apart too long. The weirdness would surely wear off by the end of the day.

Amber weaved through traffic. "Do you wanna go straight to see Dolly or stop by the house?"

"Home first, let me unpack and get a quick shower. I didn't wake up early enough to take one this morning."

Amber leaned in closer. "Smell good to me."

Garrison pointed ahead. "Better keep your eyes on the road."

"And my hands?" Amber asked, putting one hand on his thigh.

"I think they go on the wheel, but there's no rule about the passenger's." She giggled as he tickled her side. This was more like it. This banter was comfortable.

But Garrison's comfort fled when Amber pulled up to the last house on Meadow Creek Drive. The house of his childhood. A house held up by his memories. Mostly good ones, but those hurt the most to remember.

He'd only been away from home for two years when his parents died, but when he returned here the night of the accident, he realized he'd have to make it home again. It was where their things were, where their scents were, where their lives had been. How could he trade that for some crappy apartment in a bad neighborhood?

"Garrison, come on." Amber stood at the door. "I don't have my key with me. I hope you don't mind, but I cleaned the place a little when I brought the mail in yesterday."

A little was an understatement. It looked cleaner than it had since October, maybe even cleaner than it *ever* had. The air was rich with the scents of clean linen and fresh cut flowers. "Why would anyone mind this? Thanks, Amber, you really are the best."

"Good practice I guess, cleaning up after you." She said it like she needed reassurance. He put his hand on her shoulder.

"I'm sorry everything we planned has been put on hold. But that's all it is, a hold. It will still happen."

She lifted her head to kiss his cheek. "I love you, Garrison."

"Love you too. I'm gonna take a quick shower, but no more cleaning allowed, okay?" He tossed his dirty shirt onto the floor. "I still want it to look like a man lives here."

Amber scratched at her neck. "While we are on the topic..."

Garrison's shoulders tensed. Why couldn't she leave well enough alone?

"Well, no pressure. But Dad says it's a seller's market now. He's certain someone would snatch this place up within a month. Then he could help us find a new house, one that could be ours."

This was not the conversation Garrison wanted to have right now. It was not the conversation he wanted to have ever again, but Amber had once again torn open the Pandora's Box of their relationship.

"Amber, *this place* will be ours. I told your father I'm not ready to sell. Why are you bringing this up again? Why right now?"

"Because that was months ago. I thought after time passed, you'd see how unfair you are being. This house and everything in it belonged to your parents. And it's the same way they left it. Except for the disgusting mess you create daily." She kicked his dirty shirt across the floor. "How are you going to react when I want to take those gold birds off the wall or clean your dad's tools out of the garage?"

Garrison scrubbed a hand over his face. "I don't use the tools, and I don't care about the decorations."

"And that's why you keep their room locked up like a shrine? Why you hoard their belongings?"

Her words were like a knife, shredding his insides. It was hard to believe the cherub-faced, glossy-lipped Amber could be so cruel. "I'm sorry for grieving the loss of my parents. It hasn't even been a year, Amber." He waved his hands around. "This place is all I have left of them."

"It's not." Her voice and face softened. "Memories are worth more than a pile of bricks. I'm sorry, Garrison, but I think I've been patient and accommodating. Have I not?"

She had, but he was too angry to admit it, so he shrugged.

Turns out that was a mistake. Amber leaped from the couch as if it had caught flames, but the only sparks were the ones shooting from her eyes. "This is one thing I'm not budging on. I will *not* live in this house."

Heat stained Garrison's body. Unfortunately, it wasn't just his face that reddened when he was angry or embarrassed. His chest looked nearly as red as the shirt he'd tossed on the floor. Amber stood with her arms crossed and her lips drawn back in a snarl.

"Then we're done talking," he said. "I'm going to take my shower so I can see Grandma. You remember the way out, right?"

Amber yanked her purse from the couch, riffling through it for a Kleenex. "You're being a jerk, you know? You have been for a long time. The problem is that you're angry, and you don't know where to direct it. There's no drunk driver or faulty brakes to blame, so you hurl it all at me."

She had a point. He was angry. Angry his mom had let his dad drive at night without his glasses. Angry his dad took that curve so fast. Angry at God, who sent the rain that made the road slippery. Seemed he knew just where to direct his anger: two dead people and one deity. "I see those psych classes are paying off." Garrison pushed past her. "Thanks for the diagnosis," he added, slamming the bathroom door behind him.

He heard her crying, but he wasn't going back in there until she left. For all he cared, she could cry a river that swept away all the gold birds she despised. He switched the fan on and turned the water full blast. He could no longer hear the sobs, but the bathroom's noises weren't enough to drown out the crash of the slamming door.

***

Dolly was crocheting when Garrison arrived. He stood in the doorway and watched her work the needle and yarn the way she once had, the way she hadn't in years.

"Grandma?" He couldn't keep his voice steady.

The needle fell to her lap when she saw him. "Garrison, you're here."

"I'm here, Grandma." He moved in closer for a hug, kicking a pair of slippers under the bed.

"It's been so long since I've seen you!" She took his face between her hands. "Where have you been all this time?"

Garrison knew the more appropriate question was where *she* had been all this time. But maybe it was better she thought he didn't come around much rather than realize she'd forgotten a year of visits. She started to cry, and Garrison wondered if maybe she realized it after all.

"What's wrong, Grandma?"

"My Lucy," she sobbed. "And Andy too."

It was the first time she had shown much emotion about their deaths. This was the downfall of having a memory back. It wasn't just the good ones that returned.

"It's been hard." Garrison's tears became too heavy to hold. "Every day is hard."

"They loved you so." Dolly handed him a tissue. "Your parents loved you so. Neither could stand to be away from you."

Despite his late night, a fresh energy filled Garrison. He wanted to stay and listen to stories like this. Even the ones he'd heard a million times. No way was he leaving to eat; no way he was leaving in a few days for Texas. Grandma Dolly was here, and as long as she was, he would be too.

Garrison listened to his grandma for over an hour, ignoring the bubbling of the fish tank and murmuring of residents outside her door. She shared stories of backyard campouts, birthday parties, and Christmas Eve excursions to look at lights. Garrison could practically taste the cinnamon-laced hot chocolate they drank as they drove around town for hours in Grandpa Hale's beat-up truck. It was strange how he could remember the exact feelings he'd had during those times—how the feelings were even fresher than memories.

There should be a record of today. He considered going home for the camcorder but was too scared to leave. What if he left, the clock struck midnight, and Grandma left again?

An orderly interrupted a story about Garrison's first day of kindergarten. "Dinner time."

"Oh dear." Dolly glanced at the clock. "The time's gotten away from me. Garrison, go get something to eat and go straight to bed. You've got awful bags under your eyes." She grinned. "Not that I should talk to anyone about bags."

"No, I want to stay. If I get hungry, there's a vending machine out front." Garrison helped situate her table. "But you dig in."

"Garrison, a Snickers or bag of potato chips does not a meal make. You get skinnier every time I see you. Visit your mother once in awhile and let her cook for you."

Garrison's legs weakened beneath him. He took his grandma's hand. "Mom's gone. She died in the car accident, remember?"

Dolly's tea-brown eyes searched the room. She let go of Garrison's hand to rub her head. "That's right. I don't understand why I feel so confused."

"It's okay. Sometimes I forget too," he lied.

Grandma Dolly's entire body heaved as she coughed. Garrison patted her back, unsure of what else to do. "Thank you, young man," she said when the choking subsided.

He was losing her. As much as he wanted to hear more memories, this may be his last chance to ask about Clancy. "Grandma, where did you live before you moved here?"

Her eyebrows squished together. "You mean the house in town?"

"No, before you moved to Ohio."

"Oh." She slurped a spoonful of soup. "Lots of places. Daddy always moved us, 'following the money,' he said."

"But do you remember the town right before you came here?"

"Somewhere in East Texas. Didn't stay long."

"Did you meet Grandpa Hale there?"

"No, that was here in Ohio. Met and married three weeks later."

It was a story Garrison knew by heart, but now, he had to wonder if there was more to it. Maybe there was more to all the stories she told, to the stories everyone told. His granddad was a kind man, but also a proud one. Did he know the baby wasn't his?

"Did you date much before Grandpa Hale?"

She sat straighter in her bed. "I had a few beaus but no one special."

"What about a man named Clancy Fitchett?"

Dolly dropped her spoon, splashing soup on her tray. "Oh goodness. I'm so clumsy."

Garrison laid a napkin over the tiny spill. "So, did you?"

"How do you know about Clancy?"

"Last time I was here, you mentioned his name."

"Is that all?" Dolly's face relaxed. "Clancy was a boy I was sweet on back in Texas. All the girls were. He was very handsome, very charming."

"Oh come on, I bet he liked you too."

Dolly chewed her cracker slowly, giving herself more time to form an answer. "We went together for a little while. But it wasn't serious, not to him." She shook her head. "Not that it mattered; it was soon time for another move."

"You didn't want to keep in touch with him? Try the long-distance thing?"

Dolly laughed. "I wanted to do more than that. I wanted him to give me a reason to stay, to ask me to marry him. It was a silly idea. I should have known better. Clancy would never have been faithful. And he was a reckless boy. I did much better marrying your grandfather."

"Did you meet his family?"

"Whose? Clancy's? Yes, a time or two. He had a strange brother who kept to himself and would barely look at me. Heard years later, he killed their daddy. Didn't surprise me. Not after what Mr. Fitchett did."

Garrison's pulse sped. "What did he do?"

"Why are you so interested in this?"

"Just curious. You know me; I love a good murder mystery."

"Do you?" She eyed him suspiciously. "Well, Mr. Fitchett was a brute. Clancy told me stories of horrible things he'd done."

"What kind of stories?"

"I don't remember." There was a faint irritation in his grandmother's voice. "It was so long ago." A tray crashed in the hallway, stealing her attention.

"What did he do to Joel?" Garrison knew Tom Fitchett had an alibi for the night of Joel's incident, but his friends might have covered for him.

She didn't answer, just closed her eyes and opened them again. It was past her usual bedtime already. It was time to ask the question every question before had been building to.

"Grandma," he narrowed his gaze. "Is Clancy my grandfather?"

It was impossible to read her expression because she turned her face away and coughed. A fake cough if Garrison had ever heard one. "Where did you get a ridiculous idea like that?"

"You said something about it once."

Her lower lip trembled. "I did nothing of the sort."

"Maybe you were dreaming," Garrison added. He hated he'd upset her, but he had to know. "Someone said I resemble him."

Dolly shook her head. "You don't look a thing like him. John is Lucy and Sharon's daddy. What a shameful thing to imply. Don't say anything like that in front of your mother! I don't want to upset her over this silly idea you have."

For a second, Garrison wondered if this was an act, like the cough had been—a clever way to dodge his questions. He hoped so, but something in her eyes changed—the sadness replaced by a vacant gaze.

"Mom died in the accident."

Her head shot up. "Who died?"

"Mom did. Lucy did."

"Nonsense," she said. "Lu Lu's in the backyard playing, and I have a roast in the oven to see to. Please excuse me."

"Grandma, it's me, Garrison."

She rubbed her hands on her nightgown as if it were an apron. "Mr. Hale will be home in an hour. Come back, and he may buy your encyclopedias." She barely got the words out before her eyes shut again, and her chin sunk to her chest. Garrison's own chin did the same. Maybe she'd spoken out of exhaustion, but Garrison was afraid he'd lost her again. Just like he lost Amber. The two women in his life gone within three hours. Had to be some kind of record.

He considered kissing his grandma goodbye, but he didn't want to wake her. Who wanted a kiss from an encyclopedia salesman, anyway?

***

Garrison threw open the phone book when he got home. His rumbling stomach commanded a pizza, but he had a more important call to make first. He was starving for good news more than takeout.

He found North Dakota's area code and dialed directory assistance. "There's no listing for Katherine Mencken. Got another name?" The operator sounded like she hated her job, possibly even her life.

"Frank or maybe Franklin Mencken?" He spelled the last name again for good measure.

"Please hold."

The longer stretch of elevator music raised Garrison's hopes, but the operator returned with the same news, delivered in the same flat voice.

Garrison slammed the phone down. Couldn't something go right for him? Couldn't anything be easy? The red blinking answering machine light only added to his rage. When would people stop calling? He punched play and flopped on his parent's bed.

"You have fourteen messages," the robotic secretary told him. Garrison took his dad's hacky sack off the nightstand and practiced tossing it up and catching it. Most messages were hang-ups or sales calls. The thirteenth message was a reminder for a yearly doctor's appointment his mom had made. Calls like that seemed so prevalent at first, but they were slowing down now. Garrison hated returning them. Hated saying the words again, hated the awkwardness and fake sympathy.

Garrison recognized the voice on the final message right away. He caught the ball and sprang up.

"Garrison, it's me. I'm sorry."

Well, this was new. Amber never made the first move towards peace after a disagreement. Garrison reached to push delete but accidentally played the outgoing message instead. It was still the recording his dad made when he got the machine. Garrison tried to erase it so many times, but it was the only way left to hear the voice he missed so much. On the third playback, he realized Amber was right. He was hanging on so tight, he couldn't even delete a voice on a machine.

Garrison crossed the hallway into his own room slamming the door behind him. He burrowed himself under a mountain of quilts, all stitched by his grandma. These covers comforted him but also buried him. Were his memories doing the same? Garrison threw the quilts down and stormed into the living room. He grabbed the cordless and surprised himself by dialing Molly's number.

***

Garrison awoke the next morning with a headache and realization of why Molly hadn't answered. She was on her way to West Texas to pick up her grandfather. Thank God. Calling her had been a mistake. What would he have said? His head pounded, but the ache in his chest hurt worse. He didn't know if last night's pizza caused it or the memory of Grandma Dolly slipping away once again.

He poured a bowl of cereal before remembering he hadn't been shopping. There was probably milk in the fridge—but not any fit for consumption. He pulled his shirt over his nose and opened the refrigerator door, bracing himself for the stench of rotting food, but the fresh, sweet scent of strawberries filled the air instead. A large crate of them sat beside an unopened gallon of 2% milk. Amber, he knew immediately. She had done more than bring in his mail and straighten up. He opened the pantry and found four boxes of Pop Tarts and a large bag of trail mix. He was an ass. Here she had done so much, only to have him come home and pick a fight when all she wanted was a future with him. And then she'd assumed the fault and called to apologize. And what did he do? Call another girl. Ass. He left his bowl of Froot Loops on the table and dialed Amber's number. She answered on the third ring, her voice hoarse. "Amber, it's me. Can you come over?"

***

Garrison started with an apology and ended with an assurance he was ready to move forward. He could live in his childhood home forever, clinging to every memory, or he could make new ones. "I'm ready for new," he told her. Amber promised to be patient, to not push for big changes too fast.

He considered telling her she didn't need patience. That they should pack up the house today and tell her dad to list it. Garrison didn't have to go back to Texas. He didn't need Molly or Clancy Fitchett any more than he needed the ghost of his parents. Amber was all he needed, and she was right here.

She leaned her head on Garrison and wrapped her arms around his bicep. "When will you be back?" she asked. "Did you sign up for the first or second summer session?" Though he was glad he and Amber were no longer fighting, he wished she had held off on the school question. But she had supported him looking for Clancy; she deserved more than his word she'd be his first priority. If signing up for classes would do that, he would enroll. The first session started in a few weeks. He couldn't solve a mystery in a few weeks. He should stay. His head formed the words, but they stayed there, unwilling to leave his mouth and become a binding agreement.

The ringing phone felt like a life preserver. He headed for his parents' room in case Molly was calling him back. He hadn't left a message, but what if she bought that new service that showed the number of who was calling? Talk about a terrible invention. Garrison picked up the phone, just beating the machine to it. He heard static followed by a recording informing him he had a call from an inmate at Gib Lewis.

"Yes, I'll accept the charges." He fought to untangle himself from the phone cord so he could shut his parents' door, but it wouldn't reach. Except for faint static, the line was quiet. "Hello?" Garrison's voice was unsteady.

"Howdy," Joel said. "Is this Gary?"

"Yes, it's me. How did you find this number?"

"Privacy's gone with the '80s."

"But it's listed under my dad's name and—"

"Look, kid, you're paying for this call. If you want to spend your bubblegum money asking dumb questions, that's fine by me, but I called for an actual reason."

"What do you need?"

"If I'm not mistaken, it's *you* that needs me, not the other way around."

Garrison wasn't in the mood for games. "I need your brother, and I thought you said you couldn't help me."

"Maybe I can, and maybe I can't."

The arrogance in Joel's voice made Garrison's skin crawl, but he couldn't hang up, no matter how much he wanted to. "What is that supposed to mean?"

"It means I may be willing to help you, but you've got to help me too."

In the living room, Amber cleared her throat in the way she did when she was tired of waiting for him. "How can I possibly help you?"

"It can't be said over the phone."

"It has to be." Garrison picked up a paperclip from his dad's desk and mangled it. "I'm not going back to Texas."

"Then forget it." Joel didn't sound angry or even disappointed. "Have a nice life, kid."

"No wait," Garrison said, but it was too late. The line was dead; Joel was gone. Garrison went to call him back but realized he didn't have the number. Maybe Caller ID wasn't so terrible of an invention after all. He was dialing directory assistance when he spotted the figure in the doorway. His hand flew to his chest.

"Why are you so jumpy?" Amber asked. "Who was that?"

Garrison set the phone down. "The recruiter at OSU."

"Oh." Amber smiled. "Well, did you get signed up?"

"I did." Garrison avoided her gaze by focusing on the distorted paper clip.

"Which session?" He'd never heard two words spoken with such hope.

"Second one." Garrison hated to see her disappointment, but he couldn't let her sad eyes convince him to drop what she wanted into her lap. He'd promised to register for summer classes and he would. Second session was still summer, but that phone call made him realize he wasn't through in Texas.

CHAPTER 11

Longview, Texas, 1941

Lorraine had always loved Christmas. Any holiday really but Christmas especially. It was different in Texas, hotter mostly. She missed the snow, but Clancy was a fair trade. Thank God he was here to share it with her. That he hadn't rushed off to enlist like she feared he might.

When she heard the boom of Clancy's Chevy, she ran to steal a quick kiss. "Merry Christmas, you!"

"It *is* now." Clancy went in for another.

Lorraine stepped back. "My parents might be watching. Come inside, but I have to warn you that Mother made you a stocking. Complete with jingle bells."

"A stocking, huh? I'm flattered."

She tried to pull him toward the door, but he stood in place.

"While we are dishing out warnings, Joel is coming," Clancy said.

"Oh. Well, he was invited. Did you two make things right?"

"No. That's what's strange. We've all but ignored each other these past few weeks. I called Daddy before I came to give directions, and he said he would pick up Joel and be here by 4:00."

"Suppose Mr. Fitchett talked him into coming?"

Clancy shrugged. "Maybe."

Lorraine detected the worry in his voice but knew all would be fine. Joel was a doll. She didn't know what he and Clancy had gotten so worked up over, but siblings fought, and that was that. The sooner they put all this behind them the better, and Christmas was a perfect day for that.

Birdie took Clancy's coat when he stepped through the door.

"If it isn't the man of the hour," Lane called from the kitchen. "I've got a Coca-Cola waiting for you. Bought up a dozen cases. With sugar rationing on the horizon, these may soon be extinct."

"Should we start with the presents now?" Lorraine asked.

"She's no better at waiting than she was as a girl." Daddy chose a small wrapped box under the tree and handed it to her. "Dig in."

Lorraine exchanged the package for a slightly larger one. "I want Clancy to open his first."

Clancy shook the package and turned it over in his hands. "Feels like a book."

"Shhhh!" Lorraine held a finger against her lips. "If you guess what it is, you can't keep it."

Clancy only wore a slight smile as he held up the gift. "*The Sun Also Rises*, my favorite." He crumpled the discarded paper into a ball. "Thanks, Lorraine."

She had expected this. He wouldn't be impressed yet. "Open it!" She drummed her hands on her lap. "Look on the first page."

"First edition," he said. "Wow! That's something."

"That's not all." She stood and flipped the page for him. "Read the inscription."

"*To Clancy Fitchett, all the best wishes, Ernest Hemingway.*" Clancy blinked rapidly. "How?"

"Never mind that. Just say thanks," she said, even though the silly grin he wore was thanks enough.

"Thanks! This is incredible. The only way I could love it more is if he would have written something nasty about Fitzgerald in it."

"I would have marked it out." Lorraine sat back in her chair. "Do you need to run out and buy me something else? I think it's safe to say I've topped you this year."

"Don't be so sure." Clancy's wink turned her knees to water. As much as she loved Christmas with her family, she suddenly wished she and Clancy had some privacy.

"Sounds like a challenge." Daddy sat on the fireplace. "Let's see what Clancy brought, and Birdie and I will judge who did best."

"I don't have it," Clancy said.

Lorraine pressed her lips tight. What did he mean he didn't have it?

"I don't have it *yet*. My old man's bringing it when he comes."

"Hooey." Lorraine crossed her arms.

"Hey, any good story needs suspense, I thought writers understood that."

He had a point. Not that she remembered anything about writing. She'd barely managed a few sentences this month. "Okay then," she said. "Let's see about getting the rest of these opened."

***

Joel overslept, a fact he blamed on last night's celebratory bottle of wine. But his spirits were high. Yes, today was Christmas, the day Clancy would propose, but Joel would arrive with a new face. Probably not scar free, but well on its way.

He'd avoided his reflection as much as possible since he started the treatment. The doctor said the silver would take the full two weeks, and Joel didn't want to get discouraged. But he had stolen a few glances and was sure it was fading.

Joel ripped off the bandage like wrapping paper. Like it was his first gift of Christmas. He leaned closer to the bathroom mirror and screamed. The scar was not only still there, but it didn't look different, no matter how many ways he turned his head.

Joel took the empty silver bottle and threw it against the mirror. The tiny container smashed, but it wasn't enough. The towel rack left a hole in the wall as he yanked it free. He brought it over his shoulder like a ballplayer at bat. He thought about Daddy, Clancy, and Lorraine, imagining all their faces in the mirror circling around his own. His bat connected with all of them, but he saved the hardest hit for his own reflection.

When he finished, sweat dripped from his neck, and shards of glass encircled him. He picked up a piece the same size as the one that had caused all this trouble for him. He remembered the unbearable burn as the glass sliced his skin and the fountain of blood that soaked his white t-shirt. And he remembered the doves. They circled like vultures.

Though Clancy barely had a scratch on him that day, he'd passed out when it was all said and done. Joel had to forget his pain, pick up his brother, and stumble until he found help. And he'd been carrying Clancy ever since. But not anymore.

***

All morning Clancy doubted his decision. Was Lorraine the last girl he'd sleep with? Even flirt with? It wasn't too late to change his mind. He could call his dad and ask him to bring a gift that entailed no extreme commitment. He and Lorraine hadn't talked about marriage, not seriously. She wasn't expecting a proposal. But then again, why should he change his mind? Lorraine was a great gal. He didn't want to live without her, and this war pushed things along faster than normal.

When he watched Lorraine, he imagined what she'd be like as a mother. He'd never thought about a girl like that before, beyond the here and now. But now he wanted his children to have a mom like he had, a mom like Lorraine would be. Wanted to live in a house that smelled like brown sugar and hot chocolate every Christmas. And the thought of having Lorraine in bed beside him every night didn't sound so bad either. Hell, even Hemingway settled down. Of course, he had settled down three times now, so he probably wasn't the best example.

When Lorraine went to help her mother, Clancy followed Lane to the patio for a pre-dinner snack of Milk Duds and Coca-Cola. Good thing Daddy wasn't here yet. Tom Fitchett would be horrified by Lane's sweet tooth.

Clancy scooped out a handful of the candy. "While we are alone, I have an important question to ask."

Lane removed his hand from the column he was leaning on. "Should I sit?"

"Wouldn't hurt."

"Nothing's wrong I hope?" The uncertainty on Lane's face didn't look natural.

"That's up for you to decide."

"Well, now you've got me curious." He looked at his half-empty bottle. "Do I need something stronger?"

The candy had already started to melt in Clancy's clammy hand, so he tossed them into his mouth. "Depends. Just how attached are you to Lorraine?"

Though Clancy was sure Lane suspected what was coming, his face was unreadable. "Very attached. Couldn't ask for a better girl."

"So, you'd be opposed to someone taking her away?"

Lane took a thoughtful sip before he answered. "Depends on the person taking her away—and their motivations."

"And if the person is me?"

Lane raised an eyebrow. "I don't suppose you are asking about taking her on a weekend vacation?"

"No, sir."

"You know, son...." The word son hung in the air. Clancy wondered if he'd chosen it on purpose. "I've imagined this moment before, a young man asking for Lori's hand, but I've never pictured it like this."

"Let me give it another go then." Clancy squared his shoulders. "Sir, I love your daughter. It's been fast, but she loves me too. I may never make her a lot of money, but I can make her a lot of happiness. So, I'd like your permission to ask her to marry me." Clancy's mouth was bone dry, but he'd gotten the words out almost exactly like he practiced.

"Lorraine doesn't need money; she's already got that," Lane said. "She needs to be cared for in a different way, and I trust you will. Of course, I'm the easy one, the pushover, as Birdie always says. Lorraine may have the harder questions to ask you."

"I'm ready for them, sir."

Lane raised his bottle. "Then here's to a beautiful future."

Clancy raised his own and downed half of it in a single gulp. He looked at the sky and smiled. A father's blessing, a cold drink, and not a single dove in sight.

***

Staring Joel down across the table wasn't helping Clancy's nerves. Why had he come if he was only going to sulk? At least Daddy was trying to keep the conversation going and to control his alcohol intake. When Tom Fitchett did better at those two things than someone, it was saying something.

"Can I get you anything else to drink, Joel?" Lorraine asked.

Clancy touched Lorraine's knee under the table. A silent signal she seemed to mistake for affection.

"Another glass of wine sounds good," Joel said.

Clancy squeezed her knee harder.

"What?" she mouthed.

Joel's eyes burned into Clancy. "On second thought, got anything harder?"

"Name your poison." Lane pushed away from the table.

"Gin sour," Joel said.

"And for you, Tom?"

"Just water."

Well, thank God for that at least. That Daddy saved his drunken stupors and blackouts for home.

"Clancy tells us you're a dentist?" Birdie dabbed the corner of her mouth with her napkin. "That must be so interesting."

"It can be. Fixing cars really interests me, but fixing teeth pays the bills."

"Fixing cars pays the bills too," Joel said. "Pays a pretty penny to our landlord, doesn't it, Dad?"

Lane arrived with the drinks, saving Tom from having to answer. Joel threw back the Gin Sour before Lane sat back down. "Say, Lane, any more where this came from?" he asked, mouth still puckered.

"Sure," Lane said, but without the enthusiasm of a few minutes before. "Be right back."

Lorraine looked at Clancy again, her eyes registering understanding. "We should have dessert," she said. "Alma made two cobblers yesterday. Her pies are divine."

"That sounds like a plan," Clancy said. "I'd love to try the peach one."

Lorraine and Birdie stood and collected plates in perfect synchronization.

"No, no, you ladies sit down." Joel's words slurred. "Let Alma get them."

"She's off today." Birdie kept her head down.

"Think you can keep her? With the war on?" Joel asked.

"Joel, mind your own business." The china rattled. Whether Daddy bumped against the table or the thunder of his voice made them clatter, Clancy wasn't sure.

"Must be nice to have a maid. We never have—unless you count Mama. She worked for the Harris family a few years after Clancy started school. Remember that, Old Man?"

"Those were hard years." Daddy took a sip of water. "We did what we had to do."

"Well, of course." Birdie stopped gathering dishes to fan herself. "It's a fine a job as any."

"But how would you feel if your little Lori didn't have a maid—or worse yet, became one?"

Birdie laughed uncomfortably.

"That would be fine," Lane said on her behalf.

Clancy opened and closed his fists under the table. Is this why Joel was here? To ruin the proposal?

Joel turned to Lorraine. "You talk about helping the have-nots, but are you ready to become one?"

"That's enough." Clancy's nails bit into his palm.

"It's fine." Lorraine patted Clancy's arm. "It wouldn't bother me to be poor, Joel. There's more to life than money."

"Here here!" Joel raised his empty glass. "Damn! Gone so soon. Time for another."

"No more," Daddy said. "It's time we leave."

"Well, if you don't care about money, Clancy's your man. He's never supported himself. Daddy's the reason he got a job—and the reason he keeps it. Yet, in spite of the steady paycheck, he has no money. Mysterious, right?"

Clancy's muscles twitched. "Shut up, Joel."

"Come on, now. Lorraine deserves to know about your gambling habit. Have you met his buddy yet, Lorraine?"

Clancy tried to stand, but Lorraine grabbed the pocket of his trousers, tugging him back down.

"His name is Crawl," Joel said. "C-R-A-W-L. Strange name, right? He got it from this sick game he plays. When someone falls out of his good graces, he makes them *crawl* through the swamp." Joel walked his middle and index fingers toward Clancy. "Then it's either, BANG!" Joel slammed his hand down on the table, causing everyone to jump. He grinned, dragging his hand back across the table. "Or a lucky few get to *crawl* to the other side."

"Crawl who you saw at the movie?" Lorraine's eyes and voice were accusing.

"Yes, but that story is a dumb legend. He's a big craw fisherman, so his buddies called him Craw. Somewhere along the way it became Crawl." Clancy could tell by the wide eyes and gaping mouths around the table, it was Joel's story everyone believed.

Daddy stood. "Thank you, Mr. and Mrs. Applewhite, for a lovely meal. We'll leave you to your evening now."

"Thanks for coming." Lane leaped from his chair. "And for the wine. Can I get you a piece of pie to go?"

"No, we're fine." He took a hold of Joel's arm. "Come on, son."

Joel didn't budge. "I like my pie with ice cream, and that won't keep all the way home. Go on ahead, Daddy. I'll catch a ride with Clancy."

"I'll be late." Clancy tried to speak over the pounding in his ears. It took everything inside him not to reach across the table and grab his brother's throat. Show him that the hit he got in at Daddy's was just a lucky shot.

"No rush." Joel settled back in his chair. "My schedule's all clear."

"It's not a choice. Go home with Daddy or else," Clancy said.

A strange crow-like cackle escaped Joel. "You and your threats. Has Lorraine witnessed your violence yet?"

"That's it." Clancy pushed his chair back, ready to show his brother how violent he could be, but Joel's next words stopped him in his tracks.

"Have any of you heard the story of this scar?"

Sweat dripped down Clancy's spine. He wanted to turn and run, but that wouldn't stop what was coming. "Shut up!" Clancy pushed his father aside, digging his nails into Joel's wrist.

Joel shook free, but stood at least. Stood up with his fist open and mouth closed. Both good signs. As much as Clancy wanted to finish their fight, doing it in front of Lorraine and her family would only make them believe what Joel said about him. He leaned close to his brother's ear and whispered, "Come on, Joel. We promised."

"Ehh what's a promise really?" Joel asked loud enough for everyone to hear. "You've made how many to how many girls now? Haven't kept one yet."

"Stop. You're drunk."

Joel traced the scar with his finger. "Not until you tell me and everybody here that what happened was your fault."

Clancy's heart pounded erratically. Of course it was his fault. The shame from that day had corroded him from the inside out. Every flap of a bird's wing reminded him of his culpability. Clancy tried to speak, but all moisture had abandoned his mouth in favor of his eyes. The tears came faster than he could wipe them away. He despised how they stung, both his face and pride. He was supposed to be a man.

Daddy grabbed Joel's arm again with more force. "Clancy, help me get your brother to the car."

"Do you need help or..." Lane looked lost in his own dining room.

Clancy looked apologetically at their host. "Can you get the door?"

Getting Joel outside wasn't easy. He alternately kicked his legs and went limp like a toddler throwing a tantrum. Somehow, they got him into the passenger seat. Joel stopped fighting as if he wasn't capable of unlocking the door and getting back out. Clancy was glad for that; he didn't have the strength for anymore wrestling with Joel.

Daddy slammed his fist on the hood of his car. "What is wrong with that boy?" He turned to Clancy. "And why the hell are you crying? Pull yourself together and get back inside. I'll take Joel home with me." He pulled the ring box out of his coat pocket. "Sorry I won't be around to see it."

Clancy was too. Despite everything, he wanted his father here. And Joel too. Not like this but as the supportive big brother he'd been for all those years. Maybe that had been an act. Either way, his plans were shot now.

"And I'm sorry for what he said. Sorry that I brought him at all. He's drunk," Daddy added, as if that explained away everything.

If Clancy was counting right, this was the third apology in less than a minute, a record. "Yeah. No kidding."

"Go on back inside. They won't hold him against you."

Clancy wasn't so sure. He waited for his father to pull from the driveway before tossing the ring into his truck.

***

"You should have stayed last night; we have a guest room." Lorraine huddled next to Clancy under a blanket at Lake Lamond.

"It wouldn't have looked right."

"No one's paying attention to us." Lorraine toyed with a lock of hair.

"Someone is always paying attention, Lorraine."

"Well, who cares what anybody thinks? We're adults. I hated for you to leave so upset."

"Joel upset everybody." The bite in his voice took Lorraine by surprise. He obviously didn't want to talk about that awful dinner. That was fine; she didn't particularly want to talk about it either. She knew she should be angry at Joel for tainting her first Christmas with Clancy, but she couldn't muster it up within her. It must be hard for Joel, to see his baby brother so serious about someone. Jealousy was a monster; even Shakespeare said so. Pour alcohol on jealousy, and it made a worse monster than even Dr. Jekyll could create. But Lorraine would be lying if she said she wasn't more curious about the scar now. She wouldn't ask, though, not with Clancy barking like this.

It took a few minutes, but Clancy finally stopped snatching handfuls of grass, and his face returned to its normal shade. Red was a terrible color for him. "Sorry," he whispered.

"About what?"

"Lots of things."

Lorraine tucked her legs underneath her. "Name three."

"Last night, just now with my tone, and also...last night."

She took his hand. "Last night wasn't your fault."

A strong wind blew, and Clancy pulled her closer. "I shouldn't have brought you here. It's too late, too cold. We can go."

"Wyoming-born remember? I like the cold, not that this is cold."

"It's too cold for Texas. Too cold to be at a lake. Come on." Clancy stood, tugged at her hand.

She shook her hand free. "Go if you have to, but I want to stay. I like it here, breeze and all. I would like to see this place during the summer sometime. See

95

how different it looks when crowds are here to appreciate the beauty with us. Will you bring me here this summer?"

"How about every summer?"

"Every summer?" Lorraine's hopes rose.

"This isn't how I planned it. I wanted to ask you on a day you loved, surrounded by people you love. Family old and new. I'm sorry that didn't happen."

Lorraine's stomach fluttered as Clancy pulled out the ring.

"Lorraine, I fell in love that day at the station. Couldn't stop thinking of you. Then one day, I turned the corner I always turn on my way to the old house I always go to, but I saw something new. Something beautiful in the middle of a desert winter. Because there you were on my porch swing, wearing that sunset-orange dress. Do you remember?"

"I spent hours picking out that outfit. I wanted to impress you."

"You did—and not just because of the dress. I'd sat on that porch swing a thousand times and never realized someone was missing. But you were. You were missing from my porch swing, from my passenger seat, from the pew beside me at church. And it was no wonder my life had always felt so empty." Clancy looked down at her. "I think, traditionally, you're supposed to be the one standing now."

"Oh, right." Lorraine used Clancy's hand to pull herself up.

"I realize our relationship has been pretty effortless so far, but it won't always be. There's still a lot we don't know about each other. But I promise I'll love you when it's easy—*and* when it's not. To quote a little-known author, 'I don't ask you to love me always like this, but I ask you to remember. Somewhere inside me, there'll always be the person I am tonight.'"

Lorraine grinned. "That's Fitzgerald."

"So it is." Clancy dropped to his knee. "Lorraine, when your book gets published, can the name on the spine say Lorraine Fitchett?" Lorraine bounced on her toes as Clancy brought the ring closer to her finger. "Marry me, Lorraine. I talked to your Daddy, and I didn't quote Hemingway, so there's no reason to say no."

Lorraine sensed this moment would become a story she'd tell again and again to her children and grandchildren. She tried to form a clever response, but in situations like this, only one word would do. "Yes." Lorraine barely recognized her shaky voice, so she repeated her answer with more confidence. "Yes!"

Clancy's hand trembled as he slipped the ring on her finger. "This was Mama's."

"How perfect," Lorraine said. And it was. Both the fit and the sentiment.

Clancy rose to kiss her. Right where they'd had their first kiss. How far they'd come in such a short time.

Above them, Lorraine spotted a pair of birds building a nest. It had always fascinated her how birds built homes. It was troublesome, though, that these doves chose such a flimsy branch to build on. She hoped it would hold up to the strong Texas winds.

"I know it's a small diamond, but those are real pearls," Clancy said.

"I love it." Lorraine held the ring protectively against her chest. She looked back at the birds just as a hawk swooped down. The poor dove with a twig still in his beak never saw it coming.

"What are you staring at?" Clancy looked up.

"Nothing." She pulled him closer. "Nothing that concerns us, anyway." And it didn't. Brothers could fight, hawks could prey, and the world could go on fighting their war. She had Clancy, and nothing could touch them.

CHAPTER 12

Gib Lewis Unit, 1991

Garrison almost felt like a regular here at Gib Lewis. Too many faces were familiar. One inmate's girlfriend even winked at him. But considering the jerk he'd been to Amber, maybe these women were on to something. At least men behind bars couldn't take another girl to watch *Drop Dead Fred*.

He hadn't talked to Molly since he'd left, even though she was all he thought about. He needed to wait and see what Joel wanted. Calling with news seemed more appropriate than calling just because.

Joel was already waiting for Garrison. Kicked back in the chair, his uncuffed hands were positioned comfortably behind his head. He made no move for the phone until Garrison picked up the one on his side.

"What do you want?" Garrison asked.

"Good Morning to you too, Gary. Things are good, thanks for asking. Did you have a nice visit home?"

"I don't have time for chit-chat. You're lucky I came back at all."

Joel propped his chin on his free hand. "You were always going to come back. Don't put that on me."

"What do you want?" Garrison repeated.

Joel's expression gradually sobered. "I want her. I want Lorraine."

That Garrison wasn't expecting. Hadn't Joel said he'd spent fifty years trying to forget her? What had changed? "Me too," Garrison said. "Can you help with that?"

Joel groaned theatrically. "If I knew where to find her, I wouldn't need you. It's up to you to find Lorraine. Find her and bring her to me."

"Bring her here?" Garrison wrinkled his nose. "To prison?"

"I doubt they'll let us go to Red Lobster."

"Even if I can find her, you really think she'll want to see you? After building a life with Clancy?"

"I'd hope so. She loved me. Once upon a time." Joel stared down at the table. "Anyway, I'm not asking her to be my cellmate. I just want to see her. I just *need* to see her."

"I know about how you tried to steal her—when my grandpa was fighting." Garrison hoped the negative spin on the story would encourage Joel to set the record straight. It was hard not to be curious about the three of them, especially given this turn of events.

"Easy on the grandpa talk. You don't know Clancy is your grandpa any more than you know about me and Lorraine, so cool it."

"So, tell me. I'm a good listener."

For a minute, Garrison thought Joel might actually share. He looked relieved that Garrison asked. Like he'd been waiting fifty years for someone to. But he just shook his head. "Not now. Not till you find her."

"Well, she doesn't live around here. Earl Rogers said her folks flew out all the time."

"Earl Rogers?" Joel snickered. "That old SOB is still around? Too uptight to die, I guess. Your well must be pretty damn dry if you're tapping into that old coot for information. He don't know nothing. Never did."

"Then who does?"

"Ask the warden. Somebody puts money in my account every month, like I'm a damn bill they gotta pay. Can't imagine who else would do that but Lorraine."

"I'll ask." Garrison opened the spiral he'd brought and wrote a note. "Who else might be in touch with her?"

Joel shrugged. "She had friends, but I don't even remember their names." His eyes locked on the notebook. "She was a writer. Maybe she got her book published."

"Okay, I'll check." It was a long shot, but if she had been published, the few sentences in the back of a book about the author almost always said where they resided.

"Wouldn't that be something if she's an author?" There was a longing on Joel's face that was almost uncomfortable to witness. Garrison had never seen him look so vulnerable. He turned away, worried that Joel would assume he was looking at the scar.

"He had the most appalling cut." The witness's words popped into Garrison's head. But that couldn't be. Joel didn't have a cut in 1945. He had a scar. Maybe Garrison had the wording mixed up.

Garrison tapped on the glass to bring Joel back from whatever memory he was visiting. "Hello? Any other ideas?"

"I have a picture if that would help." Joel reached into his pocket and looked at the photo before holding it to the glass. "This is her; this is Lorraine."

The black-and-white photo had captured Lorraine mid-laugh, head thrown slightly back as she lay propped up on her elbows. Even though she was dressed for winter, she appeared to be at a lake. Cold or not, she was happy. On a date maybe. Whether it was with Clancy or Joel, Garrison had no idea.

"I can have the guard give this to you."

Garrison could tell by Joel's tense grip on the picture, he didn't want to let it go. "No thanks. She won't look like that anymore. It's better for you to keep it. Thanks for showing me though. Beautiful lady."

Joel's face relaxed as he folded it carefully to put back in his pocket.

"So, if I find her, why should I bring her here?" Garrison asked.

"Because it's an old man's dying wish."

"Dying?"

"Look at me. I'm sure you can tell I'm approaching my expiration date. It's only a matter of time before I'm gone—or she is. You're already looking, so what's the big deal?"

"Not interested." Garrison folded his arms. "You said you had information that could help me, and you don't. You haven't been helpful at all."

Joel rubbed his hand over the front of the white surgical scrub. Garrison still hadn't got used to the white. Weren't prisoners supposed to wear orange? White suggested a purity that these men at Gib had obviously lost along the way—Joel especially.

Joel's Adam's apple bobbed as he took a few deliberate swallows. The way he grabbed his chest made Garrison panic. "Hey, are you all right?" Garrison asked.

Dropping the phone, Joel downed a glass of water. "Interview," he said when he finally picked up again.

"What?"

"How green are you, Gary?" Joel yelled into the phone. "I said I'll give you an interview. I've gotten more interview requests than love letters. If you find Lorraine, I'll give you an interview. Then you can sell it to CBS or NBC or whichever combination of three letters offers you the most money."

Garrison wasn't interested. Once he knew where Clancy was, why would he care about anything Joel had to say? But then he remembered Molly. Molly who loved journalism as much as she loved Joel Fitchett. What could it mean for her future?

"I have a friend, Molly Hamilton. She's written you. Can she do the interview?"

"I'd rather it be you."

"She believes you're innocent," Garrison said. "And she likes you more than I do."

Joel raked his hand all over his face and growled. "Fine. But only if you get Lorraine here."

"Deal," Garrison said. "I'd shake your hand, but..."

"Yeah about that. While you are talking to the warden about the money, maybe mention you would feel safe seeing me in the visiting room again. Then we could play that Loony Tunes Rummy game."

"Loony Rummy? I thought you said it sounded lame?"

"Well yeah, it *is* lame. But what else do I got to do?"

Garrison liked Joel better behind a barrier, but now that he was needed, maybe Joel wouldn't try to kill him. "I'll talk to him. But I won't be able to be here every week. I'll need to spend more time in Longview, do more digging."

"Do what you need to do. This ain't some adopt-a-felon program. Come when you can, write when you can—or don't. I don't care."

Joel could say what he wanted, but a different story was written on his face. He cared—cared enough to trade a lifetime of secrets for a few hours on a Saturday.

CHAPTER 13

Longview, Texas, 1942

The muddy lake waters distorted Clancy's features the same as looking into a tarnished mirror. Sometimes, if he stared long enough, the reflection morphed until he was staring into the face of a blonde-haired boy on a picnic with his mama.

In those times, it wasn't a tarnished mirror so much as a magic one.

"Clancy? Are you listening?"

He jolted like someone woke him from a dream. He'd almost forgotten Lorraine was here—forgotten he was here to plan a wedding. "Sorry. Guess I'm distracted."

Lorraine sighed. "I knew we shouldn't do this here. Too many memories at this lake to steal you away. Far fewer memories at my kitchen table."

"There are memories there too—and not good ones."

Lorraine waved her hand. "Let's not talk about that. Joel apologized. Water under the bridge and all that."

If only it were that easy. Joel could blame the alcohol all he wanted, but Gin Sours didn't create words. They had been inside Joel already; the alcohol just breathed life into them. Clancy saw the truth now—that Joel hadn't forgiven him—that whatever he had done to protect his brother had not been enough.

"Take care of Joel," Mama had told him on her final day when her voice was as unrecognizable as she was. And just like that, she used her last words to anoint Clancy as his brother's keeper. It had once been the other way around.

"Mother needs your guest list by Friday," Lorraine said. Early enough so our Wyoming friends can make arrangements to be here in June."

June. Clancy's stomach clenched. June would be too late. It was now or never. Clancy took her hands. "Lorraine, what would you say to moving the wedding up?"

She smiled. "You're only thinking of the honeymoon. Speaking of, with gas rationing coming, I'm thinking somewhere close. San Antonio? The River Walk sounds divine. There's a night parade and a river carnival. A real carnival on the river! Wouldn't that be something to see?"

"No." Clancy couldn't let her continue talking a blue streak. "June won't work."

Lorraine's face scrunched. "The church is booked, and the woman Mother spoke to about the cake could barely squeeze us in as is. Anyway, it's good luck to be a June bride."

"No, Lorraine. I know you are used to getting your way, but just this once, I'd like to be heard."

"What does that mean?" Lorraine released his hands. "A few minutes ago, I couldn't squeeze any input out of you. So, don't get fussy with me for not hearing you when I've been trying to get you to say anything all morning."

Clancy rubbed his hands through his hair. "You're right. I'm sorry." He bit the inside of his cheek. Hot blood mingled with the words he needed to say.

"What's going on, Clancy? You haven't been yourself in weeks. You never act... I don't even know the word. Stressed maybe? It's not like you."

"I'm joining the Marines." Clancy let out a breath he'd been holding since his shaky hand signed his name.

"You're what?"

"I'm enlisting."

"No." Lorraine squeezed her eyes shut. "They'll send you overseas. Right to the middle of the war."

"That's the idea." Clancy reached for Lorraine's hand, but she pulled it back. "Please, don't be like this. America needs me."

"*I* need you."

"That's what made this decision hard. If it wasn't for you, I would have signed up the day after Pearl Harbor like everyone else. It's the right thing to do—the only thing to do. If I stay, everyone will call me a coward."

"So that's what this is about? What other people will think? Not everyone is enlisting. There are valid reasons many can't."

"It's not just about what others think. It's about what I think, about my honor and—"

Lorraine threw up her hands. "Men and their honor. You sound like you stepped right out of *Gone With the Wind*. Those men were fools, and if you do this, so are you."

Clancy stood. "For all your talk about the greater good, I'm surprised at your response. Are you even concerned about the Jews? The Germans are putting them in cages."

Lorraine squeezed the bridge of her nose. "Cages? What are you talking about?"

"Camps, but that's just another word for cages. And what about Pearl Harbor? Aren't you a little worried about whether or not America can survive another attack? The next one might be a little closer to home. Does that scare you? It should."

Lorraine lowered her eyes. "Of course, it worries me. But why do you want to leave when we are at such a crucial moment in our lives?"

"So, you're content to send others' fiancés but not your own?"

"Yes!" Lorraine raised her voice. "Yes, I'm a hypocrite. Is that what you want to hear?"

It wasn't. Clancy had never expected this to go well but prayed she would see beyond herself. Lorraine was usually so good at doing that.

"Please," she muttered. "Please don't do this."

Clancy looked away. "It's done."

"What's done?"

"I already signed up."

Lorraine jumped up, sending the stack of papers filled with flower names and wedding cake flavors flying. "Without even talking to me? You asked me to be your wife, to share our lives together and then you go and make this life-changing decision without asking?"

Clancy knelt and gathered the papers. "Please, Lorraine. This is the right decision. I can't see what Hitler's doing—what Japan did—and continue living inside a bubble, pretending the world is right. I'd never ask you to compromise your beliefs. Please don't ask me to do it either."

"There are other ways to make change, Clancy. Collect scrap metal, grow a Victory Garden, buy war bonds."

Clancy shook his head. "It's not enough."

Lorraine seemed to wilt in front of him. "Am I enough?"

Clancy didn't answer; he couldn't answer. He saw her point; she should be enough. In every way a woman could be, she was, but this desire was a separate one, unrelated to her—an itch she couldn't scratch, a thought she couldn't extract from his mind with all the love in the world.

Lorraine swatted tears away. "If you can't answer, I already know the answer." She twisted the ring several times before tugging it off her finger. "Here you go."

Clancy's brain felt like the eggs he'd scrambled for breakfast. "No. That's not what I want. Keep it. I want to get married before I leave."

Lorraine kept her hand extended and her face stoic.

"Is it a big wedding you want?" Clancy's chest ached. "Then wait till I get back, and we'll go all out. Biggest party you've ever seen. Anything you want. Don't do this."

"I didn't do this." Lorraine took Clancy's hand and put the ring inside.

"Let me drive you home," he said. But she was already gone. Clancy wanted to run after her, but he stood frozen, watching Lorraine until she was only a blur of yellow curls and a fluttering emerald dress. He opened his hand and looked at the ring. Joel might get it after all. Because if not Lorraine, there was no one else for him. Clancy knew that like he knew the sky was blue, that cages were wrong, and that signing his name on that paper yesterday had been the right decision.

***

Joel didn't recognize the vehicle out front, but he could tell by the frantic knocking something was wrong. The door wasn't even halfway open before Lorraine spilled into the living room. She looked awful—matted hair, smeared makeup, and torn stockings. "Lorraine, what's the matter? Are you hurt?" Outside he watched an unfamiliar car back out from the driveway. "Who's that?"

"A gentleman who gave me a ride."

"A ride? I thought you were with Clancy. Is he hurt?"

Lorraine shook her head. "Can I get some water?"

"Yeah have a seat." Joel brushed away the laundry he had never got around to folding. "Be right back."

The cup was so full that water splashed across the kitchen floor. More spilled when placed in Lorraine's shaking hands. She set it down and ran to the bathroom. Joel listened to her vomit. What had Mama always brought when they were sick? He went back into the kitchen and searched the cupboard. No crackers. He dampened a dishcloth and waited outside the bathroom door till the toilet flushed. "Here's a cold towel and your water."

"Thanks." She wiped her mouth. "I'm so sorry. I'll clean up in here."

"No need. Can I help you back to the couch? Do you need a trash can or—?"

"I think I'm okay. You wouldn't happen to have a spare toothbrush?"

"Just a few dozen." Joel pulled open the drawer. "Dad's a dentist, remember?"

She thanked him, covering her mouth when she spoke.

"If you need anything, I'll be right outside," Joel said.

The ten minutes outside the bathroom door dragged on forever. Joel's mind raced with possible scenarios that had brought her here like this.

When she finally emerged, the makeup was scrubbed from her face and her wild curls pinned back. She handed him an empty water glass. "Can I get a refill?"

Joel got a clean glass, careful not to fill it so full this time. He found her on the couch, head between her legs. He set the glass down, then considered picking it back up so he'd have something to occupy his hands. He put his handkerchief on her knee.

"I shouldn't have come here," she finally said.

"No, I'm glad you did. Can you tell me what's wrong?"

Lorraine used his handkerchief to wipe her face. "I'll give you one guess."

Joel noticed then that she wasn't wearing Mama's ring. Clancy must have given her the boot. Joel wasn't sure why that made him angry. This was what he wanted. But it was hard to take pleasure in seeing Lorraine heartbroken.

"I can try to talk to him." Joel had done his best to avoid Clancy since the Christmas fiasco, but for Lorraine, he would try.

"He's already signed the papers," she said.

"Papers? What papers?"

"You don't know?"

"Obviously not." Suddenly the room seemed hotter.

"Clancy enlisted in the Marines. He's going to war." Lorraine heaved and sobbed again. Joel tried to position himself to put his arm around her but knocked over the glass of water in the process. She jolted as if he had detonated a bomb.

Joel used a shirt he had shoved to the floor to wipe up the mess. "Where's Clancy now?"

"At my house. We were at Lake Lamond when he told me." She stopped to blow her nose. "I ran off. That man drove me home, but I saw Clancy's truck and couldn't go in."

"Your folks might be worried. Clancy probably explained what happened, and they'll go looking for you. Let me call them."

She held up her hand. "No, please. Then Clancy will come here. I can't see him, Joel. I can't."

He gently lowered her hand. "Then you call. Tell them you're okay, that you're with a friend."

"But what if Clancy comes back here?" She looked frantic. "Then what?"

"We'll go somewhere else. Anywhere. I'll take you home when you're ready. Please call."

Lorraine clasped her hands together. "You're right. Hopefully Daddy will answer. I can't deal with Mother right now."

Joel led her to the kitchen and stepped back into the living room to give her privacy. He banged his head against the wall. The Marines!? How could Clancy be so stupid? Joel had spent his entire life trying to keep Clancy out of trouble. Now with one signature, Clancy had undone it all—had finally stepped beyond Joel's reach.

***

Lorraine read the same sentence four times before tossing the copy of *The Last Tycoon* on the floor. There was nothing wrong with the book, but she knew it had no ending. Fitzgerald left behind only half of a story when the heart attack took him. If there was no closure in actual life, there should at least be in literature.

Two weeks had passed since she'd given Clancy the ring back. Two weeks. Yet she still looked at her hand expecting to see its sparkle.

She pushed the curtains back, hoping to let the sunlight in, but dark clouds overtook the sky. She needed to get dressed today. Needed to rid herself of this colossally low mood. She couldn't let all this business with Clancy be the end of her. There was another life somewhere out there, and meanwhile, she'd pour the pain onto the pages. Without a wedding to plan and a man to distract her, she could finish this novel. Wouldn't that be something? To see her book in print this time next year? Then she would look back on these days and wonder why she got so worked up over a tiny setback.

Lorraine longed for the gift of hindsight. Because no matter how hard she tried to stay positive, every time she thought of Clancy, her entire body went cold.

The rumble of thunder shook her. It was raining now and hailing so hard she almost didn't hear the knock. "Can I come in?"

"Sure, Daddy."

"Stay back from the glass. The hail shattered Mr. Allen's window."

Lorraine moved to her vanity.

"Time to get all dolled up?" Lane asked.

"Yes, going to fix my hair and color my face so you and Mother will stop worrying."

"Good girl." He put his hand on her shoulders. "Clancy came by again, this morning."

Lorraine sunk further down into the chair. The rain hissed louder. "What did you say?"

"Same thing I always do. That you aren't ready to see him."

Lorraine turned her chair to face her father. She had to speak louder due to pings of hail that seemed to be hitting the house from all directions. "And then?"

"He said he's leaving. This afternoon. He wants to talk to you before then."

"Well, he can't."

"Come on now, Lori. Don't do something you'll regret."

"What's left to say?"

"He seems to think quite a bit seeing as how he calls or shows up here at least twice a day, every day."

"I can't face him, Daddy. Clancy made a fool out of me."

Lane sat on Lorraine's bed. "I don't see how he's done that. Clancy's doing what's right. If he didn't enlist, the government would have drafted him. It's happening to all the boys at work. I understand you don't want him to leave, but you act like he chose this war over you."

"Well, of course, he did."

"Clancy didn't end the relationship. That was your decision. And you are so stubborn, you won't change your mind, no matter what your heart says."

Lorraine wasn't used to this, her daddy calling her out on something. "I don't want him to go to war, obviously, but it's not just that. He didn't even ask me. How dare he make this huge decision without asking? What kind of marriage would that be?"

"A hard one." Lane chuckled. "But they *all* are. Do you love him?"

Lorraine walked back to the window. The storm was over, but the clouds were still dirty. Hail the size of baseballs covered the ground. The shrubs sagged, and glass shards from the neighbor's window littered their yard. Odd how short storms were, but how much damage they left behind. "I do," she whispered, "love him."

"Then give him a reason to stay safe out there." Lane stood. "I better survey the damage. Just remember one thing. It's too late for Clancy to change his decision now."

Lorraine rolled her eyes. What was the point of saying that? Of course it was too late. She picked up her brush and fought against her tangled curls. But her emotions were putting up the real fight. She had decided two weeks ago, but it only felt final now—now that there was a time limit. Clancy would leave today. She couldn't even sleep on it.

How could she manage the coming months and years not knowing if Clancy was alive or dead? In fifty years, would she be sitting on a porch swing wondering whatever happened to Clancy Fitchett?

Her father was right. It was too late for Clancy to change his mind—but not too late for her to change hers. She couldn't unsign a name, couldn't stop a war, but she could give them a fighting chance

"Daddy!" she yelled, wrestling on a dress. "Did Clancy say when the train leaves?!"

***

Tick Tock, Tick Tock. There was nothing to do but watch time escape. Clancy broke through the silence. "Should we go?"

"Train leaves at 2:00," Joel said. "I'd give it a little longer."

"Okay." Clancy fumbled with his bag. "Thanks for doing this."

Joel shrugged one shoulder. "It's just a ride."

"No, I mean, thanks for letting me go."

"You don't need permission. You're a grown man."

"Well, thanks for not giving me hell the way Daddy did, the way Lorraine did. You're the only one who's taken me seriously. They act like I'm a six-year-old who wants to play Cowboys and Indians."

Joel didn't know what to say. He didn't support this. But it was done.

"Sorry I don't have any money to leave for rent. I'll try to send a little each month."

"Don't worry about rent. You'll have better things to worry about." Joel was curious why Clancy had gone to see Crawl last night if he was short on money. But why pick a fight now? Maybe a night of cards was what Clancy needed to take the edge off today.

Clancy twirled a tassel dangling from the lamp. "I realize I don't say this enough. Hell, maybe I never have. But you're a damn good brother. I'm sure it must feel like all I ever do is ask, but there is just one favor I need before I leave."

"Anything."

"Keep an eye on Lorraine. I get that she's not my concern any longer, but I need to know she's safe."

Joel glanced around uneasily. "I'm not sure that's a good idea. Lorraine probably wants to move forward."

"She came here, so she must consider you a friend. You don't have to make it obvious to her. Just check in now and again—drive down her street, make sure nothing looks fishy."

"Why would anything be fishy for Lorraine?"

"It won't be. It shouldn't be. I'd just rest better knowing someone's watching out for her."

"I'll look in on her. Don't worry about anything but staying down out there. Don't do anything crazy."

"You mean besides going in the first place?"

"Besides that." Joel glanced again at the clock. It was time to leave now, but he didn't want to say so. He wanted to sit a few minutes longer. He wanted to go fishing. They used to love fishing. Why had they ever stopped? "We should go fishing."

Clancy gave a blank look. "Huh?"

"When you get back, I mean. We should fish again."

"Yeah. Okay."

The clock chimed a reminder it was too late to go fishing, too late to sit and talk about fishing.

Clancy wiped his hands on his pants legs. "Time's up I guess."

Joel hoped not.

***

The crowd at the station was overwhelming. Scents of smoke and sweat choked Lorraine as men shoved past her, all too eager to ride into destruction. The women weren't so eager, gripping their soldiers' hands. Their diamonds gleamed as they wiped their eyes. She nearly had a shotgun wedding too. It was too late for that now, but if she found Clancy, maybe she'd get back the ring and the promise behind it. But where was he? She longed to smell his cologne instead of these other scents assaulting her.

Lorraine searched the crowd, again and again, losing focus in the ocean of faces. Men were hanging out of the train; handkerchiefs were waving, and steam was rising. Her eyes blurred with tears, making the faces even harder to distinguish. She needed to sit down before she passed out. It was too hot here, too loud, too futile. She turned around and finally saw something familiar. A scar. Joel. Clancy was here. Her body regained a sense of purpose as she pushed through the crowd. "Joel!"

He turned his head. He'd heard her.

"Joel!" she said louder, standing on her tiptoes and waving with all the range her arms could manage.

He turned, motioning someone ahead. Clancy stopped mid-stride when he saw her. Joel gave him a small push forward, and Lorraine didn't stop till she was in his arms. "Clancy," she cried. "I'm sorry."

He pulled her closer and pressed his lips against the side of her head. "Lorraine." Her name had never sounded sweeter. "You came."

"I should have sooner. Shouldn't have been so stubborn." The sound of a train whistle tore their gaze away from each other.

"I'm supposed to board now."

"I know," she said but held on tighter.

Clancy pulled back to look into her eyes. "You coming here. Does this mean you forgive me? That we're okay?"

She nodded. "Will you write?"

The answer was a kiss that made her forget the noise and heat of the station. He readjusted his pack and walked backward through the crowd.

"I love you," she mouthed as he jogged for the train.

Joel stepped beside her.

"Oh, Joel. I'm sorry. You didn't get to say goodbye." She looked for Clancy again, but he'd disappeared. "You might find him if you head towards the train."

"I said goodbye at the house. It's fine. But what about you? Are you okay?"

Had Joel not asked, she might have held herself together all the way to the car. But instead, she dissolved into a crying mess. Joel put his arms around her, allowing her tears to soak his shoulder. Lorraine appreciated the comfort his tight hold brought, but it was no substitute for Clancy. She wanted to be in his arms, to taste his kiss again. A line from a book she loved, *Brave New World*, came to mind. "I want to know what passion is. I want to feel something strongly." She wished she had written those words because it summed up the human experience.

Now she understood what passion was. What she felt for Clancy was passion. This feeling that caught her blood on fire was passion.

Lorraine pulled away from Joel as the train growled forward. "I'm sorry." She went to wipe her eyes but stopped short, noticing her still-empty ring finger.

"I'll get it back for you," Joel said as if he'd read her mind.

She meant to say thank you but found herself in Joel's arms again. She stayed there until both the train and crowd disappeared from the station.

CHAPTER 14

Longview, Texas, 1991

Garrison pulled into Molly's driveway without checking back into his hotel. He hadn't even made a pit stop on the two-hour drive from the prison despite the three bottles of Gatorade he'd downed. He couldn't wait to talk to her. It was only when a stranger answered the door that Garrison considered the advantages of calling ahead. The guy was about his age but at least twice his size and wearing only a pair of striped swimming trunks. A boyfriend?

"Can I help you?"

Garrison pulled his eyes away from the man's arms and met his face. His neck was only slightly smaller than his biceps. New plan: get out of here as soon as possible. Well, ask to borrow the restroom then get out of here as soon as possible.

"Who is it?" Molly appeared at the door, barely visible behind Hercules. The annoyance on her face dissolved when she recognized Garrison. "Hey!"

"Am I interrupting anything?"

"No. Come in, come in." She pushed open the storm door. "I see you've met my brother?"

Brother. The word brought too much relief. "Not officially."

"Garrison, this is Lewis. Lewis, Garrison." There was no hint of enthusiasm in her voice.

"Just Lew." He extended his hand. "Nice to meet you."

"Likewise." Lew looked different from the school pictures Garrison had seen. Bigger mostly. But standing next to Molly, it was easy to see the resemblance. They had the same sharp cheekbones and high foreheads.

"We were about to swim if you want to join us," Lew said.

Molly flung her arm across her brother's chest. "Very funny."

"She doesn't swim," Lew said. "Scared to death of water," he continued, undeterred by Molly's hand over his mouth. "Take a chill pill, Mol." He pushed

113

her away. "Didn't mean to embarrass you in front of your man. If I wanted to do that, I'd show him your Barbie collection."

"Not before I go show your girlfriend the diary I found when you moved out."

"It was a journal."

"It had a unicorn on it."

Lew threw open the French doors leading to the pool. Garrison noticed a long-legged blonde in a small bikini reclining in a lounge chair. "I don't think she can read anyway," Lew said.

Molly gave the door a shove and twisted the blinds closed. "Sorry. He's a pain in the ass."

"Barbie collection, huh?"

"Secrets out. I played with Barbies. But I only kept the holiday ones."

"No judgment here. I still have my favorite G.I. Joe in my dresser at home."

"I used to steal Lew's G.I. Joes so they could date my Barbies."

"No Ken?"

"Just one. But he couldn't handle dating all my Barbies, even if he was a Malibu Ken."

Garrison heard coffee brewing in the kitchen. The sound of the boiling water made him squirm. "Got a bathroom?"

"Third door to the right." Molly pointed down the hallway. "Want some coffee?"

"Do you have any Tang?"

"Tang?" Molly's head flinched backward. "No, I'm not an astronaut, sorry."

Garrison laughed. "Alright, coffee it is."

On his way back to the kitchen, Garrison heard Lew trying to impress his date with his cannonball skills. He wished it was his own skin feeling the sting of the water and burn of chlorine. Wished it was Amber lounging in that chair. A perfect pool and a pretty girl. If there was a better combination for a blistering summer day, Garrison didn't know what it was.

"First swim of the year?" Garrison asked.

Molly tightened her ponytail. "Yeah. Lew doesn't take care of anything else around here, but he makes sure that pool is ready the minute he's home for the summer."

"You really don't swim? With a pool like that in your backyard?"

Molly busied herself with the coffee pot. "I nearly drowned as a kid. But you're welcome to use it while you're in town."

"I may just do that. Beats the one at the Value Inn for sure. I was on the swim team in high school and taught lessons every summer. I'd be glad to work with you."

"Cream or sugar?"

"Yes and yes."

"Oh, that's right. You put so much cream and sugar in your coffee that it's barely coffee."

"We can't all be John Wayne." Garrison took the cup from Molly. "So, are you interested?"

"In what? Conquering a silly childhood fear?" Molly chewed on her bottom lip. "Maybe not today." She poured herself a cup. "So how was home? You were gone longer than I expected."

"Miss me?"

A corner of her mouth lifted. "No, just wondered if you'd fallen into a black hole."

"If I did, I'd look like a noodle."

"Huh?"

"There's an actual term for it, spaghettification, believe it or not. The tidal force would stretch me like a piece of spaghetti."

Molly leaned over the counter, resting her hand on her chin. "Fascinating. Let me try this again. How was your trip home?"

"Sorry." It was like Amber always said, obscure space facts don't interest everyone. "Trip was good. And not good, but mostly good. But before we talk about that, I have a question. Remember the statement from the witness who saw Joel fleeing the crime scene?"

"Yeah, what about it?"

"She said the killer had an appalling cut on his face, right? Cut not scar."

A shrill squeal carried in from outside. "Ugh, I hate the summer." Molly turned to shut the window but stopped short. "You're right! Joel didn't have a cut; he had a scar." She brushed a finger against her parted lips. "It's proof. How did I miss it?"

"I wouldn't call it proof necessarily. She might have misspoken. What are the odds someone else would have a fresh cut that matched Joel's scar?"

"All this time it's been right under my nose." Molly pulled out a chair. "It's not near enough to get his conviction overturned, but it's a step in the right direction."

Garrison took the seat beside Molly. "And that's not even my good news." Molly's eyes twinkled, but Garrison didn't pretend it was for him. Joel Fitchett made her eyes sparkle. It was probably the same goofy look he got when talking about the solar system. "Joel called me."

"What? When?"

"When I was in Ohio. Said he needed something from me, but he wouldn't tell me what over the phone."

"You are going to meet him, right?"

"I already did. Sorry for not calling you before. It happened pretty fast."

Molly grabbed his wrist. "What did he want?"

Garrison explained as best he could while trying to ignore Molly's rose-petal soft skin on his own. He saved the best news for last. "And if we bring Lorraine to Joel, he's promised us an interview."

Molly's mouth fell open. "No way." If Garrison had thought he'd seen her eyes sparkle before, he'd been wrong. Her entire face brightened.

"And seeing as how you're the journalist slash lawyer here, I figure you'd be better cut out for that job than me."

Molly jumped up. "Me? Garrison, no. Connie Chung, sure, but not me." She took a slight step back and forced the excitement out of her voice. "What's the catch?"

"Catch? Not one on my end."

"I don't understand why you'd hand over an opportunity like this."

"It means more to you. I just want to find my grandfather."

"What are Joel's parameters?"

"His what?"

"For an interview, what are his limits? Things I'm not allowed to ask?" Molly paced frantically across the kitchen.

"I don't know. None."

Molly held up a finger. "Did he say no limits? Or did you assume? We'll need something in writing."

Garrison took his coffee cup to the sink. "You are really sucking the enjoyment out of this, Hamilton. Just say thanks and drink your cup of coffee so you can get to your second, and then we can get to work."

The hug caught him off guard. As did the heat coursing through his veins. He didn't want to let go, and considering she made no move to separate, maybe she didn't either. "Thanks," she whispered, too close to his ear.

"Am I interrupting something?" The voice sounded too gruff to be Lew's.

Molly recoiled. "You scared me, Pappy. Thought you were napping."

"I can't sleep with that damn splashing and squawking out there."

"Pappy, this is Garrison."

"Ray Gillard." He shook Garrison's hand. Ray's skin was tan and weather-beaten and his hair a shaggy gray.

"Garrison is the one I told you about, the one looking for Clancy Fitchett."

Ray groaned. "Molly, you are too wrapped up in those folks. Your class is over and you got an A. Let it go. College is for having fun." He waved to the window. "Like that knucklehead out there."

"Don't mind Pappy. I bored him the entire way home with talk about the Fitchetts."

"No need for the country music then?" Garrison winked.

Molly's smile was short-lived, fading when the telephone rang. "That will be Mom. Do you want to say hello, Pappy?"

"Nah, tell her to enjoy their trip and not to scurry back on my account."

"Oh, they won't." Molly spoke under her breath, but Garrison heard the anger in her voice. What kind of people had raised this great girl but didn't stick around to enjoy her company? Maybe they assumed they were giving her enough things that she didn't need them. Yet Molly didn't seem to care about things. Far as Garrison could tell, she survived solely on coffee and ponytail holders.

"Stick around, Garrison. I'm cooking." Ray pulled a pack of bacon from the fridge. "How does a BLT sound?"

"Thanks, but I gotta check into my hotel."

"Hotel? Don't let me kick you out."

"Oh no." Garrison tugged his cap down. "I'm not staying here."

"It's okay. It wasn't so long ago I was young. Her folks stay away all summer." He mimed zipping his lips. "And I won't say a word."

"It's not like that." Heat crept into Garrison's cheeks. It was natural Ray assumed they were a couple. That hug was three miles past friendly. Still, Ray giving him permission to have a summer-long sleepover with Molly felt awkward.

"Fair enough. Sleep in the guest room. It will give me a chance to get to know you better."

Staying here wasn't the worst idea. He and Molly had a lot of work to do, and the hotel was kind of a dive. "All right. As long as it's okay with Molly and Lew."

Ray grinned. "Lew doesn't count. And I spent a full day in a cramped vehicle with my granddaughter. She only stopped talking about you to pump gas and drink coffee. Trust me when I say, having you here will be more than all right with her."

***

Ray was right. Molly seemed excited at the idea of Garrison staying, maybe too excited. Garrison promised himself he'd be more careful what he said to her. He didn't want to lead her on. But he had never slept better than he did last night under that goose down comforter in the guest room. And coming in from morning laps to the smell of homemade breakfast wasn't bad either. The only thing he hadn't worked out was how to tell Amber.

He dialed her number and waited for her answering machine to pick up. He was a coward to call when she was at work, but if there was ever a conversation that needed to be one-sided, this was it. "Hey, Amber. Made it to Longview. Couldn't get a room at the same place, but I'll call you in a few days. Hope you enjoy lifeguarding. Save lives, but use mouth to mouth sparingly. I love you."

There. He hadn't lied nor given too much information. He'd eventually have to talk to her, and she'd ask for the hotel's phone number, but at least he bought more time.

Eggs sizzled as Ray dropped them into the hot grease. Garrison couldn't help but notice how pale and weak Ray looked as he moved between the griddle and stovetop.

Molly took a plate of bacon and pancakes to the table. "Come sit, Pappy. We'll finish the rest."

A violent cough escaped Ray. Molly helped him sit, and Garrison grabbed him a paper towel. Ray pulled out a bandanna to spit into. "I'm fine," he said with a hoarse voice. "No need to fuss." Garrison peeked at the bandanna, but its red color made it impossible to see if Ray had spit up blood.

"You really don't need to cook. It's not like when we were kids. Lew and I stick to cereal and sandwiches these days," Molly told him.

"I said I'm fine. I realize I'm an old man and there's a lot I can't do, but I can still cook breakfast for my grandchildren."

"And a fine one at that." Garrison loaded his plate. "Guess we better save some for Lew."

"Don't bother." Molly put a single hash brown on her plate. "He won't be up till 11:00. Just in time to flirt with the new housekeeper. Don't worry, Pappy. I made sure the nurse we hired is in her fifties. That way you don't have to share her with Lew."

"I don't need a babysitter." Ray tried to hide another cough by keeping his mouth shut, but it produced a sound almost worse.

"She's not a babysitter; she's a nurse. She doesn't start until tomorrow, but I'll be around today to help."

Ray ambled back to the griddle. "This may surprise you, young lady, but just last week, I lived alone and took care of myself."

"I know that. But we don't have a game plan today. The trail is cold."

"We just need a good brainstorming session. Find a new lead." Garrison looked out the window. "Maybe over burgers? Weather is nice, and my burgers taste as good as this breakfast."

"Is that so?" Ray threw down a tray of eggs like a gauntlet. "I'd love to try them, but there's nothing in that freezer but ice and corn dogs."

"I wasn't kidding when I told you that Lew and I didn't cook," Molly said. "Hope you like takeout."

"I'll go to the store." Garrison put an egg on his plate. "Just point me in the right direction."

"I can take you. It's confusing to explain directions, and it would be faster if I came." Molly rushed her words.

"That works too. Good day to put the top down."

"Guess that means I'm driving. Do you mind if we leave you for a few minutes, Pappy? If you need Lew, throw cold water on him."

Ray poured gravy on his plate. "Go on. Just bring me back a couple packs of Marlboros."

"Pappy, no. You're already so sick. Those things will kill you."

"Darling, there's not much to relish in this life that won't kill you, and I'm too old to break habits."

Molly clenched her jaw.

"Oh, relax and eat." Ray stabbed his fork into a pancake and dropped it in front of her. "The sooner you finish, the sooner I can get my new pack."

***

"So, is your mom Ray's only child?" Garrison asked.

"Unfortunately for him, yes. The way I see it, everyone needs three or four. Odds are, at least one of them will be willing to take care of you someday."

"Well, Ray's lucky to have a grandkid that does."

Molly shrugged and kept her eyes on the road.

"So, you spent time every summer in Odessa?"

"Pappy never lived anywhere long. Work took him everywhere."

"What kind of work?"

"Oilfield. What else is there?" she asked sarcastically. "But it worked out well for me and Lew. We got to see a lot of the country. Oilfield country but still country."

Garrison pointed outside, "Did he work on those?"

"On what?"

"On those machines. The ones that move like elderly woodpeckers."

"Pumpjacks?" Molly bent over the wheel laughing. "I've heard them called a lot: nodding donkeys, thirsty birds, but never an elderly woodpecker." She wiped a tear from her eye. "Yeah, he worked on the woodpeckers."

Garrison smiled. He loved Molly's laugh, even if it was at his expense. "What about your grandmother?"

"She and Pappy weren't ever married. She took off when Mom turned three. He married twice after, but neither stuck. Some men are built to be bachelors. Judging by the divorce rate, probably most of them."

Garrison considered telling Molly marriage had worked out well for the men in his family, but that didn't seem like something to rub in. "So, what about you? Are you from here?"

"Longview? No. We moved here from Carthage when I was twelve."

"Carthage to Longview? Your life sounds eerily like the Fitchetts."

Molly tapped the steering wheel. "Hmm, interesting observation. Maybe that's why I'm abnormally interested."

"You get back to Carthage much?"

Molly chuckled. "Why would I?"

"It's where Joel and Clancy grew up. Who knows what we might find."

"A subtropical climate, pine trees, mosquitoes. Not much different from here."

"Come on now. Try spontaneity. It may look good on you. We can find the house they grew up in. Could be kinda cool."

"Like Fitchett Graceland?"

"Exactly. Or we can make it a Fitchett-free day where you show me the sites of your childhood."

Between her poker face and sunglasses, it was hard to tell what Molly thought of the idea. Garrison realized his circumstances made him overly sentimental. He'd made his memories his own personal Graceland.

"Getting out of town does sound nice. Even if it's just to Carthage. I get tired of seeing the same thing day in and out. But I don't want to leave Pappy that long."

"Tomorrow then? When the nurse is on shift?"

"Okay, tomorrow." Molly only drove a few more miles before veering into a gas station. "Actually no. It's time for Lew to pull his weight." She pulled a twenty from her purse. "Fill up the tank. I'll be Lew's wake up call."

"Road trip!" Garrison pumped his fist up and hit the Porsche's roof until Molly let the top down. There were more clouds than sky, it seemed. He turned the radio dial until he found a country station. "Brother jukebox, sister wine," Garrison sang with his best Texas accent.

"No." Molly turned to another station playing a commercial.

"Oh, come on! It's what? A half-hour drive?"

"Closer to an hour. Let's go inside." She reached to kill the ignition just as the commercial ended.

"Wait, wait!" Garrison turned up the volume. "Friends in Low Places! What are the odds you'd turn to another country station?"

"In Texas? I'd say pretty good."

"Come on; don't act too good for Garth." Garrison didn't know all the lyrics but struggled through the first verse as best he could.

"Fine, fine." She held up her hand to silence him. "You pick the music, but you owe me a bag of Cheetos and a Pepsi for my troubles."

"A small price to pay."

Molly rolled her eyes but didn't kill the engine till the song was over.

***

Garrison leaned back in his seat and watched the telephone pole wires dance just the way he had as a boy on road trips. They seemed to widen, then narrow, cross, and straighten like some elaborate game of Double Dutch.

He sat up when they passed the blue "Welcome to Carthage" sign. He liked the small town feel right away, the neighborly way people in passing cars took the time to wave.

121

Molly said little, but Garrison didn't probe. She was taking it in. Hometowns had a way of resurrecting buried memories.

"Is it strange to be back?" he finally asked.

"A little. It's even smaller than I remember—but also prettier." She drove a few more miles and turned down a narrow road. She parked in front of a house that sat far back from the curb, nearly swallowed in a forest of pine trees. It was small with plain brown brick, but well-maintained.

Molly rolled down her window. "This was our house."

Garrison couldn't hide his surprise. "Wow, would not have guessed that."

"Yeah. This was our pre-promotion, pre-move, pre-oversized, and over-decorated house. Back when we had nothing to prove. Back in the good old days." Molly's voice trailed off as she spoke.

"Fitting then that it's surrounded by an actual picket fence," Garrison said.

She kept her eyes out the window. "Dad put that up to keep the deer out. Our backyard was covered in rosebushes, and deer were constantly eating the blooms. I used to love waking up early to watch them." She sighed. "It's been too long since I've watched a deer stroll through a forest of roses."

Garrison unlocked his door. "Want me to go knock? I'm sure they won't mind you looking around."

"Nah." Molly put the car into drive. "It's just a house, not a time machine." She managed a tight-lipped smile. "Besides, one of my elementary schools is up the road. I'd rather see that. Not sure how long it's been around, but maybe Clancy and Joel went there. They might have records. If not, it'd be cool to say hello to old teachers."

When she pulled into the school parking lot, the melancholy look on her face disappeared, replaced by a smile that made her eyes crinkle at the corners. Obviously, the memories here were less bittersweet.

"Wow. Now, this is a blast from the past. My third-grade teacher was amazing. I wonder if she's still here."

Garrison scanned the empty parking lot. "My guess would be no."

"School must already be out. Let's go see if it's open somewhere."

"Like breaking and entering?"

"If it's not locked, it's not breaking. I just want to look inside."

When the front door didn't budge, she set off for the back. This was certainly a new side of Molly. Garrison had pegged her as a rule follower.

They made it as far as the playground before she stopped. "They got new equipment," she said wistfully. "I know I was shorter, but our monkey bars were bigger than these."

"Doesn't seem right, does it? They actually tore down my elementary school two years ago. It felt like they should have at least asked me, you know? It's kinda sacred ground or something."

Molly studied the rest of the playground. "That slide's the same. And the trees." Her face lit up. "Follow me; you've *got* to see this."

She found a tall oak tree and lay underneath, squinting into the sunlight. "Come on, a little grass and sticks won't hurt you."

The sticks weren't a problem. Garrison had spent plenty of time in his backyard staring at the night sky. It was more the proximity to Molly, the intimacy of lying beside her that gave him pause. But they were on a school playground. What could happen?

He lay next to her and followed her gaze upwards where sunlight danced through swaying branches. A bright sunburst crept through, growing larger and larger. Just when it looked like it would swallow them up, the light drew back. It came for them, again and again, pulsating like a variable star. Smaller, translucent circles of yellows, pinks, and greens flashed in his peripheral. This riot of colors felt almost otherworldly.

Molly broke the silence. "No better kaleidoscope than a tree. You know, I had my first kiss here. Not when I was a student, but years later, a boy brought me back."

Garrison laughed to himself. So there was the answer to his question about what could possibly happen on a playground.

He turned his head to face her. "I can see why." He meant due to the general beauty of the setting, but with the light streaming on her, Molly looked ethereal.

"It was awful," Molly said.

"Most first ones are. But they still make good memories."

"No running from the memories here, I guess."

"No need to run. Sometimes memories are all we've got."

Molly looked back up. "Guess I stay busy looking ahead. Maybe I need to find a balance."

"Maybe we both do." He sat up. "Let's check that door."

Molly ran ahead of him. Her shoulders sagged as she pulled. "Locked."

Garrison cupped his hands to stare inside, but the halls were dark, no handprint projects or A+ spelling tests on the walls.

"School ended." Though the voice was kind, the surprise of it made Garrison jump.

A frail man stopped to pick up litter surrounding a trash barrel before pushing his walker to the bench beside them. The plastic bag wrapped around his wrist rustled in the wind.

"Do you need help?" Garrison asked.

The man lowered himself on the bench and leaned forward on his walker until he resumed normal breathing. "I'm okay. I live with my boy and his family right across the street. Walk here on nice days to have lunch."

"You look so familiar," Molly said. "Did you work here?"

"Cleaned those halls till 1982. Now my son's the principal." He gave a satisfied smile. "What's your name, young lady?"

"Molly Hamilton. And you're Mr. Nevins!"

"Small world," Garrison said.

"No, just a small town," Mr. Nevins said. "What brings you back?"

"Memories I guess." Molly looked at Garrison. "Well, memories and a pair of infamous brothers."

Mr. Nevins pulled a sandwich from his bag and took a bite. "Let me guess," he said, mouth full of peanut butter. "Fitchetts?"

"Yes." Molly sat beside him. "Did you know them?"

Mr. Nevins wiped his mouth on his sleeve. "Yes, ma'am."

"Did they go here?"

"Well, here wasn't *here* back then. But I knew them from the old grammar school."

Garrison felt a fresh jolt of energy. Maybe the coffee was finally kicking in. "Were you friends?" he asked.

"Friends? Ha! I was sixteen when I started scrubbing piss off toilets. I wasn't allowed to mix with students, nor any of the white staff either. I only remember him because of what happened my first year working at the school."

Garrison sat on the other side of Mr. Nevins. Of all the days for Molly not to have her notebook. "Did you hear anything about that?"

"There were lots of rumors and teasing. Children will always be children."

"Poor Joel," Molly said.

Mr. Nevins attempted to get a ragged nail under the tab of his Diet Pepsi. "You mean, poor Clancy. Everybody thought he did it. I paid no mind to that. Ain't no way a little boy could've done such a thing." He shoved the can in Garrison's face. "Give an old man a hand, will you?"

Garrison popped the tab and handed it back. "Anything you heard that may have been more than a rumor?"

"Just what little Jack Monroe said." He took a slow sip. "Still haunted by that child."

Molly and Garrison exchanged confused glances. "Who's Jack Monroe?" Molly asked.

"He went to school with the Fitchetts. He was a good kid, but no one thought so. Can't expect a ten-year-old boy to sit still and listen when he hasn't eaten a good breakfast. He never had a lunch either. So, I left mine at the place he sat. He caught me once and struck up a conversation after school. I wasn't supposed to talk to him, but that poor boy needed someone to care, someone to notice the bruises."

"Was he friends with Clancy or Joel?"

"I think I was his only friend." Mr. Nevins pulled out a handkerchief and blotted his forehead. "But Jack missed several days of school after Joel was hurt. When he came back, he was white as bleached sheets. Said he'd been sick, but it was more than that. He came back with jumping beans in his belly. A damn bluebird could fly by and he'd cower like bombs were falling from the sky."

Molly leaned forward. "And did you ask him why?"

"He wouldn't say. Not at first. But after Joel and Clancy came back, I noticed how nervous he'd act whenever they came around. I asked him, but he swore he wasn't involved."

"And you believed him?"

"Had no reason not to. I told you he was a good boy. I asked him if he witnessed what happened. I saw the answer in his eyes before he spoke. So, I demanded he tell me who did it."

Garrison's stomach fluttered. "And..."

"He said he couldn't tell me that. Told me it wasn't Clancy, but I couldn't get much else out of him."

Garrison felt an unexpected release of tension. It hadn't been Clancy. Of course, it hadn't.

"Did you tell him to go to the police?" Molly took over the questioning.

"I knew he'd never do it himself, so I did. Can't blame little children for being scared. But I wasn't scared, so I visited the station myself. Officer took one look at me and asked if I was there to turn myself in for something." Mr. Nevins's nostrils flared. "Can you believe they said that to me when I was the only one trying to help little Jack?"

"Unfortunately, I can," Molly said. "Nothing evil in this world surprises me anymore—especially racism in Texas. Did they ever listen to you?"

"No. I begged them to ask Jack about what happened to Joel Fitchett—told them to check the cupboards for food while they were at his house too. They told me to mind my own business, but I wasn't gonna leave till they filed a report."

"Good for you," Molly said.

He pressed a dent in the Pepsi can. "But then the officer said, 'How do we know you ain't got something to do with this, Jed? You got a record.' I did. Petty crimes, but still. Then he said he heard what was going on between me and the boy. I thought he meant us talking during my workday, but he meant more than that. Said we had an inappropriate relationship—that they could put me in prison for it. Of course it wasn't true, but who would take my word? How could my grandma survive if I got locked up?"

Molly flinched. "How awful."

"Looking back now, the worst part is they knew Jack was being abused and didn't care to stop it. Just used it as a weapon to shut me up." Mr. Nevins' eyes widened. "I shouldn't have shut up."

"You were a boy yourself." Molly patted his knee. "A brave one. Did you talk to Jack after that?"

"I was too scared. I stopped leaving him lunch. Avoided him altogether. Then come fall, he was gone."

"Gone?" Molly asked. "Like his family moved away?"

"Never came home from trick-or-treating. Some said it was a kidnapping, but knowing how his home life was, I assumed he ran away."

"A ten-year-old?" Garrison asked. "Where would he go?"

"Ten was older back then. No offense to your generation, but we were tougher stock."

"Did they ever find any leads on what happened to Jack?" Molly asked.

"Nope. It was news and then it wasn't anymore. His parents gave up and so everyone else did. They might have killed him, but I choose to imagine otherwise."

"And the Fitchetts?" Garrison asked. "Ever heard any more about them?"

"Just what everybody did. Bout Joel killing their daddy."

The unmistakable sound of pea gravel being dumped down a metal slide made Garrison look up. At some point, three small children and their mother had arrived.

Mr. Nevins looked at his watch. "That's my cue to start home. Rest of the mom's group will be here soon."

"Can we give you a ride?" Garrison scooted his walker closer to him.

"Nah. Doc says I need to walk fifteen minutes a day."

"It was nice to see you again, Mr. Nevins." Molly put her hand on his slumped back. "Sorry for all those messes I made."

"Ha! Messes kept me in business, young lady. Just do me a favor and keep out of them when you can."

"Okay," Molly said. It was good advice, but Garrison knew they were doing a lousy job of following it.

***

"Here it is!" Molly tapped the screen.

Garrison scooted his chair closer and read the article detailing Jack Monroe's disappearance. He'd taken his sister trick-or-treating and come home around 8:00. When his mom went to wake him for school the next morning, he was gone. Nothing missing from his room except the pillowcase full of candy he'd collected.

"He probably went back trick-or-treating and someone kidnapped him," Molly said. "He wouldn't run away without packing a suitcase."

"A pillowcase full of candy might be all a ten-year-old would bring to run away."

"I don't buy it. Let's keep looking." Molly reached into her bag. "Not a word," she warned, putting on a pair of thick glasses.

"You look cute," Garrison said without thinking. He didn't look to see her reaction but shifted his body to make sure they were not touching.

It had been Molly who insisted on coming to the library today. Finding Jack Monroe was probably a fool's errand, but Garrison didn't have another kind to run. Jack might shed light on one mystery, even if it wasn't the one he most needed solved. Garrison sniffed the air. "You ever notice how all libraries smell the same?"

Molly kept her eyes on the screen. "Musty carpet."

"And pencil shavings."

"Here's another one." Molly leaned forward as Garrison read over her shoulder. He was in the middle of the second paragraph when Molly deflated in her chair. "Nada."

"You already read it? How do you even comprehend at that speed?"

"You need less Tang and more coffee."

"Maybe so, but I did find something you missed."

Molly squinted at the screen. "What?"

"His sister. Said she was only five. Roxanne Monroe isn't the most common name. Maybe we can find her."

"And you say you aren't a journalist." She wrote down the name and continued to search. "Unbelievable," she said a few minutes later. "The story just stopped. The crime section got taken over by this Clyde Lawson trial. Some local who killed his brother."

"He's the reason the stories about Joel's attack stopped too, back when they first found his brother's body."

"Media hog."

"Too bad Clancy isn't."

Molly rubbed her eyes. "I can't see straight. I think we're done here."

"Better run by the store. Don't want your Pappy to run out of smokes. Plus, I promised to cook dinner."

"You did. Let's head that way. I'd say we put in a good day's work."

It had been a good day. Good because Carthage was a great little town, a town where smiles were wider and days were slower. Good because they were coming back to Longview with two new names, two new leads. But even though Garrison felt guilty admitting it, the good was mostly because of who he'd spent it with—and the night was still young.

CHAPTER 15

Longview, Texas, 1942

Have you looked in on Lorraine?

Day two since Joel received the letter, and he still couldn't escape that single line. Clancy had completed boot camp. That meant six weeks had passed without Joel seeing Lorraine. He'd hoped his brother wouldn't need him to check on her now that they were back together—together and no doubt pouring their hearts out to each other on page after page. But this letter proved he wasn't off the hook.

When Joel opened Clancy's door, a burst of warm air escaped. Without the scents of his brother's aftershave and cologne, the air smelled stale, like his own breath blowing back at him. He considered cleaning, but a stroke across the dresser told him there was no need. No dust, no piles of dirty laundry, no Clancy.

Joel searched but already knew the ring wasn't in here. He'd turned the entire room upside down weeks ago. Still, he couldn't visit Lorraine empty-handed. He'd have to write Clancy and ask. He had promised Lorraine after all. Promises. Seemed they caused all Joel's troubles lately.

The phone rang just as Joel returned from getting the morning paper but not the two short rings followed by that shrill endless one that indicated the call was his. For some reason, the other homes that shared his line were getting an awful lot of calls this Tuesday morning. It reminded Joel of Pearl Harbor, and the memory turned his stomach. He pushed away his cereal bowl and his irritation at the busy line. Not like anyone would call him anyway.

Joel found the explanation for the active phone on the paper's front page. The headline, *Gregg County Draft Numbers and Names* might as well have been written in blood. Maybe it was a good thing his phone wasn't the one ringing.

Joel ran his finger down the list. So many familiar names. Charles Johnson? Mr. Rogers just hired him to take Clancy's place. Joel picked up his coffee. That should make work interesting today. Work. He glanced at the clock. Only twenty minutes till eight. He was halfway off his chair when his eyes caught a familiar name. His own.

But it couldn't be. He sat down to look closely. His name. His address. Joel dropped his coffee cup, and black liquid smeared the matching ink erasing many names, but not his own.

Joel tried to take a deep breath, but his chest tightened. He pushed open a window, sending a cloud of dust into the kitchen. He took a few gulps of fresh air before stumbling back to the paper again. The words had not changed.

Of course, he understood this was a possibility. Registering with the Selective Service was a requirement, and there had been a drawing on St. Patrick's Day. Joel read about it in this very paper. They'd used green capsules and a mechanical mixer rather than a wooden spoon. Like the festivity and technology would make it better if your number was written on that bile colored capsule. But Joel hadn't even been worried. Clancy was fighting. America needed soldiers but not badly enough to wipe out an entire family's lineage.

The phone kept ringing. Twice in a row for Joel, but he didn't answer. He knew why they were calling. He rubbed his face, scraping rough hands against the rough pattern on his skin. Maybe the scar would be a problem. Unlikely, but Daddy said they rejected men for bad teeth so anything was possible. Did a scar like his pose an infection risk? So what if he was being selfish? Was it wrong to wish the scar might be good for something? That someone would see it and pity him, realizing he had already suffered enough?

***

Lorraine lived for 10:30 in the morning and 3:30 in the afternoon, the times the mail came. She could tell by the mailman's wide smile that he had a letter for her today. "Thank you!" She hugged him, sat on the curb, and tore open the envelope.

Dearest Lorraine,

I am a Marine. Throughout my life, I've been decent at many things but exceptional at none. Until now. Five weeks of training have made me an expert killer. I'm trained to take a life with a gun, a bayonet, or even with my own hands. I don't tell you this to worry you; I intend it to do the opposite. To show you when a moment of danger arrives, my skills will not fail me.

130

My skills nor my Model 1903. This rifle is no longer a burden but an extension of me, eight pounds of power to make up for the weight I've lost running.

I ache for you and for the warmth of home, but I have survived. Survived humiliation, torture, and reprogramming. I've been called a sonofabitch and a lily-livered bastard so many times, that it feels strange to be called a Marine. Strange to be respected. Don't tell the girls at college you are marrying a gas station attendant; tell them you are marrying a Marine. I only wish I could say when. I will ship out soon, and I don't know when I'll be home. But the hope and expectation of a life with you will aid in my survival just as much as my new skills will.

Love,
Clancy

***

Sleep had eluded Joel since reading his name in the paper. Wine helped, but didn't tuck him in the way it had before. It calmed the shaking hands at least. He sat against the hard boards of the back porch step and sipped from his glass. Across the alley, vines of fiery orange flowers dressed the fence. Flowers he'd never noticed. A memory rose up and choked him. Similar blossoms covered Katie Montgomery's fence many springs ago. Joel and Katie would pick them as they walked the benches surrounding her deck. He hadn't thought about Katie or those carefree days in so long. Where was she now? Why hadn't they stayed in touch? She was the first real friend he'd had. Come to think of it, she was the last real friend he'd had too. But it didn't matter. Now was no time to rekindle a friendship, not when he wouldn't be around to enjoy it.

The official notice arrived two days ago. He'd report Friday for examination.

Who would care for the house when he left? Daddy couldn't water the grass every day, not from Carthage. Joel had always taken pride in his green lawn, but now the blades would turn brown as an old penny. No, the grass would not be greener than it was right now, and that knowledge felt like a knife twisting in his stomach.

Joel reached for the wine bottle. Practically empty. Not enough for the night, not enough for the nightmares. He went inside and grabbed his keys. The market was still open. He would get some candy bars too—might as well before the army put him on the basic training diet. The Army. He wasn't suited for it. Maybe he should ask if he could be a Marine so he could look out for Clancy. But he was even less suited for that. Plus, one explosion, and Tom Fitchett would never have the grandkids he claimed he wanted.

Joel took his time at the store, wandering each aisle until he was satisfied, his cart cradled enough alcohol and sugar for the long night waiting for him.

Only one line was open, and a woman about his age was working it. Joel gripped the cold metal of the shopping cart and kept his eyes down. That was how he noticed the glittering ring on the hand of the woman ahead of him. He wasn't sure if it was the wine or his sentimental imagination playing tricks on him, but it looked like Mama's ring. It couldn't be, but who else would have such a bright hoop of diamonds circling a translucent pearl? It pulled Joel towards it. "Excuse me, ma'am."

"Yes?" The woman with a turned-up nose pulled her purse closer when she noticed Joel's scar.

"Nice ring." Joel detected a slight slur in his speech. "Looks like my Mama's."

"Oh." She took her change from the cashier. "Have a nice evening."

"Where did you get it?"

Her eyes drifted to her hand. "You'd have to ask my husband. It was a gift for our tenth anniversary just last week." She took her bags and jogged out as fast as she could in her three-inch heels.

The cashier totaled Joel's items, but it was the story about the ring that wasn't adding up. She'd only gotten it last week, and Mama's ring was missing. And why had she been in such a hurry to get away? Joel needed to see the ring again, needed to check inside for Mama's initials.

"I'll be right back," Joel told the cashier.

He found the woman loading her bags into her back seat. "Mind if I take a closer look at that ring?"

She stood rigid. "Don't come any closer! I'll call the police!"

"I don't want to hurt you, I just—"

Her door slammed, and the engine sputtered. Joel was sure now that something wasn't right. He jumped into his truck, tires howling as he pulled out from the parking lot.

Joel followed her Pontiac through the streets of Longview, trying not to lose her, but also trying to stay far enough behind so he wouldn't be seen. She never spotted him, not even when he parked across the street from her house. The home was enormous and in a good neighborhood, but having nice things didn't exempt people from stealing. Joel rang the doorbell.

The woman answered. "John!" Her voice was breathy. "Someone followed me home."

An overweight man with an uneven mustache shielded his wife. "Is there a problem?"

She gripped her husband's arm. "This man harassed me at the store and followed me! Call the police!"

"Where did you buy her ring?" Joel asked.

John's face wrinkled. "None of your business." He tried to close the door, but Joel wedged his way into the frame.

"I'm not crazy. But that ring looks just like my Mama's ring that's gone missing."

"I bought this ring fair and square," the husband said.

Joel wrung his hands. "Please, can I see it?"

The woman peeked over her husband's shoulder. "How could he know just by looking? Not like it's one of a kind." The disdainful way she spoke of it made Joel's body tense. If the ring meant so little to her, why was she guarding it like it was the Hope Diamond?

"Mama's has her initials, NAF, engraved on the band." Joel stepped backward. "If those letters aren't there, I'll leave."

John didn't look convinced, but he held out his hand. His wife made a show of tugging it off but eventually handed it over. John held it to the light then looked at Joel dejectedly. "Oh hell." He opened the door wider. "Come inside."

***

When all was said and done, Joel didn't feel like going home. He didn't have the wine he had set out for, but the ring was in his front pocket. The button secured it, but he patted his chest every few minutes to be sure it hadn't escaped.

He knew he needed to take it to Lorraine, but somehow, it felt like it should be his now. He had paid for it—paid twice the price it had cost John at the pawnshop in Shreveport. That fact that it was in Shreveport left no doubt that Clancy had either sold it or lost it to Crawl. How could he gamble with something so precious? How could anyone be so careless? The more Joel stewed over it, the more determined he was to call Clancy out for it. But this wasn't the sort of thing to say in a letter, so he'd have to wait. Joel didn't know how he'd manage. It already felt like a volcano had erupted inside him. It would surely stain everything red by the time Clancy came home.

Joel turned on Lorraine's street, not sure he would stop. He might not have, but Mr. Applewhite was out watering the lawn and saw him.

"Well, hi Joel." Lane frowned as he approached. "Is everything all right?"

"Everything's fine." Joel closed the truck door. "Is Lorraine home?"

"Sure thing. Come on inside. Birdie's turned in early with a headache. She'll be sorry she missed you."

Joel wasn't sorry. The last time he'd seen Mrs. Applewhite had been to apologize for Christmas. Lane had slapped his back and laughed. Who hadn't had one too many Gin Sours? But Birdie said nothing. She stared at Joel, scrunching her eyes like she wasn't sure what to make of him. Like he was a blurry letter on an eye chart.

Lorraine's face looked similar when she saw Joel at the bottom of the stairs. She walked stiffly, gripping onto the banister. "Is it Clancy?" Her voice trembled.

"No, Clancy is great. I got a letter from him a few days ago, and he asked me to check in on you."

Lorraine sagged against the wall. "Thank God."

"How about you, Joel?" Lane asked. "We...uh...saw your name last week."

Joel looked at the floor. "My exam is Friday."

"Well, you'll let us know, won't you?"

"Sure."

They made an awkward trio, standing in silence, avoiding each other's eyes. Joel wished he wouldn't have come. He was eyeing the front door wondering how to announce his exit when he felt Lorraine's hand on his elbow. "Can we step outside?"

"Right." Lane walked towards the hallway. "Good seeing you Joel and um...Godspeed."

"Sorry about that." Lorraine led Joel to the back porch. "Daddy just doesn't know what to say."

Joel passed the patio chairs and sat on the swing, hoping Lorraine would too. "Do you? Know what to say?"

The hair on Joel's arms stood when Lorraine sat beside him. "No, I guess I don't. But I did try to call."

"What? When?"

"The day we saw the paper."

Joel had assumed Daddy had been trying to reach him all day or maybe Mr. Rogers wondering why he wasn't at work. Lorraine calling never crossed his mind. It made him feel better somehow, knowing she cared.

Birds clamored above them, beating their wings and squawking. There were more trees back here than in a forest. Joel had to consciously force his limbs to relax. When Lorraine finally spoke, Joel was sure he heard her wrong. "What was that?"

Lorraine looked away. "There are ways to make sure you fail the test. I'm terrible for suggesting that, aren't I? You're surely itching to go just like Clancy."

"I'm not." Joel felt the tickle of a ladybug as it crossed his arm. "I'm not against the war." He looked up. "I'm just scared to death of it." The words were no surprise to him, but the ease at which he voiced them was. Intimacy didn't come easy for Joel, but it was different with Lorraine. *He* was different with Lorraine.

"Of course, you are! I'm scared for you. As Clancy pointed out, I'm a hypocrite about the whole matter. Besides not wanting him to fight, there's the economy. America has been in a crawl since the Depression, and the war has solved all that. Industry and technology are booming. Anyone who wants to work can, but look at the cost."

"Daddy thinks since I'm a mechanic they might use my hands for repairs instead of destruction."

"Maybe, but I still hate the idea of it—of you being gone so far away."

"Why?" Joel craved words to carry with him to war—words to replay in his mind as he replayed the memory of how she looked at him now. Even if it was all part of a fantasy, so what? Sometimes fantasies kept people alive.

Lorraine picked at the chipping paint from the swing. "Because I'm fond of you. We'll be family soon, but I'd like to be your friend in the meantime. I haven't made many good friends here. The girls are fun, but I can't talk to them the way I talked to my friends back home—or the way I talked to Clancy."

Joel pressed his palms into his lap. "So how do I fail the test?"

"I feel awful even talking about this."

"Don't." Joel brushed his hand against her leg. Her skin was cool and smooth. "I thought if I stayed, I'd organize a scrap drive. Could have the biggest one in Texas with all Daddy's car parts lying around."

Lorraine looked at him. He wondered if she saw through him. Wondered if she realized scrap metal had nothing to do with why he wanted to stay. "I heard they ask a question, and if you answer it a certain way, it's an automatic no."

"What's the question?"

Lorraine turned her head, but Joel saw her left cheek redden. "They ask if you like girls."

"Oh." Joel felt his own cheeks warm.

"It's a silly idea." She brushed her hands across her dress. "If you end up going, we'll at least go out before. Have a proper send off. But I'll pray they will let you stay here...with me."

Lorraine's enticing smile made Joel eager to erase the distance between them. They had been here before. Different porch swing but same parting lips, same fixed gazes. Clancy had ruined it then, but he couldn't now. How much could Lorraine mean to his brother if he'd given away her ring? Joel leaned in closer and raised his hand to push a stray curl off her forehead. Lorraine took hold of his hand but lowered it back to his lap. Her touch was gentle but her expression sharp. "What are you doing?"

Joel jumped to his feet. "Nothing."

"I must have given you the wrong idea. We can be friends, but I love your brother."

Joel's brain sifted his memories for proof she had wanted him to kiss her. But what did any evidence matter when she was telling him no?

Joel needed a fresh glass of water to quench his dry throat, but more than he needed a drink, he needed an escape. He ran for the gate. The last thing he wanted was to risk seeing Mr. Applewhite again.

"Wait!" Lorraine stood and pulled at her dress. "It was only a misunderstanding. Please stop."

But Joel didn't stop—even as he saw Lorraine shouting and waving in his rearview mirror.

***

College wasn't so bad. Lorraine's time would be better spent writing, but knowledge was never a bad thing. The other girls complained about the papers they had to write and the lack of handsome boys to sit beside in their classes, but not Lorraine. She was good at writing and had her own handsome fiancé to send love letters to. But for tonight, the only writing she had time for was school related, an essay comparing a literary character's fatal flaw to her own.

Lorraine set her pencil down when the phone rang. It was Lu; she said she'd call when she found out when the movie started. Lorraine needed to know so she

136

could show up late. She didn't want to sit through another war newsreel before the film. Things weren't going so well for the Allies, and Lorraine couldn't stomach more bad news. Maybe knowledge was sometimes a bad thing after all.

"Lorraine, telephone!"

"Coming!"

Mother handed Lorraine the phone, but she shook her head disapprovingly. Lorraine hoped her friend hadn't said something off colored. There was never any telling where Lu was concerned.

"Hello." Lorraine twirled the cord around her fingers.

"Hi, Lorraine."

She nearly dropped the phone when she recognized the voice. "Hi, you! How have you been?"

"Real good," Joel said. "I got news today."

Lorraine looked at her mother's calendar over the stove. Today was Friday, and she hadn't even said a prayer. "Did you already report?"

"I did." Joel couldn't hide the cheeriness in his voice. "And I can't serve."

When Lorraine exhaled, she felt an unexpected and unnerving relief. She knew she would be glad if he stayed, but should she be this glad? Especially considering she had somehow led him on. "That's wonderful news. Was it...that question or...?"

Joel laughed. "No, I told the truth on that one. The medical exam caused the 4F classification. Seems I have a ruptured eardrum."

"Goodness! And you didn't know?"

"Happened when I was younger diving in the lake. Doctor said it would heal. Guess it never did. I'm prone to ear infections, and Clancy complained I kept the radio too loud, but other than that, the ear has never given me any problems."

"All that worry and fuss for nothing. I'm so glad it's over for you. Thank you for calling."

"Thanks for your kindness." Joel's voice was a whisper. "I'm sorry about before. Too much wine mixed with too much emotion never bodes well for me around you."

"Please don't worry about that."

"Nothing like that will happen again."

"Of course not. Really, don't mention it. I'm glad you called so we could sort this out."

"Me too." Joel's voice grew loud and chipper. "So, let's celebrate me being a shirker?"

"You aren't a shirker! They rejected you."

"I doubt anyone else sees it that way, but I'd be lying if I said I wasn't relieved. I picked up supplies to make a celebratory root beer float if you want to join me."

Lorraine nearly said yes but remembered Lu. "I'd like to, Joel, but I've already made plans tonight." She was about to suggest tomorrow, but she had the paper to write. Plus, she didn't want to sound over-eager.

"Oh, okay." She hated the disappointment in his voice. She liked how he sounded earlier, so light and happy, so unlike how he usually sounded. "Another time then?"

"Sure! Just call me."

"Bye Lorraine."

"Joel, wait. Are you all right?"

But he was already gone. She had failed at a fresh start, all thanks to a movie she didn't even want to see. But he would call her again, and they would be friends. Clancy would come home, and then Joel would become her brother. No need to tell Clancy what happened because really nothing had. Almost didn't count.

She ought to find a good girl for Joel. Might be a hard sell at first, but they'd come to see what a catch Joel Fitchett was. Maybe Lydia! She had the biggest heart of anyone Lorraine knew. She trotted back up to her room plotting about how she could introduce them but stopped herself. If Joel and Lydia hit it off, that wouldn't leave any time for Lorraine to spend with him. Better to wait till Clancy came home.

She sank into her desk chair, disappointed in herself. Pages of her essay were strewn in front of her. Pride. That's what she'd identified as her fatal flaw. Yet, given recent events, she wondered how she had gone eighteen years without realizing how completely selfish she really was.

CHAPTER 16

Longview, Texas, 1991

Garrison barely caught himself before tumbling backward over the coffee table. Not like an intruder would put the coffee on or be reading the paper, but he hadn't expected anyone else to be awake this early.

"Didn't mean to scare you."

Garrison moved his hand from his heart. "Geez, Ray, ever heard of a light switch?"

"I can see fine in the dark, but flip it on if you want. Don't want anybody else jumping out of their skin."

"Just surprised me is all." Garrison twisted the cord to the Venetian blinds. Cool light poured into the room, painting ellipses across the lush carpet. "Anything good in the paper today?"

"Is there anything good in here ever?" Ray threw it on the coffee table. "I just like to stay in the know. Plus, reading keeps you sharp. Since you're up, you ready for an omelet?"

Garrison pointed to his swimming trunks. "Need to get a few laps in."

"Work off last night's burgers?" Ray patted his stomach. "Those hit the spot."

"Thanks. Dad taught me a lot about grilling. Some of it stuck."

"Where do your folks live?"

Garrison stared at his sandals. Why had he brought up his dad? He wasn't even sure how to answer. In the ground? In heaven? Somewhere among the cosmos?

"They died. Car accident, last fall." Garrison was so used to saying that phrase, he wondered how he'd ever break the habit when a new fall came. Car accident, two falls back didn't roll off the tongue in the same way.

"Well, hell. I'm sorry. Makes sense now why you are on this quest for a grandfather." Ray patted the seat beside him.

Garrison eyed the pool but sat down anyway. He didn't want to talk about this, didn't want to talk about anything.

"You're a young man," Ray said. "Young enough to make a family. My folks were worthless, and my sister and I never knew any grandparents, no aunts, or uncles. But I had a child of my own, and with Adele, I secured a family for myself. I realized if I treated my girl right, she'd be in my corner the rest of my life. And she has been."

Garrison could have asked how Ray figured Adele was in his corner when she was in the middle of the Pacific, but it wasn't his business.

Ray lit a cigarette. "There's my two cents; take it or leave it."

"I appreciate it," Garrison lied. "I understand I can't put all my hope in Clancy Fitchett. He may be a jackass."

"Hell, that don't matter. He might be Wally Cleaver, but that don't mean he will roll out the red carpet for you. What's his wife gonna make of all this? About this reminder of another woman Clancy shared his bed with?"

"I guess I assumed she was too old to be tortured by the green-eyed monster."

"In my experience, a woman is never too anything to be immune from jealousy. Look, I don't mean to discourage you. But if it's a family you want, no need to search the Continental United States for a stranger. Narrow your gaze; see what's in front of you."

"You mean...?"

"Molly." Ray's voice warmed. "Ever think the universe used the Fitchetts to bring you two together?"

"I think the universe, with its billions of galaxies, has more to worry about."

Ray set his cigarette down and pulled out his handkerchief. His cough sounded even harsher, and this time, Garrison was sure he saw blood. He got a glass of water. He knew Ray hated to be fussed over, but he had to do something.

Ray nodded his thanks and took small drinks until the coughing relented. "Say what you will," he croaked. "But everything happens for a reason."

"Maybe." Garrison looked at the blood-soaked handkerchief. Cancer, car accidents, were there reasons for them too? "Then again, maybe it's all random."

"It appears that way sometimes, but things aren't always what they seem." He pointed outside. "Take the sun. Seems so large to us, but that's only because it's close. It's really just an average sized star. We look at stars ten times the size of the sun and sing *Twinkle Twinkle Little Star*." Ray laughed. "Little. Our limited perspective don't change what is."

"You're right," Garrison said, although he wasn't sure what the size of the sun had anything to do with him and Molly.

"I've always had a fondness for stars," Ray spoke longingly as he gazed through the glass. "Anyway," he looked back at Garrison, "Even if it's not cosmic forces bringing you two together, sparks are flying."

Whenever Garrison heard someone talk about sparks, he thought about white holes. The opposite of black ones, white holes spewed out matter and light. Or that was the theory. Was that what the reaction between he and Molly looked like? Or was this just a nosy grandpa playing matchmaker? Either way, Garrison couldn't stand to sit in this algae-colored room when a crystal pool awaited him. "I better get that swim in."

"Yeah, best to get out there before Lew wakes up and turns it into the Playboy Mansion. But before you go, I didn't have time to ask last night about the trip to Carthage. Find anything interesting?"

"Not really." Garrison didn't see the point in talking to Ray about something he obviously didn't support.

"But did you have fun? With my granddaughter?"

"Yes." Garrison picked up his towel. "We had a lot of fun."

Ray's eyes were half closed, a lidded look of satisfaction. "Well, there you have it then; there you have it."

***

Being in the water always liberated Garrison. He could push back his problems as easily as he pushed back the water. There was no better therapy.

And there was plenty of pushing back to do after that conversation with Ray: his parents' death, the futility of finding Clancy, white holes. And there was Amber. He needed to call her back. He couldn't go an entire summer leaving vague messages on her machine.

The answer came to him as he backstroked across the pool. Lew. He would tell Amber he was staying with Lew. Give Molly's story to her brother and Amber wouldn't know the difference. Garrison felt better already. With his head back in the water, he only faintly heard the hum of the air conditioner and song of the blue jay. During the third lap, an unsettling sensation crept over him. The feeling he was being watched by more than morning birds. He made a few more strokes toward the shallow end and flipped over.

"Don't let me disturb you."

Garrison was relieved to see Molly instead of Ray. While the old man seemed nice enough, Garrison couldn't shake the feeling that something was a little off about him. And he always seemed to be keeping his eye on Garrison.

"Good morning, Hamilton." He squinted. "You're up early."

She held up a Styrofoam cup. "Went for coffee and donuts."

He tipped his head to drain a waterlogged ear. Got any with sprinkles?"

"What other kind are there?"

Garrison pulled himself out of the water. Was it his imagination, or did Molly steal a glance at his chest? Not that there was much to look at, but still. He wished he had brought a shirt out or that he had a better tan. He covered himself with his towel and sat at the patio table, trying not to notice how cute Molly looked in shorts and a tank top.

Garrison reached into the box. "Oh, a chocolate one with sprinkles. Bonus."

"And that's not the best surprise." Molly twisted a strand of hair. She'd worn it down again, and it fell perfectly on her freckled shoulders. Beautiful might not have been the word he'd used to describe Molly when they first met, but he saw now that she *was*—beautiful like a patch of wildflowers is beautiful—no tending nor fancy vase needed—just organic, ungoverned beauty.

"A better surprise than donuts?" He peeked into the box. "Did you get cinnamon rolls too?"

Molly held up a pink Post-It Note. Garrison littered the table with sprinkles as he leaned forward to read. "Who's Laura Hendricks? And why do I need her phone number?"

Molly reclined in her chair. "Nobody. Just the daughter of Katie Mencken. The daughter, Katie currently resides with."

"Wait? What?" His feet were drums against the gritty concrete. "How do you know?"

"Earl got it for me; believe it or not. Seems he's got a little sweetheart there at the home with a connection to Katie. They did a little investigative research of their own, and voila."

"Wow, what are the odds? No way I can repay you for this and chocolate sprinkled donuts."

"Sure you can. It's called a sit-down interview with Joel Fitchett."

"Working on it. This will help. But what else? Want me to buy you this year's Holiday Barbie or something?"

She winked at him, and the patio chair suddenly felt wobbly.

"Great idea. And maybe...." She plucked at her shorts. "Nah forget it."

"No," Garrison shook his finger at her. "That's against the rules of friendship. You can't start a sentence and then say never mind."

"So, you're saying we're friends?"

"Sure we are." Garrison wondered if Molly wanted to be more. If that's why Ray kept bringing it up. Maybe she thought he was flirting right now. Maybe he was.

"Well, I was going to say that I enjoyed watching you swim." Molly's voice was thin. "It looked relaxing. It's probably time I at least tried to be comfortable in water."

"Heck yeah. Come on. No time like the present."

Molly hid behind her hair. "I don't have a swimsuit."

"So, get one, and we'll give it a go this afternoon." Garrison didn't want to give her enough time to change her mind.

Molly bit her lip. "I don't want to swim when Lew's around. He'll give me hell. Plus, I'll be busy showing Pappy's nurse the ropes today."

"How about tonight? After Lew and Ray are asleep?"

"Is that safe?"

"Sure it is. The pool has lights, and I have every safety certification under the sun, or in this case, the moon."

Molly peered over her coffee. "Think there's hope for me?"

"Of course. Believe it or not, teaching people to swim is what I do best. Next to lining up interviews with felons and grilling burgers, that is."

"I'm afraid you may have met your match."

Garrison raised his chin. "You or Joel Fitchett?"

"Both." She grabbed the last sprinkled donut and stood up. "See you tonight."

***

Garrison called Katie from the guest room. Thank goodness for cordless phones. See, privacy hadn't completely gone with the '80s.

His heart drummed against his rib cage with each ring. He expected her daughter, Laura, would answer the phone. But the voice on the other end sounded too brittle to belong to a middle-aged woman.

"May I speak to Katherine?"

"You are." There was a slight annoyance in her tone. Like she had already written him off as a salesman.

Garrison fumbled around his bag looking for a notebook and pen. "Hi, Katherine. My name is Garrison Stark, and I'm calling you about Clancy Fitchett." Her silence was concerning. "Do you remember him?"

"We were acquainted…years ago. Who did you say this was?"

"My name is Garrison, and I think Clancy is my grandfather." Garrison suppressed a laugh. It sounded like a bad opening line from an AA meeting.

"Oh goodness." Katherine's tone was friendlier. "Clancy and I lost touch ages ago."

Garrison's stomach dropped. "When did you last talk to him?"

"A lifetime ago. Umm….Forty-five years, give or take. How did you find me?"

"Long story." Garrison considered thanking her for her time, but something told him to dig deeper. "Forty-five years ago?" Garrison did the math. "So, you two kept in touch into adulthood?"

"Not exactly. I moved to Shreveport, and our families lost touch. But I saw him once after. See, I met my husband, Frank, after the war. He got transferred and asked me to marry him so I could come too." She laughed. "I hardly knew him. This is embarrassing to admit, but a part of me wanted a reason to stay. I was always sweet on Joel, so I looked him up. It was stupid, but I hoped there might be…"

"White holes?"

"Huh?"

"Sparks?"

"Yes, I guess so. But the visit didn't go as planned. Talk about bad timing."

"What do you mean?"

"I visited the boys the day before Joel killed Mr. Fitchett," Katherine said.

Garrison swallowed his gum. "Mind telling me about it?"

"Well, Clancy acted strange. He faked friendly, but his eyes were dull—like the light had been snuffed out. He reeked of whiskey, and the house wasn't fit for rats."

"What about Joel? Did you see him?"

"He came out just before I left. I don't expect he would have had he known I was there. He was out of his ever-loving mind. I wonder now if he was mixed up with drugs or something. Such a shame. They had been such good boys, such good friends." Garrison couldn't be sure, but it sounded like Katherine was crying. "And seeing that cut all fresh on Joel's face again, well it was too much. I left quick as I could."

Static roared over the sound of her voice. He shook the headpiece. Freaking cordless phones. "Did you say the cut was fresh?" Garrison thought about the police report and how the witness described the scar as a cut.

"Suicide attempt. It wasn't the first time—or so I heard."

"He tried to kill himself by cutting his face?"

"I suppose. Looked like he'd taken a blade and traced over the original scar. I didn't dare ask, but it was the talk of the town soon after. Joel lay in bed, hoping he would bleed to death, but Clancy saved him."

"Wow." It was all Garrison could say. He felt a surge of sympathy for the callous man behind bars. Joel was obviously struggling with some dark stuff long before he murdered his father. And he *had* murdered his father. As much as Molly would hate to admit it, the description of a cut no longer eliminated Joel. But something still didn't wash. There were more efficient ways to end a life. Maybe it had been a cry for attention. "Did Clancy mention he and Lorraine were planning on getting married or leaving town?"

"Not that I remember." She yawned. "It was a long time ago. Had I known what was coming, I would have listened more carefully—paid more attention to what was going on underneath all the piles of clothes and dirty dishes. I was too busy thinking about how dumb I was to go there. How I needed to accept the ring from Frank."

Katherine sounded tired. Garrison knew he should call her back another day but couldn't stop himself from pressing further. "The report said you were at the Fitchett's house that night in 1932. Do you remember anything about it?"

Silence again. "A little," she finally answered. "Do you know you're the first person ever to ask me about that night? Guess the police didn't figure I could tell them much. They were probably right."

"I'd still like to hear what you remember."

"Clancy wasn't home at first. I didn't mind. He was always picking on me. And I was glad for the alone time with Joel. But about an hour later, his father charged in demanding that Joel find Clancy. I wanted to go too, but I didn't dare ask Mr. Fitchett. I was scared to death of that man. He was cruel to those boys."

"Abusive?"

"There wasn't much talk about abusive parents in those days, but looking back, yes, I'd call it child abuse. He was too hard on them in every way."

"Do you think Mr. Fitchett had anything to do with what happened?"

"No way he could have. He was there the whole night. Well, until he and my dad left looking for the boys. And I remember how upset he was at the hospital—hysterical almost. Had Clancy by the shoulders like he could shake the truth out of him."

Garrison paced across the room. "What about Clancy? What part do you think he played?"

"None!" she practically shouted. "He was a pest, but he wouldn't have done anything so terrible. Not to Joel."

"Any thoughts on why Joel killed Tom?"

"Besides the fact that Mr. Fitchett was a monster? No. As I said, Joel wasn't right that day I saw him. Who knows what was going on in his head? But it's still hard to accept. Joel was a gentle soul. My dad swore he was innocent. Had this conspiracy theory but not much to prove it."

"What was his theory?"

"We had another house in Shreveport. Dad rented it out to a man. I don't know his real name, but everyone called him Crawl. Strange name for a strange guy. Mom wanted him evicted, but there was a war on, and renters who paid were scarce. Crawl didn't pay one month, and Dad found the house abandoned. Not unexpected for Crawl's type, I suppose, but when you consider it was two days after Mr. Fitchett was killed, it made Dad wonder."

"Did he tell the police?"

"Yes, but the officer said they were about to arrest Crawl for selling drugs. Figured he must have found out and left. Makes sense to me."

It did to Garrison too, but something nagged at him. Hadn't Earl said Clancy was hanging around a Louisiana boy that caused trouble? "Was Clancy friends with this Crawl guy?"

"I don't believe Crawl had any friends, just messed up folks wanting a fix. But after seeing Clancy and Joel that day, nothing would surprise me."

It was unlikely, but Garrison couldn't help but wonder if he'd stumbled into something. "Do you have any of your dad's records that would have Crawl's real name?"

"No dear, I'm sorry. I'm sure our lawyer did, but he died years ago." She yawned again. "I'm afraid it's time for my pills and nap. Sorry I'm not more help."

"You were very helpful. Thanks for your time, Katie."

"Katie." She giggled. "Nobody has called me that in years."

"Sorry, Katherine."

"No, I like it. I like feeling young again. Enjoy it while you can. The fire of youth may feel unquenchable, but it's not. It will burn out on you when you least expect it."

"Oh, I don't know. You seem to have some sparks left."

"A few embers, maybe." He heard a smile in her voice. "Thanks, Garrison, and good luck."

Chapter 17

Longview, Texas, 1945

February 20, 1945

Sweet Lorraine,

In two days, it will be three years. Three years a Marine. It's a title I'm proud of but not as proud as soon having the title of husband. I can't wait to marry and start a family, even if you don't approve of my name choice for a daughter. Brett is a fine name! If you had read The Sun Also Rises without your Hemingway bias, you'd find Lady Brett Ashley a fascinating character with admirable strength. Still, I'd be beside myself if you wanted to name a daughter after Fitzgerald's vapid Daisy Buchanan, so I'll concede.

How do you feel about the name Rosalind? I've never read much Shakespeare, but publishers have sent us pocket editions of their books to keep us company here. Having read all that interested me, I tried those that didn't, and have found a new kinship with Shakespeare. I just finished As You Like it, and I really admire Rosalind's spark. What say you?

What is life like for me, you ask? I'll admit I've tried to keep that a secret. I prefer discussing happier things, but I will answer a few of your questions now. Yes, there are plenty of rations. They taste like cat food, but we eat them. No, the fighting is far from constant. I spend as much time battling humidity, insects, and drenching rains as I do the enemy. But I am safe, kept alive by God and my desire to make it home to you. And that is all that matters.

On this anniversary of my service, I try to remember what kind of man I was when I began. The words cocky and ignorant come to mind. I assumed training made me an expert killer. I wasn't then but am now. Not that it's anything to brag about. The blood on my hands will never wash off. It is enemy blood, blood necessary to shed, but I have to live with the stained hands nonetheless.

How are you, Lorraine? Tell me about your studies and one more time the plans for our wedding.

Forever Yours Darling,

Clancy

To read the letter now always upset Lorraine, yet she couldn't make herself stop. She counted the months on her fingers. Six. Six months of silence.

Missing in action. That's what the telegram sent to Mr. Fitchett said. Lost like the pearl earring Lorraine had searched her jewelry box a hundred times over for. But Clancy was not a trinket that might fall behind a dresser. How could the Marines lose a person? Still, a temporary loss was better than a permanent one. Missing was better than dead.

Lorraine stacked the letter on top of the others in her desk drawer. Had Clancy even received her reply? Did he know she adored the name Rosalind and had finally settled on wedding colors? Maybe she'd call Clancy's dad again today. Poor old dear. He was probably as lonely as she was. She should bring him a nice home-cooked dinner. And Joel too.

Joel. Lorraine didn't like thinking about him any more than she liked reading Clancy's letter. But she had no self-control when it came to either. Why had he never called back to make plans to celebrate the 4F stamp on his file? How had three years gone by so quickly?

She'd seen him around once or twice, but he was always in a hurry to get away. But they couldn't keep this up forever, not when they would be family.

When the phone downstairs rang, she wondered if it might be him, but it was only Sally. It hadn't been Joel in three years, why should it be now?

"You're coming out with us!" The smack of Sally's gum was amplified on the phone. "We miss you!"

Not this again. Lorraine should have faked a headache and gone to bed already. "I'll see you girls next week when classes start again."

"Ugh, don't even talk about school. I only enrolled to catch a beau, but with the war on, it might as well be an all-girls school."

Lorraine massaged her temples. "Really Sally? Boys? You realize there's never been another time in history where women have as many opportunities as we do?"

"Easy for you to say. You're engaged." Sally said engaged like it was a dirty word. "We don't want to see you at school; we want to see you having fun again."

Fun, like that was possible anymore. All Lorraine wanted to do tonight was write. After two years of struggle, the pent-up words were unstoppable now. But Sally and Lu had been calling for three weeks. They were taking shifts and would not give up. "If I go tonight, do you promise to give me some space?"

"Sure thing!"

Lorraine didn't believe her, but it would make her parents happy to see her going out again.

"Get yourself dolled up, and we'll be there in half an hour."

"No don't do that. I'll just meet you wherever."

"No way! You're not going to stay an hour then run right back home."

Lorraine slumped against the wall. "Am I that predictable?"

"See you at seven, doll."

***

Joel didn't like loud noises, flashing lights, or crowds. But when a Ferris wheel and cotton candy were thrown in, chaos became tolerable.

Fairs were scarce since the war started, but they had once been a family tradition for the Fitchetts. Joel was only four when he first walked through this grassy field, but the sensory overload he'd experienced that night was a memory as vivid as any. "Those are rides!" Mama said. "And there is ice cream!" Rides meant nothing to Joel, but he understood ice cream and would have been satisfied with his vanilla cone and nothing more. But Daddy took him to the carousel and steam train before circling back for a second ice cream cone, washed down by a glass of lemonade so big Joel's hands didn't even fit around it. He had never loved his father more. Daddy took them back every year and never seemed as happy or as generous as he did at the fair. Joel and Clancy took advantage of the permission to ride, eat, and play whatever they wanted. But the clock always struck midnight. The benevolent stranger turned back into to their father, griping about wasted money and cavities.

Joel realized it wouldn't feel the same tonight. But even one good memory (and one candied apple) would be worth the drive and thirty-five cent admission price.

The first face he recognized produced no such memory. He ducked his head and turned, but somehow, he still ran smack into Crawl.

"Hey, what's the hurry?" Crawl grabbed Joel's wrist, depositing a sticky residue. "Sorry about that." Crawl wiped his hand across his pants then licked it. "Damn Cotton candy."

The saliva turned the film on Crawl's hand red. It reminded Joel of blood, and he shivered despite the summer heat.

"Look here, Joel. I'm sure we are both remembering last time we were together, but let's not dwell on the past." Crawl put his hand to his heart. "No hard feelings here."

"Here either." Joel shoved his hands into his pockets, absently jingling some change.

"Let me prove it to you." Crawl motioned two women forward. "Donna, Peggy, this is Joel, Clancy's brother."

The brunette looked him up and down. "I see the resemblance now that you mention it."

"Donna and Clancy were *friendly,* if you catch my drift." Crawl winked.

Donna tugged at her too-tight skirt. Were these women prostitutes? They looked like it—or at least how Joel imagined prostitutes would look. Why would Clancy be with a girl like this? Worse, had he cheated on Lorraine with her? Surely this is not what Crawl meant by "making it up" to Joel.

"There's really no need."

"I insist." Crawl pushed Donna forward. Had Joel not put his hands out, she would have landed in the dirt.

"Are you all right?" Joel helped her stand on her own.

"She's fine." Crawl grabbed the other girl's hand. "Just clumsy. Donna, pull yourself together. I need you to perform a personal favor to show my friend that all is good between us."

A personal favor? If Crawl thought Joel was anything like Clancy, he was wrong. Joel leaned back. "I'm seeing someone, so I don't want to..."

Crawl held up both hands. "Wait a minute here, what are you suggesting?"

Joel's face, neck, and ears felt impossibly hot. "I thought you meant..." He couldn't bring himself to say it.

Crawl's entire body convulsed as he laughed. He rested his hands on his knees until he composed himself. "Who do you take me for? I was going to send Donna to get you lemonade."

The girls giggled. Joel wished he never would have come here tonight—wished he was home listening to his favorite radio drama, *The Shadow*. Or at the very least, he wished he had the same power The Shadow possessed—the power to cloud everyone's minds, so they couldn't see him.

Donna pushed her hand in the pocket of Crawl's Levi's, but he slapped it away. "I said get us a drink."

"I'm really not thirsty," Joel said.

"Then go get me one." Crawl released Peggy's hand. "Both of you." He put his arm around Joel. He smelt of stale beer and aftershave. "Let's walk."

Joel's stomach churned like he'd just been on the Loop O Plane, but it's not like he could take off running.

"I'm glad I saw you here." Crawl spoke over squealing breaks and clanking ride chains. "I haven't gotten a letter from your brother for a while and was..." Crawl tapped his chin. "Worried."

"Clancy writes you?" Joel asked.

"Every month usually." Crawl had to raise his voice even louder as they passed The Fun Slide. "Why? Doesn't he you?"

Joel's collar chafed his neck. He pulled the fabric away from his skin. "He writes," Joel said, even though he could count on one hand the number of letters he'd received in three years. "But he's been missing since March."

"Crawl!" A uniformed police officer slapped Crawl's back. If there was any justice in the world, he would have slapped cuffs on him instead. "Thought you were going to take me fishing, you old dog."

Joel took advantage of the distraction. "I'll let you know if I hear from him," he said, already heading towards the exit.

He was nearly to the gate when he spotted her. Somehow, in the blur of color and lights, she came into perfect focus. He couldn't leave without at least saying hello. "Lorraine!" he called. "Lori!" he said louder, forgetting all about Crawl.

Maybe it was wishful thinking, but she seemed to brighten when she recognized him. Excusing herself from a group of girls, she jogged toward him. "Hi, you!" She gave him a quick side hug. "It's been what? A hundred years?"

"Something like that, yeah." She looked different. Her hair was shorter, and Joel had never seen her in jeans. She was prettier now—or he'd just forgotten how pretty she always was.

"Well..." She put her hands on her hips. "Catch me up."

Joel kicked gravel. "Not much to tell, just working."

"Working's good. Glad the gas and tire rations haven't hurt the business too much. Are you still doing Clancy's job too?"

"No, Mr. Rogers hired someone else last year. Just until he comes back," Joel said confidently.

Lorraine wrapped a few of her curls around her finger. "Ah, so you're kept locked up in the garage again."

"Just like Quasimodo."

She grinned. "Stop it."

Joel looked to the group of girls, now staring at him. "Enjoying the fair?"

"Not as much as I used to. I see the parachute drop and bomber ride, and it feels a little too real now."

Joel wiped his sweaty hands down the side of his pants. "I understand that. And it seems most of these rides are meant for two."

The silence made him wonder if he'd said too much. Did she assume he was asking her to ride with him? He crossed then uncrossed his arms, put his hands in his pocket, and then took them out. He had no idea what to do with his body and even less idea what to do to carry on the conversation, so he stood mute, listening to the balls rolling up and thudding down the game shoot behind him.

"Lori! Come on!" a grating voice finally yelled.

"Well, it was great seeing you, Joel." She put her hand on his shoulder. The lingering touch made every nerve-ending stir. He had to stop this, had to get over her. "Keep in touch, will you?"

"I'll try," Joel said. "But fair warning, I'm terrible at friendship."

"I haven't been so great at it myself lately. But promise you'll call if you hear anything about Clancy. Good or bad."

"Okay." Joel pressed his lips tight. Of course Lorraine only wanted to hear from him if it involved Clancy.

"Lori! Come on!" A short redhead took a few steps from the crowd and motioned to Lorraine.

"Guess I better get a wiggle on." She jogged backward. "Goodbye, you!"

Joel held up his hand. "Bye, Lorraine."

She strutted back to her friends, back to the faces she belonged with. They were giggling. Probably wondering why their Lori was spending time with a toad like him. Joel looked at the caramel apple line. It was short, but maybe he should just get out of here before he ran into Crawl, or worse, Lorraine again. He needed to be home. Home where no one could see him. Home where no one could hurt him.

***

"Well, isn't this swell? Sally kicked the tire. "Flat as..."

"Your chest?" Lu crouched to fluff her hair in the side view mirror.

Sally adjusted the padding in her bra. "Not funny."

"Oh, relax. You've got a spare tire, don't you?"

"Yeah but who's going to change it? Any of you knuckleheads know how?"

"Let's go back in," Lu suggested. "We just passed Mark Steven's car. He's in there somewhere."

"Gross." Lorraine faked a shiver. "Mark Stevens is a complete meathead."

"Maybe so, but he's a cute meathead and one of the few fellas under fifty around to show us a good time," Lu said.

That wasn't true. Lorraine knew there were better men around than Mark Stevens. She bent down to exam the tire. She thought of Joel, but asking him for a favor didn't seem right. The tire didn't look like an easy fix, but she could figure it out.

"Oh, come on, Lori, don't futz around with it. You'll get dirty, and you are not getting out of going with us for drinks." Sally opened the car door. "Sit and relax, will ya?"

"I'll just walk down the road to the payphone to call my brother," Maggie offered.

"In those shoes?"

"If I can jitterbug for three hours in these shoes, I can make it a few miles down the road."

Lorraine couldn't listen anymore. "Joel can fix it." Humbling herself before Joel had to be better than getting eaten alive by mosquitoes. Better than listening to Sally and Mags bicker while Lu reapplied her lipstick for the hundredth time.

"Great idea!" Sally slapped the hood of her car. "If he saves the night, I'll buy him a drink."

"Oh, Joel won't come with us to the bar," Lorraine said.

"Well, at least invite him. For saving our butts."

"Hey, isn't that him there?" Lu pointed across the giant parking lot. "Joe!" she called. "Help us, Joe!"

"It's Joel." Lorraine shut the car door with more force than was necessary.

"He knew who I meant; look, he's coming over."

"Wow, he looks so much like his brother." Sally raised her eyebrows. "Creepy."

Lorraine had never seen a strong resemblance. Maybe because she had spent hours memorizing Clancy's face. And though she'd only looked into Joel's eyes a few times, she'd recognize them in a lineup. They were so different from Clancy's eyes, so different from anyone's. Glittering blue fringed with eyelashes long enough to make any girl jealous. She shook her head. *Stop thinking about his eyes!*

"Everything okay?" Joel looked straight at Lorraine. Through her almost.

"Flat tire. Can you help?"

"Sure, I can. Got a lug wrench?"

"It's not my car." Lorraine looked at Sally.

Sally shrugged. "A lug what?"

Joel smiled. He had such a good smile, even if it was out of practice. "I'll get my tools."

"I'll help," Lorraine said, happy for another chance to talk to him. She should have offered to ride with him earlier. She'd been such a creep, and now he was saving the day. "Why are you leaving so soon?" she asked.

"Not much to do."

Lorraine swatted away a buzzing fly. "We should have ridden something together. I was dying to try the roller coaster, but the girls were big chickens about it."

Joel stopped digging around in his truck. "I would have liked that."

The fly was gone, but Lorraine's ears were still ringing. Her feet were sore, and sweat made her shirt cling to her back. But still, she couldn't let Joel fix Sally's tire and go back to his empty house. "Let's do it then; we can go back in."

"What about the tire?"

"After the tire. I don't want drinks with the girls. I'd have more fun with you. We need a proper catch-up. None of this 'hi, goodbye' stuff we've settled for."

"Will your friends be mad?"

"They won't mind. They'll make you swear not to take me home until I've had fun, but they'll hand me over."

Joel climbed out of the truck. "Okay. But I don't break promises. So that means I won't take you home until I'm convinced you've had actual fun. Sure you can manage that?"

Lorraine felt her body relax as the awkwardness evaporated between them. "Shouldn't be a problem," she said. "Not with you."

***

Lorraine had been right. Her friends released her to Joel with strict instructions to keep her out till at least eleven. Joel wished he understood Lorraine's motivations. Did she want to spend time with him or was he just a free ticket away from her friends? Either way, she seemed to be enjoying herself.

"Let's do the Ferris wheel again." Lorraine clapped her hands together. Joel would have preferred a third go on the roller coaster, himself. He liked the way she held on to him during those sharp curves, but the Ferris wheel offered a beautiful view of the full moon.

"Want to get your cotton candy first? Stand's right over there." Joel pointed it out.

"That's for the ride home. I don't want sticky hands for the rest of the night."

"Not much left of the night. The crowd is thinning, and it looks like a storm's coming. The place will shut down soon."

"Then we better hurry."

"You sure you want to be in a metal wheel in a stormy sky?"

She helped herself to the last of his lemonade. "Live a little, Joel."

"I'd like to live a lot." Joel looked at the sky. "That's why I suggest avoiding this particular ride right now."

"Oh, come on! Just once more! Then we'll get my cotton candy and go home. I swear."

"I'm not in any hurry to leave," Joel said. "I enjoy spending time with you." He brought the lipstick stained straw to his mouth. There was nothing left except melted ice, but the temptation for his lips to touch the spot Lorraine's had was irresistible.

Lorraine's shoulders sagged as she stared at something beyond Joel. "You're right. Let's go. We shouldn't be here, spending money, eating sugar, and laughing when Clancy is God knows where going through God knows what."

Joel looked around. A soldier in army green stood in the cotton candy line with a bright-eyed girl on his arm.

"I wonder if he's on leave or if he's hurt?" Lorraine stared without blinking; her voice wistful. "Either way, I envy that girl all the way down to my toes."

Joel tossed his cup in the trash. "Do you really think Clancy would object to you smiling? No matter what he's going through? He'll be home soon. War is over in Europe. Can't be much longer in the Pacific."

"I hope you're right." Lorraine pulled her eyes away from the couple, like she was waking from a trance. "Sorry, I'm spoiling our time. Come on, let's get in line."

The line for the Wonder Wheel was so short they got up right away. It only circled once before stopping at the peak. "Best seat in the house." Lorraine's eyes gleamed.

Below them, a too tired toddler cried as her balloon drifted away, shiny horses moved hypnotically on the carousel, and game vendors called out to guests. Joel pointed to one. "Did you visit that guy? If he guesses your weight wrong, you get a prize"

"No way am I stepping on the scale after all that fair food."

Joel smiled. She looked fine from where he was sitting—which happened to still be at the wheel's peak. Maybe it was too many rides or too many sugar-dusted donuts, but he suddenly felt nauseous. He tilted his head to focus on the single, steady silver light instead of all the flashing, brightly colored ones.

"Thinking of your mom?" Lorraine asked.

"Huh?"

"Oh, I just remember Clancy saying she was interested in the stars."

"She was." Joel closed his eyes to stop the spinning. "But I wasn't thinking about her. Just about keeping that last caramel apple down."

Lorraine laughed. "You should have said something. Want me to yell at the carny? He may have fallen asleep."

"I'll be all right." He gripped the paint chipped safety bar. "Plenty of fresh air."

"Indeed." She rested her hand on his knee. Joel forgot his stomach. "And if not, don't worry. I threw up in front of you once. Fair is fair." She leaned her head back on the seat. "So was your mom into astrology?"

"No, not Mama. She said seeing the stars made her feel close to God."

"That's beautiful."

"A beautiful thought anyway."

"You don't believe it?"

Joel shrugged. "I'm not sure what I believe anymore. It would be nice if a caring God was looking out for us. Just hasn't been my experience."

"Maybe you aren't looking hard enough."

Joel looked at her hand still resting on his knee. "Maybe not."

Her hand remained even as they made their descent back to earth. Joel stared at the operator and tried to relay a telepathic message. *One more time around, please, bud?* Maybe he read Joel's mind or his pleading expression. Or maybe he just wanted to finish his cigarette, but the ride didn't stop, and Lorraine's hand did not move.

"Shooting star!" She bumped against his shoulder. "Did you see it?"

Joel shook his head. "Looked down too soon."

"Exactly." Lorraine's smile was slight and closed-lip. "Maybe you always look down too soon to see the miracle." It sounded like something Mama would say. She would have loved Lorraine. "So, my friends insisted you join us for dinner next Friday. As a thank you for the tire."

Joel shook his head. "That wasn't a big deal."

"Sure it was. You'll come, right?"

"I don't know, Lorraine. I don't want them to laugh."

She moved her hand away and then her entire body. It was not even an inch, but Joel felt it. "My friends aren't like that."

"They were sure giggling tonight."

"They weren't laughing at you." Lorraine's voice was like a foghorn. "I'll admit the girls can be frivolous and boy-crazy, but they are good girls, all of them. I wouldn't be friends with them otherwise." Joel wanted to believe her, but it's not like she would admit if he was right. "We should go home." Lorraine scooted another half inch. "It's late."

Joel pressed a fist against his mouth and puffed out his cheeks. He had offended her. One simple statement and she'd transformed completely. He should be used to it by now. Lorraine Applewhite never held a mood for long.

"Let us down, will you?" Joel called. He needed to be back on solid ground, out of the clouds, out of the fantasy of his own making.

***

The night should not be ending like this. With Lorraine huddled against the truck's door. They should be laughing and leaving cotton candy's sticky remnants on everything they touched. Why did Joel say what he did when things were going so well? When she was having fun, real fun, for the first time in forever?

"Look, I said I was sorry, and I am. It was dumb, but why let it ruin the whole evening?"

She turned towards him. "You know, it's bad enough you think I'd be friends with people who would laugh at you. What's worse is you think I'd stand there and allow it. Or did you assume I was joining in?" Joel's silence sped her pulse. "Did you?" she yelled.

Joel's veins strained against his skin. "Yeah, maybe I did! And if you were in my shoes, you'd be just as suspicious of others' laughter."

Lorraine froze. She'd never heard Joel yell. "People laugh at you? Adults?"

"Fun for all ages." Joel's voice was as flat as the road he kept his eyes glued to.

"How cruel."

"I'm sorry I mistook you for one of them, it's just..." He slammed his hands against the steering wheel. "When I got hurt, everyone was sympathetic at first, but that turned quick. So not only did Clancy and I have the horrific memory to deal with, but we also had to develop thick skin. Luckily, Daddy had already helped a lot in that arena."

"Clancy too? He was teased? For your scar?"

"Everyone assumed he did it. That was the talk for awhile."

"Well, that's ridiculous. Clancy would never." She gazed at Joel, searching him for any sign she was wrong. She knew Clancy would never hurt him on purpose, but it could have been an accident. Joel's face gave nothing away.

"We both escaped after that. Clancy into his books, me deeper in myself. Built up walls and assumed everyone who wanted in wanted to hurt me. Never grown out of it." Joel slid down in his seat.

"I'm sorry for all you've gone through. Sorry for how horrible people can be. And I'm honored you felt safe to share your feelings with me, but you can't shut everyone out. Can't assume the worst of everybody."

"I know."

"Joel, what happened that day?" She knew the question was a flipped penny. Heads, Joel would keep telling her things he had told no one. Tails, he'd switch his temper back on. But she couldn't help herself; she'd wanted to know since she met him.

Joel jerked his head in her direction. "What did Clancy tell you?"

"Nothing."

He looked back at the road. "Good, let's leave it at that."

Tails it was then. Given how the night had gone, she decided not to press anymore. "Well then, since you admit it's time to let people in, let's give it a go. Friday night, six sharp at the Shake Shop."

"I don't know."

Lorraine felt bold. "I do. You're going. If you don't enjoy yourself, I won't ask you to come again."

"Fine," Joel whispered.

Lorraine cranked the window the rest of the way down and closed her eyes. After a night of so much motion, with so many ups and downs, it was nice to take things slow and steady.

CHAPTER 18

Longview, Texas, 1991

Garrison dipped his feet into the pool. The water was only beginning to cool from a day spent under the merciless Texas sun. He wasn't sure if he'd ever get used to this muggy heat. The wind rustled the blooming rose bushes, carrying their scent to the pool where it mingled with the stronger stench of chlorine.

It was 9:30, and he still hadn't talked to Molly alone. Between showing the nurse around and swimsuit shopping, he'd barely seen her. Then Ray stayed up an hour later than usual. Thankfully, Lew was spending the night at his girlfriend's, or this might have turned into a midnight swim.

Molly didn't leave him waiting long. She wore a cover- up, but thanks to the sheer material, Garrison saw the swimsuit underneath. It was a modest, black one-piece but hugged her in all the right places. Garrison turned away as she shed the cover-up. It was ridiculous how uncomfortable he felt. He was supposed to be a professional.

"You ready?"

Molly's whole body shook. "I'm not sure about this."

"It's okay. Just come sit; put your feet in."

"You aren't going to pull me in or anything?"

"No tricks. If this is as far as we get tonight, so be it."

She didn't look confident but lowered her feet into the water.

"Not so awful, right?"

Molly gripped the edge of the pool.

"Is this where the accident happened?" Garrison asked.

"Yeah, summer we moved here. I was playing outside, and then I was waking up in a hospital."

"So, you jumped in?"

"They thought so. Mom found me face down. But I had never learned to swim and was always a cautious kid, so it was surprising. Dad insisted on running tests, and turns out, a heart murmur caused me to faint at the worst possible time in the worst possible place."

"A heart murmur?" Garrison gripped the edge too. "Did it go away?"

"Nope, still there." Molly swirled the water with her foot. "I know you're thinking I should be scared of my heart and not the water."

"I wouldn't blame you if you were scared of both."

"I'm not dying or anything. I take medication, get a yearly checkup, try not to over exert myself. Not a big deal."

A dark figure brushed across the water then disappeared. "What kind of bird was that?" Garrison asked.

"The bat kind."

"A bat?" Garrison searched the skies. "Are those um...common here?"

"Don't tell me you're scared of bats?"

"Not scared really."

Molly elbowed his side. "Come on, I told you mine."

"Okay, a little scared. When I was ten, we vacationed in New Mexico. Went to Carlsbad Caverns and watched the evening exodus of the bats. Thousands of them, chattering, ready to prey. I cried, cowered behind Dad, and have tried to avoid them ever since. The whole scene was pretty disturbing."

"I see." Molly bit down on a smile.

"I know what you're thinking. Close encounter with bats, dead parents, but no, I'm not Batman."

Molly's laugh caused her to relax her grip on the pool's edge. Not wanting to do too much too soon, Garrison filled her in on his conversation with Katie.

"This Crawl lead sounds promising," Molly said when he finished. "Did you take good notes?"

Garrison pointed to his head. "It's all up here."

"Oh Geez, Garrison. I'll get my notebook."

He put his hand across her lap. "Nope. Let's move this conversation to the steps."

Molly surprised Garrison by following him to the lowest step. She sat but popped right back up, holding her neck like the water was a switchblade. "I don't like the water close to my face."

Garrison scooted up another step. "Try here."

The water hit Molly right above her chest. She still didn't seem comfortable. He was going to suggest moving up one more but stopped himself. Given the thoughts bouncing around his head, it was probably best Molly kept her chest below the water.

"This is better, thanks." Molly cautiously patted the water. "So, who do we find first? Crawl or Roxanne?"

"Roxanne will be easier, but maybe Joel knows Crawl's real name, and if he's the same Louisiana boy Earl described."

"Why don't you visit Joel, and I'll focus on Roxanne."

It made sense, but Garrison didn't want to split up. "I hoped we'd both go to Woodville. I realize you aren't on the list to visit Joel, but I can drop you off at the mall or something."

Molly flinched. "Mall? Do I seem like a girl who wants to spend the day at the mall?"

"Library then? Hastings? Courthouse?"

"I think it makes more sense for us to go different directions this weekend. Then we can compare notes."

They stayed on the steps awhile, but Molly eventually let Garrison lead her around the shallow end. The slide was their cue to turn around before the pool sloped. She released his hand the third time around. A great step for a student, but a blow to someone who enjoyed the physical contact with her.

"You're doing great. Let's try one more thing before we call it a night."

Molly stopped walking. "I'm not ready to go under."

"How about floating?"

"Same thing."

"No, it's not." Garrison demonstrated. "Everyone can float. Just takes a little practice and a lot of relaxing."

"Relaxing won't happen if my head is in the water."

Garrison stood up. "I'll hold you."

"Yeah, I get how that works. Kinda like when Pappy promised he'd hold on to my bicycle. He let go and I crashed into a rose bush."

"Same thing happened to me, but fortunately no rose bush was involved. I won't do that. No letting go unless you give me the okay."

"All right." Molly shook out her arms. "What do I need to do?"

"Turn around," Garrison put his hands under her. "Put your head back and arms out."

Molly tried, but when the water met the back of her head, she jerked up.

"It's okay. I've got you," Garrison reassured. He helped her lay back again, but this time, she rested her head on his shoulder. "Just look up," he instructed. "Watch for bats."

Molly's body was tense. It took five minutes of pulling her around the pool to convince her to open her eyes. When she did, she relaxed. "No bats, but the stars are beautiful tonight."

Garrison glanced at the sky. The stars were always beautiful to him. "Did you know when you look at the stars you are looking back in time?"

"Because they are millions of years old?"

"Because they are so far away, it takes their light a long time to reach us. Even the light from the closest star takes over four years to get here. So, when we look at it, we are seeing how it looked four years ago, not necessarily how it looks tonight. Others, you are seeing how they looked hundreds, even thousands of years ago."

"Wow. Who knew seeing into the past was so easy?"

"If only we could look back on Joel and Clancy's lives with such ease."

"What about the moon?" Molly asked. "Are we seeing a past version of it too?"

"No, it's pretty much live, a second or so delay. The beauty of the moon is witnessing the phases."

"Crescent tonight," Molly said.

"Waning Crescent."

"Same difference."

"Not exactly, but I promise not to bore you with the details if you let me move your head onto the water. I'll still hold on, but your ears will be under. Good news is, it won't cover your face, and you won't hear me babble anymore."

Molly swallowed. "Okay." Garrison lowered her head and moved his hands to her lower back to help her feel secure. She tensed only slightly when the water cocooned her ears.

The moonlight highlighted Molly's high cheekbones as Garrison tilted her chin slightly. He couldn't remember ever wanting to kiss someone as badly as he wanted to kiss Molly right now.

He closed his eyes, tried to picture Amber, but only saw Molly. How had he mistaken her eyes for light blue all this time when they were gray? Not a dull gray but almost silver in the way they held and reflected light. Maybe if he took his hands off of her, something would give. "Want to try it on your own? Just for five seconds?" Garrison tried to sound professional but was sure his cracking voice gave him away.

Molly kept her eyes set on his. "Okay."

"Stay calm," he said for himself as much as for her. He lowered his hands first, and then moved them away. She continued to float even as he stepped back. "You're doing it."

"Has it been five seconds yet?"

Garrison reached under her to help lift her. He kept his hand on the small of her back too long. When he removed it, he made no other move to distance himself.

His fingers ached to touch her again. He tried to hold eye contact but was suddenly drawn to her lips. He swallowed. "Great job, Molly."

She fidgeted with her swimsuit strap. "Thanks, you're a great teacher." A slow smile built. "Actually, you're pretty great in general."

If there was ever a perfect time to kiss Molly, it was now, right now. Right here in this warm water, underneath a crescent moon and time-traveling stars. He wanted the kiss, but did he want all that came after? All the hard decisions and conversations? He didn't, but his body leaned in anyway. It was as if the two created a magnetic field from which there was no escaping. It drew Molly in closer too. Garrison's fingers weaved into her wet, tangled hair. He pulled her in so close that the features of her face were no longer distinguishable. He only saw light. Light like a white hole. But before his lips met hers, Molly's body tensed. Something was wrong. He had misunderstood. "What is it?"

"Lightning." She pointed up. "Close."

Garrison turned just as thunder growled a warning. "Come on." He took her hand. "Let's get out." He wrapped a towel around Molly's shivering body. "Go inside. I'll get the pool covered."

Leaves swirled around Garrison as he fought the pool cover. He had never been one to search for signs, but what would someone like Ray say about this one? A near kiss foiled by near electrocution. That couldn't be a good omen for a relationship, but then again, he could just as easily blame the lightning on the sparks flying between them. And there *were* sparks. Ray had been right about that. But Garrison wasn't this guy. The one who cheated. As much as he wanted to finish what he started, he couldn't. He needed to shoot straight.

He found Molly on the couch in the same tank top she'd worn this morning and a pair of ripped jeans. Garrison forgot the words he wanted to say, and the only sound was the dripping of his wet swimsuit.

"Thanks." Molly folded her legs beside her. "For doing that, out there. I mean, the cover."

"No problem."

"Want a cup of coffee?"

"Nah, it's late."

"Something else then? I actually bought some Tang today. Saw a can when I bought the swimsuit and couldn't resist." She picked up the remote. "We can make popcorn and see what crap comes on this late. Or even make a Blockbuster run."

"I'm tired." Garrison heard the coldness in his voice. Why was he doing this? Why couldn't he tell her the truth instead of acting like he didn't care?

"Oh, okay." Molly's voice dropped. "If you still want company to go visit Joel, I'll tag along."

"Nah, you were right. We should split up, cover more ground."

"I see." Molly's jaw stiffened. "Thanks for the lessons. What do I owe you?"

"Nothing." Garrison jammed his hands into the pockets of his suit. "Of course, nothing."

"No, I'd like to know what you charge." She reached for her purse. "I don't want it to seem like I'm taking advantage of you."

As much as he hated the shift in Molly's attitude, at least he knew he'd gotten his message across. "I'm staying here for free, so I come out ahead."

Molly clutched the remote. "Right, well about that. The Super 8 down the street is running a special if you stay an entire week. You're welcome here, naturally, but I thought you might be more comfortable elsewhere." Molly's eyes had turned to stone. It was like the two of them were in a contest to see who could be the biggest jerk. He had won, obviously, but Molly was definitely competition.

"Okay. I'll check in there when I get back from Woodville. Goodnight."

Garrison went back to his room and picked up the cordless phone off the bed. Hopefully, it had enough juice for a call to Amber. He dialed collect. No way was he talking to his girlfriend on Molly's dime after what happened. Actually, it was what *hadn't* happened that seemed to be the bigger problem.

"Garrison!" Amber sounded like she'd been running.

"Hey, Amber. Sorry I haven't called."

"I've been trying to reach you. Calling every hotel listed."

Garrison hadn't expected Amber to go that far to find him. "I'm sorry. Let me explain."

"Garrison, please." Her voice didn't sound like it belonged to her. "Listen!"

"Okay." Garrison plopped back on a pillow and braced himself for the yelling or crying to come. Judging by her tone, his money was on yelling.

"Something happened."

Garrison sat back up. "Are you all right?"

"I'm fine. Oh, Garrison, I hate to tell you this on the phone when you are so far away."

"Just say it, Amber. Whatever it is. I'll be okay."

When he heard her sniffling, he was sure she was breaking up with him. She had probably cheated on him. Why didn't that thought bother him more? The phone beeped. "Amber, what is it? The phone's dying."

Static infiltrated the line so loud that he pulled the phone away from his ear. When he put it back, he heard two unfamiliar voices. "Amber, are you there? We're picking up someone else's conversation. Let me call back."

"I'm so sorry, Garrison." Her voice was loud and clear now.

"Sorry for what? I couldn't hear you."

"Grandma Dolly. She passed away last night."

The phone sounded a final time and died. Garrison tried to turn it back on, but it made a long series of beeps and switched back off. He slammed it against the wall.

Garrison tumbled out of the room. "Where's another phone?"

Molly craned her neck down the hallway and stared like he'd gone crazy. "There's one in here."

Garrison collided with the coffee table but didn't feel the pain. He picked the phone off its cradle and tried to steady his hands enough to dial.

"What's going on, Garrison?" Molly asked.

He didn't bother with collect this time; he just dialed. His fingers stopped moving when it was time to press the last two numbers. Was it 56 or 65? How often had he called Amber only to forget her number at a time like this? He tried 56 and listened to the familiar series of beeps that preceded a wrong number message.

Molly's hand pressed against his shoulder just as he pressed the phone's switch hook to try the call again. "Are you okay? Do I need to call someone for you?"

Yes, he needed her to call Amber, whose number ended with 65, but he couldn't get the words out. His body shook. He felt the weight of the phone on his bare foot and the weight of the first tear he'd cry grieving for his grandma on his cheek.

Molly wrapped her arms around him. He would call Amber back later, but he already knew. That same heaviness he'd felt when he learned of his parent's death was back on top of him. He knew he must seem like a master of mixed signals tonight, but he also knew that right now, Molly's arms were all that were keeping him from crumbling.

CHAPTER 19

Longview, Texas, 1945

Joel checked his watch again. Lorraine promised she'd be here by six, and it was fifteen after. Her friends were probably inside, but he wasn't going in without Lorraine. It would be hard enough to talk to them with her there.

Joel spotted movement from the corner of his eye. Lorraine's squished face against the glass caught him off guard.

He opened his door. "Nice face there."

"You looked too serious. Come on inside; that's where the fun is."

Joel brushed his jeans off.

"Wow, look at you!" Lorraine said, but she was the one who looked good. It was easy to get behind fabric rationing when seeing Lorraine in a dress that short. He forced his eyes up. *Your brother's wife, your brother's wife.* Joel realized he'd need to keep that mantra looping in his head for the next few hours.

Lorraine led Joel toward two joined tables near the back of the restaurant. There was a pair of free seats together, but they were right in the middle of the group.

"Bout time." Sally kissed Lorraine's cheek.

"I'm only 15 minutes late."

"More like 15 months." The man beside Sally hugged Lorraine.

"Hey, Tyler! I know, I know. It's been too long. This is my friend, Joel."

Tyler shook Joel's hand and introduced him to the rest of the group. Joel forgot their names before he sat. It was overwhelming to have so many eyes on him, so he kept his own eyes on the well-scratched tabletop.

"Did you meet Lorraine at school?" one girl asked.

"No." Tyler shook his head. "He's Lori's brother-in-law, remember? Well, future brother-in-law."

"What do you do for a living?" the bullnecked man across the table asked.

"I'm a mechanic."

"Oh yeah? So is my old man. Do you enjoy it?"

Joel had barely finished answering before Lu leaned in to ask what might cause the humming noise when she started her Chrysler.

"Where are you from?" Tyler lit a cigarette. No one seemed familiar with Joel's story. An advantage of befriending transported college students. The questions came at him like rapid fire from a Tommy gun. Joel had no time to formulate carefully worded answers, yet everyone acted interested in everything he said. And he never once caught any of them staring at the scar.

By the time the food arrived, the two sides of the table had split into separate conversations. Joel was glad to have the attention off him. He and Lorraine had barely spoken. He turned to her seat to find it empty.

"Ladies room," Lu explained.

The bells hanging on the entrance crashed against the glass as a group of teenage boys burst in. They obviously wanted to announce their arrival to the entire restaurant. Chairs screeched against the linoleum as they slammed bags on the table right behind Joel.

The sound of Lorraine's heels drawing closer was more welcome than the whistling that followed. "Sounds like you have some fans." Joel stood until Lorraine sat.

She rolled her eyes. "I hope I never acted that obnoxious."

"I'm sure you didn't. I'm sure no one ever has. But in spite of them, thanks for letting me come tonight."

Lorraine opened her mouth, but a loud crash stole her response. The kid who'd been balancing on two legs of the chair had fallen backward. Joel offered his hand, but the red-faced boy pushed it away.

"Don't mind him," Lorraine said. "He's embarrassed. But that's how things go, isn't it? If you want something badly enough, you usually get it. *It*, in this case, being attention, but you don't always get it in the way you hoped."

"Let's get the check and split." Lu rubbed her forehead. "We can go someplace quieter. All this noise is giving me a migraine."

A quieter place wasn't a bad idea. Joel leaned in towards Lorraine. "What are you doing later?"

She frowned. "A paper. First week of the semester and a paper already. Can you believe it?" Joel stopped listening, distracted by the boys again. This time, it wasn't their volume that got his attention.

"You shouldn't have let that freak touch you, man."

"I didn't! I told Frankenstein to go chase himself."

"Ha-ha! Yeah, says you, buddy."

Joel's chin trembled. He was a twenty-five-year-old man, but a few comments from stupid kids, and he was twelve again.

Nobody else seemed to have heard, except Lorraine who stared over her shoulder.

Joel tried to get her attention back. "Well, you're a writer, so the paper shouldn't be hard. How's the novel going?"

"I wonder if the Nazis did it?" The boy raised his voice.

"Bet so. It does kinda look like half a swastika."

"Just like those damn Nazis to not finish the job."

Lorraine pushed her chair back. "I'm sorry, but I won't sit and listen to this. Their parents must not have taught them respect, but I'm sure I can get through to them."

"Please, don't. Nobody's listening, but if you speak up, everybody will be."

Lorraine gave a long, low sigh. "I see."

"They're dumb kids. Best to ignore them."

Lorraine scooted her chair back under the table. Joel tried to listen as she talked about her writing, but he couldn't tune out the voices behind them. He only stopped hearing their jokes when Lorraine put her hand on his knee. His stomach and brain faltered. What was she doing?

She kept her hand there for less than a minute before pushing her chair out again. Joel feared she might say something despite his pleas. Suddenly, everything sounded underwater.

"I've got to fix my lipstick." Her voice was lively and loud. "Order us a milkshake to share, won't you, sweetheart?"

Joel looked around their table. If anyone noticed, they weren't acting like she'd said anything unusual. Maybe she called everyone that. It wasn't until he heard the boys again that he understood.

"Holy joe! There is no way *she's* with him!"

The other boys snickered. "And she gave you the brush off when you whistled at her, Mickey."

The taunts continued but were directed at Mickey for striking out with yet another girl. As much as Joel wanted Lorraine's affections to be real, the way she defended him without embarrassing him was pretty incredible.

The boys were gone before Lorraine made it back from the bathroom.

"Thanks," Joel whispered. "The whole place thanks you."

"No big deal." Lorraine looked around. "Where's our waitress? I need my check."

Joel pulled out his wallet. "I'll get it. I owe you."

She slung her purse over her shoulder. "No, you don't, but thank you. My treat next time."

"Milkshake included?"

Lorraine smiled. "Of course." She made her way around the table saying her goodbyes. Joel watched her hug every person until she got to him. She looked like she might, but seemed to decide against it. "Bye Joel. Talk to you soon."

She stole one last glance at him as she walked out the door. Joel wasn't upset she hadn't hugged him. It was the opposite actually. Hugs meant comfort, and she was comfortable with her friends. But when feelings were involved, even slight ones, there was some discomfort. When the waitress came back, Joel paid the entire table's tab and went home happier than he had in years.

***

There was nothing like the first shower after being sick in bed for three days. Lorraine inhaled the steamy shower air, glad for the ability to breathe again.

The pipes shook and gurgled as she turned the water off and wrapped herself in a soft towel. She raked a brush through her hair but set it down after the first painful snag. Her tangles could wait; her stomach could not. Maybe she could finally eat without the sensation of swallowing needles.

She dressed and ran into the kitchen, grabbing a piece of bacon before even taking her seat. She could always count on bacon a few times after they'd received their new ration books. To remember they'd had this glorious breakfast treat anytime they wanted before the war was nearly incomprehensible.

Daddy looked from his paper. "Looks like you feel better."

"Much," Lorraine said with her mouth full.

"Then you ought to consider coming with us. I figured you'd jump at the chance to go home for two weeks."

So had she. But when her parents explained they'd be going home to lay a dear family friend to rest, she'd had no desire to tag along.

"I'll be fine, Daddy. Travel interferes with the war effort."

"The war is as good as over." He pushed the paper in front of her.

171

"Atomic Bomb Hits Japan," she read the headline aloud and skimmed the rest of the article. "Scientists win four-year victory? Harnessing the powers of the universe? Equal to 20,000 tons of TNT?"

"Happened Sunday night. President Truman announced it yesterday."

"My God." Lorraine shook her head. "Three days in bed and I woke up to a new world."

"Had to be done," Lane said. "They wouldn't surrender."

"But still." Lorraine looked at the paper again. "That radiation will kill for years to come. There must be alternatives."

"Like bombing them conventionally for a few more years? Risking more and more lives? This bomb may be Clancy's ticket home."

Lorraine understood that, but she couldn't be proud that her country had opened Pandora's Box to win a war.

Lane sipped his coffee. "So now will you come? Since you can't use the war as an excuse?"

"Daddy, I have class."

He took a piece of bacon and pushed the rest to Lorraine. "Are you sure this has nothing to do with Joel Fitchett?"

Lorraine froze. "Why would it?"

Her father raised an eyebrow. "We've noticed how much time you've spent with him. Practically every night before you got sick."

A tingle swept up Lorraine's neck and across her face. "Not *every* night."

Daddy thumbed his ear. "It's fine. Mother's just worried you're getting yourself confused."

"And you? Are you worried too?"

"I don't know, Lori. This relationship stuff is above my pay grade. All I will say is be careful. Things can get confusing quickly."

"Well, I'm not confused." Lorraine looked away. "Joel and I are both worried about Clancy, and it's nice to have someone who understands."

"Okay," Lane said, but his expression called her a liar. Was she? If only a common grief joined her to Joel, why did her pulse turn into a turbojet every time the phone rang? Why did she get so angry when Lu suggested setting up Joel with her older sister? But none of that was the worst of it. The worst was that when she was with Joel, she didn't fret about Clancy as much. She told herself it was normal for pain to lessen with time, but what if it wasn't time? What if it was Joel? Her stomach twisted. So much for breakfast.

Her father held up the paper again. "Just be careful, sweetheart. You don't want to be the girl who comes between brothers."

The way he hid behind the headline and the absence of his usual stoic tone connected dots in Lorraine's mind. She shoved his paper down. "Uncle Rick?" She made his name a question. "You told me you had a falling out, but never what caused it. Was it a girl?"

Lane's brows furrowed. "It's an awkward thing to tell your child you had a past life and past lovers, but yes. Before I knew your mother, I was engaged to a gal named Judith Hayes."

Aunt Judy, Lorraine realized. She'd never met her aunt or uncle, but they sent her birthday money every year.

"She left me for Rick. They ran off one week before the wedding, settled in Montana." Lane's eyes went glassy. "Talk about an atomic bomb."

"Oh Daddy, how awful."

"Well, it worked out fine for me," he said, and his voice and face settled again. "Met your mother a few months later, and now here we all are. Happy as clams."

"If that's true, why haven't you spoken to Uncle Rick since?"

"Hurt feelings I suppose. The fact that it turned out okay doesn't take away the sting of it."

"Even all these years later?"

"Oh, I don't know. I'm not so angry anymore, just figured it would be awkward to try to change things now."

"Awkwardness is better than regret."

Lane stood. "Probably right about that."

"Then you ought to look him up. Montana's not so far from Wyoming."

"Guess not." He dropped his plate into the sink. "I better finish packing. Forget what I said earlier about Joel. I know you better than that."

***

Joel couldn't believe his luck. He had just been daydreaming about Lorraine, and now she'd materialized at his door. "All better?" he asked.

"Finally." She touched her stomach. "Want to go eat somewhere? I was so busy helping my parents pack I forgot lunch."

"I'm cooking dinner, but there's enough for two."

"Oh, no, I couldn't. Not when you used your stamps."

"I'm making chicken. No rationing on poultry. Help me with the cooking, and we'll call it even."

"Ha!" Lorraine followed him inside. "You'd come out ahead taking my stamps. I can't cook."

"Sure you can." He led her to the kitchen. With his hand on her back, he didn't feel hungry anymore, not the traditional hunger anyway.

Lorraine looked around the kitchen. "I can give it a go, but you won't make me touch *that* will you?"

"It's somewhat essential to touch a chicken when cooking chicken. Just reach on inside and pull everything out."

Lorraine rolled her shoulders violently.

"Have you really never done this?" he asked.

"Well, no. But so what? Have you ever written a book?" She tried to look serious, but she had no poker face.

"No, haven't done that."

Lorraine shrugged. "Well, me either, but I *am* working on it. Why are you smiling?"

"I'm surprised you've made it twenty years without touching a chicken. Didn't you used to work in a soup kitchen?"

"Yes. Just soup, no dead birds. And I only served the food. I'd much rather roll up my sleeves to help the homeless than to pull out chicken organs."

The stray toast crumbs on the counter stole Joel's attention. A reminder of Clancy and the messes he left. For a moment, the guilt was so strong he considered asking Lorraine to leave.

"Come on, what else can I do?" She pointed to the kettle. "Tea? A salad?"

Joel pushed down the guilt. "Salad sounds good." He was tired of feeling bad for spending time with her, for liking her. They had done nothing wrong. Clancy would be home soon, and nights like this would only be a memory.

Lorraine pulled a head of lettuce from the fridge. "I'll need more than this."

"There's a garden out back." He handed her a basket. "Pick whatever you need."

"A victory garden?"

He looked down. "It's nothing."

"I'll be the judge of that." She scrunched her nose at the chicken. "Take care of that thing while I'm out."

Joel shoved his hand into the chicken.

"Eww!" She reached for the doorknob. "Be sure to wash your hands. Or else I won't hold them, even to say grace."

Joel realized she was teasing, but when he finished preparing the chicken, he turned the hot water on and scrubbed his hands till they turned red.

***

"This is delicious." Lorraine wiped her mouth with the napkin, smearing cherry red lipstick all over it.

"Glad you still want to eat it after seeing it in its natural state."

She held a piece of grilled chicken on her fork. "As far as I'm concerned, this is a chicken's natural state."

Steam and the unmistakable smell of rosemary wafted to his nose as Joel cut his first bite. It was too quiet, but also too hard to talk and eat simultaneously. Music. They needed music.

"Want to listen to the radio?" he asked.

"Sure!" She swallowed another bite. "This chicken is amazing. If I come around enough, you might make a cook out of me. I'm sure Clancy will thank you for that."

The kitchen lights flickered at the mention of Clancy. Lorraine gripped the table. "What happened?"

"It's windy. Might be a storm coming."

Lorraine released her grip, her knuckles now as white as the tablecloth. "Sorry I'm so jumpy."

"Don't apologize. I half expected to hear the air raid sirens myself."

"That's the world we live in now, isn't it? A light flickers, and we run to pull the blackout curtains." She squeezed a tomato between her fingers. "A world with atomic bombs."

"That was necessary." Joel echoed her father's words. "Japan refused to surrender."

"And they still haven't."

"They will. This is a victory."

"So they say." She set down her napkin. "I used to marvel at the advances in science and technology, imagining the world my grandchildren would live in. But knowing the world of my imagination can be wiped out at the drop of a bomb makes it hard to see the future as anything but frightening."

Joel excused himself to turn on the radio. The conversation felt too serious, and they were both thinking about Clancy again. "Save room for dessert."

"I'm full as a tick."

"Oh, come on, just Jell-O. Or I may have enough sugar for a batch of brownies."

"Don't trouble yourself. Jell-O is...."

"What is it?" Joel listened for any sound that would alert him something was wrong, but all he heard was the melody of the Glenn Miller Orchestra.

"I love this song!" Lorraine was already on her feet. "Dance with me!"

"Let me get that Jell-O."

"No, please. Before this song ends. I can't remember the last time I got to do a proper Lindy Hop."

Joel undid the top button of his shirt. "I can't."

"Can't what? Do the Lindy? I'll show you." She turned up the volume.

"I can't dance at all," Joel said over the music. "I've never even tried."

"Then how do you know you can't?" Lorraine pushed up her sleeves. "You are teaching me to cook; I can teach you to dance. Even Stevens."

"But you started with a salad. Starting with the Lindy Hop seems comparable to starting with your hand shoved up a chicken."

"Fair enough." She pointed a finger at him. "But next song..."

"Next song," Joel said. "Next non-Lindy Hopping song." He knew he should be excited to have Lorraine's arms around him, but all he could think about was the million ways it could go wrong.

The melody that began next was familiar. A ballad. Joel wondered if a slow dance would make Lorraine drop the whole idea altogether, but she wasn't deterred. She placed one of his hands on the small of her back and held on to the other. He wondered if she noticed his body shiver at her touch.

"Follow my feet," she said. "A lot of swaying, a little turning. No fancy footwork required. Definitely the salad of dancing."

I'll be seeing you in all the old familiar places, Billie Holiday bellowed.

"Is this okay?" Joel felt like he was crowding her.

"You're doing fine."

Joel tried to concentrate on Lorraine's feet, but it was impossible when they were connected to legs like hers.

"See, you're a natural."

Her scent overwhelmed him this close. She smelled like the honeysuckle that covered the walls of his childhood home. Her kiss would surely taste as sweet as the nectar straight from those bulbs. *I'll be seeing you, in every lovely summer's day...*

When she rested her head on his chest, Joel wished he had closed the blackout curtains. They were only dancing. It wasn't like he had made a pass at her. But they were standing at a diving board's edge—one more step and they'd be in over their heads. *I'll be looking at the moon, but I'll be seeing you.*

Lorraine lifted her head. Her eyes and cheeks glowed. He thought about leaning in but then thought better of it. He'd misread her last time, so who's to say he wasn't again?

She hooked two fingers in the loop on the back of his pants where a belt should go. "Have I ever told you how beautiful your eyes are?" she asked.

He gnawed on the inside of his cheek. "The first day we met."

"Well, they are really something."

"You're the only one who's ever..." Joel struggled for the words. "Who's seen beyond the scar."

A heavy thud at the door jarred them out of the moment, out of each other's arms. It took a minute for Joel to collect himself. It was after eight. Who would come this late?

"Expecting someone?" Lorraine's face was ashen. He knew her fear, that whoever was behind that door came with bad news about Clancy. But that would surely arrive in a telegram. And it would go to Daddy. Still, Joel's hand shook as he twisted the knob.

There was no somber serviceman holding a letter outside, but an unwelcome visitor all the same. "Crawl?"

"Hi-de-ho." Crawl sipped from his flask. "I was in the neighborhood."

Joel looked around outside to make sure Crawl had come alone. "What do you want?"

"Can't I stop by for a visit?" Crawl asked.

Joel didn't understand what Crawl was up to but assumed it had to do with money and Clancy. The war was ending, and Clancy probably still owed something. How that was possible after giving him Mama's ring, Joel didn't understand. But he couldn't ask with Lorraine here. "Come back tomorrow."

"Who's there?" Lorraine appeared behind him. Joel hadn't even heard her footsteps.

Crawl gave Lorraine a once over. "Well, what do we have here? Or rather, whom do we have?"

Something about the way Crawl looked at Lorraine made Joel panic. Made him remember the knife he hid under his mattress. A gift his daddy had made for his 18th birthday. Joel hated it. Knives, like doves and broken glass, would forever be tied to the worst of all memories.

"This is Lorraine," Joel said.

Crawl reached for Lorraine's hand. "Delighted."

"Likewise. Are you a friend of Joel's? We were about to have dessert. Care to join us?"

"That's all right." Crawl stomped his feet. "Got muddy boots. Lorraine, you said?"

"Yes, and you are?"

"Getting on my way," Crawl said. "I came here for something, but seeing you, I've suddenly forgotten what it was."

"Don't leave on my account." Lorraine looked at Joel. "If you two need to talk, I can go."

"No, don't do that," Crawl said. "Not before dessert." He winked at Joel. "See you around, though." Crawl lifted his hand in a slight wave. "Both of you."

Joel shut the door, locked it, and checked to make sure it wouldn't open.

Lorraine frowned. "I should have gone. Whoever that was obviously didn't want to talk with me around."

"No, I'm glad you stayed. In fact, you ought to stay the night." Joel was too worried to care how his suggestion must have sounded.

She touched her throat. "Stay here?"

"In Clancy's room, I mean. While your folks are gone."

"Oh, nothing to worry about there. I'm fine being home alone. Not to mention, Mother insisted she would call at 9:00 sharp every night to check on me. Sneaky of her, right? A way to enforce a curfew from across the country." She grabbed Joel's hand and twisted it to see his watch rather than look at the clock. "Yep, I better go. I'll have time for a hot bath before the warden rings."

Joel didn't want to push her, especially when he might be overreacting. Whatever Crawl wanted probably didn't concern Lorraine, but Joel worried that by having her here, he had somehow pulled her into Crawl's grisly world.

"Thanks for coming." Joel looked in all directions as he followed Lorraine to her car.

"Sure, it was fun. Sorry you got gypped on the dance lesson."

"Next time." It always seemed to be next time with them.

"Yes, next time."

He stepped awkwardly around Lorraine to open her door. She thanked him but didn't get in.

"Everything all right?" he asked.

"No, not really." She held on to the top of her door. "I have a question, but you have to promise not to laugh."

"Okay."

Lorraine blew a strand of hair out of her face. "Do you believe in ghosts, Joel?"

That he wasn't expecting. "I'm not sure. Do you?"

"Well, yes, I think I do."

Joel rocked on his heels. "I thought you believed in heaven and all that."

"It's possible to believe in both, you know?" Lorraine replied.

Joel didn't know that. Nor why Lorraine was talking to him about ghosts in his driveway. And just when he thought she couldn't make less sense to him.

"You want to laugh, don't you?" Lorraine asked.

"No. I'm just wondering what made you think of ghosts." He looked around. "Right now."

"You can't say you didn't notice it. The way the lights flickered right when I said Clancy's name?" She shivered at the memory.

"Yeah, I noticed. But it was a coincidence, Lori. That's all."

"That's one thing I don't believe in."

"You're wondering if Clancy's a ghost," Joel said.

"What if he didn't want me here tonight?"

"So, like a jealous ghost?

Lorraine sank into her seat. "I knew you'd make fun."

Joel crouched beside her. "I'm not making fun. Clancy's not a ghost. He's alive."

"How can you be sure?" She began to cry. In Joel's fantasy, he liked to forget how much she loved Clancy, but there was no denying it in moments like this.

He handed Lorraine his handkerchief. "A gut feeling."

"And if you're wrong?"

"Then he's in heaven."

She wiped her eyes. "Thought you didn't believe in that?"

"Who knows? But whether he's dead or alive, or a ghost or an angel, he wouldn't be upset you are here. He made me promise to keep an eye on you."

Lorraine handed Joel back his handkerchief. "Thank you for telling me that. I'm sorry for being silly. I hope I didn't spoil your evening."

"Are you kidding? You made the evening great."

"Let's spend time together tomorrow. No strange knocks at the door, no ghosts. Maybe even a Friday night movie?"

"Yes, to all the above." Joel stood. "Goodnight, Lori; see you tomorrow."

He closed her door and watched her drive away. He didn't want to go back inside. It was a nice night, and he had a lot of reflecting to do. He walked to his vegetable patch. Wind slid through the leaves, carrying the pungent smell of tomatoes through the night air. He strolled around the perimeter, proud of the carefully tilled rolls of healthy plants. No, he hadn't gone to war, but he had created and nurtured life.

Joel knelt to snap a pea from the vine and saw the dips where Lorraine's heels had dug into the earth. But close by were other prints, boot prints, far bigger than his own feet. He stood, remembering the thud of Crawl's muddy boots on his front porch. He'd been back here, watching them.

Joel's lungs constricted. He ran inside and haphazardly grabbed a few items: a jug of water, a box of crackers, a blanket, and a flashlight. He piled them by the door. He pulled a random paperback from under Clancy's bed before retrieving what he kept under his own mattress, though he hoped he wouldn't need it.

There was a perfect place to park across the street from Lorraine's house. He would stay awake as long as he could. Hopefully the book would help. But if not, he'd always been a light sleeper. If a car so much as drove down the road, he'd hear. The sunrise would wake him, and he would be home, showered, dressed, and at work before Lorraine even woke up. She'd never even know he was there, but he would know she was safe.

CHAPTER 20

Ohio, 1991

It took less than three hours for Garrison to plan his grandmother's funeral. It had taken three days to do the same for his parents. He was better at it now. Knew the papers to find, the calls to make, and the songs to choose. Elvis, of course. Grandma Dolly always said she'd only fallen in love twice, once with Grandpa and again with Elvis. Garrison realized now there was likely one prior she forgot to mention.

He watched the slideshow through blurry eyes. How strange to see his grandma so young and beautiful. She posed with a hand on her hip and a spark in her eye he'd never known his mild-mannered grandmother to have.

The church wasn't full, but it was a decent-sized crowd, a nice amount of flowers. Not enough to mask the smells of wood polish and musty carpet, but several arrangements on both sides of the casket. Garrison hadn't even remembered to buy flowers, but Amber took care of that. She'd taken care of so much the past few days. Her parents arranged for their church to bring Garrison food for an entire week. It was only day three, and the fridge overflowed with leftover casseroles. At least his buddies brought a more practical offering of beer and hot wings.

Garrison curled and uncurled the program as the preacher spoke, a lump thick in his throat. He scraped a knuckle beneath his eye to catch a single tear, but blinked back the rest until Elvis bellowed those final notes of *How Great Thou Art*. Then the tears began with no sign of stopping. How often had Grandma Dolly played that song? Not as many times as she'd played *Burning Love*, but the First Baptist Church would probably frown on that song choice.

As he stood to exit, Aunt Sharon blew into her handkerchief for at least the sixth time during the service. Garrison was surprised she'd come. She hadn't seen Grandma Dolly in at least ten years. Sharon worked as a nurse in third-world countries. Out saving AIDS patients in Africa while her own mother wasted away in a nursing home.

Garrison removed his suit jacket at the graveyard. Today was warmer than the last time he stood here, shaking hands and accepting condolences, but the heaviness inside was the same. Once the crowd dissipated, Garrison raised the coffin lid a final time. He understood why some didn't want to see dead bodies, but he needed to. If he hadn't looked at his parents in their coffins, his last memory of them would have been the way they looked at the morgue. He needed to see his mom and dad put back together, wearing clothes not stained with blood and brain tissue. The funeral home did their best, but couldn't cover all the scrapes and swelling. But Grandma Dolly looked better than she had in years. Peaceful, like she was lost in a perfect dream.

A hand settled on Garrison's back. "Mama looks beautiful." Aunt Sharon sniffled. "And the service was too."

"Glad you came," Garrison said.

"Well, of course. I'm so sorry I didn't when your folks..." She stopped and wrapped Garrison in a hug. "Oh, you poor thing."

"It's okay," Garrison said. He was so messed up during those days, he wouldn't have noticed Sharon there anyway.

She pulled away and attempted in vain to straighten her wrinkled skirt. "I ought to find a hotel and get unpacked. I'll be in town a couple more days if you want to get together."

"Um, yeah absolutely."

"Got any hotel recommendations?" Sharon kneaded her shoulder.

"The Value Inn is decent. But if you want something nicer, my girlfriend might know." Garrison motioned Amber over. "What's a nice hotel here?"

"Value Inn is nice enough for me," Sharon said. "I spend most nights under a mosquito net, remember?"

Amber's brows snapped together. Garrison knew her well enough to understand everything she wasn't saying. Sharon was family, and Grandma Dolly would have wanted them to get along. Knowing Amber, the sheets in Garrison's guest room were already washed.

Garrison sighed. "On second thought, Aunt Sharon, how do you feel about casseroles?"

***

Amber left Garrison's house around eight. She never slept over in the summer when she was out of the dorms and back under her parents' roof. He wished she would have tonight. Conversation came naturally for her.

182

There should have been plenty to discuss. Sharon had missed Garrison's entire life, but after fifteen minutes, Garrison struggled. He was about to excuse himself to take out the overflowing garbage when Sharon shifted from casual conversation to a pointed question. "What's this Amber mentioned about you looking for Clancy Fitchett?"

Garrison went rigid. "That's a long story."

Sharon stood. "I'll put on a fresh pot."

As Garrison watched Sharon, something bothered him. It had been bothering him all night. She and his mother didn't look anything alike. And it wasn't just Sharon's tan skin and pixie haircut. Besides their full lips, neither sister looked much like Grandma Dolly. But Sharon had Grandpa Hale's deep-set eyes and square chin. But who did Garrison's mom look like? Maybe Aunt Sharon had wondered too.

She set a steaming mug in front of Garrison. "Ready when you are."

The first sip burnt Garrison's tongue. He blew into the cup, but it was no use. As much as he wanted to keep drinking and delay this conversation, he'd have to talk while it cooled. "Grandma lost her memory near the end. She said a lot that didn't make sense, but one thing stood out. She said Grandpa wasn't mom's real father." He set the bitter coffee down and looked Aunt Sharon in the eye. "Crazy right?"

Sharon pressed her lips together. "Not so crazy."

"What?"

"It's true, sweetie."

A flush of adrenaline tingled through Garrison's body. This was the news he'd been waiting for. His fuzzy brain couldn't string words to form a coherent sentence, so he waited for Sharon to continue.

"Your Grandpa Hale wasn't Lucy's daddy. Well, he *was*. He was the only dad she ever knew. He treated us the same."

"How do you know?"

Lines formed on Sharon's forehead. "Growing up, your mom always said she must have been adopted. Claimed she was so different from the rest of us. I assumed she was fishing for attention. It never occurred to me there was any truth to it. We were just kids. Dorothy was our mom, John was our dad, and that was that." Sharon drank her first sip. "But one night, I overheard a conversation between our parents. Well, let's call a spade a spade; they were fighting." She looked into her coffee cup. "Say, do you have any cream?"

"In the fridge. What did they fight about?"

"It happened the night Lucy got kicked out of prom for drinking." She spoke from behind the refrigerator door. Garrison had never heard that story. He'd have to remember to ask Aunt Sharon for the details on that later. "Mother barely got her up the stairs before she passed out." Sharon set the creamer down. "Would you like some?"

Garrison shook his head. The coffee needed cream and a lot of it, but there was no way he could drink it now.

"Mother and Daddy were as furious as I was curious. I sat on the stairs and listened to them fuss. Daddy said Lucy had too much of her father in her, that she always had. Mother had a fit. I heard her say that Clancy was a fine man, that he'd never even raised his voice to her. That only got Daddy yelling louder."

"I can't imagine Grandpa Hale yelling. Any more than I can imagine Mom being drunk."

Aunt Sharon's eyes brightened. "Oh, the stories I could tell you. Anyway, Daddy's yelling scared me back into the room. I never heard any mention of Clancy again."

"Wow. Wow. Wow. Did you ever tell mom?"

"Could never quite find the words. It wasn't my news to tell anyway."

Garrison held on to the chair so he wouldn't collapse out of it. It was all true. None of these last months had been in vain.

"Why do you want to find Clancy so badly?" Aunt Sharon asked.

"To solve the mystery," he said even though that wasn't true anymore. Somewhere out there he had a grandpa, a family. He couldn't live the rest of his life without a family. It wasn't just curiosity fueling him now; it was desperation.

Sharon saw right through him. "It's more than that."

Garrison plucked at the cuff of his shirt. He had always been a terrible liar. "No offense, but I'd like a family."

"I see." She tapped her fingers on the table. "What about your dad's folks?"

"I barely know them. They never came for a single birthday or Christmas, not for graduation. They mail an occasional sweater, a check when I'm lucky, but they aren't family." Garrison stopped. It was weird to tell Aunt Sharon this because she'd also been absent from his life. "And they had no reason not to," he added. "They live on investments and real estate and are loaded. Dad said his grandpa basically raised him."

Garrison thought of Molly. His grandparents would have fun cruising the Caribbean with her parents. He wished Molly could have met his dad. The ache to have them both around the table was, for a moment, overwhelming.

"But you don't know Clancy either. What if he's no better? He didn't marry Mother when—"

"Grandma may not have told him. You shouldn't assume!"

"It's possible." Aunt Sharon spoke with the gentle voice one might use to talk a jumper off a ledge.

Garrison squirmed in his chair. Sharon was not the enemy. "He might have known, but my gut says otherwise."

Sharon put her hand on top of Garrison's. "I hope you find Clancy and he's all you are looking for. I'm sorry I've missed out on knowing you. But life takes us to different places. I'm fulfilled. Sometimes growing up means going your own way—alone even. Remember that, should this not turn out the way you hope."

"Okay," Garrison said but was already wondering if he'd find Clancy in time for Christmas. He wasn't sure he could bear it alone this year.

Sharon reached into her bag behind the chair. "On any account, let's keep in touch. I can leave the international calling card I used to call Mother with sometimes."

"I'd like that."

"Let me know how it goes with Clancy if you find him."

If. There were no more ifs. Ifs were gone with the uncertainty of whether Grandma Dolly had told him the truth. She had. Clancy was his grandfather, and Garrison would not stop until he found him.

***

"Is it true you offer special rates for extended stays?" Garrison fumbled for his wallet. "Great, let's start with three weeks." He read his credit card number and searched for a pen to write the confirmation number. He'd just had one. These are the times his mom would say, "It didn't grow legs and walk away." But Garrison suspected pens and car keys did just that.

Amber stepped through the doorway. He covered the phone's speaker with his hand. "Got a pen?"

She reached under one of the throw pillows on his parents' bed and retrieved the lost pen. Amber had a knack for finding things, and that worked out well for someone like him.

Garrison didn't want to keep the Super 8 waiting any longer while he found paper, so he wrote the confirmation number on his arm. When he hung up the phone, he noticed the purse slung over Amber's shoulder.

"You leaving?" he asked.

"I assume that's what you want since you stopped watching the movie."

"Oh, sorry. Just wasn't into it."

She jutted out her hip. "You don't have a clue why I chose it, do you?"

Garrison scratched his head. He was obviously missing something special about *Look Who's Talking Too*. "I guess not."

"Our first date?" Amber tugged at her sunflower necklace like it was choking her. "Oh, come on. You kept the movie stubs! We watched *Look Who's Talking*, and you really liked it."

"I *said* I really liked it. It was a first date; you say you like everything."

"So, you lied?"

Garrison clasped his hands behind his head. "No, it was fine, better than this one. Sequels are generally awful."

"Well, I'm sorry for picking such an *awful* movie. I thought it would mean something to you; it did to me."

"It's a movie, Amber, come on. Are we actually fighting about a movie whose plot revolves around talking babies?"

"That depends." Amber looked at the numbers written on his arm. "Who was on the phone?"

Garrison poked his tongue into his cheek. "Other girl's phone numbers don't typically start with 000. I made a hotel reservation."

"Hotel? For when?"

"Tomorrow night...and a few more days." Garrison hoped she hadn't been standing in the doorway long enough to learn the truth. "Don't worry, I'll leave the name and number this time."

"No." Amber crossed her arms. "You can't go back. Classes start July 8th."

Garrison looked away. "I'm not signed up for any classes. It's too much right now. Maybe fall."

Amber threw her arms up. "This is unbelievable, Garrison. Another lie."

Garrison laughed. "Look, I get why you're upset about school, but you're going to have to let this *Look Who's Talking* thing go."

"Can you blame me for being angry? I mean, this is a new development. Not that you are a liar, but that I'm just figuring it out."

"It was our first date! The same date you told me you liked sports and were a supportive person."

Amber's stomped her foot. "I have watched sports with you, and I *am* supportive!" Her shrill voice reminded Garrison of a smoke alarm's low battery warning.

He lowered his voice. "You have been supportive. I need you to keep it up a little longer. Aunt Sharon confirmed Clancy is my grandfather."

"And?"

"And nothing. Don't you get how huge that is?"

"But she doesn't know how to find him?"

"No, but—"

"Then stop, Garrison! Enough is enough. Dolly hasn't even been in the ground two days, and now you're leaving again?"

"Yes, she is in the ground, which means she doesn't need me any longer. Thanks for the reminder." Garrison chewed on the pen's cap hoping having something in his mouth would stifle the urge to yell.

"Have you ever considered that I might need you around?"

Garrison threw the pen down. "You were the one who said not to give up!"

"That was...that was," Amber fumbled her words. "That was before you got so obsessed! This isn't healthy. Just look at you." Amber flung her hand at him. "Have you even showered since you've been in town? You certainly haven't shaved."

Garrison detected an edge in his laughter. "Sorry, didn't realize there was a dress code in my own home."

"This is crazy. I'm not going to stand here and argue with you."

"Good, tonight's my last night here for awhile; I don't want to waste it. Let's calm down and go grab a milkshake." He sniffed his shirt. "I'll change."

Amber held up her hand. "No, Garrison. I don't want a milkshake. I want you to call and cancel the hotel. Stay here."

"You know I can't do that. It's unfair to even ask."

"What's unfair is how you're treating me. I get that your parents' death left you with some sort of need to be nurtured that sent you on this wild goose chase. I've tried to be patient, supportive, understanding. But I'm tired of waiting for you to move forward with the life we planned."

Garrison scratched the stubble on his cheek. "So, you're saying..."

"If you leave tomorrow, we're through."

Garrison flinched. It wasn't so much her words that surprised him, but the resolve on her face, the complete absence of tears. Amber didn't appear to be bluffing.

"I'm too close. Stopping now would make this all in vain."

When Amber closed her eyes, Garrison thought she might take the threat back, but she exhaled harshly. Her face calmed as if she'd expelled all the anger and love for him in that single breath. "Okay." She fished keys from her purse and removed the one to Garrison's house. "I'll get my things and leave." She tossed the key on the bed and barged across the hall to the bathroom.

Garrison lay back on the bed. He should try to stop her, but what was there to say? Amber's platform shoes pounded as drawers opened and closed. He'd miss the pop of color her purple toothbrush added to the gray bathroom and the lingering smell of her Guess perfume. But he would not miss it enough to change his mind. If he loved Amber, he'd *want* to stay. If he loved her, he wouldn't be thinking about Molly and the similar thud her Doc Martens made on ceramic tile.

He never heard Amber cry as she packed, only a faint sniffle before the door slammed. They'd fought before, but she'd never given the key back. Garrison brushed his hand across the bed searching for the key, but like the pen, it eluded him. Amber wouldn't be around to find what was missing any longer, but that was okay. He didn't need to find a missing pen or key; he needed to find Clancy.

CHAPTER 21

Longview, Texas, 1945

As soon as Lorraine was alone inside the dark, empty house, she regretted not inviting Joel in. But the poor guy was exhausted. Soon as the theater dimmed the lights, he'd passed out quick as he'd touched a spindle.

Lorraine checked the clock. Thirty more minutes to soak in the bathtub until Mother phoned. The warm water relaxed Lorraine's muscles, but even with a paperback in hand and bubbles to her ears, she couldn't quiet her mind. Strange noises drifted from the bedroom but stopped each time the water did. The price of a writer's imagination, she supposed, but she got out of the tub just the same.

Lorraine froze in the doorway and stared at the fluttering drapes. She stepped backward then remembered cracking the window before the movie. Not the smartest idea when a summer storm brewed. She unstuck her legs and pushed back the curtains, surprised to see the window, not cracked, but fully open. Had she done that? She must have.

With one hand holding her robe closed, Lorraine grabbed for the nightgown with the other. She ran a hand over the quilt several times before ungluing her eyes from the window. It was not on the bed. Maybe she'd forgotten how wide the window was open but was certain she'd laid her peach gown out before getting in the bath.

Someone had been here. Someone may be still.

Lorraine unlocked her knees and ran downstairs. She meant to call the police, but she dialed a more familiar number.

"Someone stole my nightgown!" The phone shook in Lorraine's hand.

"From the line?" Joel's voice was raspy.

"No, from the bed."

"Take a deep breath." He sounded more awake now. "How would someone have gotten in?"

"The window is open."

"And your gown, you say? Is anything else missing?"

Lorraine did a quick inventory of the living room. "Nothing looks out of place."

"And you're sure you laid it out?"

It hurt that Joel didn't seem to believe her, but maybe she planned to set the gown out but hadn't. Sometimes ideas masqueraded as memories. With so much on her mind, anything was possible.

"I'm almost certain. And I only cracked the window; it's completely open now."

"Call the police."

Lorraine pulled at her hair. "Is that necessary?" She imagined her embarrassment if the officer pulled the nightgown from under the covers. Plus, Mrs. Brown across the street had the number to her parents' hotel. If that old biddy saw the police at the house, Lane and Birdie would be home before morning.

"If you want, I can check things out," Joel offered.

Yes, that was exactly what Lorraine wanted. Joel right here and right now. She was glad for his uncanny ability to read her mind. "Please."

"Can you go to the neighbors?"

"I don't want to frighten anyone without reason."

"Okay. Lock yourself in the bathroom downstairs. I'm sure it's fine, but best to be safe." Lorraine heard the cracks beneath the calm Joel tried to exude.

"There's a key under the mat."

"Be there in five minutes."

Lorraine said thanks, but Joel didn't answer. That was good though because it meant he was already on his way.

***

The pounding rain made it impossible to hear anything else. Lorraine pressed an ear against the bathroom door, but she might as well have been standing in Niagara Falls. Where was Joel? She moved to the toilet and watched under the door for the hallway light to come on.

She tied and retied her robe a dozen times, hoping it wouldn't slip open when Joel arrived. Why hadn't she grabbed another nightgown? A crash of thunder nearly jolted her from the toilet. She needed to calm down. She tried to take in a deep breath, but the air was stale and reeked of mildewed towels and hairspray.

The walls were closing in. Joel could have been murdered in the entryway for all she knew.

She picked up a seashell from the shelf above the commode and pressed it to her ear, but the ocean inside was silent. No doubt drowned out by a Texas summer storm and her own pounding heartbeat.

A stream of light finally beamed from under the doorway. Lorraine may not have heard the ocean in the shell, but she felt like a ship drifting in it now. A lost ship finally spotted by a lighthouse. "Joel?"

"It's me." Lorraine unlocked the door and spilled into Joel's arms, but his embrace was rigid. "Let's leave."

"What's happening?" Lorraine's eyes filled with tears. Crying had always been an involuntary reaction to fear.

"Crawl."

"Crawl? The one you mentioned at Christmas?"

"Yes, I think he was here."

"Is he still?" She clasped the robe again.

"No, his car is at the bar up the road."

Lorraine peeked out the front curtains, but only saw the world in flashes. She'd heard the storm's sounds but was finally witnessing the severity of the rain and lightning. She turned to Joel. His damp and over bright eyes were startling. "Should we call the police?"

"I don't think it would do any good where someone like Crawl is concerned, but we can decide that later. We need to leave in case he comes back."

Though Lorraine had a million questions, she trusted Joel. "Okay." She glanced at the clock. 8:55. She couldn't leave before Mother called. "Can I pack?"

"Did you understand what I said? You are in danger!" Joel snapped.

"I have to get dressed." Joel looked down as if he hadn't noticed the robe she was still strangling.

His face turned as red as her daddy's hanky. "Okay, I'll go check the windows and doors. Hurry."

Lorraine pulled so hard on her dresser drawer, it came off its hinges. She let it fall and scrounged for underwear and a pair of two-piece pajamas. She put them on without bothering to close her door and stuffed extras in her bag along with a dress, hairbrush, and her notebook.

"Are you dressed?" Joel waited outside her door.

"Yes, come in."

"All locked up. Ready to go?"

"Just about." She shoved on a pair of shoes.

Joel snatched her bag and turned off the light.

"Wait! Do I need my keys?"

"No, I've got the spare house key. Leave your car. It's better he doesn't know where you are."

They were halfway down the stairs when the phone rang. "Leave it," Joel demanded.

"It's my parents. I can't."

"Call them back from my house."

Lorraine grabbed the phone. "Hi, Mother."

Joel pounded his fist against the counter. "One minute." Lorraine mouthed. "Mother? Are you there? There's a storm and the connection's terrible. Can we talk tomorrow?"

Lorraine finished with her mother just as the front door flew open.

"All clear." Joel was soaking wet. She hadn't even noticed him going outside. He flipped the porch switch and grabbed her hand. They were running so fast she didn't even feel the rain. "Crouch down," he said once inside the truck. "At least until we pass the bar."

It was on the floor of the passenger seat when the cold caught up to her—the cold and the realization this Crawl fellow had been in her room while she showered. Her entire body shook.

"Come here," Joel said.

"No," she cried. "Not till we pass the bar."

"No need to huddle on the floorboard. Lay on the seat. Put your head on my lap." Lorraine struggled up as Joel pulled a blanket from behind the seat. She lay down, the heat from Joel's body warming her more than the cover. "It will be all right." Joel ran his fingers, through her wet, tangled hair. "I'm going to take care of this, and I'm going to take care of you." The way he said it made her believe him, made the shaking stop.

***

As if the first one and the subsequent rain hadn't done the job, Lorraine took another bath at Joel's.

She caught the glimmer of a knife on Joel's bedside table as she walked down the hall. The weapon showed his fear even more than the obsessive door checking did.

There was a quilt and warm cup of coffee waiting for her in the living room. She was grateful to be here. This smaller house felt safer somehow.

"Thank you." She held the hot coffee mug between her water-wrinkled fingers.

"Sounds like the rain is slowing down."

"I don't want to talk about the rain, Joel. Tell me about Crawl."

Joel stared at his feet. "Not much to tell."

"Oh really? That's why you rushed me out of the house? Why you have a knife?"

Joel glanced up only briefly, but Lorraine caught a glimpse of his bloodshot eyes. "He causes trouble in Shreveport."

"Why did he come here?" Lorraine set her coffee cup down, hands sufficiently warm. There was no way her stomach would calm enough to drink it. And she certainly didn't want to throw up all over his bathroom again.

"I don't know. Clancy spends a lot of time with him. He found me at the fair and then showed up last night."

Lorraine tried to remember Crawl's face. He hadn't looked at all dangerous. Strange, maybe, but not dangerous. "Why would Clancy spend time with him?"

"He makes sports bets with Crawl." Joel stood and took a few slow steps away from her. "I think Clancy has an addiction."

"Addiction?" Lorraine's throat burned. "To gambling?"

"He's lost a lot," Joel said with his back still turned. "I don't know if Crawl's coming around because Clancy still owes him or what. Either way, I don't like the way he looked at you."

"What would he want from me?"

"He likes getting a rise out of people, but with someone like him, you never know. You're safe here, though; try not to worry." Joel covered his mouth, but Lorraine saw the yawn.

"We ought to go to bed," Lorraine said.

"No, I'm fine." Joel rubbed his eyes. "I bet I won't be able to sleep anyway."

Lorraine stood. "That's a bet I'll take."

Joel reluctantly wiggled the door as if it had unlocked itself while they sat. "I'll put fresh sheets on Clancy's bed."

"Don't trouble yourself; it's fine."

"Okay. You packed in a hurry. Need anything?"

Lorraine patted her head. "I don't suppose you've got rollers?"

She saw Joel's smile for the first time since the movie. That seemed so long ago given the rest of the night's events. "I don't. Lipstick either."

"Darn. Guess I'll settle for one of those spare toothbrushes."

"Help yourself. If you need me, I'll be right across the world's smallest hallway."

Lorraine liked the narrow hallway, liked her proximity to Joel. Liked that he kept his door open. She had never cared for closed doors. Growing up, her parents shut hers when they were entertaining guests or having a disagreement. But she'd always open it back up. It didn't matter how loud it got, how happy or aggravated they were, their closeness comforted her. She felt the same now, hearing Joel snore.

But open door or not, it was strange to be back in Clancy's room, back in his bed. Clancy. Where was he? Two atomic bombs and no surrender. What were the Japanese waiting on exactly? A strange desire tugged at her. She longed to lie in Joel's arms and forget the realities of today, of her life right now. But she couldn't do that now, couldn't do it ever. Not if her prayers for Clancy to come home were answered.

***

The sun filtrating into the room disoriented Joel. Was it morning already? He pulled on his robe, cursing himself for sleeping the entire night.

There was no sign of Lorraine in Clancy's room, but the unmade bed assured him last night hadn't been a dream.

He found her crossed legged on the back porch. "Good morning," she said without looking at him. "Hope I didn't wake you."

"You probably shouldn't be out here."

"I need fresh air."

Joel sat next to her. He would have preferred this conversation inside, but Crawl would have already done something if he was going to. And it was the perfect time of the day. Before the sun stole the sparkling dew from the grass. "How did you sleep? Not as good as I did, apparently."

"I slept fine." Her tone was icy. "What's the plan today? Hide me out longer, or do I get to go home?"

Her ungratefulness stung. "You're not a hostage."

Lorraine took a bite of toast from the plate beside her. "I didn't mean it to sound that way."

"You've been through a lot. We'll figure it out." Joel watched sleepy birds scavenge for food across the lawn.

"Will we?" Lorraine tore the crust of her bread and threw it in front of her, drawing the birds closer. Joel blew out a series of short breaths, an attempt to gain control that failed him. "You okay? You are as white as chalk."

"Let's go inside."

The birds scattered when they stood, and Joel instantly relaxed. Like the imaginary hands choking him withdrew.

Lorraine gave a slight shake of her head. "What's with you Fitchetts and birds?" Joel didn't know how to begin to answer that.

Lorraine stopped short of opening the screen. "Do you smell smoke?"

Joel sniffed the air. "Yeah. Smells like it's coming from inside. Stay back from the house." He pushed past Lorraine to check the furnace and stove. The odor was stronger, but he couldn't locate the source.

"Joel! Out here!" Lorraine banged against the front door.

Heat attacked Joel as he stepped outside. Behind Lorraine's white, wide eyes were dark, billowing flames rising from Clancy's truck. "Call the fire department."

"Okay!" Lorraine said. "Do you have any buckets I can fill?"

"Stay inside!"

Lorraine flinched like he'd attacked her. Joel looked up from the hose he fought to untangle. "It's early, Lori. I'm in my robe. What will people think?"

She nodded. "Right. I'll call."

Joel stretched the hose as far as he could, but the stream of water barely reached the fire. The smell of lighter fluid was overwhelming, as was the taste of ash. The growing flames drew out neighbors. A few tried to help; others watched in fascinated fright. Joel wondered if Crawl was among them or had slunk back into Shreveport. The heat coursing through his body grew hotter than the flames.

At least his truck was in the garage. He rarely parked there but had last night to protect Lorraine from the neighbor's prying eyes. He would need his truck to get to Crawl. And he *would* get to him. He'd have to wait for the fire department to force these flames to surrender. Wait for the police to ask their questions. Wait to find a safe place for Lorraine. But when the waiting was over, Crawl's cat-and-mouse game would be too.

***

Lorraine sat on Joel's couch, kicking at her suitcase. It was nearly six. In ten minutes, she'd phone the police. What was Joel thinking? How could he fear birds and not confrontation with a man like Crawl?

Joel would be angry she'd come. But she couldn't sit at Lu's and listen to her friend ramble for another second. Couldn't stomach the needy cat rubbing against her stockings. Definitely couldn't listen to Lu's clock, louder than any ticking crocodile. For six hours, it reminded Lorraine that Joel was in danger.

She'd gone to her own home and packed a bag but couldn't stand to be alone there. But depending on how it went with Crawl, staying at Joel's may be riskier. So, she had a backup plan.

If she and Joel needed a place to hide tonight, they would find it in a simple hotel room in Kilgore, booked under a false name. Hopefully, he wouldn't find the idea scandalous. It was completely innocent, two beds innocent, but at least they'd be where Crawl couldn't find them.

She'd call her parents from the room and say she was spending the night with Lu. She'd done it before, and her mother didn't have Lu's number. Hopefully, she wouldn't ask.

It was one minute till six when a door slammed in the driveway. Lorraine pulled back the curtains, never so glad to see Joel's beat-up truck. But seeing a beat up Joel stumble out of it made her blood run cold.

Lorraine fumbled with the lock, but her sweaty hands failed her. She wiped them on her dress and somehow twisted the lock and then the doorknob. When Joel spilled in, she had to bite down on a scream. His face was nearly unrecognizable.

"Lock the door," Joel said before collapsing. Lorraine crouched beside him and raised his head. His right eye was black and blue, and his nose was obviously broken with a trickle of blood running into his mouth. "Check my stomach," Joel groaned. "It hurts."

Lorraine lifted his torn shirt. "It doesn't look as bad as the rest of you." She noticed bruises covering his arms and blood seeping through the knee on his jeans. Joel pressed his fist to his lips when she touched his stomach. She backed away, unsure what to do. Everything was moving too fast to process. "Can you stand? I can help you to the couch."

Joel did his best, but it was a struggle for Lorraine to get him across the room. He pointed down the hallway. "First-aid kit, bathroom."

A first-aid kit didn't seem near enough to fix the damage, but Lorraine grabbed the bandages and peroxide anyway. She leaned on the bathroom counter. Though it went against everything she felt, she had to stay calm. Had to handle this. Had to pretend this situation with Crawl hadn't just gotten bigger than the both of them.

***

"Don't fuss. I'm okay."

Lorraine examined Joel. "I think I got the worst ones covered. And the nosebleed stopped. Should we go to the hospital? Check for broken bones?"

"I'm okay." Joel leaned back, his face twisting like he was lowering himself onto a bed of needles rather than a couch cushion. "If you haven't guessed, I found Crawl."

Lorraine bit the inside of her cheek. "What happened?"

"I blocked the road leading out of his property and waited. Knew he'd have to leave eventually, and I wanted to talk without his entourage."

"Talk huh?"

"Started that way. I told him I knew he set the truck on fire and stole your nightgown. I asked if he stole the ring too."

"Ring? What ring?"

"Mama's ring," he said, so faintly she wondered if she had misheard. "I mean your ring."

"Crawl has my ring?" Lorraine looked at her empty finger.

"No, I got it back."

"Tonight?"

"No. Long story. Crawl told me Clancy lost it to him in a bet."

"Why would he do that?" Lorraine's chest hitched.

"Don't know. I told him to stay away from Crawl. I paid everything he owed, and he went back for more."

Lorraine dabbed a soaked cloth on a deeper cut on Joel's forehead. "Why would Clancy be friends with someone so dangerous? Why would he give his money away and my ring? Is that how little I meant to him? How little your mother meant to him?"

Joel grimaced and pulled away from Lorraine. "You're pressing a little hard."

Lorraine set the cloth down. "Now I feel like I'm the one who's been punched in the stomach."

"I'm sorry too. Sorry, that Clancy has gotten us both tangled up with him now. I can handle myself, but I can't keep letting him slip through your window." Joel slammed his bandaged hand on the coffee table Lorraine sat on. "I can't let him hurt you."

Lorraine prided herself in being self-sufficient, the captain of her own soul and all that. But Joel's words sent warmth radiating through her body. But it only took the thought of Clancy to turn her cold. Here she'd been waiting for him, loving him. Loving who she thought he was. But now it appeared he had another life he'd never bothered to share.

Joel touched her exposed forearm. "I shouldn't have told you about the ring. But it's just that I'm so...I'm so..."

"Angry." Lorraine finished for him. "I am too. Angry Clancy left me, that he's got us both into a mess. And call me a terrible person, but I'm especially angry about the ring."

"You aren't so terrible. I've been mad at him since we were boys." Joel spoke through his teeth. "It was always on me to watch Clancy, to make sure he didn't get into trouble. But sometimes I didn't want to be the big brother. Sometimes I just wanted to be a kid." He let his head fall back. "Feels good to say that."

Lorraine scooted the coffee table closer to Joel. "Then say more."

Joel hit a stray tear like it was a mosquito. "I always covered for him at work, covered for him with Daddy, paid his bills. I've always resented it. All of it, but I never stopped."

"You were just trying to help."

If Joel heard her, he didn't acknowledge it. "I'm mad because he was there when Mama died. I was with her the day before but knew she was holding on, holding out for Clancy. She always loved him more."

Something seemed to break inside of Joel. His shoulders quaked as he sobbed. Lorraine dug a tissue from her purse. He took it without looking at her. She knew he had more to say, so she took his head and raised it to meet hers. "Go on."

He took a pair of her fingers and used them to trace the rigid scar across his face. "I'm angry at him for this." He let her hand fall.

"Why?" She squeezed his arm. "Did he do it, Joel?"

"No."

"Then why are you—"

"Because this scar should have been his!" Joel's yell was the most chilling sound Lorraine had ever heard.

She pulled away. "Should have been his?" She kept her voice soft.

"He ran off." Joel rubbed the heel of his palm against his chest. "We were cleaning the yard before dinner. I said I was gonna help Mama set the table. But I didn't. I wrote a letter. A letter!" Joel's laugh was unsettling. "If I hadn't, Clancy wouldn't have left, and nothing bad could have happened."

"A letter?"

Joel's shoulders curved over his chest. "Asking Katie Montgomery to be my girlfriend. Planned to slip it into her bag when she left. It was stupid."

"That's sweet. You can't blame yourself for Clancy leaving. He was too old to need constant supervision."

"That's not what Daddy thought. When he found out Clancy was gone, he shook me till I couldn't see straight. Then he knocked me across the back of the head. Barely missed hitting the rake when I fell."

It was so hard for Lorraine to reconcile the man Joel and Clancy described with the Mr. Fitchett she knew. "How awful. It wasn't your fault."

"I was too scared to admit I'd lost him. Told Daddy he'd gone to pick berries. It wasn't the first time Clancy took off, so I wasn't worried. He always came back. But this time, he didn't, so Daddy sent me looking."

Joel stopped talking. He wasn't crying or yelling anymore, but his eyes looked feverish. Lorraine moved beside him. She wanted, *needed* him to finish the story. Partly to satisfy her own curiosity, but also for his own good. She was sure he'd never said these words aloud before and equally sure he needed to.

After a few minutes, he continued. "It wasn't how we were born or raised that made us the men we are today. It was what happened that day that set the rest of our lives in motion."

"What do you mean?"

"I got the scar. Clancy got everything else: the looks, the charm, the girls. The one before you, her name was Dorothy."

Lorraine opened then closed her mouth. This wasn't where she wanted the conversation to go. She didn't know any names nor stories of the girls before her and wasn't sure she wanted to. Ignorance being bliss and all that.

"I saw Dorothy first." Joel gave a scornful laugh. "Sounds petty right? But I saw her at the station and wanted to ask her out. Clancy encouraged it, but I was a coward. Just like I'd been with Katie Montgomery. Later that night, he's shuffling me into my room because he's got a date coming over."

"Dorothy." Lorraine slowly shook her head. "He brought home Dorothy."

"That night and every one after. Not sure she even knew I existed, locked in a room like a fairy tale monster."

Lorraine shifted in her seat. "Every night?"

"Until she stopped. I didn't ask what happened to her. It was standard."

A bitter tang took over Lorraine's mouth. She had never pretended she'd been Clancy's first, but the knowledge there had been so many made her want to take a third shower. She'd been a fool not to ask.

"But what I'm most angry about is the girl who came after Dorothy." Joel's puffy eyes locked on hers.

Lorraine took a minute to understand. "Me?"

"I realize he saw you first. I know he must love you. He never wanted to marry those other girls. But I'm furious because I don't think he deserves you. I'm even angry he asked me to look in on you because it's made it all harder."

"Made what harder?" Lorraine already knew the answer; she'd known for some time but wanted to hear it just the same.

Joel turned away. "Forget it."

"I don't want to forget it." Lorraine reached for his hand. "Because I'm angry about that too."

Joel's head whipped toward her. "Why?"

Lorraine considered the implications of what she was about to say. The words could change everything, but Joel had a right to know. "Clancy and I should already be married with a baby or two." Joel's hand went limp, but Lorraine continued. "I shouldn't be sitting here with you. Shouldn't have to shove down my feelings while I wait for him to come home or not come home. He put us in this position."

"Feelings? Joel pointed to his chest. "For me?"

He said it as if it were an impossibility. Like some silly scar made him a beast. Lorraine longed to take him in her arms and show him he was wrong. She imagined the two of them tangled in the hotel sheets, and her mouth watered with anticipation the same way it did when she smelled overripe strawberries.

Lorraine kept her face down. She didn't have to see Joel to know he was waiting for an answer. An answer she didn't have. Her feelings were too complicated for words. So, she didn't use any. She raised her head and pressed her lips against his.

It had been her experience that most first kisses started slow, a spark building to a fire. It was not so with Joel. Devouring flames erupted instantly. The smoke stench covering his clothing was Crawl's doing, but this heat was all them. The blood in Joel's kiss reminded her he was hurt, that she needed to slow down, but when she tried, he kissed her harder. "Do you want to go somewhere?" she whispered as he moved to her neck.

"Where?"

She remembered the hotel but didn't want to risk the night air cooling this heat. Taking his hand, she led him down the hallway. She was so disoriented, she turned toward Clancy's room. It brought to mind a night much like this four years ago when she'd led Clancy from that same couch down this same hallway. Her memory recoiled. Joel tugged her towards his own room, but her feet stuck to the floor. She was seducing her fiancé's brother just as she'd seduced him. What was wrong with her? Who was she? She needed to escape before the walls smothered her. "I can't."

Joel blew out a breath like he was extinguishing birthday candles. "It's okay," he said. "It's fine if you're not ready. But please don't..." He pointed his finger back and forth between them. "Please don't take this back. This with you and me, it's right."

"How can it be right?"

"Because...because I love you."

Her first instinct was to say it back. Her second was to let him lead her to the bedroom. She was ashamed of her impulses.

"You don't have to say anything. We don't have to *do* anything until we talk to Clancy. Until we explain. He'll be okay. He'll understand...eventually," Joel said.

Lorraine thought of her dad and Uncle Rick. "No, he won't. Not ever. And I can't be the one who comes between two brothers," she said, even though she knew she already had.

"Let's sit and talk this out. We can make it right somehow," Joel said breathlessly.

Lorraine stepped back, separating Joel's hands from her shoulders, separating her feet from the rose-patterned carpet. She had to make the next move. She could go to the couch, talk with Joel, try to untangle these knots, or she could go to the bedroom and make more. But neither of those options would make things straight again. So, she took one step and then two, until she was running out the door.

CHAPTER 22

It was 9:30, and Lorraine still wasn't home. Nor was she at Lu's or anywhere else Joel could think to look. Something must be wrong for her to miss her mom's 9:00 phone call.

Losing her was his fault. If he hadn't misplaced his keys, he could have followed her. For five years, he'd kept them on the table by the front door, but not tonight. And the five minutes it took to find them were five minutes in which anything might have happened to Lorraine. Joel's stomach ached. It felt like Crawl was still kicking him. He didn't want to drive around any longer, but he needed to stay in the vicinity of Lorraine's house. He settled on Mike's, a grimy bar up the road. There was a payphone, and after tonight's developments, a drink didn't sound half-bad either.

One drink turned to two, which turned to five. Joel stopped driving by Lorraine's after the third drink, stopped calling after the fourth. "Want another?" the wrinkled man behind the bar asked.

"Sure, why not?" It was only beer. Joel couldn't wait for whiskey to be available again. He would have forgotten about Lorraine altogether with enough whiskey.

"This one's on me." Joel turned to the stranger beside him. The three-piece suit and Fedora didn't exactly blend in here. And Joel was sure the seat had just been empty. Maybe he was drunker than he thought. "I'll take one too." The man swiveled his seat towards Joel. "Name's Norman Holden."

"Joel Fitchett." Norman's hand sweated like a cold beer. Where were those beers anyway?

"What brings you here?" Norman asked.

Joel grabbed the bottle before it hit the square napkin on the counter. "These."

"Good enough." Norman ignored his own drink, reaching for a briefcase instead. "Joel, I can tell by looking you are a man who likes to cut to the chase, get right down to business." He clicked open the case. "Forgive me, but that's quite the scar."

Joel clenched his fist. "What's it to you?"

"Business. It's business to me." Norman's voice and manner were matter-of-fact. "Helping people is how I earn a living."

A salesman. The greasy mustache should have given him away. Joel despised salesmen, and he hated Norman. Even if he had bought him a beer. "Not interested."

"Even if I told you what's in this case should clear that scar up overnight? Money-back guarantee."

Joel traced the lines on the beer bottle. "Whatever you've got, I've tried."

"Doubtful." He handed Joel a blue glass bottle with no label.

Joel turned it sideways, sloshing the liquid inside. Even without opening it, an acrid smell filled the air. "What's in this?"

"A special blend proven to heal scars. Newly discovered. FDA won't approve it. Not without further testing, but that's good for my business."

Joel handed the bottle back. "Proven? Heard that before." His tongue suddenly felt too big for his mouth. He should make this his last beer. Just in case Lorraine needed him later.

"You may have heard it before, but have you seen it? Norman pulled back the lining of his briefcase and handed Joel a small stack of pictures. Joel rolled his eyes but took them anyway. He couldn't *not* look.

The first in the pile showed a photo of an old man with a scar on his leg. In the next picture, the scar had disappeared. Joel laughed. "Nice try. But how do I know this one wasn't taken before he got the scar?"

Norman smirked. "You know, no one has even thought to ask that. But since you did, take a look at the next set."

Joel set the pictures side by side. In the photo on the left, a small girl had what looked like a nasty dog bite scar on her hand. It had not only vanished in the picture on the right, but the girl had aged at least a year.

Norman held two more photos against his chest. "I don't normally show these, but I want to be honest with you. Not all results are well…as perfect as those." He set the pictures on the bar but kept his hand over them. "Don't say I didn't warn you."

Joel shoved his hand away. At first glance, it looked like a photo of himself. The stranger was about the same age and build as Joel and had an eerily similar scar on his face. Joel picked up the next photo and held it to the light. The scar was still there, but just barely. A faint trace. Joel could live with a trace. He rubbed his eyes and looked again.

"You're not drunk." Norman opened his own beer and handed it to Joel. "Well, you might be, but what you are seeing isn't an illusion."

"How much is it?"

"Special bargain for today only, one hundred."

"Dollars? You're kidding."

Norman gathered the pictures. "You don't fool me, Joel. I know you have it, and I know you'd pay more."

"How did you find me?"

"By accident. Headed home to Tyler, got thirsty."

"And you just happen to have the oil with you?"

Norman pulled out a wallet from the briefcase. "I carry everything in here." He tossed a dollar on the counter. "Listen, I've got to be on my way, but here's a card if you change your mind."

Joel considered ripping the card up but stuck it in his wallet instead. He couldn't stop thinking about those pictures. You could fake claims, but not pictures.

Joel glanced at his watch but couldn't make out the time. The numbers blurred together. He needed to get home. He tried to stand but swayed like a withered tree.

"Easy there, fella." A wiry woman with hair the color of winter grass helped steady him. She pushed Joel back into his seat. "I think the scar is sexy." Her voice was gruff and her breath stale, but she was cute. If only Lorraine could see him now.

"Really?"

"You betcha. Shows you're a real tough guy." She squeezed his bicep. "That and the blood on your shirt." She propped an elbow on the bar. "You want to buy me a beer?"

Joel's stomach churned. "I don't think I can drink another one."

"You didn't hear me. I said buy *me* a beer. I mean, where else you got to go? You ain't rationed are you, sugar?"

"Huh?"

"Got a girlfriend?"

Joel picked at the label on his bottle. "Not too sure about that at the moment."

The woman stroked his forearm, her cloying perfume growing stronger as she leaned closer. "Well, seems if you're here and she ain't, she don't deserve you."

She had a point. How often was Lorraine going to do this to him? Start something and then run away like she was a victim of it? And it wasn't every day he met a girl attracted to him. No harm in one more drink. He reached for the stool next to him and dragged it close beside his. "Two more," he called to the bartender. Joel ignored the disapproving look on the old man's face and focused instead on his new friend's legs.

***

Joel sat straight up in bed. A decision he immediately regretted. Sudden movements were a bad idea. His head and stomach ached from the beers, and the rest of him hurt even worse. Crawl had a good arm on him, no disputing that.

"You gonna answer that?" a voice grumbled beside him. "Between that and the phone, it's hard to get sleep around here."

Joel flailed, knocking the lamp off his bedside table. "Who the hell are you?"

He might have slept through the phone, but her cackle made his ears ring. "I realized you were drunk, but not *that* drunk." She sat up, holding the sheet to cover her body, her *naked* body. The memories seeped in. Memories of what had almost happened with Lorraine, what had happened with this woman. With...

"Jillian?" he asked.

"In the flesh." The laugh again.

Joel rubbed his head. "This is a mistake. I love someone."

"Fair enough. But you had a good time, right?" Joel couldn't remember. Jillian let her sheet fall as she reached across him for her cigarettes. "You gonna get the door?"

"The door?" Joel hadn't even been awake enough to realize that had been the sound that awoke him. He tumbled out of the bed. "Lorraine," he knew instinctively. "Please go, Jillian."

He threw on a pair of jeans, tossing the lace bra under them to Jillian. He looked out the window and cringed when he saw Lorraine's car in front of the house and an unfamiliar one in his driveway. "Where's my truck?"

"At Mike's. I drove you back here."

Well, he was sunk. There was no way Lorraine hadn't seen Jillian's car. He hoped that she wouldn't ask, or he could think of a lie before she did.

He turned back to Jillian. "Can you sneak out the back? I'm sorry."

Jillian hopped on one foot, shoving a shoe on the other one. "Lighten up. You don't have to be sorry." Maybe not, but he was. Sorry for becoming the guy he despised. He was no better than Clancy.

As soon as Jillian closed the back door, Joel opened the front. "Lorraine! Come in!" His voice sounded too loud, too eager.

"Whose car is that?"

Joel felt his ears burn. "I had too much to drink, got a ride home."

"Oh." She looked over her shoulder using a hand to block the sun. "Should I go or..." The sunlight was glaring, but through it, he saw Jillian climbing into her Ford Deluxe. He leaned his head against the doorframe, anticipating Lorraine's reaction, but her face remained stoic. "So, can I come in, or not?"

Joel stepped out of her way. "Sure. Can I get you something?"

"I'm fine. I've been calling since four this morning."

"From where? I looked everywhere last night. I was worried."

"Obviously," Lorraine's scoffed.

Joel crossed his arms over his chest, suddenly very aware he wasn't wearing a shirt. "Okay, I deserve that. But I only ended up at the bar after one hundred miles down your road, after a thousand unanswered rings."

"I was in Kilgore." Lorraine used her hair to hide her face.

"Kilgore?" Joel raised his voice. "You didn't have to go so far for me to leave you alone. I just needed to know you were all right."

Lorraine crumpled onto the sofa. "I had a hotel booked earlier, for us."

Joel's heart hammered against his ribcage. "Us?"

"Yes, but only so we could be somewhere Crawl couldn't find us. I didn't plan on what happened here last night. I let my emotions get the better of me." She crossed her legs, clasping her hands over her knee. "I started something I couldn't finish, so I can't blame you for finding someone else who would."

"That...that..." Joel hunched to appear shorter. "That wasn't your doing. I'm a grown man, and I should have more self-control."

"Still, I'm sorry for running out." Lorraine's grip on her knees whitened her knuckles. "It was the only way I knew to assure something stupid wouldn't happen."

Joel took an uneven step away. *Stupid?* That Lorraine would regret being with him just as he regretted being with Jillian was an unexpected blow. At least he'd seen Crawl's fists coming.

"Joel, do you understand? What happened was a mistake."

Joel turned his back to her. "I'm tired of being a mistake."

Lorraine stood. "But you're not a mistake. What *happened* was. There's a difference."

He felt Lorraine's hand on his shoulder, her warm, sweet breath on his neck. He put his own hand on top of hers. "It didn't feel like a mistake, still doesn't."

Lorraine yanked back her hand. "But it is. And you know why."

Joel faced her. "But if Clancy wasn't in the picture?"

"Don't, Joel."

"I need to know the truth. If you were hurting, and I was here, say so. But if it was more than that, even a little more, say that too."

"Why?" Lorraine's fingers made small, jittery movements against her sides. What good will it do you to know? Because either way, we can't be together."

"I'm done being confused." He pointed outside. "You've confused me from day one on that porch swing."

"Have I?"

"Yes. A little then, a whole lot now."

"I don't know what you want me to say. If it weren't for Clancy, we'd have never met."

Joel shook his head. Lorraine was dodging, and she was good at it. "You know what I mean."

"Was I emotional last night? Yes. And lonely." She rubbed her forehead. "I've been so lonely. But I can't blame only that. I have had…desires. Dreams even. I'm fond of you." She looked at the carpet. "More than I have a right to be."

"What kind of dreams?"

"Dreams of another world." Her cheeks turned pink. "Please stop. I can't talk about this. I won't. Clancy and I are in love. We are getting married. That's the world we live in. That's the world that is real."

"But what if?"

"No more what ifs. Not ever again."

Joel wanted to change her mind, wanted to push, but he was afraid he'd push her out the door again, out of his life. "Okay. You answered me. I won't ask again, but please, sit back down."

"Why, Joel? We can't just go on like none of this happened."

"We can," Joel said, but he knew he couldn't. Knew he didn't want to. He needed to remember her touch last night, her words tonight. It may be all of Lorraine he'd ever hold onto.

She looked at him like she could see straight through him and put her hand on the doorknob. Joel needed to show her he was serious about honoring the line she'd drawn.

"Wait," he said, backing into the hallway.

Joel navigated the mess in his room to get Mama's ring from the dresser. His shaky hands dropped it twice, requiring him to dig through dirty clothes and sheets to retrieve it.

Lorraine was still at the door when he returned. Slipping it on her finger wouldn't be appropriate, so he held it out. Like a peace offering. "This is for you." She narrowed her eyes at him. "From Clancy, of course."

She let go of the doorknob to take the ring. "Thank you."

"I'm sorry I took so long to get it back to you."

"Considering the journey it's been on, I can hardly blame you."

Lorraine glanced at the clock. Joel realized she wanted to leave, that she needed to even, but an almost manic energy surged through him. He had to know he'd see her again. "I'm off Tuesday," he said. "Going to Carthage to get my teeth cleaned. Want to tag along?" Joel knew it was a strange thing to ask, but it would mean he'd get to see her again, and a dental appointment was hardly something she could consider inappropriate.

"Okay." Lorraine stole a glance at the ring in her hand again. She was being kind not putting it on in front of him. "I'd love to see your dad," she added. She opened the door then closed it again. "Since you're up, why don't you get dressed and come to church with me."

Church. Joel didn't care to go there any more than Lorraine probably cared to watch Daddy scrape plaque off his teeth, but this was how it had to be. These were the safe ways they could be in each other's lives. And it felt okay for now.

***

The war ended on a Tuesday. Lorraine would always remember that. Her pastor had prayed it would end on Sunday, and on Tuesday, it did. She'd been with Joel on both days. When they got the news, Joel threw up his hands and cheered; she broke down crying. And here she was seventy-two hours later, still crying. Equal parts relief and fear overwhelming her. What if they could not find Clancy? What if they did, but him being back didn't squash her feelings for Joel like she was counting on?

"He'll be back," Joel had assured her. "It will take time, but they'll get him home. And everything will be fine." Lorraine loved him all the more for saying that. He could have been disappointed their time together was ending. Worse, he could have hoped Clancy didn't come home at all, but Joel didn't know how to be selfish. He was always so good. Better than she was.

She wished he could be with her today. Lately, she needed his calm reassurances like she needed air. But he was working, so she drove alone to Lake Lamond, the place she'd been avoiding four summers. It finally felt safe to be here, safe to remember the moments she and Clancy shared under these trees. She needed to write the final chapter of her novel and hoped she could glean some inspiration from nature.

The roar of a nearby motorboat drowned out the noise of an approaching car, then approaching footsteps. It wasn't until Lorraine heard breathing, heavy and close enough to raise the hairs on her neck, she dropped the pen. She went to retrieve it, but someone beat her to it.

"Oopsy Daisy."

Lorraine recognized the voice first, then the face. She jumped up, her foot tangling in the blanket beneath her.

"Nice ring," Crawl said.

Lorraine stumbled backward. With the war ending, her parents' arrival, and the mess with Joel, she hadn't even thought about Crawl. Hadn't been careful like she should have. "What the hell are you doing?" She tried to sound tough, tried to keep her voice steady.

"Just wanted to chat. Have a seat, won't you?"

"Is this about money? You won't get a dime from me or my family."

Crawl knelt to straighten the blanket. "With all due respect, Miss Applewhite, I think you'll reconsider when you hear what I've got to say..."

CHAPTER 23

Gib Lewis Unit, 1991

Garrison's eyes kept straying to a table across the room. Today it was filled with board games and coloring books, a makeshift visiting corner for prisoners and their children, but two months ago, it had been where he'd met Joel Fitchett. He had learned a few things since his first visit: a suit wasn't necessary, and Joel Fitchett wasn't as scary as he wanted everyone to believe he was.

"I hate to admit this, but I'm impressed." Joel pulled out his chair. "How did you swing this?"

"The contact visit?" Garrison shrugged. "Just talked to the Warden."

Joel smiled. "What did it cost you?"

"A generous donation. Designated for use towards new, top-of-the-line alarms, similar to the ones at Huntsville."

"Uh-huh. Warden's still in a pissing contest, huh?"

"Good thing for you, I guess."

"Yeah, good thing." Joel edged his chair closer to the table. "Say, did you find out if it's Lorraine putting money in my account? I've been thinking, and I'm sure they have to pay with checks. Checks have addresses."

"I tried, but even bribery wouldn't buy me that information."

Joel tucked in his upper lip. "Oh well."

"But contact visits are reinstated," Garrison said, in a *look at the bright side* tone. "And not just for today. Well, as long as you keep your hands to yourself."

Joel held a cigarette between his teeth and waved over a guard. "How about you don't say anything that would justify me using my hands."

Garrison hoped nothing he had to say could provoke Joel, but leading with questions was never a good idea. He looked back at the kids table and spotted a deck of cards. "How about a game?" Garrison waited until the second hand to discuss anything that didn't involve runs and sets. "I ran into someone in Carthage who remembers you."

"Bet lots of folks in Carthage remember me."

"You'd be surprised. People know the story, but there aren't many left who know you."

Joel's hand hovered above the ace Garrison had discarded. "Oh hell, I'll take those sons a bitches."

If Garrison's dad had taught him anything about this game, it was to never hold aces in an early hand. But Garrison would not offer the same advice to Joel. Taking risks suited some men. Garrison decided to take one of his own.

"Do you remember a boy named Jack Monroe?" Garrison asked.

Joel looked up. "Your play."

"He was a kid from your school who went missing. Do you remember?"

"Vaguely. Why are you asking me about some runaway from a million years ago?"

"Because a friend of his told me Jack acted strange after..." Garrison searched for a way to say it without mentioning the scar. "After July 1932."

"He always acted strange, the whiny little puke."

"Well, his parents were abusive."

"Oh sorry, Oprah. I forgot that parents are to blame for all society's woes. Hell, my daddy was abusive too. Maybe it's his fault I'm here." Joel chuckled when he caught the irony.

"What do you think happened to Jack?"

"I always suspected the Boogeyman myself." Joel propped his chin on his fist. "You gonna draw?"

The ace Garrison drew could play into his run, but he discarded it as a gesture of goodwill. "It was so soon after what happened to you, I wondered if there was a connection."

"How does any of this wondering lead you to Lorraine?"

"I don't know." Garrison set down his cards and rubbed his forehead. "I don't know how anything fits in. That's why I'm asking. Jack told someone he saw whatever happened to you; then he disappeared. Clancy also saw, and he disappeared too. Albeit years later."

"I doubt they joined witness protection together if that's what you're asking."

"What about Crawl?"

Joel's eye twitched. "Crawl? What do you know about him?"

"He disappeared too. Right when Clancy and Lorraine did. Who was he?"

"A sonofabitch."

"But he and Clancy were friends."

Joel set his own hand down and looked at Garrison like he'd grown a second head. "Hell no, they weren't."

Garrison waited for elaboration, but Joel picked back up his cards and played his turn.

"Joel, I can't help you find Lorraine if you won't be honest with me. Earl told me Clancy got mixed up with a Louisiana boy. That was Crawl right?"

"They weren't friends." Joel's thundering voice made Garrison squirm.

"Okay, okay. They weren't friends. But they were acquainted and left town at the same time. Coincidence?"

"Yes."

"I thought we were playing Loony Rummy, not Bullshit."

Joel hit the table. "Just stop! The less you know about Crawl the better."

Garrison restacked the draw pile Joel had disrupted, a question turning over in his mind. A question with a fifty percent probability of landing him on the floor again. "Why did you hate Crawl so much? Did he do this to you?" Garrison asked, hoping Joel understood what *this* meant.

"No."

"Then why; who is he?"

"He saw it, okay?" Joel scanned the room. "Now pick up your damn cards. Guards are watching us now."

Garrison collected his cards but didn't bother re-situating his hand. Crawl was there when Joel got the scar? But Mr. Nevins had said..." Garrison's head jerked up. "I'm asking about the same person, aren't I? Jack Monroe *is* Crawl."

Joel didn't answer. He didn't have to. The puzzle wasn't a complete picture yet, but pieces were sliding into place.

"And Clancy getting involved with Crawl...that was blackmail?"

"We didn't think there were witnesses." Joel's voice was calmer now. "We should have known nobody gets off that easy. Crawl ran into Clancy on his 18th birthday. Told him what he saw, threatened to go to the law if Clancy didn't pay every month."

"And Clancy told you?"

"It's your draw."

Garrison drew and discarded without even looking at the card. He had no idea what he needed for his hand anymore. "How long did Clancy pay?"

"Years. Right until he got captured and couldn't anymore. That's when Crawl unleashed hell." Joel laid down his cards. "I'm out."

"What did Crawl see? What was worth paying so much for?"

"Save it for the interview, Geraldo."

Garrison jotted down his score. Nice to know Joel had as much knowledge of television personalities as he did. "Tax dollars well spent," his dad would say.

"But you don't have any idea where Crawl headed when he left Louisiana? Or why he left right after Tom's murder?" Garrison asked.

"Nope. Never sent me a postcard."

"Could Clancy still be paying him?"

"I think we took care of that a long time ago." Joel divided the cards into two piles. "But with a man like Crawl, who knows. I wouldn't be surprised if he's found Clancy. Or if he never lost him."

Garrison dropped his pen. "So, if I can find Crawl, I can find Clancy?"

"I didn't say that." Joel mis-shuffled, sending cards flying. Garrison reached across the table to help, but Joel pressed down on Garrison's hand. "Whatever you're thinking, don't. Crawl is dangerous, and I don't want *you anywhere near him*." Joel let go and glanced toward the guard, making sure he hadn't seen the physical contact.

"If Crawl's still alive, he's not the person you remember. He's an old man."

"So am I." Garrison listened to the whoosh of the cards as they cascaded back into a single pile. "And I still got your skinny ass on the ground easy enough, didn't I?"

"Touché."

Joel looked at the clock. "Twenty minutes left. Time to do less yakking and more playing." He pushed the pile across the table. "Your deal, Gary."

Garrison had to ask him what hand they were on and lost count twice on the deal. Eighteen minutes till he could get out of here. Two hours to get back to Longview. He realized he'd been a jerk to Molly, but maybe she'd be interested in helping him devise a plan to get from Roxanne to Crawl and then Crawl to Clancy. Or maybe she'd just want to go on a date. With what he'd learned today and Amber out of the picture, suddenly everything seemed possible.

***

Two hours and eighteen minutes later, Garrison stood on Molly's porch, throat closing as the door opened. A door he fully expected would slam back in his face.

"Oh hey, man," Lew said. "Come in."

"Molly around?"

Lew craned his neck. "Pap, is Molly upstairs?"

"Welcome back, Garrison." Ray ignored Lew. "Sorry about your grandmother."

Garrison stuck his hands deep into his pockets. "Thanks. On both counts."

Ray nudged Lew with his cane. "Go get your sister." When Lew cupped his hands, Ray whacked him harder. "Don't yell at a woman. Use your legs while you still can." He turned back to Garrison. "Speaking of, you don't mind if I sit?"

"Of course not." Garrison was about to suggest the same. Ray seemed to be gasping for air, and he looked like he'd lost at least ten pounds in the last week.

"How was home? Get your affairs in order?" There was something about Ray's tone that suggested he'd known another girl was in the picture all along.

"I did." Garrison looked him straight into Ray's hollowed eyes. "Everything is in order."

"Good. So, it's safe to say you are back for Molly, not Clancy?"

Garrison's throat constricted again. Couldn't he be here for both?

"Garrison!" Molly flew down the stairs, saving him from having to answer. She looked like she'd stepped off the set of 90210 with her denim button shirt and black leggings. Her hair fell down around her shoulders, curled and teased. His instant jealousy made it hard to appreciate how good she looked. She hadn't known he was coming. All this was for someone else.

"Hey! Hope I'm not interrupting anything."

"Not at all."

Ray struggled back up. "Excuse me, but it's time for my nap. You two need to catch up."

Garrison waited for Ray to hobble out of the room before he hugged Molly. He was surprised to find it was still awkward, even with no guilt about Amber.

Molly pulled back. "Are you okay?"

"I'm fine."

"You don't look fine."

He grinned. "Thanks."

"Nothing a shower and a shave won't help." She touched his cheek, and he still felt the electricity. "May need a couple razors."

"Yeah okay." Garrison rubbed his scratchy chin. "I've been distracted. I promise I'll take a shower as soon as I get checked in the hotel."

"You're staying at a hotel?" Molly's voice dropped with the question. "Guess that was my idea, huh? Sorry."

"Don't be sorry. Let me be sorry. Sorry for how I acted after the pool. Sorry for not calling since. I haven't had my head on straight."

"How's it now?"

"Spinning a little," he said. "I talked to Joel today."

Molly's eyes widened. Why did she have on so much eyeliner and mascara? He'd never seen her wear eye makeup. "What did he say?"

"We should discuss that caffeinated and over French Fries." He looked at her face again. He could actually smell the makeup. "Unless you already have plans."

"Oh." She pressed a hand against one side of her head, flattening her hair. "My friend Lauren is responsible for this. She's back home for the summer."

"That's great." Garrison nodded vigorously. Molly didn't seem like the type to get makeovers at sleepovers, but at least she wasn't dressed this way for a date. "Did you girls have fun?"

"Not really. Turns out the lunch was an attempted set up. I should have known when she insisted on putting me in this ridiculous outfit."

Garrison kicked lightly at the coffee table. "Oh, well you look nice." His clenched teeth caused a dull ache in his jaw.

"I look terrible." Molly took a Kleenex and wiped off her lipstick. "Lunch was terrible. I'd love to forget about it over a pot of coffee."

A slow smile spread across Garrison's face. If he wasn't worried Ray was watching from the hallway, he might have kissed her right there. But given that it had been over 48 hours since his last shower, waiting felt prudent. "Ready when you are, but you better bring your notebook."

Molly grabbed her notebook from the back of the couch. "I had it out last night when I tried to call Roxanne."

"You found her?"

"Hold the enthusiasm. All I managed was to say I was calling about her brother."

"She hung up?"

"My bet is on slamming the phone down."

"We'll figure something out. It's not bad news. She knows something or she wouldn't have hung up. I mean, what if you were saying you had found her missing brother?"

Molly rubbed her forehead. "Is it hot in here?"

"Not really." Garrison notice the shine had faded from Molly's face, and her lips, just wiped of red, now had an icy blue tint. "Are you okay?"

"I think so," she said but stumbled forward a few steps.

"Molly, you need to—" He didn't have time to finish. He barely had time to catch Molly before her head hit the coffee table. "Lew!" He screamed, feeling for Molly's pulse. "Help!"

Lew dropped his Game Boy when he saw Molly. "What happened?"

"Call 911!"

Garrison was situating Molly on her back when Ray appeared. He dropped his cane and cried out in pain as he lowered himself to the floor. Garrison hoped he wouldn't need an ambulance for both of them.

Ray leaned his ear close to Molly. "She's breathing. What do we do?"

Garrison couldn't remember. All the years of first aid training, all the lives saved and now when it was personal, nothing. He brought a shaky hand to his forehead. "Um..."

Ray gently slapped Molly's face. "No, don't do that," Garrison said. "It won't do any good." But Ray only slapped and shook harder.

Watching Ray lose it, somehow helped Garrison regain his own composure. "Check her airway; then loosen her belt, anything tight." Garrison grabbed several couch cushions and propped up Molly's legs.

"It's her heart." Ray unbuttoned Molly's collar, as his tears dripped on her face, now as blue as her lips. "Hold on, Molly," he said. "Hold on, baby. Pappy's here, and help is coming."

***

Garrison watched the machine's green lines spike up then down. The steady beeps comforted him. Assured him that Molly's heart was still beating. Any deviation of the pattern caused his own heart to patter irregularly. But the nurses never acted alarmed by the squiggly line movements, so he tried not to either.

Molly was asleep now, but stable. Garrison hadn't been here when she woke earlier. Only two visitors allowed in the room, and Lew and Ray were family.

It wasn't that late, but Garrison couldn't keep his eyes open. He tried to get comfortable on the paper-thin cot they'd rolled in for him, but it was no use. No matter what time of night, hospitals were never really dark, never at all quiet. And the smell, a strange combination of over-bleached sheets and death, choked him. He switched the lamp back on and was searching for the remote when Molly stirred.

217

"Garrison? What are you doing here?"

He blinked to free his dry contacts from the insides of his eyelids. "I've got the night shift. Need anything?"

"French fries," she croaked.

"Pretty sure the night nurse will have my head if I bring you those. I got Cheez-Its from the vending machine, and she eyed me like the saturated fat would seep through the air and clog your heart valves."

Molly smiled. "Thanks for being here."

"Anything to get out of the shower I promised to take tonight." He spotted the plastic cup and straw beside her bed. "Here, drink water."

"Got any coffee?"

"You have a better chance of getting fries. You're supposed to be limiting your caffeine."

"They always overreact. All for a little heart murmur."

"You know, I'd like to believe you, but the doctor said you have a heart valve disease. That's something I don't remember you mentioning. Nor that you will need surgery."

Molly wriggled up in her bed. "Surgery is an *option*." Garrison was relieved she didn't ask how he knew such confidential medical information. If they didn't want anybody reading the charts, they shouldn't have just left them lying out in the door slots.

Garrison fluffed the pillows behind her. "You need to take care of yourself."

"I do. Stop sounding like a dad."

"Well, according to Ray, your actual dad and mom are cutting their trip short and will be here next weekend."

"Fabulous." The tray wobbled as Molly slammed down her cup. "If anyone can make me have a full-fledged heart attack, it's Mom. But let's not talk about her. I want to hear about your visit with Joel."

Garrison pulled the corner chair beside her bed. The screech surely jolting another weary visitor from their sleep. He felt like Goldilocks, trying to situate himself in the well-worn chair as he filled Molly in on his morning.

When he finished, Molly brought her IV free hand to her mouth. "Holy crap. To think Jack was involved in their lives for years. He still might be making Clancy pay."

"Joel mentioned them handling that. I didn't fully understand."

"And you didn't ask him to clarify?"

"He's not exactly an open book. I know that you semi-worship the guy, but he can be a huge jerk."

"Roxanne." Molly ignored the insult. "Roxanne's the answer. You gotta make her talk. She must know where Crawl is."

"Easy now, Hamilton. I'm not with the mafia."

"You can find a way," she said. "Tomorrow."

"Not tomorrow. I'm not doing anything till you are better."

"Garrison, I'm fine. There is something to this. Crawl fleeing right after the murder. What if he and Clancy were in it together?"

"Slow down, will you?" Molly looked like she was seconds away from unplugging herself from the machines and going to talk to Roxanne herself. "I understand you want to exonerate Joel, but you're reaching."

"Or Crawl could have killed Tom because Clancy stopped paying. We are so close to finding out. So close to finding Clancy. You don't see how big this is!"

"I see how big it is, but I also see how big that nurse is. And if she was upset over the Cheez-Its, I shudder to think what she would do to me for raising your heart rate."

"Okay." Molly's voice lost its power. "I promise to chill out, promise to rest as long as I can trust that you are doing the work."

"I'll go visit her sometime this week, as long as you keep improving."

Molly bounced a curled knuckle against her mouth. "If you are here, that must mean Lew is staying with Pappy tonight. Do you mind going back to help? Lew doesn't know to give him his sleeping pill or—"

Garrison stood. "It's handled. Jill's staying tonight, and I hired another nurse from the same agency to start nights tomorrow until you're able to go home. Everyone and everything is taken care of." He unbunched the blanket from the end of the bed and covered her. "Your only priority is you."

"Okay. Okay." The bed creaked as Molly rolled onto her side. "Goodnight, Garrison. Thanks for everything."

"Goodnight, Molly." He switched the lamp off and settled back in his cot. He looked forward to a time when he could kiss her goodnight and fall asleep beside her. But until then, he'd settle for the melody of her heartbeat lulling him to sleep.

CHAPTER 24

Longview, Texas, 1945

Everything had changed. Lorraine marveled at how the same life could look so different, unrecognizable really, in a matter of weeks. Six weeks since the war ended, three weeks since Clancy came home. Lorraine opened her diary and tried to find the words to describe these three weeks and two days. Upheaval came to mind.

She'd been so relieved when Mr. Fitchett received word of Clancy's whereabouts. Thinking of Clancy in that horrible camp turned her stomach, but he was alive. He could come home and all would be well.

And it had been. The minute Clancy wrapped her in his arms, she knew everything was just as it should be. Watching Joel hug his brother only confirmed her belief. Whatever turmoil between the trio fled in the presence of the familiar.

Of course, it wasn't all familiar. Though Clancy claimed to have gained 15 lbs. in the hospital these past weeks, he was still a skeleton. But he still smiled the same, still held her hand the same way. No, he hadn't wanted to talk about the war, but that was normal. Not something she had any right to force.

Returning to work so soon had been Clancy's idea. Said he needed to stay busy. He rode with Joel while Mr. Fitchett fixed up an old car for him. Joel told Clancy his truck had caught fire but spared the details about why. Clancy didn't need to worry about Crawl anymore. He hadn't been back, and Lorraine suspected that after the conversation at the lake, he wouldn't be.

The trouble started on a Friday. Clancy huddled in the work restroom and refused to leave. When Mr. Rogers tried to intervene, Clancy punched him. By the time Lorraine arrived to pick him up, Clancy had calmed, but Mr. Rogers, holding an ice bag against his face, decided Clancy needed another week off. It had sounded like a good idea, but in hindsight, Lorraine wasn't so sure.

For every day since, Clancy drifted further away from her, further away from everyone, except maybe the devil. He stopped wanting to go out then stopped wanting to get dressed. There were regular nightmares, ones he couldn't seem to fully wake from—and a temper that turned faster than the Texas sky.

When Joel came down with the flu, Lorraine's father offered Clancy their guest room—a decision he surely regretted after being awoken three nights by Clancy's screams. Lorraine found Clancy each time drenched like the Sandman had baptized him and impossible to calm. Is this what Joel had dealt with since Clancy returned? Is this what she would deal with always?

Lorraine slammed the diary closed when her door creaked open. "Clancy! What are you doing? Mother and Daddy will murder you if they find you here."

"Can we talk?"

It was hard to look at him and see anything besides the black circles framing his red, hollow eyes, but he was dressed. Out of bed and dressed before ten. That was something. "Can we do this downstairs?" She felt childish to worry about Clancy in her room. They should be married already. Did Clancy even want that anymore? He hadn't mentioned the ring, the wedding, or the marriage. Was she being impatient or was he being unfair?

"It won't take long." Clancy straddled the chair to the vanity. "Want to go out today? If you don't have class?"

She had class. They had discussed this last night, but she was so thrilled Clancy wanted to go out, she didn't care about class. Even if it was her last semester.

"Yes! I'd love to!" she said too loudly. "Give me just a minute to change."

Not wanting to give Clancy time to change his mind, Lorraine skipped the shower. She put her engagement ring on before thinking better of it. That was a conversation she wasn't ready for, so she exchanged it for her grandmother's ruby ring. Just wearing any ring made her feel better than she had all week. A ring on her finger and breakfast with Clancy. Just like old times. She dared to wonder if maybe the worst was behind them.

***

Joel hurt all over. His throat, nose, and stomach seemed in competition to be the sorest place on his body. Just when he thought his nose won, a coughing fit set his abdominal muscles on fire. For the last three days, he'd filled a pitcher of water and set it with a fresh box of tissues beside the couch. Buried under four blankets, he slept when he could and listened to the radio when he could not.

Joel hadn't felt like eating today, yet when the phone rang, and he pictured Lorraine on the other end, he found the strength to stand.

"Hi there. Just checking in."

Joel collapsed against the wall. "Hi, Daddy. Nice of you to call." It *was* nice. Joel didn't have the right to feel disappointed. At least someone cared. Three days and not a peep from Lorraine. He should have known she'd forget all about him when Clancy was back to keep her bed warm.

"I won't be well enough for Sunday dinner," Joel said. Even the flu had its perks.

"Let's reschedule for next Friday. We'll make a big deal of it, go all out for Clancy's birthday."

Clancy's birthday. Joel had forgotten. Yet Daddy hadn't, even though he had no trouble forgetting Joel's every year.

"Are you sure he will come?" Joel asked.

"According to Lorraine, he will."

Joel perked at the sound of her name. "You talked to Lorraine?"

"Briefly. She and Clancy were heading off for a day on the town. Look, son, I've got a patient. Glad you are better."

Better? He felt worse. A day on the town? Must be nice to have a girlfriend to pay all your bills. Well, not *all* of them. Joel was still on his own for the rent, he supposed. He'd missed three days of work and didn't get paid for sick days. He'd sort it out like he always did, but it would be nice for Clancy to consider him. It wasn't even his brother's behavior that bothered Joel most. It was Lorraine's. How could she claim she cared and not even check on him? She had forgotten him, and that realization caused his heart to hurt worse than the rest of him combined.

***

Something wasn't right. Clancy couldn't put his finger on what, but he wasn't himself. Didn't feel like he was in complete control of his limbs. And felt even less control with his emotions. He should be thankful. He was home. Home to a great gal and supportive family. So why wasn't he happy? He owed it to all those men who didn't come home to be happy. He had to try harder. Had to do better. Had to bury what happened to him. Had to stop the waves from crumbling a perfectly good castle. Had to. Had to. Had to.

"Anywhere special you want to go?" he asked Lorraine, who held his hand as they strolled along Tyler Street. She squeezed too tight, walked too close, but how could he tell his fiancée she was crowding him?

Lorraine looked into a bakery. "I told Mother I'd get a loaf of bread. Want a bagel?"

Clancy wasn't hungry, but the smell of yeasty bread and melted butter might restore his appetite. And if not, so what? It would make Lorraine happy, so it should make him happy too.

But when Lorraine set the tray on their table, his stomach turned. So much for getting his appetite back. It would just take time. Just like so many other things would— sleeping, looking in the mirror, wanting to live.

"Plain or salted?" Lorraine asked him.

"Either is fine. I could have paid."

"I wanted to. It's nice to order without worrying about having enough ration coupons."

"Huh?"

Lorraine bit the salted bagel. "The coupons used during the war. It was nothing. Nothing I should complain about."

"I understand times were hard here too."

"Not hard compared to..."

"Hey, it's not a contest. We survived. That's what matters."

Lorraine smiled, and Clancy tried to return it. He ran his tongue across his chapped lips. He needed water but thought coffee might kick this week-long headache. As he reached for the cup, his watch bumped the receipt, causing it to drift like the leaves falling outside the window. "I got it." He crouched under the table but froze when he saw the number written on the paper.

Be rational, Clancy told himself. It was a list of prices: two coffees with cream, 22 cents, one plain bagel, 15 cents, one salted bagel, 15 cents, a loaf of bread 09 cents. But every time he looked, his eyes read the last column vertically. 2559. Six months as a prisoner known only as number 2559, and now here it was again. That cursed number taunting him.

Lorraine met his eyes under the table. "Everything okay?"

No, it wasn't okay, but she'd never understand. "Just fine." Clancy sat up too fast, and for a moment, the bakery went black. "So, no class on Friday?" Small talk was all he had the strength for.

"Actually yes, my class meets on Fridays, but today is just review." She fidgeted with the sugar dispenser's spout.

"You should have said something."

"I did. Last night. Don't you remember?"

"Oh, that's right." Clancy forced a bite of the bagel into his mouth. "I remember." He didn't. He forgot a lot of things lately. Things like his address, what happened in the last chapter of the Steinbeck novel he was reading—and apparently an entire conversation with Lorraine last night. Lack of sleep might have been the culprit. But Clancy couldn't help but wonder if some tropical bug had crawled into his ear. Right now, it could be eating holes into his brain like it was a Banana Leaf.

"So, your father called this morning. Wants to celebrate your birthday on Friday. Sound good?"

Clancy eyed the receipt under the table. "Sure."

Lorraine clapped. "Great! What kind of cake would you like? I don't even know your favorite kind. That's a shame, isn't it? Let's see, we could do…"

Clancy drummed his fingers on the table as she spoke, tapped his foot, pushed his chair out, and then scooted back in. It was like when he was seven, and that ant colony took up residence in their back yard. "Just keep moving," Daddy had said. "Keep moving and they won't get you."

Clancy had been resting when the Japs captured him. It couldn't have been more than five minutes he'd been still, resting in the grove of palm trees.

Lorraine perched her elbows on the table. "Do you remember my favorite?"

Clancy beat his ankle against the leg of his chair. He had to keep moving, or the ants would ascend. "Chocolate?" he guessed.

"German chocolate, thank you very much. And yours?"

German chocolate. Germans. Those bastards tattooed numbers on Jews' wrists. At least Number 2559 wasn't burned into his flesh. But it was a part of him just the same. "Any kind is fine."

"But you must have a favorite."

"Vanilla." Anything to make her stop.

"All right if that's your favorite. A dull choice, I hoped for more of a challenge."

"I haven't forgotten everything. You hate cooking, so I didn't want to give you anything too difficult." He tried to remember if this was how to flirt.

"I'll have you know, Clancy Fitchett, that I took a few cooking lessons."

"Is that so? At school?"

"Mother wishes. She tried to get me to study home economics. Actually, Joel taught me."

Joel, huh? The thought set wrong with Clancy, and he couldn't say why. Jealousy maybe? Not about Joel and Lorraine, but imagining them enjoying themselves while he was trapped in a place where burying bodies became as normal as washing dishes. "Sounds fun," he said through gritted teeth.

"I wouldn't go that far, but it's not completely awful. Baking is downright enjoyable as long as someone else cleans up the mess. Can I count on you for that?"

Clancy sensed someone behind him. His chest tightened. Why had he sat with his back to the counter? Never turn your back. Lorraine droned on about cooking mishaps, not even realizing the danger. Had she always been this self-involved?

"I made a few messes, but I didn't burn a thing!" she chirped.

What *the hell* was that sound? Why was someone just standing there instead of moving through the line? Clancy clenched his fists and spun around. But there was no danger lurking in the shadows. Just a pair of teenagers leaning against the tall glass case filled with donuts. The girl held a muffin, crinkling the paper between her fingers.

"Clancy, are you okay?" Lorraine touched his arm.

"Sorry. What's that you said about brownies?" Clancy couldn't listen to her. Not with all this noise: an oven timer dinging, the slide and catch of the cash register, the chime of the bell on the front door, and still that goddamn muffin wrapper. There was a buzzing that rose above the rest of the noise, like the sound wind made in a tunnel. But before he could cover his ears, came the worst sound of all. Familiar words, but not comforting ones. Words that raised the hair on every inch of his body. Japanese words. There was a Jap in here. Clancy whipped his head around the bakery, taking in every face.

"Clancy?" Lorraine stood. "What's the matter?"

The voice grew louder, but Clancy could not locate the source. Was it coming from outside? From a baker in the back?

Lorraine touched her stomach. "I'm not feeling well. Let's get some fresh air."

Sweat soaked Clancy's collar. How could the voice be this loud when its source wasn't close enough to be seen? He was hiding.

He was checking under tables when Lorraine grabbed him. "What on Earth, Clancy?"

"There's a Jap," he whispered. "Hiding."

"A what? No. No there isn't. You must be daydreaming.'

"I heard them! Someone is speaking Japanese." Clancy tried to yell louder than the disembodied voice.

"We are in Texas. What you're hearing isn't real." Lorraine stood on her toes to get closer to his ear. "You're making a scene, Clancy."

He let her pull him out the bakery, but the voice didn't quiet. Maybe it was a ghost. Clancy didn't know what scared him more, that one of his captors had found him, or if a ghost of a man he'd killed had. Either way, someone was still torturing him. His knees gave, and he hit the pavement with a thud. Lorraine crouched beside him speaking words he didn't understand any better than he did the Japanese ones.

She eventually stopped talking and stroked his arm till the spinning stopped. Till the voice stopped. Clancy lifted his head, blinking in the sunlight. Lorraine's face was red and smeared in makeup. A crowd circled them. "Do you need me to call a doctor, miss?" someone asked.

Clancy waved his hand. "I'm all right." Lorraine's ring dug into his skin as she helped him stand. Mama's ring? He spun the band around to reveal a single ruby. Not Mama's. Crawl had that. Crawl. Clancy crossed his arms over his chest. Forgetting his birthday was one thing, forgetting Crawl was another. Collateral. That's what Crawl called the ring. Clancy wasn't getting his paycheck while a prisoner, but Crawl wouldn't care. He'd surely sold the ring by now. What if he'd gone to the police?

Clancy grabbed Lorraine's arm to steady himself. "I need you to drive me somewhere."

"Huh?"

"Shreveport!" He pawed through his wallet to see if he had enough to make it right.

Lorraine lowered Clancy's wallet. "It's taken care of," she whispered. "Crawl is taken care of."

***

Lorraine wanted to call Joel. She needed to talk to someone about Clancy, and he was the only one who would understand. And she missed him. Missed him so much she knew calling wasn't smart even under the pretense of discussing only Clancy.

She was putting rollers in her hair when her father peeked in. "Are you turning in?"

"Yes, it's been a long day."

"So, I gathered."

Lorraine froze. "What do you mean?"

"Mrs. Davidson called your mother. Seems Mrs. Horowitz told her about an incident at the bakery today."

"Clancy was tired." Lorraine resumed rolling. "Exhausted really."

He nodded. "Well, Mother is worried. Especially after finding him drinking wine in the middle of the night."

"So what? Wine helps everyone sleep. No one fusses at Mother for her glass *or two* at bedtime." Lorraine didn't understand her own defensiveness. Didn't understand why she couldn't just tell the truth.

Her father stepped through the door. "It's not the first time. I found an empty bottle of whiskey in the trash Wednesday."

"If you didn't want Clancy to drink your alcohol, you shouldn't have told him to make himself at home."

"I'm not worried about dwindling liquor; I'm worried about Clancy's state of mind."

"What's to worry about?" Lorraine avoided Daddy's eyes. "Don't you think I'd notice if something was wrong?"

"A breakdown at a bakery sounds like something *is* wrong."

She opened her mouth to argue, but what could she say?

"It's nothing to be ashamed of. A lot of soldiers are coming back with that battle fatigue. Some are even seeing doctors."

Doctors. Lorraine liked the idea of a doctor treating Clancy's mind just as they'd set a broken bone. But she'd never convince him to go. "Clancy doesn't need a doctor. He needs our support."

"Well, he's got it. One hundred percent. Get some shut-eye."

Lorraine would have cried, but she couldn't keep her eyelids open for it. She needed rest as much as Clancy did. If he suffered another nightmare, he would need her, and after today, she wasn't sure she had anything left to give.

***

A shrill scream jolted Lorraine straight up in bed. So much for a good night's sleep. She rubbed her eyes, disoriented by the sunlight peeking into the room. It was already morning, late morning. And it wasn't Clancy screaming; it was her mother.

227

"Just calm down," Daddy's voice rose up the stairs. "No one needs to get hurt."

Lorraine set off for the kitchen, almost hoping it would be an intruder, hoping it would be anybody but Clancy.

She found her mother pressed against the stove, shaking uncontrollably. Daddy stood in front like a shield, his pounding pulse visible in his neck. "Move away, Lori!" Her mother yelled.

Lorraine grabbed the counter when she saw Clancy. He looked like a rabid dog—a rabid dog holding a kitchen knife. An actual burglar might have been less frightening. Clancy waved the weapon. "You can't keep me here! I'm an American!"

Lorraine took a small step closer. "Clancy, you aren't a prisoner. Daddy let you stay here since Joel is sick. Do you remember?"

"Lorraine, get away!" Daddy stepped towards them.

But it was too late. Clancy grabbed her by the back of the hair, yanking her body against his. She shivered at the coldness of the steel against her neck and the agony of her mother's scream.

"Stop right there!" Clancy pulled Lorraine closer. "If you take another step, she's dead."

Lane raised his hands in surrender. "Drop the knife and leave. Nobody will follow."

The kitchen blurred through Lorraine's tears. What was happening? Was this her own nightmare? Maybe she'd be the one to wake up screaming.

Clancy's grip choked her. "Please, Clancy. You're hurting me." She brought her hand up and pushed the knife away. It was a risk, but so was feeling her neck indent beneath the blade.

Clancy went limp, and the knife clinked against the floor. His eyes searched the room frantically.

"It's okay." Lorraine tried to stroke his damp hair, but he charged for the back door.

She turned to follow, but another set of arms enveloped her. "Let him go, Lori," Daddy said. "He's not right. You can't help him."

He was right. Clancy was beyond her reach right now. But she wouldn't just sit here either.

"Let me go; I need the phone."

"Good idea, call the police." Birdie closed the drapes above the sink. "He headed south."

Lorraine dialed Joel's number instead.

"Hello?" Joel's voice sounded frailer than even hers. She was probably draining the last of his strength, but she desperately needed to siphon it.

"Joel, I need you. Something has happened."

The response came without hesitation and without questions. "Be there in five minutes."

***

Joel was glad Lorraine called. Even if the reason was Clancy, as he suspected, it was nice to be needed. Nice to be outside again. The air smelled damp and earthy. It was the first day it really felt like fall, and chill bumps covered Joel's arms as he approached Lorraine. She was still in her pajamas and didn't appear bothered by the cold. "You okay?"

She fell forward into his arms, warming him. It was so good to hold her again.

"Clancy's gone," she said into his shoulder.

"Gone? Where?"

Lorraine pulled away and then pulled herself together enough to explain what happened. It almost sounded unbelievable.

"A knife you say?" Joel's fingers splayed like a fan against his breastbone.

"Yes." She crumpled onto the porch step. Joel didn't sit beside her for fear he couldn't get back up. His muscles were heavy, and his eyes shut involuntarily. He needed to stay up, stay moving.

Joel looked into the house. "Is everyone okay?"

"Everyone but Clancy."

"Did he take the knife?"

"No."

Joel offered his hand. "Come on, let's go get him."

"I think it's best you go alone. My parents will worry themselves to death if I go, but promise to call."

Joel hated his disappointment, hated how he longed for a few minutes alone with her again. "Okay. Try not to worry." He wished he could take his own advice. What if Clancy was with Crawl? Joel had been no match for him in perfect health. There was no way he would survive a fight today.

Lorraine reached for his hand and squeezed it. "Find him, Joel."

229

He squeezed back. It wasn't enough, but it was all he could do. "I will," he promised.

A carpet of leaves crunched under his feet as he made his way back to his truck. Others scattered into the road, blown one way then the other by the fickle wind, seemingly as confused as Joel about which direction to go.

***

Joel walked back through his door late that night. He hadn't found Clancy, but ten hours into his search, the tired hit him like the fist of Joe Louis. In spite of the exhaustion, he felt better than he had all week. Maybe he was on the final leg of the flu, or maybe the fresh air did him good like Mama always claimed.

Lorraine was probably worried, but he would let her call. If he slept on the couch, he'd hear the phone. It was late, and he didn't want to wake Mr. and Mrs. Applewhite, not without good news.

He hadn't been asleep long when something woke him, the sound coming from the door instead of the phone. Disoriented, Joel fumbled to turn the lamp on. "Clancy? It's unlocked." The doorknob twisted, but there was a brief hesitation before it pushed open.

"It's just me." Lorraine looked at the loveseat as if she expected to find Clancy crammed there.

Joel wiped the drool off his chin with his shirtsleeve. "He's not here."

"Sorry I couldn't help earlier." Lorraine pulled Joel's jacket from the hook. "Mother and Daddy didn't think I should, so I waited till they were asleep."

Joel checked his watch. Nearly midnight. "They don't know you're here?"

"I left a note. It's fine." Lorraine tossed the jacket at him. "Come on, let's look."

"I've looked, all day."

"He's not right, Joel! We can't leave him somewhere overnight."

"Clancy's not a ten-year-old anymore. It's not my responsibility to find him." Joel hated himself for yelling, but sometimes Lorraine didn't know when to quit.

She made an odd noise in her throat. "Fine, I'll go myself."

Joel kicked off the blanket. "Lorraine, wait. I'm telling you, he's not out here. Not anywhere you can find. I've checked the hospital, called Daddy, even asked the police. I didn't file a report, but will if you want."

"I don't want him to get in any trouble."

"I don't think he will." *He never does.* "But I promise if he's not back by morning, I'll search again. With fresh eyes."

230

Lorraine sat on the couch's opposite end. Her face was turned, but Joel could tell she was crying.

"He's embarrassed," Joel said. "I don't know where his friends live. He may be with one of them. He needs time."

"What about Crawl?"

Joel couldn't pretend he hadn't been thinking the same thing. "I don't think he's there. Shreveport would be quite the trip on foot."

"Unless he got a ride." Lorraine's shoulders heaved, but despite her tears, Joel kept to his side. One touch and they'd be back where they swore to never go again. That is all it would take for him, anyway.

"You need rest. Go home and sleep. I can pick you up at seven, and we'll look again."

Lorraine pulled at her jacket collar like it choked her. She didn't seem to notice the button that snapped off, flying across the room. "I don't want to go home. I won't be able to sleep, and I don't think I can be alone with my thoughts right now."

"You can stay here." Joel hoped she didn't detect the desperation in his voice.

Lorraine tipped her head, weighing the idea. "But you're sick. You look exhausted."

"It's fine," Joel said, already on his way to put the coffee on.

***

Bright headlights shining through the front window woke Joel. His arm tingled. When he tried to move it, he realized why. Lorraine was laying on it. He replayed the night in his foggy brain. They had sipped coffee and talked. Then what? His last memory was leaning against the arm of the couch, fighting to stay awake. Apparently, that was a fight he'd lost. But why was Lorraine next to him? His entire body tingled. She didn't fall into his arms accidentally.

He didn't want to move, but outside, a pair of doors slammed in near unison. What if Lorraine's parents were here? He couldn't let Mr. Applewhite find them together like this. He wriggled his arm free and struggled to climb over Lorraine. She stirred but didn't wake.

Joel didn't recognize the Pontiac Streamliner in the drive nor the woman it belonged to. But that was Clancy, bent over in her arms. Joel charged for the door, just beating them to it.

Clancy stumbled forward. "You gonna let me in?" His entire body reeked of yeasty beer.

"Dammit Clancy," Joel hissed. "Keep it down! Lorraine is here."

"Is she?" Clancy spilled into the living room, but Joel put up his arm, blocking the frizzy-haired blonde. "She's not coming in. How could you, Clancy? Lorraine's worried sick."

Clancy weaved toward the couch and leaned too close to Lorraine. "Don't look so worried."

Joel left his post at the door to pull Clancy away from Lorraine. "Don't touch her."

"Relax! It's fine. I went to Carthage and had a drink." He laughed. "Had a drink a few times."

"Carthage?"

"Yeah, Carthage." He pointed to the loveseat where the woman now slouched, making herself at home despite Joel's wishes. Her uncrossed legs revealed light pink underwear, and her skirt would surely split in two if she spread her legs another inch. "Libby gave me a ride home." Clancy's eyes went right between her legs, and Joel's skin crawled. She was such a contrast to sweet Lorraine nestled on the couch.

"Well, she needs to leave."

"That's his girl?" Libby sneered. "Looks like a fun one." A wad of white chewing gum slipped from her mouth as she laughed.

Joel grabbed Libby's arm, yanking her from the couch.

"Hey, let her go!" Clancy yelled.

"Fine." Joel did, and Libby crashed to the ground. Clancy ran to her aid, but she pulled him to the floor. They made a pathetic pair down there, trying to stand, giggling with no sign of stopping.

"See how he rushed to my side?" Libby composed herself enough to speak. "Always a perfect gentleman. You can tell Sleeping Beauty there I said so."

Joel handed Libby the keys that had fallen from her pocket. She was in no position to drive, but she was the least of his worries right now. He turned to Clancy. "Get up. Do you want Lorraine seeing you like this?"

"Too late," a whisper of a voice said behind them. 'Too late."

***

Lorraine wasn't sure how long she'd been sitting on the back porch. She was tired of hearing Clancy carry on. Tired of Joel trying to force him to bed like an obstinate toddler. The sounds of boisterous crickets and arguing neighbors were preferable—but just barely.

She pushed away the blanket Joel brought her. She didn't feel the cold. How could Clancy do this? Yes, he was confused this morning with the knife, but bringing another woman home? That was deliberate.

When Joel opened the back door, she no longer heard Clancy's yelling. All day she'd wanted to hear his voice, but now she was glad she couldn't anymore.

"Clancy's asleep. He swears nothing happened with that woman. He was adamant that I tell you."

"Right. Sort of like how nothing happened between you and the woman I saw leaving here?"

Joel broke eye contact. "I never claimed nothing happened."

Lorraine brought her legs close to her body. The night's events obviously unearthed an old hurt. "You're right. And I have no right to be angry about that."

"Yes, you do. I'm sorry. That's not the kind of person I —"

"But I *do* have the right to be angry about this." Lorraine let her head fall into her hands. "What are we going to do, Joel?"

"Maybe Doc Banks can give him something to steady his nerves. We don't have to figure it out tonight. It's 2:00 AM."

"Is it?" She jumped up. "I need to leave."

"You don't have to."

"We need to get some sleep."

Joel pushed his hands into his pockets. "We were."

"Don't read something into that, Joel." Lorraine shook dirt from the blanket. "I was upset and tired. It wasn't like—"

"I'm fully aware of what it wasn't. But it *was* nice."

It had been nice. Lorraine missed the comfort only Joel gave her. Would she still be missing it had Clancy come home complete? He'd brought comfort once, hadn't he? Did the war render him incapable now or had he never made her feel what Joel did? It was hard to be certain. Young lovers only wore rose-tinted glasses or even blindfolds, never bifocals. All she was sure of was that Joel hadn't changed. He was still a rock. A rock for Clancy and for her.

What if Clancy never snapped out of this battle fatigue? Would she always wake up to screams, or worse, his hands around her throat? It would be a life of locking wine cabinets and hiding knives, of always looking over her shoulder. That uneasy image contrasted sharply to a life with Joel. A life of falling asleep in the arms of the one person you knew would do anything to protect you.

She shook her head. It was too late to think about this. "I need to go home. I'll just use your restroom and be on my way."

Joel didn't respond, but when she came back to the living room, he was lying on the couch. Why wasn't he sleeping in his own bed? And was it her wishful thinking or was he leaving room for her? *You don't have to leave.* His words echoed in her head.

But she did. She had to be in her own bed before Daddy woke up at 6:30. Joel was sick, and Clancy was right down the hall. But then again, would it be so terrible if Clancy sobered up and found them together? Maybe it would make him realize he could lose her. Or maybe he would lose her. Either way, a change in her life's trajectory didn't sound half-bad at the moment.

She slipped her shoes off and kicked them under the coffee table. "Is there an alarm?"

Joel smiled. "In my bedroom."

If Joel thought she'd sleep in his bed with him, he was wrong. She wasn't a fool. She brought the alarm into the living room and set it for 5:45. Neither said a word as she switched off the lamp and lay beside him.

The last thing she remembered was the warmth of the blanket and the scratch of Joel's whiskers as she edged closer to him. She slept sounder than she had in months and was back home by sunrise. Her parents and Clancy none the wiser.

CHAPTER 25

Longview, Texas, 1991

Molly had improved considerably by Thursday. The talk was that she'd be released in the next few days. Garrison was glad, of course, but had actually enjoyed these last three days with her. Long talks and slow walks around the hospital corridors by day, sitcom reruns and card games by night.

Garrison was disappointed when Ray arrived to relieve him early that morning. He offered to stay—he wanted to stay, but Molly wouldn't let him.

"Pappy's well enough to sit here for a day with me. It's the 4th of July. Go celebrate," she's said.

Garrison didn't feel like celebrating, not without Molly, so he used the morning to move out of her place and back into the Value Inn. Her parents would be home tomorrow, and while Ray insisted they'd be fine with the arrangement, Garrison didn't need to add any awkwardness. Living there with Ray was bad enough without throwing parents into the mix.

He spent the morning in the hotel's pool, but it was overrun with kids. Kids didn't want to swim. They wanted to scream and splash.

Garrison wasn't due back to the hospital till eight that night. He tried to watch television, but couldn't stomach it. He'd go crazy if he had to hear the results of one more paternity test or watch the silver-haired judge settle one more ridiculous dispute.

With a daytime swim and daytime television off the agenda, there was nothing left to do but what he'd been avoiding, visiting Roxanne. After all, he'd promised Molly he would, if she would rest and improve. She'd held up her end of the bargain; now it was his turn.

He had a plan, sort of. There was a good chance it wouldn't work, but at least he could tell Molly he tried.

Garrison changed into his grungiest clothes. Wasn't hard since that was the style nowadays, but he needed to look even younger than he was.

He borrowed Lew's truck and loaded their lawnmower in the back. The drive took longer than he expected. He had to pull over twice on the way to check his map.

The house he stopped at had lost two of the address numbers, but it had to be the right one. It was the color of washed out jeans, covered in crusty paint peels and multicolored graffiti. It looked abandoned with two boarded up windows and shards of glass littering the yard, but a car sat in the driveway. If you could call that junker a car.

Garrison trudged through a labyrinth of weeds and stray grocery bags to the front door. A loud bang startled him. He hoped it was a firework, but in a neighborhood like this, one could never be sure.

A piece of blue painter's tape stretched over the doorbell, so Garrison tried the screen door. Locked. Banging on the screen made little noise, but it did summon an army of dogs.

The door opened just enough for a woman to peek through. "You the landlord's boy? Tell your daddy to go to hell. My brother sent the check last week." The door closed in his face. Her brother? This was a good start. Well, despite the slamming door.

"I don't know your landlord." Garrison struggled to be louder than the yappy dogs. "I'm here to mow your lawn."

The warped front door scraped open. A small Pekingese with matted fur jumped against the screen, nearly pushing it open despite the lock. "Dammit, Madge!" She picked up the dog and threw it behind her. "The lawn, you say?"

Now in full view, Garrison got a good look at Roxanne. She looked familiar somehow even though he was sure he'd remember seeing her before. A wisp of a woman, five feet at best, gained another two inches by spiked gray hair. She tried to hide her age with spandex shorts and a halter-top, but the weary and weathered face gave her away.

"Yes, the lawn." Garrison pointed to the lawn mower.

She pulled her glasses down and looked over the leopard spotted rims. "Did my brother pay for it?"

"No, but..."

"Well, I ain't got any money."

"It's an outreach my youth group is doing. Just making my way down the street to find someone I can um...bless."

Roxanne's face transformed, became softer, younger even. "God bless you for doing the Lord's work. Bible says the young are supposed to care for the orphan and widow."

"Are you a widow, Ro...?" Garrison stopped short of saying her name.

She unlocked the screen "More or less. Sonofabitch ran out thirty years ago. But he may be dead. Hope so." She stepped out and waved her cigarette, flinging sparks. "Do you pull weeds too?"

Garrison figured he didn't have much of a choice. No way those suckers were coming down by lawn mower alone. "Yes, ma'am."

"Good. I'll let you get to work. Need anything?"

Garrison studied the yard. "Got a trash bag or two?"

***

Three hours, and well over two trash bags later, Roxanne's yard was trash and weed free. When he hauled the bags to the dumpster, he caught a glimpse (and smell) of the backyard, obviously used solely for the dogs' bathroom. Thank God his imaginary youth group only required front yard service.

He knocked on Roxanne's screen again. She stepped outside with the passel of dogs that nipped at Garrison's sweaty socks. "Holy crap!" Roxanne said. "Don't even look like my yard."

It didn't look like a yard that belonged anywhere in this neighborhood, actually. "Glad you like it."

"Missed a little by the sidewalk, though."

Garrison's lips pinched together. Was this lady serious? The yard had been a jungle when he showed up. "I didn't bring an edger."

"Next time then." She whistled at the dogs, now scattered and sniffing around their new yard. "Get your little furry butts back in here, girls." She looked at Garrison. "Well, thanks. Do I need to call your priest or somebody? Tell him you done good?"

There was no way Garrison worked the last three hours to leave with nothing. "Mind if I come in for a glass of water?" He used his shirt to wipe the sweat from his face. "Pretty warm out here."

"Sure! You'll have to forgive my manners and the mess. Don't get many visitors."

Garrison covered his nose when he stepped in. At least the smoke stench slightly masked the unmistakable odor of dog piss.

Roxanne wiped fur off a faded plaid couch, covered in burn holes. "Sit down. I'll get you a drink. Don't think there's any Kool-Aid left. Just water and whiskey, but I guess God don't allow you to have the latter?"

"Water's good." The floorboards gave and bent beneath him with each step. The couch wasn't any sturdier, and he sank into it like quicksand.

The room was cluttered with various knickknacks, all dusty and cobweb-coated. They were mostly ceramic mice, but it was likely real ones leaving the tiny pellets along the floorboards.

A stack of mail on the coffee table called to Garrison. As soon as Roxanne left for the kitchen, he leaned over to snoop. The top envelope looked like an overdue bill. The faded coffee cup stain suggesting it served as a coaster for a while. He noticed the name: Ms. Della Hunt. Della Hunt? Had he spent his afternoon in the wrong yard?

"Looking for something?"

Garrison jumped. "Just realized I didn't remember your name, so I cheated. Della is it?"

She handed him the water. "Nah, that's my crazy neighbor. Keep forgetting to take it over. I'm Roxy."

Garrison exhaled. Close call. He sipped the water, trying to ignore the dirty glass. Or maybe the water was dirty. What did it matter at this point? "I'm Tony," he said. It was the first name that came to mind. An obvious pick with a last name like Stark. Iron Man had always been his favorite comic.

"Glad you stopped in this neighborhood, Tony. It's like I won the lawn lottery."

"I can imagine it's tough to take care of a house and lawn like this by yourself."

Roxanne pulled the ceiling fan's cord. "I ain't no damsel in distress."

"No, it's a lot of work for anybody. Did you say your brother helps?"

"From time to time. I'm on a fixed income. He's got more money than he knows what to do with, so he throws some at me sometimes." She lit another cigarette. "His idea. I don't ask for charity."

Says the woman who asked Garrison to come back and edge her yard for free. He tried to ignore the growling dog climbing his leg. Between the five (or six?) dogs and smoke, Garrison probably had about ten minutes before he dropped dead from an asthma attack. "Does your brother live nearby?"

"Nah, he's back west."

Garrison sank even further into the couch. "West like California?"

"California?" She said it like a foreign word. "Hell no. West Texas."

Garrison smiled. "Right. Where else is there but Texas?"

"I sure as hell don't wanna find out. Mother and Daddy didn't raise us to be no tree hugging hippies."

"Do you see him often?"

Roxanne glanced at the water-stained ceiling. "Nah. He doesn't get out this way much, but we talk on the telephone."

Garrison considered for the first time she may have more than one brother. One born after Jack ran away. "What did you say his name was?"

"I didn't." Roxanne snuffed out the cigarette. "Excuse me, but I gotta let the girls out before they ruin the carpet. Then it'll be time to get dinner in the microwave so..."

Garrison stood. "Right. I'll get going. Mind if I use the bathroom first?"

"First door on the right." Roxanne prodded and kicked the animals outside. She turned back to Garrison. "Come back again and remember the edger."

As soon as she left, Garrison shuffled through the pile of mail, checking the back door often. The whirl and rattle of the ceiling fan made it impossible to hear anything else, and he couldn't afford to get caught again. But there were only bills and junk mail, nothing from Jack Monroe.

Garrison headed straight into Roxanne's bedroom. It was obvious she wanted him to leave, that she didn't like chit-chat. Short of edging her yard, she wouldn't invite him back. All he had was now. The room smelled like a college dorm room, the odor of pot mingling with the smells of sex and unwashed socks. He held his breath and dove in, searching for more mail, photo albums, maybe even an address book. The messy room made it both easier and harder. Hard to find what he was looking for, but he didn't have to worry she'd notice anything out of place.

He was elbow deep in candy wrappers and romance novels when Roxanne whistled for the dogs. He slammed the drawer and ran for the bathroom. After a quick flush of the toilet, he ventured back into the hallway. He paused by the shelf that held the telephone, disappointed to see a picture hanging where others may post a list of phone numbers. There was something haunting about the small and barefoot set of children in the black and white Polaroid. The solemn expressions didn't fit them any better than their too-small clothing did.

"That's me and my brother."

Garrison jumped. Roxanne had a knack for appearing out of nowhere.

"Sorry." She nudged him playfully. "Easy to sneak without those damn dogs following me."

"That's alright. I'm just admiring this picture."

"It's a good one ain't it? Me and Jack." She leaned against the wall. "On my seventh birthday."

So it was Jack, a nine or ten-year-old Jack, Garrison guessed. Possibly the last picture taken before he ran away. Garrison was surprised he hadn't seen it in the papers. It would be plastered in grocery stores and on milk cartons nowadays.

"He made me a cake." Roxanne gave a slight smile. "Course he stole the eggs from our neighbor, so Daddy whipped him. Jack stole a lot, but he was like Robin Hood. Robbing from the rich to give to the poor. It was my first cake."

Seven years without a birthday cake? Garrison usually got two. One on his actual birthday, one for a weekend party with friends. He would have sacrificed one for someone else if he'd known not everyone had it as good as he did. Maybe Robin Hood and Jack Monroe were on to something.

But feeling sorry for the kids in the photo wouldn't give Garrison the answers he needed. "Sounds like a great brother. When's the last time you saw him?"

"Been a long while. He came back for my 50th birthday and made me another cake. I got a picture of that day too." She turned to the opposite wall. "Same kids, but in color. Sad story to only have two pictures of your big brother." The other photo, a framed 5X7, hung crooked on the wall. Besides all the polyester, the first thing Garrison noticed was that somewhere in the forty-three years between the first and second photo, Jack and Roxanne had learned to smile. Roxanne's eyes were squeezed closed as Jack squeezed her in a bear hug. Only Jack's profile was visible, but he looked so familiar. If you took away the sideburns, it almost looked like...Garrison stepped closer and stared till his vision blurred. It couldn't be. His pulse sped.

The man in the picture looked younger, stronger, happier, but it was him. "Ray." It came out almost involuntarily. He looked to Roxanne, sure he'd given himself away, but she looked as confused as he was. "Ray? No. That's Jack. That's my brother Jack. Who the hell is Ray?"

Garrison was beginning to wonder the same.

***

Garrison needed time to think. He drove aimlessly around Longview, windows down, listening to the whistle and bang of fireworks.

His first instinct was to confront Ray soon. But then he thought of Molly. If he went in with both guns blazing, he might ruin everything. What had Joel said about Crawl? That he blackmailed them? Caused trouble when he was younger? There were worse things a person could do. And even if he had been a terrible kid, it didn't mean Ray hadn't changed. He had made a good life and stayed out of trouble. Molly was crazy about him. He'd come a long way from that boy with no shoes or birthday cakes. Did Garrison want to exhume old bones? No, he didn't. But he wanted to find Clancy. Did Ray know where he was? Had he been so against Molly and Garrison's digging because he was worried they'd find out about the man he used to be? Or the man he still was? A dangerous man like Joel claimed? It didn't seem possible.

As much as Garrison tried to make sense of it all, he couldn't. There were too many missing pieces. And Ray wasn't the only one hiding something. Joel was too. He'd start there.

It might be a dead end, but something told Garrison this time it wasn't. He'd found Crawl in the most unlikely of places; maybe finding Clancy would prove just as easy.

***

"Hi there, stranger." Molly sat up in bed. She looked even better tonight. Her face had more color and she'd washed her hair. Had to be the telltale sign a girl felt better. Even one like Molly who swept it into a ponytail before it had time to dry.

"Hey, Hamilton. Feel better? You look it."

"I've been fine all along; they wouldn't believe me. You look better too."

Garrison rubbed his smooth face. "A shower and shave work wonders. Any word on the last of the tests?"

"Results tomorrow." Ray's voice made Garrison's scalp prickle.

"Hey, Ray. Didn't hear you come in."

"He's sneaky like that," Molly said. She had no idea.

Ray stared down Garrison like he realized something had changed. Like he could see right through him. Garrison bent to tie a shoe that didn't need tying.

241

"Well, young lady, Lew should be out there waiting to take me to watch the fireworks. You know anything, Garrison?"

Garrison's head snapped up. "Huh?"

"I asked if you need anything?"

"Oh no, I'm good." Garrison stood. He needed to calm down. Ray knew nothing. He'd been here all day, and it wasn't like he and Roxanne were close. She didn't even know he moved back.

Garrison waited till Ray left to take Molly's hand. "So, are you really doing okay?"

"Yes. Pappy took good care of me." She twisted her hospital bracelet. "Just dreading tomorrow. Lew picks up my parents in the morning." She looked back at Garrison. "I guess you won't be around as much now?"

He sat on the edge of her bed. "I figured I'd give you time with them this weekend, but I'll be back."

"Be back from where? Are you going to visit Joel?"

Geez. Molly really didn't miss anything. Well, except for her grandfather's fake identity. "No, I'm going to Tyler. Check out the planetarium there. I hear it's pretty sweet."

"A vacation? I thought you said you'd talk to Roxanne."

Garrison wanted to tell the truth. Molly had been his teammate from the start, but he couldn't tell her this. "I tried, Molly, but she wouldn't answer the door."

Molly plopped back on a mountain of pillows. "Okay, so now what?"

Garrison didn't know what to say. He couldn't keep talking about this, not when he couldn't be honest.

He grabbed the remote. "Let's see if we can find some fireworks to watch."

"On TV?"

"Sure, why not. DC sure has some pretty ones."

"Pretty? Come on, Garrison. Fireworks are a package deal. You've got to smell the sulfur in the gunpowder, hear the deafening bangs, and see the lingering smoke."

Garrison laughed. "Good point. "I mean if it doesn't feel like you are in the actual Battle of Bunker Hill, what's the point?"

"Exactly. Well, if the Battle of Bunker Hill involved lawn chairs and a cooler of beer."

Garrison looked out the window. "Well, I doubt they will let you drink any beer, but maybe I can convince them to let me wheel you out to the lawn when the city display starts."

"Okay, but it won't be dark for another hour and a half at least."

Garrison turned on the TV. "*90210* or *Wings*?"

"Do you think this is the best use of our time? Let's skip TV tonight and figure out Plan B before you take off for the weekend."

"I'm positive laughter is the best possible use of our time tonight," Garrison said, flipping the channel to *Wings*.

Garrison sprawled out on the cot and turned up the volume. He wasn't paying much attention to the antics at Tom Nevers Field Airport, but he laughed when the show's laugh track cued him to. He couldn't talk to Molly tonight, so she had to believe he was lost in the Hackett family instead of his own.

His own and her own, as it turned out.

CHAPTER 26

Longview, Texas, 1945

The ride to Carthage was mostly quiet. Clancy was mostly quiet these days. "How's your day been so far?" Joel threw out a topic like a boomerang, knowing it would come right back to him. Having a two-sided conversation with Clancy was impossible nowadays.

"Good, you?"

"What does my day matter? It's your birthday." Joel had tried to make Clancy's day special with omelets for breakfast and a new hat. That was something, or it should have been anyway.

Clancy leaned his head against the window. "I messed things up, didn't I?"

"Don't ask me; ask her."

"She won't return my calls."

Joel knew that much. Lorraine hadn't returned any of his calls this week either. He blamed the Applewhite's housekeeper. She spoke little English and didn't seem to grasp there were two Fitchetts calling. Lorraine probably assumed all the calls were from Clancy.

When they pulled on to their father's property, Clancy perked up. "Hey is that...?"

"Lorraine," Joel answered, never so glad to see her car.

Clancy pulled a comb from somewhere and ran it through his greasy hair. It was amazing to watch Clancy's transformation at the site of the car. Not just the combed hair, but the way the light reentered into his eyes, the way he smiled again.

Joel adjusted the mirror to check his own reflection. He should have shaved. "Ready?" he asked, but Clancy was already outside the truck, tucking in and trying to smooth wrinkles from his shirt.

Joel struggled to keep up with Clancy. They'd raced this dirt road a thousand times as boys, and they still were. Lorraine met them at the door and greeted

Clancy with an embrace that punched Joel in the gut. He told himself it was all a show for Daddy's benefit.

"I didn't realize you were coming." Clancy appeared stiff in her arms.

"Wouldn't miss your birthday. Who else would make the cake?"

"Not me." Daddy stayed in his chair but looked over his shoulder. "Happy birthday, son. My god! You boys look so much alike now that Clancy's lost his muscle."

Lorraine gave Joel a sympathetic glance, but denied him a hug or even a smile.

"Good to see you, Lorraine. Are you okay? I've tried—"

"I'm fine," Lorraine said without meeting his eyes. "Let's go to the living room. Mr. Fitchett built a fire."

Tom stood. "Say, Joel, want to help me in the kitchen?"

He didn't. Didn't want to leave Clancy and Lorraine alone as childish as that sounded. But even though it was phrased as a question, Joel understood it wasn't one.

When Joel opened the oven to check the rolls, he saw a chicken on the bottom rack. He'd never seen Daddy cook anything besides a stew.

"Let me handle this, son. Why don't you pour everyone a glass of champagne?"

Joel opened the fridge instead. "Got any Coca-Colas?"

"You know I don't drink those."

"Yes, but Clancy likes them so I thought..."

"Well, this isn't Clancy's home." Tom flung the rolls on the stove. "I won't waste money on a crate of them for one night. Nor will I be responsible for rotting teeth."

And there was the dad Joel knew. A reassuring confirmation that he hadn't entered some alternate world tonight. "Do you have something else?"

"Since when don't you like champagne?"

"I do." Joel closed the fridge. "But I don't think Clancy needs any. He hasn't been right."

"Oh, for god's sake." Tom choked the bottle. "He's been in a war; of course it's difficult to adjust. I'd say for all he's survived, he's earned his glass."

Joel ducked to avoid the flying cork. There was no reasoning with the old man.

Daddy poured four glasses, then took a drink from his own. "Ahh, best I've tasted since before the war. I'll take Lorraine hers; you grab the rest."

Joel grabbed the remaining two flutes, but only to pour half of each glass down the drain and top with water. There were already too many issues between the four of them. Issues too near the surface. Pouring champagne on them would only make them bubble over, and Joel wasn't up to cleaning up any messes tonight.

**

Clancy only sipped champagne. He'd just promised Lorraine he would stop drinking only to have Daddy insist otherwise.

At least Lorraine came. At least she was giving him another chance. All he needed to do was get his act together and make her happy. Maybe he could be happy again too. When Lorraine squeezed his knee, he looked up to find three sets of eyes on him.

"Clancy, your father asked if you were ready for the first course."

"First course? Didn't need to make a big meal on my account."

"It's your birthday, son. Why wouldn't I pull out all the stops? Not that I didn't have help. Lorraine made tonight possible." Daddy raised his glass. "Let's have a toast to..."

Lorraine stood. "No, don't drink to me. I'm starving. Let me get the salads."

Clancy was surprised to see his father lower his glass. He would never stand for anyone else interrupting a toast. It was a marvel how Lorraine got away with things no one else could.

As soon as Lorraine set the salad in front of him, he smelled them. Radishes. Clancy hated radishes. Daddy knew that. Why was his salad full of the foul vegetable? It wasn't so much a matter of taste but a matter of a memory. Clancy felt his face getting hotter, red like the radishes. He picked around the salad, but he could not gather a bite without catching one. He set the fork down harder than he meant to.

Daddy looked at him. "Is there a problem?"

"No, sir. Just saving room for the rest."

Lorraine inspected his bowl. "Is something wrong?"

"It's fine, Lorraine." Daddy crunched down on a radish. Clancy recoiled. Both from the crunch of the vegetable and father's tone. He spoke to Lorraine just as he always had to Mama. *"It's fine, Nancy. If he gets hungry enough, he'll eat it."*

Joel swapped salad bowls with Clancy when Daddy and Lorraine went back into the kitchen. "Thank you," Clancy said, never so glad to see an empty bowl.

"No problem." Joel shoveled a fork full in his mouth. "Are you doing okay? You don't look good."

Clancy pulled at his collar. "Just a little hot."

"Everything okay with Lorraine?"

Daddy saved him from having to answer, bursting through the door wearing a smile that suggested he had done something far more substantial than cooking a bird. "Here she is." He set the chicken in front of Clancy. It smelled good. And it was nice of Daddy to make it. No need to let a few radishes ruin everything.

His new outlook didn't stand a chance when Lorraine served the next course. Clancy recognized the plate. It was from a set of china Mama loved. At the bottom of the pink dish, two gray swallows sat perched on a branch. But he couldn't see the pair now, not for all the rice. "What the hell is going on?" he asked, rising from his seat.

Tom glanced upward at Clancy. "What are you talking about?"

Clancy kicked hard against the leg of the table. "You know damn well what I mean!"

"Clancy, calm down." Joel picked up the plate like it was a grenade with a loose pin. "Get rid of this," he told Lorraine.

Daddy threw his napkin on the table. "What's this all about?"

"I think it's the rice," Joel said. "It's something he ate at camp."

An edgy, twitchy feeling crawled up Clancy. It wasn't just something he ate at camp; it was *all* he ate. "Don't Joel. Don't talk like you understand."

"You're right." Joel put his hands up. "We don't know, but nobody made rice to spite you."

"Certainly not." Daddy folded his arms over his stomach. "Don't make too much of this."

Too much? What did Tom Fitchett know about too much? He'd never been to war. Never been a prisoner kept alive by half a cup of rice. "And the salad? You want me to believe it's a coincidence too?"

"The salad?" Daddy blew out a breath that rattled his lips. "What's your issue with salad? Did the Japs feed you veggies too?"

Clancy leaned closer to jab a finger in Daddy's face. "The Japs didn't. You did!"

Lorraine tugged at his shirt. "I made the salad, Clancy. I'm sorry."

"It's not your fault," Joel said. "Let go of him. He's having another episode."

Episode? Why were they talking about him like he wasn't even here? Clancy snatched the bowl from Joel and held it below his father's nose. "What if I poured this down your throat? Would you remember then?"

Daddy knocked the bowl away, spilling salad across the table. "Is that what this is about? A dinner twenty some years ago? I have news for you. I didn't make the salad then or today. Now stop! You're frightening Lorraine."

Clancy looked at Lorraine, huddled behind Joel like she was in danger. Didn't she realize if Clancy wanted to get to her, Joel couldn't stop him? They'd proven that before. "Don't act scared, Lorraine. Just sharing childhood memories. The first time I tried a radish, I gagged. Mama said I didn't have to finish, said trying it was enough, but that wasn't enough for you know who." He turned back to face his father. "Nothing was ever good enough for you was it, Daddy?" Clancy downed his champagne in a single gulp. "He made me eat another. When I spit it out, he really came unhinged."

Tom snickered. "All right. Yes, I told you to eat. Glad you got that off your chest."

"You didn't just tell me to eat. You held me to the ground, force feeding me. Mama tried to pull you off me, but you knocked her against the wall." Clancy felt a thickness in this throat. He could still hear the awful thud she made all these years later.

Daddy gave a quick, disgusted snort. "Now, that's not the entire truth of the story. You were too young to remember."

Clancy's entire body tensed like it was on the verge of springing. "It's one of my first memories. No wonder I always hated you."

"Hate me all you want, but you were told to eat them and you refused. No discipline is pleasant."

"I was four years old." Clancy grabbed Lorraine's champagne. He didn't want to be sad; the anger was easier. Her glass tasted better, stronger than his own.

"You were willful." Daddy's stare was intense and fevered. "You've always been willful."

Clancy sneered when his father grabbed the knife. Let the old man come at him. Clancy knew a dozen ways to kill with that boning knife. But Daddy didn't fight him. He didn't even look at him as he carved the chicken. "Anyone else hungry?"

"I think it's time to call it a night," Joel said. "Lorraine just left."

Clancy pushed past his brother to the living room where he found Lorraine putting her coat on. "Where are you going?"

Her eyes bored into him. "You need help, Clancy. Please let someone help you."

"You can help me."

"I can't. You're drinking so you will only get worse. I can't watch that again, not tonight. I'll call you tomorrow."

Clancy turned away. Loraine hadn't even needed a knife to stab him in the back. If she was going to run away when things got real, the hell with her. "Don't bother," he said over his shoulder.

He stopped short of going back into the kitchen, examining his father's stocked liquor cabinet. It was his birthday, and dammit, he was celebrating. The chicken smelled delicious and so did the cake. He pulled out a bottle of Blue Bird Gin. He could make it through the evening; he just needed a little help.

***

Joel knew who would be on the other end of the line before he answered. Last week he longed for her to call; now, he only felt dread. "I told him you called, but there is no talking to him when he's like this," Joel said.

"Well, I hadn't heard from you, so..."

"You told me to call when he's sober. He's never sober."

"That's not possible, Joel."

"It is, Lorraine; it's possible." Joel might not have believed it himself if he hadn't lived in it for the past four days. Clancy was drunk by the time Joel woke up and passed out by the time he came home. Short of keeping a constant vigil outside his door, there was nothing to be done.

"I shouldn't have left the party early." Joel heard the tears she attempted to hide. "I think by abandoning him, I set all this into motion."

"The war set all this into motion."

"Oh yes, the war. Fixed the economy but broke an entire generation." She sighed into the phone. "Can't you get rid of the liquor in the house?"

"I thought I did. He hides it or buys more when I'm working."

"Well, Mother and the ladies at church are going to organize a veteran's lunch. Clancy can make friends there. Or even talk to our pastor."

"Maybe," Joel said, even though he knew Clancy would never go. His brother's stubbornness made no sense to Joel. He would have done anything to keep her.

"I read an article about the positive health benefits of having a dog. We should get him one. Might be a big morale booster."

Joel sank into his chair. He understood Lorraine needed to find a solution, but there just wasn't one. No lunch, no friend, no dog that could save his brother. Every day at the station, they heard stories of other returning soldiers having the same troubles. Joel wondered how these men survived war, only to come home and cower at the sound of an airplane or a bowl of rice. "Everyone's gotta break sometime," Mr. Rogers told him. "Maybe they were waiting for a safe place to do it."

He checked on Clancy when he got off the phone. When he opened the door, the stench of whiskey and piss knocked him back a few steps. Not to mention the body odor that could only belong to a man who hadn't showered in weeks nor washed the clothes littering the floor.

Joel used his shirt as a mask as he entered. It didn't help. Clancy's bed was empty and stripped of sheets. He found his brother wedged between the bed and wall, wearing only his underwear.

Wet sheets were crammed at the foot of the bed. They brought back unpleasant memories. Joel had always wet the bed growing up. Something Daddy couldn't beat out of him. Clancy never complained about the mess, never made fun of him.

Joel sat on Clancy's bare bed, staring at his bare walls. Did Clancy knock the pictures off on purpose, or were they casualties of a drunken stupor? Either way, it made Joel sad. Sad that Clancy would allow pictures of Mama to lie in piles of soiled clothes. Sad that the brother who once kept his books in pristine rows under the bed would live in a room like this. Sad that someone who had everything, who always had, was throwing it all away. But he was mostly sad that he'd given up on his brother. The same brother who had often woke him in the middle of the night to remind him to use the bathroom. Who once snuck out wet sheets to wash before Daddy found them. Why had Joel forgotten about those times, but remembered all Clancy's screw-ups? Some brother he was.

Joel made the bed with fresh sheets and lifted Clancy back onto it, surprised by how little he weighed now. He grabbed a basket and gathered every piece of clothing off the floor, throwing away trash as he came to it. The pictures needed to go back up and the trash taken out, but that could wait till morning. Joel flipped the light off and stood in the doorway. Nothing was back to normal, but maybe it was a start.

***

The first basket of clothes wasn't even finished when Lorraine called. But now Joel felt ready to talk to her. Ready to figure out a plan to help Clancy.

"Hey, Lorraine. Clancy's still asleep, but I'm glad you called. I've been thinking—"

"Me too." Lorraine's voice had lost its frantic edge. "I've been thinking about you." About him? Joel felt a bowling ball lodge in his throat. "I miss you, Joel."

The ball fell to his stomach. "I miss you too." He wanted to say more, but he always said or did too much when it came to Lorraine. He didn't want to turn this into something she didn't mean for it to be.

"My head's a mess, Joel. It's been a terrible mess. I realize I need to keep helping Clancy, but I'm so tired."

Tired. Joel understood that, but what did she mean she missed him? Did she miss being friends? Or miss being something more? Because they had been more, hadn't they?

"Can we meet in the morning and talk?"

"Yeah. I was actually going to call and suggest we get together to discuss Clancy—"

"Not about Clancy," Lorraine said firmly. "About us."

Us. Joel took a hard swallow. "Okay, just tell me when and where."

"Nowhere too crowded."

Joel sensed that for this conversation, even three would be a crowd. "I can pick you up. We can drive around and talk."

"Be here at 6:30. I'll wait outside."

6:30. Joel looked at the clock. Ten and a half hours never seemed so far away. "Can't we meet right now?"

"6:30," she said again. "Don't worry. I won't change my mind, not again."

***

Joel bounced around his house, unsure what to do with the excess energy. His thoughts bounced similarly. Back and forth between the sensible and the fantasy. Lorraine always turned to him when she was lonely or sad, but she always turned right back to Clancy. Still, what if this time was different? That thought would have been easier to stomach a few hours ago before this sudden sympathy for Clancy settled on him. But Clancy might be relieved. He'd barely mentioned Lorraine since he'd been home from the war. A lot could change in three years, including his brother's fickle feelings.

There was no way Joel was getting any sleep tonight. He needed a shower, though, and a shave. He stroked his stubble, and the scar itched again. It was itching a lot lately. Maybe lotion would help. Getting rid of an itch had to be easier than getting rid of the scar itself. He'd given up on that. Well, he hadn't really given up or he wouldn't still be holding on to that business card. When he thought about Lorraine, calling Norman Holden didn't sound like a completely ridiculous idea. He dug the card out of his wallet and imagined meeting Lorraine tomorrow with a new face. What would she think? Sure, she acted like the scar didn't matter, but she was only human. She'd prefer someone without one. She'd preferred Clancy, after all. Imagining the surprise and delight on her face was the final push he needed to make the call.

***

There was no light outside when Joel awoke, but the singing birds outside his window suggested dawn was imminent. That meant the oil should have done its job. Norman said it would only take around six hours. The burn had almost been too much to bear at first, but now it was just a light tingle. Maybe because the scar was gone? But he tried not to get his hopes up yet. Tried to remember that if his face looked the same, he had only lost one hundred dollars, not Lorraine. He'd still get to meet with her and hear her out. But he wanted it to work. Lorraine always said everything happens for a reason. Maybe he'd been destined to meet Norman Holden. Had the scar's incessant itch the past three weeks been a reminder?

When Joel stood, he saw spots. He assumed the black floating ones were caused from sitting up too fast, but what were the red ones dotting his pillow? He stared at them, unable to blink until he settled on an explanation. The oil had a reddish tint. Some must have leaked from the bandage.

Joel stumbled into his bathroom, lightheaded with excitement. When he tried to peel the bandage, he felt the sting again. He counted to three and tried again, but the gauze remained cemented to his skin. Joel splashed water on his face, once, twice, three times before the bandage fell into the sink. Joel cringed seeing it smeared with red. And he smelled it now—not the musky, acidic scent of the oil, but the unmistakable odor of blood.

Joel ripped off the rest of the bandage without noticing the pain. Not only was the line still there, but it looked split open. Almost like it had the first time he saw it. And the blood. So much blood. When Joel opened his mouth, a primal scream escaped—a sound he didn't know he could make.

This had to be a dream. Nothing could have caused this reaction. It was the stuff of Grimm's fairy tales, not real life. Joel splashed more water, pinched his skin, but he did not wake up. His face had not been made new as Norman promised—his scar had. It was a punishment he could never escape, a reminder of what he'd done.

His knees buckled beneath him. He hoped he hadn't woken Clancy. He needed help but didn't want it. This was his own fault for being a fool. He was not destined to meet that snake oil salesman; he was destined to have this scar. Trying to erase it only reopened it. He crawled back into his bed, letting the salt from his tears sting the fresh cut. The more tears, the more pain, but he couldn't stop. With no strength left to stand, he let his pillow absorb all that was left of him: blood and tears.

CHAPTER 27

Gib Lewis Unit, 1991

"I wasn't expecting you." Garrison heard the cold indifference in Joel's tone and knew nothing would come easy today. "You realize I get strip searched every time you visit?"

"It's not exactly pleasant getting in either. I wouldn't have come if I didn't have news."

Joel shifted in his chair. "Did you find her?"

"No, but—"

"Of course not." Joel kicked the table leg.

"But I found Crawl."

The table stopped shaking as Joel stilled. "Have you talked to him?"

"Not yet."

"Good. Don't. I can't have a dead kid on my conscious. It's full enough already."

Garrison wondered if he should disclose that he'd been talking to Crawl since May and was still alive. "Come on, you really think he's that dangerous?"

"I really *know* he's that dangerous." Joel's voice was strained. "If he knows where Lorraine is, he won't tell you. But it may get him wondering about her. The last thing I want is to cause them any trouble."

He was probably right; Ray wouldn't tell. He hadn't yet. But if Garrison knew the truth, he could use it to make him talk. Of course, it was possible Ray hadn't kept up with Clancy and Lorraine after all, and Joel was just paranoid.

"But if you don't believe he's still blackmailing Clancy, why would he keep up with them?"

"He keeps an eye on people who can get him in trouble."

"Trouble?" Garrison put his hands on the table, palms up. "What could he get into trouble for all these years later?"

"Last I checked, there isn't a statute of limitations on murder."

Garrison's chest stuttered. "He killed someone?"

"He killed a lot of someones. Most of them had it coming. The ones sleeping in the glades with broken necks can blame themselves for being stupid. Play with fire, get doused with swamp water. Or something like that."

Garrison squirmed in his chair. Imagining Ray as a troublemaker and a blackmailer was one thing, but a murderer? "If everyone he killed had it coming, why are you still afraid of him?" Garrison asked. "Do *you* have it coming? Does Clancy?"

"Crawl may think so." Joel's eyes flitted around the room. "And it's not like everyone he knifed deserved it. Some were revenge killings; others, it seemed, he killed for sheer enjoyment."

There was no reason not to believe Joel, but Garrison didn't want to. "Why is he not in jail?"

"He's smart. Smarter than me, smarter than you. He doesn't leave evidence and always has a fall guy."

Garrison crossed his arms. "Well, I can't *not* talk to him. He's the best chance I have right now. I'm going there when I leave unless you give me a reason not to. A solid reason. No vague talk about how he might be a threat to me or to Clancy. I need to hear the truth—all of it."

Joel gave an exaggerated throat clear. "I need something to drink." He used his hand to fan himself. "Get me a coke."

Garrison didn't want to lose any time, but time might be what Joel needed to realize Garrison wasn't bluffing.

As the coins fell into the machine, Garrison tried to force his emotions into place too. He took a deep breath in through his nose and out through his mouth. Ray likely knew Clancy's whereabouts. But would he admit it? What if Ray killed Clancy? It would explain why they both had gone missing simultaneously. Clancy at the bottom of the swamp, Crawl fleeing punishment.

Garrison leaned against the machine for support. No, that wasn't possible. Clancy married Lorraine after Tom's murder. Clancy was alive somewhere, possibly with proof of one of Ray's crimes. But then again, Joel said Crawl never left evidence. That he always had a fall guy. The thought turned over and over in Garrison's brain. Left no evidence, always had a fall guy. Wait…

"You ain't the only one thirsty." The raspy voice brought Garrison out of his head and back into the prison visiting room. How long had he stood here hitting the Coca-Cola button without noticing the empty light was on? He punched the button underneath, not caring what it was.

Cold beverage in hand, he weaved through the maze of white jumpsuits and blue plastic chairs back to Joel. He opened his mouth to speak, but Joel beat him to it.

"If you insist on talking to Crawl, play dumb. Say I mentioned he and Clancy were old friends and may still be in touch. Don't let on that you know—"

"That I know what? Who killed your dad?"

Joel's eyes widened. "What?"

"You didn't do it." Garrison's eyes flooded with tears, and he wasn't sure why.

Joel stared incredulously. "Sit."

Garrison did. He felt the coldness of the plastic through his shorts. "Does Clancy know you're innocent?"

"We can't talk about this here," Joel whispered.

"Where else is there but here?" Garrison lowered his voice, mimicking Joel. If the guards approached, their conversation would be over. "How could he know and leave you here?"

"It's complicated, all right?"

"No. It's not. You don't deserve to be here. We have to get you out." He sounded like Molly. She'd been right all along about Joel. Yet, she wouldn't want to be right if she realized how wrong she'd been about her grandfather.

Joel squeezed the Big Red can, aluminum crinkling beneath his fingers. "I deserve what I got. I don't expect you to understand."

"Make me understand. Were you involved?" Garrison scraped a hand down his thigh. His skin felt as raw as his nerves. "Tell me what happened that day."

"It's not that day that matters." Joel scratched his forehead and down his face, following the scar. "It's another one that I'm doing time for..."

CHAPTER 28

Carthage, Texas, 1932

Joel heard Daddy's oppressive footsteps clomping down the hallway. Was it his imagination or did the vibrations shake the dinosaur collection on his dresser? Those dinosaurs had once been his favorite toys. He was too old for them now, but he still kept them. He liked to look at them, even hold them now and again. Sometimes he wished he could still play with them. But on his twelfth birthday, Daddy said he was a man. It had never occurred to Joel that childhood could end so abruptly. Someone should have warned him what was coming when he turned eleven.

Thud. Thud. Thud. Joel wondered if this was how the Triceratops shook when they heard T-Rex coming. But unlike Joel, at least they stood a chance to escape—and at least they weren't right in the middle of trying to impress Katie Montgomery.

He knew why Daddy was coming—the same reason Joel had bruises forming on his arm. Clancy hadn't come home. If Daddy had shaken him so hard when Clancy went missing, what would he do now? Now that he must realize Joel lied about Clancy leaving to pick berries. Joel just hoped he wouldn't whip him in front of Katie.

"Son, supper is nearly ready. Go get your brother."

Joel jumped to his feet. "Yes, sir." Daddy's voice was stern, but he wasn't yelling, and he hadn't taken his belt off. "Be right back," Joel told Katie, wishing she'd offer to come along.

He kept his head down as he walked out the back door, avoiding the glares of Mama and their guests. He noticed the maroon rug wasn't in its usual spot by the door. It was his job to clean it. Had Mama left it outside for him to beat and he'd forgotten? The last thing he needed was another reason to be in trouble.

Joel cursed Clancy with each step. He and Katie never got time alone. Clancy owed him and owed him big.

Even though Joel didn't find his playmate in any of their usual hiding places, he wasn't worried until he reached the patch of trees outside the Abbot's farm. They rarely ventured further than this. The sun would set soon; Clancy knew better than to be home after dark. They had broken plenty of their father's rules before. They couldn't take over three steps or two breaths without breaking one, but they'd *never* break this one. It was a sacred sort of rule.

A dove swooped on the path in front of Joel, pecking the ground for seeds. Joel stooped down. "Are you hungry, little fellow?"

He's not eating it; he's storing it for later. Clancy's words from last week came to mind. On the way back from Rover's Diner, they'd come across doves pecking around the Lawson brothers' land. Joel wasn't sure where Clancy learned so much about birds, but he knew there was an awful lot of grain on the Lawson property. "Bait," Joel told Clancy. "See there? They trap them and put them in that holding pen." Clancy's face whitened. "You aren't surprised, are you? You know they're rotten drunks. When you can't keep a job, you've got to eat what you catch."

Clancy had mentioned those doves several times in the week since. Joel didn't understand why those caged birds gnawed on his brother like they did, but it made him wonder. What if Clancy had gone back there? Surely he wouldn't be so dumb, but Joel had nowhere else to check.

Tall grass slapped against the skin of his leg as he cut across the Abbots' farm. A nearby tractor threw up a plume of dirt ahead of him. The dust in his throat made him cough, but he didn't slow down. He still had another mile to go, and he needed to beat the sun.

Joel didn't stop till he came to the fence surrounding the Lawson's property. He hadn't noticed the barbed wire crowning the fence last week, but it was glaring now—almost as glaring as the little boy crouched behind a scruffy bush on the other side.

"Clancy?" Joel hissed. "Clancy!"

He didn't turn around. Joel was about to shout it louder when he saw Clyde Lawson sprawled out on the porch—the rise and fall of his round belly the only indication he was alive. Joel looked at the fence again. How did Clancy get through? He searched for a break in the wire, somewhere Clancy might have squeezed through, but unlike the rest of the place, the fence stood in good repair. There was no way in—except over.

"Joel!" Clancy pressed his face against the fence.

"What are you doing, Clancy? We hafta get outta here! Daddy's waiting for us."

"Use this to get up." Clancy hoisted something over. It hit with such a thud, Joel and Clancy both looked to see if it had awoken Clyde. Fortunately, this Lawson was a hell of a sleeper. Passed out drunk most likely. Joel had seen Daddy like this before, so gone he didn't even stir when Mama threw water on him.

When the dust settled, Joel recognized that Clancy had thrown Mama's rug over the fence. "Fold it and angle it on top of the wire. It won't cut through." Clancy ran back to the bush before Joel could try to stop him.

Joel wanted to leave. Let Clancy handle the implications of a stupid decision. But he couldn't go back without him. And so Joel made a decision he would spend every day after questioning. He took the carpet and climbed.

Once hidden behind the bush, Joel punched Clancy's bicep. "What are you doing here? Are you stupid?"

Clancy recoiled, rubbing his arm. "I'm going to open that cage. Just as soon as Lyle goes inside."

"That one's Clyde." Joel didn't have a lot of dealings with the Lawsons, but he saw Clyde around sometimes. He ventured out more, popped off his mouth more. He also outweighed his brother by at least one hundred and fifty pounds. How he stayed so big on a diet of doves, Joel didn't know. "You can't stay, Clancy. Daddy's real mad. The Montgomerys are over." Joel thought of Katie, sitting crossed legged on his carpet alone and hated Clancy even more.

Clancy shook his head. "Living things shouldn't be caged, especially things with wings." Clancy's eyes were overly blue and overly bright, with no trace of fear. "You go home if you want, but I could sure use a watchman. Someone to make sure he doesn't wake up."

A knot settled deep in Joel's gut. "I don't think it's a good idea, Clancy. Let's come back next time they go into town."

"We're already here! Already over the fence. That's half the battle. Those birds will be dead tomorrow. Don't you see? It's got to be now."

Joel wiped his sticky, dirt-speckled hands down his legs. Clancy had his mind made up. The sooner he opened that cage door, the sooner they could go home. There were at least a dozen birds inside, slamming into the walls and each other. They couldn't make more noise when they escaped than they already were.

"All right," Joel conceded. "But run fast! And if you chicken out, too bad. No second chances. No going back."

"I won't need to go back. I'll get 'em all out," Clancy said in the overconfident way he said everything nowadays. "And I'll break the damn cage while I'm at it."

"Don't." Joel held up his finger. "Let the birds go, and then we'll go." Joel checked the porch a final time and tried to shrink behind the bruise-purple smoke bush. He wasn't sure how the plant got its name, but his blood did suddenly feel on fire.

When Clancy made it to the cage, Joel let himself breathe again. This would not be so bad. The birds could fly free, and Clancy could put this obsession to rest. They would be home for dinner, Katie would get his letter, and the memory of his dad shaking him would fly to the place all his other worst memories did.

Joel checked on Clyde, but a reverberating crash brought his attention back to Clancy. The cage lay sideways on the ground, the birds flapping even louder. The short-distressed coos sounded more like screams. Clancy tried to tilt the cage back up, but it was bulky, and he kept yanking his fingers away, fearful of the sharp claws and snapping beaks.

Joel knew he should help, but while his blood was on fire, the rest of him froze. The screen door's screech reminded him he was supposed to be a watchman. And now he had two men to watch. Clyde, still sleeping and Lyle standing above him, surveying the yard. Joel tried to make himself smaller, but it didn't matter. Lyle wasn't looking at him anyway; he was looking at Clancy.

"Clancy, run!" Joel didn't bother whispering now.

Lyle whipped his head around. "What's this we got here?" He kicked his brother. "Wake up, Clyde. We got us some trespassers." Clyde didn't move, but Lyle stomped toward Clancy. He was a scrawny man, but the look in his eye made him somehow scarier than big ole Clyde.

"Stay away from him!" Joel yelled, jumping from behind the bush. It got Clancy's attention at least, and he dropped the cage, sending the frenzied birds deeper into their madness. Clancy took off towards the back of the property, Lyle following behind. He was fast. He'd catch Clancy in seconds. Joel had to act now.

"Come over here." Joel tried to keep his voice steady. "Come over here to me, somebody your own size."

Joel knew it was dangerous, but it would give Clancy time to escape and get help. He spotted a rake propped against the porch and ran for it. He might have made it if not for that rock in his path. Just a tiny rock, a tiny stumble, but it was all Lyle needed to catch up.

Joel tried to free himself, but for a small man, Lyle seemed disproportionately strong.

"Not so loudmouthed now, are ya? You think it's right to sneak on another folk's property? Think it's okay to steal their dinner? Your Daddy should have taught you better."

The more Joel struggled, the tighter Lyle squeezed. And the tighter he squeezed, the blurrier the world became. The colors all bled together like looking through a kaleidoscope.

He didn't recognize the mass coming toward them till Clancy was close enough to release the rock in his hand. It connected with Lyle's forehead like the story of the giant and the shepherd Mama liked to tell. Lyle let up enough for Joel to slip through his arms. He tried to run, but the ground felt unstable beneath him. Like when Daddy shook him. Lyle seemed to be on the same shifty ground, stumbling, reaching, but never making contact.

Clancy broke up the strange dance by swinging a stick at Lyle. Though he hit Lyle several times, it did little to stop him. Joel gave up trying to stand and searched the ground for his own weapon. But the East Texas land was strangely bare beneath him. No rock or stick big enough to do any damage. As he watched Clancy swing, something beneath a stunted tree caught his eye—something glistening in the rays of the slow setting sun. A bottle. Joel scooted till he reached it and threw it without aim. It missed his target, but the glass smashing against the concrete porch got Lyle's attention.

Seeing Lyle charge at him somehow got Joel to his feet. He ran a straight line toward the porch and reached for the rake, but only managed to push it over. Lyle did the same to Joel, shoving him down beside Clyde. He tasted blood with the dirt already in his mouth as he rolled to his back. He noticed that Clyde's eye was black and his lip swollen. He'd obviously pissed off someone too—probably the same somebody Joel had.

Lyle straddled Joel and put his hands over his throat. "Open your eyes and look at me, boy!" He sprayed spit as he spoke. "If you think that..."

Joel stopped listening to Lyle when he saw Clancy. He stood behind Lyle, rake raised like a spear. He wore the same look of resolve on his face as when he told Joel he would open the cage. *Do it, Clancy,* Joel thought. *End this.*

But that's when something went wrong. Lyle loosened his grip, no longer looking at Joel, but at the shadow Clancy cast over him. In one quick movement, Lyle stood and shoved Clancy off the porch. Joel only drug himself a few inches away before Lyle plopped back on top of him.

"Stop wiggling, you sorry worm!" Joel stilled, praying he'd hear Clancy stir. But the only sounds came from the doves, still wrestling in their sideways prison. Lyle pinned one of Joel's arms under Clyde and held down the other. With his free hand, he pulled a knife from his pocket and shook the blade loose. Joel squeezed his eyes shut. He was going to kill him—and Clancy too, if he wasn't dead already.

"Please," Joel cried. "Call my daddy, or the law even, just don't kill me."

Lyle laughed. "I ain't gonna kill ya. I'm gonna teach you a lesson." As Lyle lowered the knife, electricity charged through Joel like he'd been struck by lightning. Clyde was three hundred pounds of dead weight, but somehow Joel freed his arm to knock the weapon out of Lyle's hand.

"Dammit!" Lyle tried to grab the knife, but he couldn't do that and keep Joel still. He held Joel's arms above his head then turned around and sat on them, wedging Joel's head between his own knees. Joel's legs were free to kick, but Lyle was out of his range now. Moving his arms was impossible. He wasn't sure where his strength had come from a few seconds earlier or where it had gone now, but at least the knife was gone with it. Lyle held him there for a few seconds before a delirious smile spread across his face. He couldn't reach the knife, but he did reach for something.

Lyle held the piece of broken glass, dark amber and jagged—the glass from the bottle Joel broke. "No! Please," Joel said, but it was too late.

Lyle drug the glass from Joel's forehead to the inside corner of his right eyebrow. The sting was unbearable. Warm blood dripped into his eye but was quickly washed out by his tears. Despite Joel's thrashing, Lyle continued to trace a diagonal line across the bridge of Joel's nose and onto his cheek. He paused there and studied Joel, the way an artist might consider his next stroke before twisting the glass downwards and sawing through Joel's lip. Joel's entire body convulsed. How much longer would it be before he lost consciousness? The blade would have been better. A quick, fluid slice through Joel's fleshy lips would have hurt far less than this slow carve. When Lyle reached Joel's chin, he stopped and tossed the glass into the yard.

"Take your brother and get the hell out of here. If you ever think of trespassing, look at your face and think twice."

It took a second for Joel to register he could now move his arms. Lyle had stood. Backed away even. He was letting them go. Joel sat, pressing his hand against his face, but he could not slow the blood. He stumbled down the porch steps where Clancy still lay, curled into a ball. His eyes were closed, but he was breathing. "Clancy, come on!" Joel pushed Clancy to a sitting position and shook, but seeing his brother's head bobble the way his own had at Daddy's hands was too much. He let Clancy fall back to the ground. The jostling woke him. He took one look at Joel and scampered away like he was gazing at a monster.

"They are letting us go, Clancy. Can you walk?"

"Don't even think about calling the law," Lyle warned from his perch on the porch. "Or I'll give little brother a matching one."

The threat propelled Clancy to the fence. He didn't even bother with the rug this time. Joel followed but in slow motion. He wasn't even halfway up when he heard the crunch of gravel behind him. He looked over his shoulder, bracing himself for the worst, but Lyle wasn't near the fence. He was across the yard, setting the birdcage upright again. Joel continued his climb but froze when the rattling started. Then, he looked back. Curious as Lot's wife, he looked back. He didn't dissolve into a pile of salt, but when he saw Lyle shaking the cage, something changed inside him just the same. The lid containing the darkest parts of him came loose.

"Come on!" Clancy called from the safe side of the fence. "You're almost there. You can do it!"

But Joel couldn't do it. His face no longer stung, but the rest of his body burned as rage poisoned his veins. Not rage for the birds. It wasn't pleasant seeing them knocked around, but Joel didn't care about them, not really—not the way Clancy did. It was the shaking that got him. Why did men like Tom Fitchett and Lyle Lawson think it was okay to taunt the weak? To hurt what couldn't fight back? He felt Daddy's fingers digging into his biceps. He smelled the liquor Daddy always reeked of. He'd had no right to shake Joel like that.

Joel climbed down a few steps and let go. Clancy yelled, but the rattling was louder. Joel ran straight for the knife he'd dislodged from Lyle's hand.

"What the hell?" Lyle dropped the cage and took a single step backward. Joel barreled towards him, screaming what sounded like a war cry. Just as it had been with the bottle, Joel did not aim. He swung and slashed until Lyle fell, screaming and clamping both hands over his thigh, desperate to stop the blood suddenly erupting like a volcano. Joel dropped the weapon and fell backward. How could so much blood come from a thigh? What had he done? He swallowed the vomit that rose in his throat. "Oh god. I'm sorry."

"I let you go." Lyle kept his eyes on his wound. "You little sonofabitch! I let you go!"

Above him, Joel heard the whistling of dove wings as they took flight. Somehow, in the commotion, they opened the cage door. Joel followed them over the fence, barely flinching as the barbed wire dug into his leg. He found Clancy on the ground, passed out again. He picked him up and walked. There was no time to waste.

Rover's Diner was the first building he came to. He wasn't sure how he'd made it this far, losing this much blood, but he felt light and airy now. Like he was floating. He couldn't remember how he got inside. He was still holding Clancy, so someone must have opened the door for them. But he remembered the clang of the bell against the glass. How it only partially muffled the gasps and screams. He remembered coleslaw. The fresh bowl the waitress dropped, its tangy vinegar smell wafting towards Joel just as his knees gave way. And he remembered the linoleum, its dingy blue hexagons blurring together until everything went black.

CHAPTER 29

Longview, Texas, 1945

The last person Clancy expected to see was her. Yet, when he woke up, there sat Nancy Fitchett cross-legged on the floor. "Mama?" Clancy blinked, but she remained.

She was young again, with long hair the color of butterscotch and Morning Glory blue eyes that still glittered. Just the way Clancy remembered her as a boy. Such a stark contrast to those final days.

He rubbed his eyes. He was drunk or he was dreaming. There could be no other explanation for a dead woman watching him sleep, nor for the fresh sheets and clean floors. Clancy didn't remember anything from the night before, but judging by the bottles in the wastebasket, he hadn't spent it cleaning.

Mama pulled out a bottle and frowned. Did she not realize she'd left a long time ago? That Clancy was an adult now? An adult who'd been to war?

When she dropped the bottle back into the wastebasket, it made no sound. There was no noise except the soft whisper of her voice. "You promised me you wouldn't drink."

His eyes prickled with tears. He'd nearly forgotten what she sounded like, how her voice rose and fell like the notes of a sweet song.

"It's ruining you," she said.

What could he say to that? She was right. His last coherent memory was the birthday dinner, and he wasn't sure how many days passed since. "I'm sorry. I'll stop."

She approached the bed. "And the other promise?"

Clancy wrapped his blanket tighter around him. He didn't remember another promise. All he remembered was the safety he felt in her arms. "I miss you, Mama." He reached, but she evaporated, like wispy fog. "Don't leave. I need you." He gave a strangled sob—the sort that would have summoned Mama into his room when he was young, but she continued to fade.

He was still crying when he woke up. It was only a dream. He'd suspected that, but it felt as real as the tears still wet on the pillow. Looking around, he saw that the clean room hadn't been a dream. Maybe Lorraine had been here. Lorraine. Thinking of her physically hurt. What a fool he'd been.

Joel's door was closed, so he was probably at work. That meant Lorraine might be in class, but Clancy dialed her number anyway. All these years and he'd never forgotten. It was a better number to remember than 2559. Mrs. Applewhite answered, and her silvery voice went tight when she realized who was calling. "Lorraine's not home."

"I understand she doesn't want to talk, but things have changed. This morning..." Clancy stopped. A ghost warning a wayward soul might work in a Dickens novel, but it wouldn't win back the approval of someone as sensible as Birdie Applewhite. "This morning I decided things will change. That *I* will change. No more drinking."

"Hmmm. That's all well and good, but this is not just a drinking problem. I suspect you know that."

Clancy's body went rigid. "It's most of the problem."

"It's a symptom of the problem," she said crisply. "You need help dealing with the war. With what happened there."

Clancy pursed his lips. Birdie Applewhite knew nothing of war. Yet, she seemed to know something about him—something he hadn't even admitted. "Yes," he finally said. "Yes, I do need help."

"I'm glad to hear that." Clancy heard papers shuffling. "I've done some digging. Found a doctor in Shreveport who specializes in this particular problem."

The prospect of sharing such dark thoughts with a stranger made Clancy cringe, but he could do it for Lorraine. "What's the number?" Clancy reached for a pen. "I'll call right now."

"Well, the office won't be open today. Not on Saturday. But I'm looking for it now. I'll call you back."

Saturday? Already Saturday? Clancy turned back towards Joel's room. Maybe he was still asleep. "So, can I talk to Lorraine?"

"She's really not here. Lane found her outside this morning, seemed agitated, but wouldn't say why. She eventually left." Birdie sighed. "Who knows with that one?"

"But you'll tell her what I said? About visiting the doctor?"

Birdie hesitated. "Yes. But Clancy, don't let me down."

***

266

Lorraine couldn't find the word to describe her feelings when she saw Joel's truck in his driveway. If this were her novel, she'd leave a blank and fill in the right word later. But this was reality. Joel stood her up.

She barely knocked. The last thing she needed was to wake Clancy. "Joel?" The doorknob opened when she twisted. How unlike Joel to leave it unlocked.

Clancy rounding the corner was an even bigger surprise. He was not only awake but seemed aware. "Lorraine." He stepped forward. "You're here."

He looked awful, but he hadn't stumbled. Nor was he slurring words. "Hello, Clancy. How are you?"

"I'm good. Well, I want to be. Can we talk?"

"Is Joel home?" Lorraine asked.

Clancy ran his fingers through his hair. He needed a haircut. But of course, he needed a lot of things. "He's still asleep."

Slept in? It was possible, but it wasn't like Joel. Lorraine tried not to take it personally. Maybe he didn't feel well.

"I know you and I haven't been connected since I got back, but things are going to change," Clancy said. "I'm calling the doctor Monday. I have two bottles hidden in my dresser. Go toss them. I'm tired of living this way."

Lorraine sat on the couch, her gaze ping-ponging from Joel's closed door to Clancy.

"I want to get back to work, back to church, back to our life," he continued.

It sounded good. Too good. These were the words Lorraine had longed to hear. Why had he waited till now to speak them? Waited till she was tired of waiting?

"Did you tell your brother this?" Maybe Clancy was the reason Joel hadn't shown this morning. He was bowing out gracefully or whatever they called it.

Clancy's eye twitched. "I haven't talked to him." He considered Lorraine and took a deliberate step back. "When you knocked, you called for Joel. Did you come for him?"

She twisted her hands in her lap. "Well, I'm not sure why I'd come to visit you considering—"

"But why do you want to see *him*?" Clancy widened his stance and crossed his arms.

Outside a tailpipe backfired, and the neighbor's dog reactively barked. Lorraine jumped, but Clancy didn't seem to notice. His eyes burned into her. She should lie. Say they were trying to figure out a way to help him. But it wasn't that simple. Not anymore.

"Have you been seeing Joel?" Clancy's eyes turned wild and his voice unfamiliar. He hovered over her like a storm cloud, spit flying from his mouth. "Have you?"

"Joel!" Lorraine screamed, pressing herself into the cushions.

Clancy pushed against the couch, springing back up. "It's true." He paced back and forth, his footsteps too heavy for his wasting frame. "When I was gone?"

"It's not what you think."

"To hell it's not!" He clenched his jaw.

Lorraine gauged the distance from the door, wondering if she could make it out before he grabbed her.

"I don't see it, Lorraine. You and Joel? Y'all are worlds apart. But you have something in common. The capacity for betrayal."

"Go wake Joel." Lorraine clutched her purse in front of her. "Then we can talk like adults."

Clancy pounded his hand against the wall. Lorraine was surprised it didn't go straight through. "My brother!"

"You asked him to check in on me. And we became close. That's it." Well, it was mostly it anyway. Clancy didn't need to know every detail, not when he was already breathing fire.

Clancy kicked the same wall. How was Joel sleeping through this? "I should have known." He paced again, scrubbing his hands over his face like he was trying to shed his own skin. "The way you stare at him, his nickname for you."

"His nickname for me? Daddy has always called me Lori, my friends do, even you have." She stood. "This is crazy. Joel is a friend. He was there when I needed one."

"Oh, I'm sorry I couldn't be, sorry I was fighting a damn war!"

Lorraine raised her voice. "Yes, you were, and you couldn't help being gone then, but what's your excuse now? For still being gone? For shoving me away? You aren't fighting a war any longer, Clancy."

When Clancy clenched his fists, Lorraine squeezed her eyes shut. He was going to hit her. And she would let him, but only once. One hit and she would know all she needed to know. The knife had been bad enough, but he'd been mixed up. Today, he knew exactly who she was, and he knew exactly what he was doing.

When the impact didn't come, Lorraine looked at Clancy. She knew she'd never forget the haunted look in his eyes as long as she lived. "I'm still fighting it," he said. "And I don't know how to stop."

The anger didn't leave her but did make room for pity. This wasn't a stranger—it was the man she loved. Yet, he was broken, and she didn't know how to fix him. She wasn't even sure she was up to figuring out how to anymore. "I need to use the restroom," she said for lack of all other words. It would give her a chance to compose herself and check on Joel.

The blood in the sink didn't startle her at first. Could have been a shaving accident. But the splatters on the wall and blotches on the rug…well, no razor nick could account for that.

The crimson trail led her across the hallway. She bit back a scream. There was Joel, his face down on his bed. Did Clancy hurt him in one of his fits? She called Clancy's name anyway. She was afraid of him but more afraid of what could happen to Joel without his help. It was struggle enough to roll Joel over. There was no way to get him to the hospital without Clancy.

"What's going on?" Clancy froze in the doorway.

"Joel's face." Lorraine struggled to make sense of what she saw. "The bleeding has stopped, but he's lost consciousness." She looked at the blood-soaked carpet then back at Clancy. "What happened?"

Clancy leaned over with his hands on his knees. "I...I don't know."

"Breathe, Clancy! Call an ambulance."

Clancy stood straight. "That's it!" He rushed to Joel's other side. "This is what Mama meant. This was the other promise I made."

Lorraine could not handle this right now. Joel was bleeding to death, and Clancy was carrying on about his dead mother. Why couldn't he keep his head just once? "What?" she screamed.

Clancy lowered his head close to Joel's face. "I promised to look out for him. Mama reminded me so I could save him. He's still alive. It's not too late. It's not too late, Mama."

Lorraine stood. Obviously, she would have to be the one calling for help. But before she made it out of the room, Clancy scooped up Joel with a strength she didn't know he still possessed. "Let's get him out of here."

***

The ride home from the hospital that evening was quiet, but Clancy was glad for the chance to think. Seeing Joel with the bandage wrapped around his head was eerily familiar. It had been over thirteen years, but in so many ways, Clancy still felt like that frightened 10-year-old wondering if his big brother would be okay.

But frightened or not, Clancy was functioning. Maybe even thriving. He handled the crisis like a Marine. Finding Joel this way should have tripped him off. If numbers on a receipt brought him to his knees, how was he still standing now? Maybe he'd turned a corner.

Clancy dropped off Lorraine but didn't walk her to the door. He was still furious, still wanted answers, but now wasn't the time. Once he and Joel were alone, Clancy took a chance and broke the icy silence between them. "Why Joel? Is it about Lorraine?"

Her name pulled Joel's head from the window glass. "What about Lorraine?"

"I know." Clancy gripped the steering wheel tighter. "She told me about you two."

A long silence passed before Joel spoke again. "I didn't do this." He touched the bandage. "Not on purpose."

Clancy looked back down the familiar road. "Must have been a hell of an accident."

Joel shook his head. "Forget it. I can barely believe it; no way you will."

Instead of turning down their street, Clancy kept driving. "Try me."

***

If Clancy thought he had turned a corner, he had been wrong. That night brought more memories. And if the memories weren't enough, in came the ghosts. The Schenley Whiskey in the bottom dresser drawer taunted him. He should have thrown it out earlier. But then again, after today, he deserved a drink. One final drink, he promised himself.

He unscrewed the cap and took a swing. It warmed his mouth and settled his shaking hands, but it wasn't enough. It took the whole bottle to chase away the ghosts.

***

Lorraine must have walked one hundred miles across Joel and Clancy's porch. The events of yesterday repeated in her mind like her Bing Crosby record with the scratch. Why had Joel hurt himself? Why didn't Clancy answer her calls all day? Why were neither answering the door now? Why was Mr. Fitchett taking so long? Why? Why Why? Since yesterday morning, she'd forgotten every word, but why.

The doctor certainly couldn't answer why; he couldn't even answer what. The injury resembled a chemical burn, but just over the scar? It didn't make sense, but what was the alternative? That Joel traced his scar with a kitchen knife? After he talked to her? Vomit rose in her throat.

If she wasn't so angry he'd taken so long, she might have hugged Mr. Fitchett when he finally arrived. "Thank you for coming. I'm probably overreacting, but something happened, and..." She stopped. He would see soon enough.

"It's Sunday night. They probably turned in early." Tom tried one of the million keys on his ring. "Wrong one." He examined another. "Nope. I recognize this one. Pine Tree Road. Tenants just took off last week. Still haven't gotten around to cleaning that mess." He tried to force another ill-fitted key into the lock. "At least I keep the deposit."

Lorraine tapped her fingernails against the brick, fighting the urge to rip the key ring from Mr. Fitchett's hands. She stopped clicking her nails only when she heard the click of the lock. Pushing ahead, she called for Joel and then Clancy.

Clancy appeared first, wearing only a pair of boxer shorts, guarding his eyes like the sun was suspended in the living room. Lorraine saw that he was hungover, at best. "So, you *are* here. I've been calling."

Clancy rolled both fists over his eyes. "Joel took the phone off the hook."

"Where's he now?" Lorraine asked.

"Hell if I know."

"Joel?" Lorraine jiggled the handle of his locked door.

Tom squeezed her shoulder. "It's fine, Lorraine. These boys obviously can't hold their liquor. Best to go home."

Lorraine continued twisting and pushing. "I need to check! Joel did something. He tried to hurt himself."

"Hurt himself?" There was an unfamiliar glimmer of compassion in Mr. Fitchett's eyes. He opened and shut them as if to blink it away. "Step aside then"

He threw his weight against the door until it opened. When Lorraine flipped on the light, Joel came into focus. He sat huddled in the corner, his knees pressed tight against his chest. He didn't even look up to see who burst into the room.

Mr. Fitchett took a few slow steps toward Joel like he was approaching a rabid dog. When the keys fell from his hand, Lorraine knew he saw—that he understood why she was so adamant to get in tonight. "Joel!" He brought a hand to his mouth. "What did you do to yourself?"

Joel raised his head. "I didn't do this. You did!"

***

Joel locked eyes with his father. The expression on Daddy's face was familiar. The same blend of defensiveness and rage he wore anytime someone dared to call him out.

"What on earth are you talking about?" Daddy asked.

"You sent me after him!" Joel pointed at Clancy, now standing at the door's threshold.

"What?" Tom looked to Lorraine as if she was an interpreter.

Joel stood. "Clancy wasn't my responsibility. You always put too much on me!"

Tom pinched the bridge of his nose. "This again? Good god! Want me to apologize for making you tough? The world is tough, so my sons had to be too. If Nancy had her way, you'd be frail and fearful boys!"

Joel's fist charged with no instruction from his brain to do so. But when it connected with Daddy's face, Joel was glad that he finally let rage lead reason. It was a swing a lifetime in the making.

He expected retaliation, but Daddy only gave a startling bark of laughter as he ran his fingers across his jaw. "You damn near knocked a tooth loose."

A broken tooth for a broken life. It wasn't nearly enough.

Lorraine stepped between them. "Calm down, Joel."

"Oh shut up, Lorraine." Joel pressed his face against hers. "Get a good look. That way you can stop staring."

The color drained from her face. "I wasn't staring."

"Any more than Katie was, eh Clancy?"

"Katie? Who's Katie?" Lorraine asked.

"An old friend." Clancy stepped beside Lorraine. "Stopped by earlier."

"Not just an old friend. She was my *best* friend, and today she looked at me like I was dirt!" He faced Clancy. "I planned to ask Katie to be my girlfriend."

Clancy's brow furrowed. "Today?"

"No. That night you took off. She might have said yes. Think about how different my life could be if she said yes." Joel closed his eyes as he imagined all the things a normal life could have brought.

Daddy chuckled. "So, you're still carrying a torch for Katie Montgomery? Well, I'm sorry we messed up your plans that night, but what about every night after? You can't blame anyone else for being spineless."

"No." Joel pointed to the scar. "I blame this." He looked back to Clancy. "If I hadn't followed you, this would be your face. This scar...it was meant to be yours." Clancy stepped backward, sinking onto the bed like the coward he was. "You led me to the Lawson place," Joel continued.

"Hey, hey hold up!" Daddy waved both hands in the air. "Are you saying it was one of the Lawsons who hurt you?"

"I'm sorry. I didn't know what would happen." Clancy was crying now, putting on a big show.

"Of course not. You never do," Joel said. "You do what you want and don't care about the collateral."

"He cares." Lorraine sat beside Clancy, placing a hand on his back.

Joel laughed. She switched sides like a Hermit Crab trading shells.

"Clancy cares more than you know. He's done more for you than you know," Lorraine said.

"Don't, Lorraine." Clancy looked at her, his face red and damp. "There's no point."

Lorraine stared Joel down. There was an unsettling coldness in her eyes. "There was a third boy at the Lawson's that day."

"What are you talking about?" Joel asked.

"Crawl. He saw everything. Your brother..." She stood but kept her arm on Clancy's back. "Your brother, who doesn't care, has been paying to keep him quiet."

Joel's brain fought to understand. He looked at his palms as if they held the answer. "That's why you've been throwing money at Crawl?"

"For seven years," Lorraine said.

"Seven years?" Joel asked.

Clancy kept his eyes down. "I got behind during the war, and Crawl found Lorraine. She's been paying him since."

The room spun. Joel needed air but could not fill his lungs. All that money lost. All that danger Clancy endured. It had all been for him.

"Will someone please fill me in on what the hell is going on?" Daddy asked.

"We did something." Clancy's voice cracked. "Crawl saw us."

"Saw what?" Daddy asked.

Joel and Clancy looked at each other. They had made a promise. Made a promise and kept it all these years, but Joel didn't care anymore. The burden they'd carried thirteen years had finally crushed them.

"I killed a man, Daddy." Joel's shoulders quaked.

Tom's eyes widened. "Lawson. You killed Lyle Lawson?"

Joel didn't dare meet Daddy's eyes as he backed himself into the corner that had been his hiding place all day. A broken moan escaped as he slid down the wall.

"It's okay; it's okay." Daddy's hand was ice on Joel's burning skin. "I can fix this." He looked over his shoulder at Clancy. "This Crawl fellow, what's his real name?"

"Jack Monroe," Clancy answered.

"Little Jack Monroe? My god."

"What?" Clancy asked. "You knew him?"

"Remember the secretary I employed before the war? It was Roxie Monroe, Jack's sister. She stole, and I never turned her in." Daddy stomped his foot. "I let that winch off the hook all the while her brother blackmailed my boys. I have the proof in my ledger, and it's time Jack Monroe gets a taste of his own medicine."

Lorraine removed her fingernail from her mouth. She must have bitten it to the quick by now. "What are you suggesting?"

Joel pulled his legs close. Lorraine and Daddy's voices sounded muted like he was underwater. His lungs felt submerged as well. He needed to say something. Tell him what a horrible idea it was to blackmail Crawl, but it was all he could do to just breathe.

"No, Daddy." Clancy became the voice of reason. "You have no idea who you're messing with."

"The same man you've all been messing with for years apparently," Tom said.

A sudden knock froze them all. When no one responded, it came again, louder and impatient. "Police," a voice called. "We're coming in."

Tom took charge. "Joel, get up. Clancy get dressed. Let me handle this."

Joel heard Daddy talking to the officer as Lorraine helped him to the bed. Sounded like a concerned neighbor heard yelling. Had to be Mrs. Jefferson. From what Joel could make out, the officer wasn't satisfied with his father's assurances that everything was settled now.

Lorraine handed him a handkerchief. "They will want to talk to you. Are you okay to do that?"

Joel didn't have a chance to answer. There was another knock, faint this time. Daddy stepped into the room followed by an officer Joel recognized. Jimmy Carlson was a regular at work, and his wife was the town gossip. She'd get the word out about his face quicker than if the Longview News posted a picture on the front page.

"Fitchett?" Jimmy's bug-eyes bulged more than usual. "What happened?" He surveyed the room. "Somebody hurt you? Again?"

"No," Joel said. There was no use in telling the real story. Clancy hadn't believed it—no one would. "It happened Friday night. I did it." It wasn't really a lie; Joel had caused it. He'd caused a lot. Caused the bruise developing on Daddy's jaw, caused the division in Lorraine's heart, caused Clancy to lose all that money, and caused the scar to open again. And there was no foreseeable way to fix any of it.

CHAPTER 30

Gib Lewis Unit, 1991

Even though their time was running out, Garrison waited until Joel was finished to speak. His was a story that deserved to be told without interruption—the kind that demanded a few moments of silence after hearing.

"First, let me say how sorry I am—"

Joel held up a hand. "I don't want counseling."

"Well, you need it. Legal especially." Garrison's chair scuffed the linoleum as he scooted closer. "I get that you were a kid and didn't understand various degrees of murder. But you must now. Why let Crawl ruin your life over an act of self-defense?"

"We trespassed onto their property."

"That doesn't matter. You weren't there to hurt them."

"He let me go. I attacked him." Joel put his hand on the unopened Big Red. "I asked for Coca-Cola."

"I remember reading about the Lawsons," Garrison said. "How did they get Clyde for the murder?"

"Dumb luck. When that bastard woke up, he didn't remember anything. He was beat to hell, and I guess he assumed he'd killed Lyle in one of their brawls. He panicked, buried the body." Joel turned the soda can in a circle, looking at it instead of Garrison. "Lyle didn't get out much, so nobody even missed him till Clyde got drunk and bragged to some old boy about the time he killed a man. Three days later, they dug up Lyle."

"So, Clyde is serving a life sentence for something he didn't do?"

Joel looked up. "Is that supposed to make me feel guilty? Prison was a step up for Clyde's living conditions. I can tell you that. Besides, he had a heart attack fifteen years in. I've served three times that."

"That doesn't make it okay." Garrison weaved his hands into his hair and pulled. "Fifteen years for him. Forty-five for you. Sixty stolen years."

"You don't hear me crying about it, do you? It doesn't matter who I killed. Whether Lyle or Daddy, there's no difference. Murder is murder, and when you take a life, the penalty is your own. In one way or another."

"That's not how it works. You were a child! No jury would sentence you to life for what happened. You need a good—"

"No." When Joel couldn't fan himself fast enough to stop the sweat dripping from his forehead, he stuck the Big Red can against it. "Don't try to get me out of here."

Garrison's own temperature rose. It was as if Joel wanted to stay. Like he'd told Garrison that story to ensure he could.

"Look," Joel continued, "all the evidence points to me."

"Why did Crawl do it? How'd he get away with it?"

"Another time."

Garrison looked at the clock. In less than ten minutes, he'd be on his way to talk to Ray. The need to know everything was suddenly right up there with the need for oxygen. "It's got to be now."

Joel slammed down the can." You get Lorraine here if you want the rest of the story. That was our deal. I've told you too much already."

Garrison knew Joel was right, but he also knew Lorraine was the only card he had left to play. "You agreed to give my friend an interview if I brought Lorraine. What you've shared so far has been your choice. But if you don't cooperate with me now, the deal is off the table."

"That's not your call to make." Joel leaned in aggressively. "Listen to me. You *will* find Lorraine. If you insist on using blackmail to get the information from Crawl, that's on your head. But you will say nothing about bringing Lorraine here. In fact, forget her name altogether."

With Joel leaning on the table, it was easy to see the rigid and defined muscles of his forearm and the vein throbbing beneath his skin.

Garrison drew back, tried to make himself smaller. Threatening Joel had been a mistake with the nearest guard clear across the room.

"If you find them, you will personally fly with Lorraine here and back. After that, I'll give the interview to your little girlfriend. If you don't find Lorraine, don't bother coming back. We have nothing else to say to each other." He shoved the table into Garrison's stomach. "We're all done here."

"Sit down Fitchett!" A scrawny guard smacked into a chair as he made his way to them.

Joel picked up the can of Big Red and shook. "If my story has taught you anything, Gary, it's that you ought to be careful which cages you rattle." He popped the top, turning on a hose of hissing soda.

"What the hell, Fitchett?" The red-faced guard grabbed Joel's arm.

"It's okay," Garrison said. "Just an accident." He held up his arms, studying the sticky mess covering them. The crimson splotches stood out even more on the off-white table and Joel's stark white jumpsuit. It was a scene, that to Garrison, looked too much like a story he'd just heard.

Chapter 31

Longview, Texas, 1945

Neither the hot coffee nor heavy blanket warmed Lorraine. An ice storm in Texas was certainly a surprise. A few years in the desert and she'd grown so accustomed to heat that the 35-degree night left her shivering.

"Just loaded more coal in the furnace," Joel said. "Should warm up soon." It was hard to look at him with that dark scab developing on his face. They needed to talk about it. Talk about what had gone so wrong between that late-night phone call and their planned morning meeting. She wanted to know, but she couldn't bring herself to ask.

"So, are you going to say what this is about?" Clancy sat with his elbow propped on the arm of the couch, his face resting on his fist.

"I'm waiting for someone else. He should be here any minute," Lorraine said.

"He?" Joel smirked. "No more room on this couch."

Lorraine understood exactly what he meant. Three was already a crowd.

"Come on, Lorraine." Clancy plopped back against the cushion. "Just tell us what's going on."

"Your father is coming. It's time you three had a serious talk."

Clancy groaned. "If you haven't noticed, our last few haven't gone so well."

Lorraine jerked her head toward him. "How about we try it sober?" As she suspected, that shut them both up. "Mr. Fitchett admits he made mistakes. He wants to make it right."

"Daddy says a lot of things." Clancy stood. "He's not coming. I'll call him now. Bet he's sitting by the fire drinking a Gin Rickey."

Lorraine carried her own drink to the loveseat and watched the snow. Having her back turned to Joel and Clancy was just a bonus. When had they become so negative and condescending? Maybe her parents' suggestion would be for the best. A fresh start for a fresh year in Wyoming. Yet, she hadn't even been able to tell one Fitchett goodbye; how would she manage both? She sighed. Obviously, she was the real problem here.

"He didn't answer." Lorraine felt vindicated seeing Clancy return, having left his swagger in the kitchen.

"Well, he's coming." Lorraine looked back out of the window. She loved the snow but hated this furious blowing. "The weather must have delayed him. I spoke to him before I came, and he said I'd caught him walking out the door."

"Before you came here?" Joel asked. "That was over an hour ago."

Lorraine searched the walls for a clock. "Was it?"

"Yeah, he should be here already. We better check on him." Clancy struggled with his jacket. "Daddy can't drive in bad weather."

Joel grabbed his keys. "Did he say anything else?"

Lorraine bit her lip. "Just that he appreciated me trying to help, but that he could fix everything."

"Fix everything?" Clancy went white. "You don't think he'd make good on his threat to visit Crawl?"

No one answered; no one had to. It was the only scenario that made any sense. Lorraine continued chewing until her lip bled. She should have known better.

"Can I use your car, Lorraine?" Clancy grabbed a key ring from the coffee table.

The cumbersome keys were familiar, but they didn't belong to her. "Your father must have left those here. They are for his rentals." She grabbed her purse, rifling for her own.

"We can take my truck," Joel said.

"It's best we split up," Clancy said. "We aren't sure Daddy went to Crawl's. You go to Carthage. Make sure he didn't break down somewhere. I'll head to Shreveport."

"No, there's safety in numbers when it comes to Crawl," Joel insisted.

Lorraine knew Joel was right, but she handed Clancy her keys, anyway.

"Carthage is out of the way," Clancy said. "It's faster to go through Marshall."

"Yeah, but what if I find Daddy? Then what?" Joel asked. "You think it's smart to confront Crawl for nothing?"

Clancy paced, rubbing his head like it was a magic lamp. No genie appeared with an answer, but one came to Lorraine just the same.

"What if I stayed here? As a sort of command center? Joel, you can call when you make it to your father's house. Clancy, it will take you much longer to get to Shreveport. Is there a public telephone you can stop at before going to Crawl's?"

"Yeah, there's one at the station on Market Street."

"Stop there and call me. If Joel's found Mr. Fitchett, I'll tell you to come home."

"That might work," Joel said. "Except I'll go to Shreveport. This is my fault."

But Clancy was already out the door.

***

Joel stomped snow off his boots in Daddy's still warm kitchen. "He's not here," he told Lorraine.

"And you checked the highway?"

"I went slow. I couldn't have missed him."

"Oh, Joel." Lorraine's voice faltered. "I swear it never occurred to me he'd—"

"Don't, Lorraine. It's not your fault. Daddy's stubborn. He'd be doing this whether or not you talked to him. Thanks to you, we have a chance to stop him." Even as he said the words, Joel's stomach sank. He somehow sensed they were too late. All he could hope was Crawl had left Daddy alive. "Lori?" he asked. "Are you still there?"

"I'm just so sorry, Joel." Her voice became a whisper.

"Lorraine, I already said—"

"No, not that. I'm sorry about everything else."

"Nothing to be sorry for. I knew what I was getting into. You were engaged to Clancy. You still are, I take it?"

"Not for long."

Joel swallowed. "What does that mean?"

Her breathing sounded louder than the savage wind shaking the windows. "Don't talk to Clancy till I get a chance, but I've been thinking it might be best if I move back to Wyoming come January."

Joel choked the phone's cord. "Did your dad get transferred?"

"No, it would just be me. A new start. Well, I don't guess that's the right phrase, is it? Not when you're going back to an old life."

"Don't do that." Joel shook his head furiously. "If you love Clancy, stay. It will kill him if you go." Joel was fairly sure it wouldn't feel too good for him either. Not that the alternative, Lorraine staying and marrying Clancy, would be much better. "Lorraine, I want to talk to you more, but knowing how Clancy drives, he may be in Shreveport before long. You need to keep your line clear."

"Right. Okay. Are you coming back?"

"No," Joel said. "I'll stay here in case Daddy shows, but I'll call you with any news."

Her voice cracked as she said goodbye. The image of Lorraine alone and freezing in their kitchen was nearly enough to propel him back to her. But Daddy needed him now, and it made sense to stay here.

Joel turned on the radio to distract himself. This was ridiculous. Lorraine was fine. If this is how he reacted to the thought of her shivering and alone fifty miles away, how would he ever manage the thought of her shivering and alone all the way in Wyoming?

***

"Daddy's not here." Clancy's shaky voice on the other end of the line was almost unrecognizable. "Lorraine said he wasn't there when you called her earlier. Is he now?"

"No, but it's good he's not in Shreveport. Real good."

"It's not good, Joel." Clancy rushed his words. "I talked to a gal I know here. Daddy came earlier. Told Crawl what Roxanne did."

Joel leaned against the counter. "What did he do, Clancy?"

"Crawl wanted proof. Daddy took him to Carthage to show him the ledger. Donna said they left a couple hours ago."

"Well, they should be here soon. I'll be ready for Crawl when they do."

"That's just it. I don't think Daddy keeps work records at home."

"His office," Joel realized. "I'll go there now." He left the phone dangling, left his jacket on the couch, and left Clancy yelling his warnings from a payphone in Shreveport as he ran back into the storm.

***

Even with the blinding snow, Crawl's red Mercury couldn't be missed. Had to be a good sign. He wouldn't risk bringing such a flashy car to the scene of a crime.

The office lights were off, but Joel tried the front door anyway. When it didn't open, he trudged around back where Daddy typically parked.

He spotted them talking under a small overhang by the back door. He couldn't hear the conversation over the slap of sleet against the wet ground, but it didn't matter. All that mattered was that he wasn't too late.

282

Joel approached, the snow silencing his footsteps. "Daddy," he called, but the wind carried his voice the wrong direction. When the breeze similarly blew a cloud away from the moon, Joel noticed a gleam coming from the arm of Crawl's jacket. He pushed up his sleeve, revealing the tip of a blade.

"Daddy!" Joel screamed this time, sliding and slipping through the slushy mud.

His father saw him just as Crawl pulled the knife from his sleeve and plunged it deep into his chest.

Daddy's howl was louder than the wind's, but not as loud as Joel's. He stumbled forward into Crawl's arms. For once, Crawl seemed unsure what to do. He took a few steps backward, letting Tom land face down in the sludge.

Joel ran for his dad almost as fast as Crawl ran for his Mercury. "Daddy?" Joel turned him over. "Somebody help!"

Tom made a series of grunts drowned out by the screech of Crawl's tires turning the corner.

"Hang on!" Joel said, tears stinging his wind-burned face. He watched helplessly as his father twitched and thrashed for what felt like forever. He eventually stilled. Stilled then smiled. Joel couldn't imagine why. His eyes fluttered rapidly and then slammed shut. "No!" Joel said pulling up his dad's head like he was one of those blinking eye dolls, but his eyes remained shut.

Joel examined the wound. His first instinct was to pull the knife out. As soon as he touched the handle, a strange familiarity flooded him. This weapon was familiar. The letters "JAF" were illuminated by moonlight—the initials Daddy had carved—the knife he had made. Joel jerked his hand away. How did Crawl have it?

"Hey!" A stranger's voice shattered Joel's thoughts. "What's going on here?" Joel turned and saw a man stomping through the alley. A woman, swallowed in her date's suit jacket, struggled to keep up in her heels.

Joel would spend years wondering why he didn't point and yell, "He went that way!" Wondering why he didn't check for a pulse. Daddy might have still been alive. And if he was, the last thing he heard were the footsteps of his firstborn abandoning him to die in the cold.

***

The roads made the drive to Carthage take thirty more minutes than it should have. Thirty more minutes for the worst scenarios to taunt Clancy.

When he only saw Joel's truck at Daddy's house, he feared the worst. It only took finding Joel to confirm it. "Joel?" Clancy knelt beside his soaked and shaking brother. "Joel, what happened? Where's Daddy?"

The suddenness of Joel's sobs startled Clancy. "Dead."

Clancy's insides shook. He sprang up and threw his fist into the hallway mirror. He was breaking a lot recently. Like he didn't even control his appendages anymore.

The shattering glass got Joel's attention at least. Clancy didn't even realize Joel had stood until he felt icy hands on his shoulders. "Stay with me. I need you right now."

Clancy shook out his hand. He would grieve Daddy later. For the rest of his life maybe. But now, it was his turn to do the saving. "Did you call the police?"

"No. Crawl used my knife." Terror overtook Joel's face. "I don't know how he got it. Nobody saw him, but they saw me. Right before I ran." He quivered. "I shouldn't have run."

Heat came from somewhere and left Clancy lightheaded. As much as he wanted to bury his head in the snow, he had to make this right. "Don't worry. No one got a good look at you. Not at this hour, not in this storm."

"And if they did?"

"Then we tell the truth. That Daddy threatened to turn in Crawl's sister. We just need the business ledger that shows all the money she stole."

Joel rubbed his hands haphazardly across his face. "I don't know if that's enough. Between your drinking and my supposed try at suicide, everyone assumes the Fitchett brothers are one exit past crazy."

"Well, we aren't." Clancy flipped the light on. The site of Joel's bloody shirt made him long for the dark again. He looked away. "We need to get home. Are you okay to drive?"

Joel's eyes were glazed, but he nodded his head.

"Good. Go get your truck started. I'll call Lorraine."

The phone was dangling where Joel had left it. Clancy reset it and dialed.

"Hello?" Lorraine's voice was thick with panic.

"It's me."

"Clancy! I've been calling and—"

"Lorraine, stop. Somethings happened."

"What? What is it, Clancy? Talk to me," she pleaded.

He pulled the phone away from his ear. He needed her to anchor him, not detach him. "Lorraine, please. I need you to stay calm, or I can't talk to you. I'm already on edge."

"Right." She lowered her voice. "Sorry."

"We were too late. Crawl killed Daddy, right in front of Joel. We're on our way back, so you need to leave. Go home, and say you weren't with us tonight."

"You can't come back! Crawl will come here. If he knows Joel recognized him, it's only a matter of time."

"Crawl is probably halfway to Mississippi by now."

"Why? He's never run before."

"He's never left a witness."

"Exactly. And he won't. Don't come back here. Get a hotel or...wait...Mr. Fitchett left his rental keys here. He mentioned one was vacant."

"Yeah," he said. "Out on Pine." Clancy was supposed to help his daddy patch the walls last week. One last promise he'd made the old man and hadn't kept.

"Stay there," Lorraine said. "I'll pack bags for both of you."

It was happening too fast for Clancy to argue. "Okay, pack; then, go home."

"I'll go home after I see you both. After I say goodbye."

"Fine, but Lorraine, you'll need to talk to your parents. Work out a story about tonight." He needed to hang up before the cops arrived, but the need to say words he hadn't in a long time seemed more pressing. "I love you." Clancy's voice shook more than it had the first time he told her.

There was a too long silence followed by a faint sniffle. "I love you too, Clancy."

Enough to live with the monster inside me? He wanted to ask but didn't. The sound of a distant siren reminded him there was no time to waste.

Chapter 32

Carthage, Texas, 1991

A hospital cafeteria wasn't the ideal place for a conversation like this. Even though it was between mealtimes, a steady trickling of people came and went through the swinging doors. But Molly's parents were home, and Garrison's hotel room felt too secluded, given all he'd learned about Ray.

"Test came back fine," Ray said. "Still waiting for the blood pressure to come down before they release her." He zipped his windbreaker. "I, for one, am sick of this place. Do they have to keep it so damn cold?"

It was cold. Especially here in the cafeteria. Cold and loud. The sound of sliding trays echoed, and the ding of the cash register made Garrison jump every time.

Garrison sipped his coffee. It tasted like wet cardboard. His stomach growled, but he couldn't eat and have this conversation at the same time. "Glad to hear Molly's improving."

"Something tells me you didn't bring me here to talk about her."

Garrison clutched his cup. "I didn't."

"Then talk," Ray said, his head buried in a newspaper.

"Are you Jack Monroe?" Garrison asked. It was a question there was no way to cushion.

"Yes." Ray continued reading.

"And Crawl?"

"I've gone through a few names in my life, yes." Ray looked up. "Did you tell Molly?"

"Not yet." The scents of burnt grease and sweet ketchup wafting from Ray's plate turned Garrison's stomach—or maybe the knowledge he was face to face with a cold-blooded killer was to blame. A real killer this time and there was no glass nor guard between them. "All this time I've been looking for Clancy and you never told me."

Ray's mouth curled into a sneer. "What did you expect me to say? That I milked a small fortune from your granddad?"

"How about the part where you framed his brother for a murder you committed?"

Ray laughed. "I should have known." He pushed the paper across to Garrison. "Read under Aries."

Garrison read the first line. Something about the movement of Jupiter causing an unpleasant surprise. He closed the paper before reading the rest. These things were such crap.

"First day I met you, this horoscope warned me to be wary of strangers," Ray said. "People really ought to pay more attention to the stars."

Garrison pushed the paper away. "Did your horoscope say anything about going to jail?"

"Nope, but I'll remember to check tomorrow." Ray leaned against the booth, placing his arms behind his head with exaggerated casualness. "But I suppose that depends less on the stars and more on whether you're wearing a police wire."

Garrison lifted his shirt. "I'm not."

Ray shielded his face. "You could have warned me to put my sunglasses on first."

"I wouldn't be making a joke of this"

"Oh, lighten up." Ray rubbed his hands greedily over his hamburger. "If you don't want me in jail, what do you want?"

"Answers."

Ray took a messy bite of the burger. "Okay. Ask."

So many questions tumbled around Garrison's mind, but the first one out surprised him. "Why did you kill Tom Fitchett?" He planned to ask where Clancy was straight off the bat. But finding his grandfather wasn't all that mattered anymore. Joel mattered; Molly mattered. The truth mattered.

Ray dipped a fry in ketchup and studied it. "Have you ever watched a person die, Garrison?"

"No." There was too much saliva in Garrison's mouth. He needed to spit, throw up maybe.

"It's very fascinating. The blood, the breathing." Ray stopped to reach for a napkin to cough into.

Garrison watched him stain it red and doubted Ray's enjoyment of blood extended to his own.

When the coughing stopped, Ray finished his water. "Some say the damnedest things too. 'Did I leave the oven on?' and shit like that. Others are more profound. I enjoy hearing those last words, the last firing of the brain before, BOOM! Game over. I wonder what you might say." Ray stopped again as a man in a white coat approached. "Oh hey, Doc. How's our girl?"

The doctor put his hands on his hips. "She's fine, but how about you?" He looked at the blood-drenched napkin. "Are you being treated?"

Garrison listened to Ray talk to the doctor, marveling at how easily he slipped out of crazy and back into civilized society. Was it hard to hide who he really was?

"Death always starts with panic." Ray slipped effortlessly back to crazy as soon as the doctor left. "But peace does take over. It's sort of beautiful. And with each death I witness, I become stronger. Like their energy enters me."

"You're sick," Garrison said. "Killing someone out of anger or revenge is bad enough, but for gratification...well, that's twisted."

Ray laughed. "Come on, I'm not some animal. I can suppress my urges. I only kill those who have it coming."

"And Tom had it coming because Clancy owed you money?"

"No. Lorraine was paying for him." He smiled. "Not the way I wanted her too. She was a beautiful woman. Someone should have told her there were better men to warm her bed than Clancy and Scarface Fitchett." He stirred his coffee. "But I was content with their money. Probably still would be if Dr. Fitchett hadn't shown up claiming he had proof my sister stole from his business. He threatened to go to the police if I didn't leave his boys alone." Ray gave a wide grin. "He said it like he was Roy Rogers come to save the day. But Roxanne was the only family I had, and I couldn't allow anyone to threaten her. Same goes today. Nobody messes with my sweet sister nor my sweet granddaughter and lives to tell about it." He held up a finger. "Now, correct me if I'm wrong, but I believe you have *messed* with them both."

Garrison wondered how and when Ray found out he'd seen Roxanne, but at this point, what did it matter? "So, you're saying you are going to kill me?"

Ray shrugged. "It's easy nowadays. Simple as taking a lug nut from a tire or dropping a pill into a drink. But where's the fun in that?" Ray unrolled his napkin wrapped silverware and lifted the knife. "I haven't killed in years, but I imagine it's sort of like riding a bike."

Garrison gripped the table. "I can tell Molly."

"And tarnish her image of dear old granddad? Test her belief in justice above all things?"

"There are worse things than showing someone the truth. Like letting an innocent person sit in jail."

Ray set the knife down and lined up the three utensils. "As sharp as Molly is, I'm surprised she's never put it together. You see, her obsession with the Fitchetts is sort of my fault." He raised his eyebrows cartoonishly. "I keep a box in my trunk full of newspaper articles and mementos from each of my uh…activities. Some keep love letters or yearbooks they pull out to remember. I have my box."

"Molly looked in the trunk?"

"During one of her summer visits. She wasn't alone long, so she couldn't have read much. Hell, she was only a second grader, so she could barely read at all. Or so I thought. But something stuck because by high school, she was flat out obsessed with Joel Fitchett. But I don't guess she remembers where she first learned his name."

"It's not too late for her to find out, not too late for her to find the box again."

"I ditched the articles right after that. And the souvenirs I kept wouldn't mean a damn thing to anybody but me. Besides, you said you want answers, and I'm giving them to you."

"I think you know the answer I most want." Garrison pushed his shoulders back. "You can tell me where Clancy is. You've kept tabs on him like you will on me—like you do on anybody who knows the truth."

"First of all, don't flatter yourself. Secondly, forget Clancy. Stay here." He waved the bloody napkin. "I'm dying. I'll be out of your curly hair soon enough. Then you and Molly can live happily ever after. She's worth a thousand Clancy Fitchetts."

He was right. Molly was special. And there was something special between them. But Garrison couldn't start something holding so much inside. Look what secrets had done to his and Amber's relationship. They were poison. Garrison slammed a fist on the table. After everything he'd been through, the unfairness of life shouldn't surprise him, but it still stung.

Garrison scooted till he hung off the booth. "Tell me where he is, or I'll go straight to Molly. The only way you'll stop me is by killing me right here."

Ray rolled his eyes. "No need to be dramatic. They're in Alaska. Sitka, Alaska."

"Do you have a number?"

"Look it up. Clancy and Lori Franklin."

"Franklin?"

"Lori Franklin is her pen name."

"The mystery writer?"

Ray snorted. "If you can call that writing. Not my preferred genre."

Garrison settled back into his seat. Grandma Dolly had loved Lori Franklin's books, particularly the Marcus Spade mystery series. She owned the entire set. In all the places Garrison had looked for Clancy, he'd never considered his grandmother's bookshelf.

"Why did he leave?" Garrison feared the answer. "Was he involved in his father's death?"

"Nope. Not sure why he ran. I assumed Joel told him it was me who offed the old man, but maybe not. It didn't look good for Joel. Besides the witnesses, there was the knife."

"Did it have his fingerprints on it?"

"They didn't test for things like that back then, but I suspect it did. Seeing as how it belonged to him." Ray emptied another sugar packet into his coffee. "I nearly killed Tom when he showed up at my place, but I remembered I had Joel's knife and saw a bigger opportunity."

"How did you get his knife?"

Ray's eyes gleamed. "Let's just say breaking and entering was another hobby in those days. So, I had the knife, and I knew about the fight they'd had. It seemed too easy. Like killing two birds with one stone, so to speak."

"And Joel showing up? The witnesses? Was that all part of the setup?"

"That's what they call the planets aligning."

Garrison's head pounded. He scrubbed his forehead as if he could rub out the headache. "Even if he thought Joel murdered their dad, why did Clancy run? Wouldn't he at least stay to bury his father?" Garrison paused as the only plausible explanation came to him. "Did you threaten him?"

"I had just killed a well-known doctor in the middle of a nosy Texas town. I was too busy getting my ass out of dodge to bother with Clancy." Ray put his hand over his heart. "If you want the truth, Clancy probably saw his chance to hide away with Lorraine, and he took it. She was two-timing him with Joel, so having his brother in prison certainly increased his chances."

"Just stop." Garrison stood up. He'd save the rest of his questions for Clancy.

A line etched between Ray's brows. "Where do you think you're going?"

"To tell Molly goodbye."

Garrison's heart thudded as Ray reached into his windbreaker. "And that's all you better tell her." His hand emerged empty, but he had positioned his fingers into the shape of a gun. He flicked his middle finger, symbolically pulling the trigger. "Yep," he said, narrowing his eyes at Garrison, "just like riding a bike."

***

Garrison reclined his seat, but he couldn't get comfortable. The armrests dug into his skin, and the kid behind him kicked his seat like it was covered in black and white hexagons.

He pulled out the Lori Franklin book he'd picked up on the way and opened the back flap. There was a small photo of Lorraine but obviously outdated. She didn't look like any other woman pushing seventy. He read the paragraph below the picture.

Lori Franklin is the author of over thirty Marcus Spade novels and six stand-alone mysteries. She and her husband live in Alaska where she enjoys spending time with family and volunteering. She is an active member of the First United Methodist Church of Sitka and the Alaska Democratic Party.

Garrison closed the book. Surreal to think he would meet her later today. For the hundredth time, he second-guessed his decision. He should have called first, given everyone time to process, but he was too afraid they wouldn't want to see him. They still might not, but slamming a door might prove harder than hanging up a phone.

Slipping the book into the backseat slot, he saw the safety instruction card. Thanks to the handy illustrated guide, he knew what to do in case of a water landing or loss of cabin pressure, but he still had no idea what to do about Molly. That felt like the real emergency.

He'd lied to her. Said he was going back to Ohio to handle the remainder of his grandmother's estate. He promised he'd be back. That part wasn't a lie. He'd go back but wasn't sure what would come after that. If Clancy slammed the door on his face, could he act like it hadn't happened? Pretend Ray wasn't a monster? Say he was ready to give up on finding Clancy for no discernible reason? How would he ever discourage her efforts to exonerate Joel?

The implications of what would happen if Clancy didn't slam the door were even grimmer. There would be no hiding that from Molly. Sure, he could lie about

291

how he found Clancy, but if Lorraine came back to visit Joel, Molly would expect an interview. The truth would not stay hidden forever.

Garrison couldn't blame his pounding head on the altitude. No matter how much he tried to work it out, he kept arriving at the same bleak conclusion. This thing with Molly, whatever it was, could not work now.

***

The house on Halibut Point Road was bigger than Garrison expected. But even with its three levels, the brown wood paneling gave it a much simpler vibe than Molly's house of the same size. The towering trees cradled it like a home hidden deep within the woods of a fairy tale. A dozen windows of various shapes and sizes were tossed across the face of the house with no distinguishable pattern. At least that many wind chimes dangled like earrings from the porch, providing the plain house its only ornamentation.

Garrison rang the doorbell and held his breath. A hummingbird zipping by to land on a nearby honeysuckle bush startled him. He hated his jumpiness. Everything would be okay.

When no one came, Garrison checked his watch again. Even though the bright sunlight made it seem earlier, it was almost eight. Maybe it was too late for a visit.

At last, he heard movement from inside. The slow and steady footsteps caused his heart to flutter like the wings of that hummingbird. The accumulation of his six-month singular quest waited just on the other side of this door.

He recognized Lorraine. She looked older than in her photo; extra lines were on her face, and her hair had gone completely gray, but she still looked too young to be a great-grandmother.

"Hello there. Can I help you?"

A Siberian husky slammed against the screen door, and Garrison jumped back. "Down, Kodiak!" Lorraine smiled at Garrison. "He won't hurt you."

Not any more than a hummingbird would. Garrison thought. *Pull yourself together.* "Is um.... Clancy home?"

"Clancy? No, I'm sorry. He'll be back soon, though. Is there something I can do for you or...?"

Garrison unbuttoned the top button of his new polo. He'd worn it to make a good impression, but it strangled him now. "My name is Garrison Stark, and I've traveled a long way to meet you both, all the way from Ohio."

"Oh. Are you a fan?"

"No. Well, I haven't read your books, or I'm sure I would be. I'm not much of a reader unless you count textbooks. I'm studying astronomy. Well, I was. Long story." He was babbling. This is where he needed Molly to cut to the chase.

"I see." She backed up a tiny step.

Garrison's sweaty hands overcompensated for his dry mouth. He patted his jean pockets before remembering he had left his mints in the car. Running back there didn't seem like a horrible idea at the moment, but he wouldn't give her a chance to close the door. "This is going to sound crazy," he said, "but I think Clancy is my grandfather."

***

Although visibly surprised, Lorraine unlocked the screen. "Come in, come in." She grabbed another husky by the collar. "Let me get them back outside. Kodiak, Kermode, time to get. We've got a visitor."

The house's open floor plan made it appear even bigger inside. The only division between the den and dining room was the line where the blue carpet ended and wooden floors began. And only a small bar divided the dining room and kitchen. But despite the size, the house was simple and rustic. Clean, but rumpled. The kind someone lived in, the comfortable kind.

"I don't mind the dogs," Garrison said.

"It's fine; they love it outside."

"I like the bear names."

She smiled. "You noticed?"

"Yeah," Garrison said. "I had this thing about bears as a kid. Still find them interesting."

"If it's bears that interest you, maybe try zoology."

"I'll stick with the sky. Less chance of being mauled at work."

Lorraine's boisterous laugh was infectious. "Well, there's not much night sky this time of year." She pointed to the ceiling. Garrison looked to find the light fixtures turned off, with natural light pouring through the skylights, illuminating the spacious room.

"I figured that Alaska isn't the hotbed of astronomy."

"Come back in the winter, and the days are so short you nearly miss them. Say, I was about to have coffee. Can I get you a cup? Or a Pepsi?"

"My morning started early today, so coffee sounds great." Garrison noticed the cane leaning against the recliner. "Can I help?"

"No, no, you sit. I had a knee replacement and need to walk as much as possible. I can get around without that old stick as long as I don't have far to go."

Lorraine kicked a stuffed animal against the baby gate surrounding the wood stove. "Excuse the mess. I kept a great-grandbaby this morning. It's getting harder to get up and down from the floor. There's a reason why young women have the babies."

From the looks of the pictures covering the walls, Lorraine knew a thing or two about babies. Garrison walked the den, studying each one. So many faces and names to learn. Strangers with the potential to become a family. How would it feel to go from nothing to a part of this? He felt guilty wondering. Like he was being disloyal to his parents, to Grandma Dolly, but they would want him to be happy, want him to have a place to spend Thanksgiving.

It was disappointing that Clancy was absent from all the pictures. Garrison wanted to find a picture of him, wanted to see if there was any truth at all to Earl's claim about the resemblance.

"Where did you say you were from, Garrison?" Lorraine handed him his cup. "Iowa?"

"Ohio." He waited for Lorraine to lower herself into the recliner before taking his own seat. He couldn't believe she was still making small talk, that she hadn't demanded to know everything. Maybe she was waiting for him to take the lead. "But I flew from Texas. I've been there all summer."

Her eyes had changed shape at the mention of Texas. "Oh. Well, I hate to be the one to tell you this, Garrison, but our last name is not Franklin."

"I know. It's Fitchett, right?"

"Yes." The cane fell as she shifted in her seat. "How did you find us?"

"Long story."

"I don't mind those." She gestured to the shelves of books behind her.

Garrison was more of a cliff notes man, so he tried to keep it short as he told Lorraine his story.

"You poor thing," she finally said. "So much loss for such a young man. What was your grandmother's name?"

"Dorothy Ellison, but she went by Dolly."

Lorraine looked at the ceiling. "Sounds familiar, but Clancy and I never talked about the past much. I'm sorry. But either way, no matter what, you are welcome here."

Garrison's hopes kindled, but she wasn't the only one who got a say. "That means a lot, Lorraine. Can you tell me about your family? Do your children live around here?"

"Two in town, and two others in the state. Brenda and her family live in Oregon, and Charlotte is based in California, but she travels the world for her job. Lots of our grandchildren still live here, and two greats."

"Do you all get together often?"

"We try, but it's not near enough. It's been years since we were *all* together, but this Christmas, all the girls will be here and most of the grandkids too." She slapped her hands down on her knees. "You should come. It would be the perfect chance to meet everyone all at once."

"I'd like that, love it actually."

"Wow." Lorraine blew into her teacup. "Clancy had a child."

"Well, if I counted right, he has more than one."

"I mean *another* child. An older one." Garrison detected a slight nervousness in Lorraine's laughter. "What year was your mother born?"

"1942."

Lorraine brought a pair of fingers to her parted lips. "I moved to Texas at the end of 41."

"And grandma left about the same time you got there. I don't think she even told him. Or maybe she did, but I don't have any feelings about that either way. I just want to meet Clancy."

"I'm so glad you found us. Now the only question is how?"

Garrison looked down, using his hair as a shield. He'd already delivered the biggest blow, but this seemed almost as daunting. Lorraine had been in a relationship with Joel, possibly even cheated on Clancy with him. His name alone suddenly felt powerful enough to take away the family within Garrison's reach. But he had to say it. Had to honor his promise. "It started with writing Joel."

Lorraine tried to sip from her teacup, but it shook in her hands, clinking against the tiny plate she held under it. She leaned to deposit them both on the coffee table. "You wrote Joel?"

"And visited."

"And he knows where we are?" Lorraine asked.

"No, but he helped me find out." Garrison's hand fluttered to his neck. "The thing is...he wants to see you."

Her face went pale. "He what?"

"He wants you to visit him. I understand if you don't want to—or if Clancy doesn't want you to, but I promised I'd ask—promised I'd help you if it's something you are interested in."

"After all this time?" Lorraine glanced around. "Did he say—?"

When Garrison heard the cough and rattle of an ancient truck outside, Lorraine jolted as if they'd been caught doing something wrong. "That will be Alan." She went poker faced and gripped her cane.

"Alan?" Garrison asked.

"Clancy, I mean. He goes by Alan sometimes. Middle name. He's past due for a breathing treatment, so I need to help with the groceries."

Lorraine's sudden breathlessness made Garrison wonder if she was actually the one who needed the treatment. He stood on his shaky legs. "I can get the bags."

"No, stay. Please." Lorraine's entire demeanor had changed. She probably wasn't going to help with groceries so much as to warn Clancy—to warn Alan. Alan. He'd seen Clancy's middle initial in several documents but didn't realize what the "A" stood for until now. But wasn't that Joel's middle name too? Must be a family one.

Garrison peered out a window, straining to see, but only Clancy's profile was visible. And even that was masked by a mustache and full beard, both as gray as the flat cap he wore on his head. Lorraine was talking, her hands gesturing wildly as Clancy leaned against the battered truck.

With each minute that passed, Garrison's worry increased. What if Clancy drove off, demanding Lorraine get rid of Garrison? He couldn't risk it. He opened the door and quietly walked the drive.

"Are you sure he's not a reporter?" Clancy asked. His voice sounded gravelly. Like the rough sound made when a tire drifts to the shoulder of the road. In Garrison's imagination, he'd had a kinder voice.

"After all these years? No one cares about our story anymore. He's the real deal, and as soon as you look into his eyes, you'll see."

"How much does he know?"

Lorraine did a double take when she saw Garrison. "We'll be right in, Garrison," she spoke in a too-loud voice.

Clancy whipped around, turning his back as he rifled through a paper sack.

Anger seared through Garrison. Why wouldn't he look at him? Did Clancy have the audacity to ignore him? Had he ignored the child he created with the same flippancy? "I'm Garrison," he said. When Clancy made no response, Garrison walked beside him and leaned over the cargo bed to pick up a bag. "Need a hand?" he asked. He didn't want to help; he wanted to be face to face with Clancy. Wanted to force him to stare into the eyes that apparently looked so much like his own.

But when Clancy looked up, Garrison didn't notice his eyes, nor the shape of his chin. All he saw was a scar. Not just any scar, a familiar one. Garrison dropped the sack, spilling limes into the truck's bed. Clancy leaned further over to gather them, but Garrison stood frozen, staring at the scar that was, in every detail, identical to Joel's.

CHAPTER 33

Longview, Texas, 1945

Joel woke up to unexpected warmth. But when he opened his eyes, he wasn't in his own bed. Why couldn't it all have been a bad dream?

He sat up, his back aching from the hard floor beneath him. There was no way to know the exact time, but it was still dark. If only he could rewind just twenty-four hours. Go back to when he was worried about his stupid scar and Lorraine rather than his dead father and the real possibility of a life in prison.

The fire before him whipped like a horse's mane. Clancy must have kept it burning. The empty house was so cold when they arrived, but the fire hadn't been started for warmth. Joel had choked on the excessive smoke his shirt made when Clancy offered it to the flames. Not that it would make any difference. Joel couldn't burn the knife in Daddy's chest nor the eyes of the witnesses.

Joel unzipped his sleeping bag and searched the house for Clancy. He found him sitting out in the cold, drinking a bottle of Coca-Cola Lorraine sent. She had thought of everything: clothes, toiletries, blankets, even snacks, and drinks. She'd be such a good wife. Clancy was a lucky man.

When Joel noticed another bottle, broken beside Clancy, worry snaked through him. Had his brother snapped again? He couldn't blame him for it. Not after a night like tonight.

Joel leaned out the back door. "You all right?"

Clancy kept his back turned. "Figured if I was going to drink one last Coca-Cola, I might as well have a cold one."

A last one? What was he talking about? Joel looked up at the sleet, falling like fireworks. "Come inside. Gather your things, and I'll take you home."

Clancy tipped the bottle back. "And where will you go?"

"To the station," Joel said. "There's no point in denying anything. The evidence points to me. Even if I could convince them it was Crawl, he knows I killed Lyle, so either way, I'm done."

Joel expected Clancy to talk him out of it, but he didn't. "You're right," Clancy said. "And Crawl has too many connections. If they arrested him, we'd all be dead by Christmas." Joel knew that, but to hear someone else say it made it seem undeniably final. "I've been up all night, trying to figure this out." Clancy's shoulders shook.

The cold stung Joel like a thousand bees as he stepped out the door. He touched Clancy's back. "Come inside, and we will..." He stopped, distracted by the bloody shirt at his feet. "I thought you burned my shirt?"

When Clancy turned his head, Joel screamed as he stumbled backward. The cut on Clancy's face was not as deep as his own, but the placement was exact.

"No!" Joel pinched his skin and slapped his face, but he didn't wake up in his warm bed or on the cold floor in the empty living room. He took a slow step toward Clancy, crunching a piece of the broken glass that suddenly took on a new meaning. "Clancy? What did you do? What did you do?" Joel yelled.

Clancy stood. "What I should have done a long time ago, what I promised Mama I'd do...take care of you." Acid rose in Joel's throat. He leaned over the porch and expelled all the contents of his stomach, wishing he could do the same with his mind.

***

"Why?" Joel asked, still shaking. Clancy wrapped another blanket around his shoulders. They'd been back inside ten minutes, and Joel still couldn't get warm. Still couldn't understand.

Clancy winced as a single tear fell. Joel was all too familiar with the sting of salt on a fresh wound. "It's all my fault." He pressed his own bloody shirt back against his face. "I sent you to Carthage."

"Because you thought it was safer," Joel said.

"The scar's my fault too. It was always meant to be mine."

Joel shook his head, cursing his own stupid words. "I didn't mean that, Clancy."

"It doesn't matter." Clancy began shoving Joel's things into a bag. "There's a folder in here with my birth certificate and other documents you'll need." Clancy pulled out his wallet. "Trade me."

"Clancy, what are you...?" A weight dropped on Joel's heart as it all came together. Clancy hadn't cut his face to punish himself—he'd done it to take Joel's punishment. He felt his stomach turn again. "No, I'm not agreeing to this. I won't. We just need the ledger, like you said."

"It's not there. Crawl must have taken it."

"You went back to our house for your documents and to Daddy's office? When I was asleep? How could you risk it? They probably have officers watching both."

"I was careful." Clancy zipped the bag. "Go to Lorraine's. Tell her to pack and come with you. Drive and don't stop till you are far enough away to never be found."

No. Daddy gave his life trying to save him. He wouldn't let Clancy make the same sacrifice. "Let's both leave," Joel said.

"We can't run forever. What kind of life would that be?" He put the bag on Joel's shoulder. "This is the only way they won't look for you—the only way Lorraine can lead a normal life."

"It will never work." Joel's voice cracked, his throat sore from the pleading.

"Sure it will." Clancy gently traced the line on his face. "It's only a few days newer than yours. Well, I mean it's been two days since you—"

Joel held up his hand. "I know it looks the same, but we aren't twins. Carthage is our hometown; people can tell us apart."

"I promise nobody will know. We've been gone for years now. And you said it yourself, nobody sees beyond the scar."

Warm tears dripped from Joel's eyes as he took Clancy by the shoulders. "Listen. You get Lorraine. *You* go start that new life. She loves you. Always has."

Clancy closed his eyes. "I messed all that up."

Joel shook him. "You haven't. Go somewhere you can make a new start. She wants a new start."

"Don't you see, Joel? I'm broken...defective. No matter where I go, I'll never live a normal life. Not ever again." His eyelids drooped. "See, there is this worm, and it's eating into my brain."

"Stop it, Clancy. There is no worm. With the right help, you can lead a normal life. You have to."

The fire in the grate crackled. Clancy stepped closer to it, tossing in his bloody shirt. They both watched, waiting for the flames to latch on. Joel glanced out the window. Time was running out. The sun would rise soon. The police would come—and when they did, one of them needed to be gone.

Neither Joel nor Clancy spoke as the shirt burned. They only watched the flames dance higher and higher, granting them a final reprieve from the cold and the decision they had to make.

Chapter 34

Gib Lewis Unit, 1991

Lorraine wiped a clammy hand down her pant leg. Her red pant leg. She couldn't help herself. Maybe a cherry red pantsuit was too flashy for an old lady, but he once said red was her color. She hadn't dyed her hair in a decade. It seemed silly for a woman her age to sport bleach-blonde hair, but today, she wished for it back. If she'd been alone, she might have stopped at the drugstore last night for a box of L'Oréal. At least her hair was still long, and although the curl was gone, it held on to a little wave. But even in his favorite color, with his favorite hairstyle, she was still an old woman. No way to iron out the wrinkles, erase the dark spots, or trim off the twenty-five pounds the babies added to her figure. Beauty was just a loan, wasn't it? She enjoyed and utilized hers for a time but had been paying it back in installments ever since.

How silly to be so worried about appearances; she was a great-grandmother for goodness sakes. Of course she looked like one. But it would come as a shock to someone who hadn't watched her age gradually—someone who last saw her at twenty-one. Twenty-one was different from sixty-eight. Sixty-eight! She was sixty-eight years into the only life she'd ever get. What a sobering thought.

"Everything all right?" Garrison asked.

"It's fine." She used the cane to stand. "I'll be in the ladies' room." Lorraine didn't need to use the restroom. She didn't even want to look in the mirror again. She needed to be alone. This was a lot to take in.

In decades of dreams about this day, she imagined the two of them pouring out their hearts in a secluded room. But like so many other dreams, reality would prove different. Garrison said the room would be crowded and loud. And there were so many rules. "A quick hug is fine. Holding hands across the table is okay too, but nothing else," the officer who searched her explained. "Otherwise keep to your side." Lorraine wanted to tell him there was nothing to worry about there;

she was a married woman, thank you very much. But honestly, she wasn't sure how she would react to seeing him again.

When she came back from the bathroom, Garrison stood. "The tables are still full, but because of the overflow, they will let you sit on the patio. That okay?"

Lorraine liked that idea. It would add another level of privacy. "Yes. Thank you."

"What, you aren't visiting today, Stark?" a potbellied guard asked.

"Not today. Just escorting a friend." Garrison looked at Lorraine. "Unless you changed your mind? I can always leave whenever you are comfortable. Like I mentioned, Joel can be difficult, and sometimes—"

"Violent." The guard folded a stick of gum into his mouth. "Fitchett belongs behind glass. This ain't no petting zoo."

"I can manage," Lorraine said crisply. She was tired of warnings from people who assumed they knew him better than she did.

She held out her cane to Garrison, but he resisted. "It's a long walk, Lorraine."

"I can manage," she repeated, shoving it into Garrison's hand. The gray hair and wrinkles were bad enough. No way she was accessorizing with a cane.

The walk took longer without the cane's support, but she arrived at the dingy picnic table in one piece. She was glad to sit but wished for shade. She'd forgotten the heat of a Texas summer. "Does the time start now?" she asked the guard.

"Not till Fitchett gets here." Well, that was fortunate. Since nobody seemed in any hurry to bring him out. She lifted her hair and fanned the back of her neck. She needed to calm down. What did a few minutes matter when she had already waited forty-six years?

When Lorraine spotted him, her stomach knotted. She grabbed the thin, gold chain around her neck and twisted it around her finger. He looked so different, nothing like his brother anymore. He had no hair, not even on his face. A prison rule, she assumed, since a mustache and beard seemed to be the easiest way to cover the scar, some of it anyway. And he was so stout. His were the arms belonging to a man who'd spent years lifting weights instead of babies.

She stood as he approached, the chains from his handcuffs and leg irons jingling against the pavement. Her new knees felt decidedly old again when he smiled. What was she to do now? Sit? Hug him?

"Hello," he said, and it was the same. Despite how different he looked, how different he was, the voice was the same. The guard undid his restraints. "Do you want to sit?"

She did; it felt suddenly necessary to sit. She looked at her watch. "1:15," she noted.

"So, the spell runs out at 3:15?" he asked.

"Yes." She folded her hands in her lap. "Back to pumpkins then." She could have applied for the four-hour visit, but Garrison said that might take another week. She couldn't bear another week. The two weeks between Garrison arriving at her front door and now had been torture enough.

The intensity of his stare made Lorraine self-conscious. Like he was studying her. "Wow, Lorraine, it's been—"

"A lifetime."

He sat straighter. "Just about. A lot has changed."

Lorraine bit her lip. "Yes."

"You're still beautiful, though; that's the same."

Lorraine smiled. "Sure you aren't saying that because I'm the only woman who's visited in forty-six years?"

"You'd be surprised."

She waved her hands. "Don't tell me about that."

"Then tell me about you." He laid his hand on the table, an invitation maybe?

She folded hers back in her lap. "Well, where to start? We live in Alaska now."

"Should have known. I remember how much you missed the cold stuff."

"Yes, but I wasn't counting on so much of the wet stuff." Lorraine didn't care for rain, especially since the night she left Texas with the other Fitchett brother. The storm that confronted them outside of Austin was unlike any she'd seen before or since. They barely saw the road, barely heard each other over the rain pinging against the roof and windows. And it was so dark. The only reprieve came in the flashes of lightning, near as frightening as the absolute darkness. As sheets of rain assaulted the windshield, Lorraine braced herself for it to shatter. It was as if the rain was coming for them. Like it knew what they had done. She would never hear rain again and not find herself wrapped in the same fear and confusion of that night. So the dream of living in a cold climate again turned out to be a punishment too. Who knew more rain than snow fell in Sitka? Still, being here reminded her there were certainly worse punishments than memories.

"Have you always been in Alaska?" he asked.

"No, we spent the first year in San Antonio. But it was too close."

"Too close to what? Me?"

"Yes. The knowledge you were only a day's drive was torture." Lorraine kept her eyes down as she spoke. It was hard to remember that year, harder to talk about it. It had been the worst one of her life. "What about you?" She tried to make her voice chipper. "What's it like here?"

He shrugged. "What does it matter?"

"A great deal." She brought her hands above the table. "I always wonder what you are doing; always hope you aren't just sitting around."

He appeased her. Ran through the daily life of a prisoner. It reassured her to learn there were instruments to play, equipment to exercise on, books to read, even televisions to rent. He told stories of the various jobs he'd held. The more he talked, the more comfortable she became. Not just with the prison system, but with being around him again.

It was Lorraine's turn to share next, but her days were so mundane now. "Life was busier when I was younger," she explained. "I founded a nonprofit organization helping families who are homeless or at a high risk for homelessness. I served on the board of The Boys and Girls Club for twenty years and..." She stopped. Lorraine recognized what she was doing, but it was a waste of words. No charitable deeds could make up for what she hadn't done to help him. "Anyway," she continued, "I don't do much of that anymore. I mostly keep to the house."

Lorraine caught him glancing at her watch, so she did the same. Almost an hour gone. An hour and they'd yet to move beyond the superficial. She should have listened to Garrison. Should have held out for the four hours.

"So..." He traced the crack on the table. "How's my brother?"

Lorraine swallowed. She wondered if he would ask. "Alan's fine. Experienced some health problems in '89, but he's much better now."

"Alan?"

She lowered her voice. "Well, I couldn't use his real name any longer, and I could never bring myself to call him yours."

"I see. Well, what's Alan do there in Alaska?"

"Whatever he wants these days. He retired six years ago. Before that, he worked as a crab fisherman. Then in the offseason, he did odd jobs around town, repairs and the like." Talking about jobs reminded Lorraine of what she'd brought. She turned to the guard. "Can we get the books now?"

"I'll check." He mumbled something into a walkie-talkie.

"I swear, they act like I tore the pages out and packed knives and files inside."

"Again, you'd be surprised." He rolled his shoulders. "So how about children?"

"Children? Oh yes, six."

"Six?"

"And all girls." She brought a hand to her chest. "Not my idea. Your brother wanted a boy so badly. It took six pink hospital bracelets to convince him it wasn't in the cards."

"Boys aren't nothing but trouble. He, of all people, should know that. What are these niece's names?"

Nieces. The words pierced through her heart. What a wonderful uncle he would have made. "Well, the twins came first, Nancy and Beatrice, after our mothers."

He nodded. "Mama would be proud."

"Well, Nancy's a dear girl, always has been. Bea was our handful. Then came Tess, Brenda, Jo, and finally little Charlotte." She laughed. "I say little, but they are grown now. They have children; Bea even has grandchildren."

He shook his head. "Six kids. I would never have pictured that."

"Me either. Forced me to grow up." Lorraine looked at her palms. "Hard to believe these hands have cooked ten thousand suppers since you held them last."

He made a strange choking noise then went quiet. She shouldn't have said that about holding hands, especially since his was still palm up on the table.

Luckily, a guard approached with the books, giving her a perfect out from that conversation. She pushed them across the table. "These are for you."

He examined the top book, turning it over in his hands. He gave a half smile as he opened the back flap. "Lori Franklin, huh?"

"Pen name. Agent said it rolled off the tongue better. Plus, privacy and all that."

"She is an active member of the First United Methodist Church of Sitka and the Alaska Democratic Party," he read aloud. "Good to hear some things haven't changed."

"We've been members for forty years now. Your brother is an usher and helps me teach the second grade Sunday School class."

"Does he help with democratic fundraising too?"

Lorraine grinned. "Goodness, not that much has changed."

He closed the book and stared at the cover. "Mystery, huh?"

Lorraine forced a smile. "Yes, I write mysteries."

"Whatever happened to the Sadlers?"

Lorraine winced. Hearing the surname of the fictional family from her still unfinished, still unpublished, novel stung. Whatever happened to the Sadlers indeed? "I suppose after my life became a mystery, writing them seemed natural."

"Well, I'm sure it's great."

"It's decent. I understand if you don't read it. I just hoped it might be something nice for you to keep." Lorraine knew it wasn't the best work she could do, but Detective Marcus Spade had been good to her. The series bought many pairs of shoes, paid for many weddings.

"Of course, I'll read it. I've finished most the books here. I'm glad for something new." He peeked inside the back flap again. "And a new picture too. The one I keep is a little outdated."

She forced back tears. If she let the first one fall, they'd never stop. "And I'm sure you are already familiar with that other book."

He lifted the Bible. "Think I've seen one or two of these around here."

"Do you ever read it?" Lorraine asked.

"Nah," he said, absently thumbing through the thin pages. "God abandoned me a long time ago."

"That's not true," she said. "In fact, it's likely the other way around. I've read things about the reason you transferred here. About the trouble you caused. That's not you."

"Being locked up changed me. It's sort of like how you learned to cook and change diapers. We had to adapt to our surroundings, didn't we?"

She hated the sudden coldness in his voice. "No, you don't have to adapt. You're better than that. And if you want me to leave here with any peace of mind, promise to read it, to attend chapel."

He gave a lackluster smile. "Okay, okay." It was impossible to tell if he was sincere, but at least some warmth returned to his voice. "So, you and my brother. Are you two..." He looked at the cloudless sky as if the right word might fall from it. "Are you happy?"

"Yes," Lorraine answered without hesitation. It was true, mostly true. They hadn't always been. But what couple could claim otherwise? She wondered if knowing the truth about her thoughts that night she left Longview would make him feel better or worse. From the knock on her window to the scribbled note to her parents, everything had happened so fast. The full weight of it all didn't settle on her until driving through that storm. As terrifying as it was, at least she could cry inconspicuously. She understood she couldn't talk Clancy and Joel out of this path; they believed it was the only way. But she couldn't pretend she hadn't wished that the man waiting on Pine Street for the police to take him away, was the one taking her away instead. It was a selfish, repulsive fantasy, but she couldn't help how she felt. That had always been her problem with the Fitchett boys. Not being able to help how she felt.

The worst part was that she'd wished it more than once over the years. But that didn't mean she wasn't happy. Those thoughts were normal. Greener grass and all that.

"Did you get the letter?" he asked.

Lorraine stiffened. "What letter?"

"The night you left. I sent a letter with—"

"Oh, yes, that one. I thought you meant one since."

He shut his eyes. "I've wanted to."

"You should have." She pulled out a Kleenex from her pocket, no longer able to stop the tears. "I considered writing a thousand times. How cruel to ask me not to!"

"I didn't want to make things any harder for you. Your heart had been divided long enough."

She stretched her hand across the table. "I've missed you."

"I've missed you too, Lorraine." He grabbed her hand. "So much."

"You shouldn't be in here." She slapped the table with her free hand. "It's not too late. We can get a lawyer."

"No, absolutely not."

"Crawl's an old man. The danger is—"

"Never gone," he said sternly. "I'm an old man too. An old man who's spent a lifetime locked up. What would I do out there?"

He had a point. What would he do? What would *she* do? Fulfill some buried fantasy and run away with him? No, of course not.

These feelings now reminded Lorraine of an emotional day forty years before. She'd been at the airport, returning from a meeting with her publisher, when she ran into her childhood best friend. She recognized Kirsten immediately, even though she'd moved away the summer before seventh grade.

As the two caught up at an airport bistro, Lorraine couldn't get over how much Kirsten had changed. Of course, she had too. They had missed so much. There was so much about the others' lives they didn't know. Far too much to learn in a one-hour time span.

Lorraine cried the entire flight back home. She blamed it on exhaustion and hormones. Who wouldn't cry with a pair of toddlers at home and a baby on the way, but it was much more complicated than that.

Alan noticed she'd been crying when he picked her up. "I ran into Kirsten," she said.

He rubbed her back. "Okay. Why are you crying about that?"

"Because I want to be friends again."

"Then be friends with her," he said as if it were that easy. "Did you get a phone number?"

Lorraine only cried harder. How could he understand so little? She didn't want to be friends with Kirsten now; she barely had time for friendships anymore. She wanted to be eleven years old. Wanted to walk the fence and play dolls with her cherub-faced friend for hours, never worrying about cooking dinner, paying bills or potty training. She wanted to be young and carefree, and that is what Kirsten would always symbolize.

It was the same now. Lorraine didn't want to run away with this old man staring at her. She wanted to be young and in love again. She wanted to walk on air and doodle hearts around his name. That is what Clancy would always represent to her.

"When do you fly back?" he asked.

"Tomorrow. But I wonder how hard it would be to change flights. If I stayed another week, I—"

"No, don't do anything like that. Crawl lives in Longview."

She rolled her eyes. "Him again. I'm so tired of Crawl ruining our lives."

"Ruin? You said you were happy?"

"I am. I mean obviously, he didn't ruin mine like he did yours, but there hasn't been a single day I haven't thought of you." She looked away. "If all this hadn't happened, I'd have gone home to Wyoming. That would've meant living life without either of you, but at least you'd both get to live your lives. I'd be okay with that trade."

He leaned forward. "You didn't get a choice. We made the choice for you. I made it. Don't regret your happiness."

She released his hand to blow her nose. "I'm just glad Garrison found me and brought me to you."

"Ah yes. How did Gary boy take all this?"

"With a great deal of shock."

"I bet. If he would have told me he found you before he took off, I could have warned him. He's a good kid. Take care of him."

"He's a darling. We offered him our basement apartment. He said he'll stay through the year, but he's applying at LSU in the spring."

"LSU?" He wrinkled his nose. "Aren't there colleges in Eskimo country?"

"I expect he wants to be around here."

"Because of that gal he's seeing?"

"No, not because of her. Baton Rouge is only three and a half hours away. I think he wants to be close enough to continue visiting you."

His face twisted. "Oh hell, don't let him do that. The kid wanted a family; he found one. Talk him into staying. Find him a college close by to apply to."

"Garrison is an adult. I can't force him."

"Well, you can be persuasive, if I remember correctly. Tell him he can make a yearly pilgrimage here if it will ease his conscience. That's as much as I can stand seeing him anyway."

"You don't fool me." Lorraine smirked. "I'm not surprised you are fond of him. Just that you let him visit. You turned Daddy away twice."

His expression dulled. "That was real early on. Wasn't sure how much they knew."

"And the second time? After they knew all?"

"Would have been too hard. Didn't want to see anybody associated with you. Figured a clean break was best."

"Was it?"

"A break's a break. Hurts the same no matter what. Just heals better if it's clean. Or so they say."

Lorraine wondered how he maintained such stoicism sharing painful memories. It was as if somewhere along the way, the grief hollowed him out. Meanwhile, her handkerchief was too wet to do any good, so she traded it for a box of tissues.

"What can I do?" She wiped the black smudges under her eyes. "Do you get the money?"

"End of every month. I appreciate it, but it's unnecessary. Does, umm, *Alan* realize you're doing that?"

"Yes. I've never tried to keep it a secret."

"Does he notice how much you send?"

"He doesn't need to." Lorraine's mouth set in a hard line. "I handle the finances, and we've always done well. But I'd like to do more than a check. A letter now and again? And I assume you can receive packages?"

He bounced a knee under the table. "I'm not sure. I don't want to cause any problems in your marriage."

"It wouldn't. He might even decide to write. We don't talk about it anymore, but he still thinks about you, still has nightmares."

"Well, tell him to stop thinking about me. Tell him I stand by the decision I made."

She caught another glimpse of her watch. It hadn't stopped ticking or even slowed down. That was the trouble with clocks; they were just too damn reliable. "Will they give us a five-minute warning before they take you away?"

"A guard will tell me it's time to go. We'll say goodbye, and that's that."

"That's that," she repeated.

He took her hand again. "Hey, enough of this crying. Let's talk about happy times."

Happy times. She just wasn't up to it, not today. But she let him share. Although it was nice to witness his eyes brighten as he recalled their first meeting, she closed her own. Both to more clearly imagine the memory and to hold the tears in. She kept them shut as he shared another memory and then another. When he stopped talking, she opened her eyes, afraid she'd see a guard standing there. There wasn't one, but she spotted the reason for the abrupt silence just the same. A dove had landed a few feet away. She sighed. Clancy and Joel had always been so funny about doves. Her poor Tess had cried all day when she caught Daddy throwing away the bird feeder she'd made in Scouts. It took two scoops of ice cream to make it right. Men could be so fussy, couldn't they? What happened wasn't the fault of doves.

While they both stared, another dove joined the first. The pair cooed back and forth as they preened each other's feathers.

"A couple," he observed. "Doves mate for life."

"Really?"

"Yeah. Read it in a library book here," he said, keeping his eyes fixed on the birds.

"Well, that's refreshing. To see that sort of loyalty still exists. It's near extinct in humans." She cringed. She was one to talk, wasn't she?

"It's not a foolproof system," he said. "Sometimes a dove dies; sometimes they are separated."

"And then what? The other remains alone?"

"Sometimes. The dumb ones will stand watch over their mate's dead body, pluck out their own feathers even."

"And the smart ones?

"Move on," he answered quickly. "Find another mate. Build a new nest. Hatch eggs, avoid hawks."

"Times up."

Lorraine jumped. She'd been so focused on the doves, she hadn't noticed the guard.

"But I'm not ready!" She squeezed his hand harder. He stood and pulled her into him. His arms still felt like home. The guard let them stay that way longer than she expected, probably longer than he should have. She pressed her mouth against Clancy's ear. "I love you."

"I love you too."

Though he turned away, Lorraine glimpsed the tears in his eyes. They hurt her almost as much as the click of the handcuffs.

"Thank you," she said. "We both thank you. For everything."

He looked over his shoulder and met her eyes a final time. "Goodbye, Lorraine."

"Goodbye, you," she whispered as they led him away.

***

Lorraine sat at the table for a while. It was a long walk back to Garrison, and she was in no state to do it carrying on like this.

She forgot about the birds until a hawk screeched. That's when she noticed one of the doves was gone. She searched the skies but saw no signs of a predator. The dove was probably fine. Perhaps back in the nest or off gathering food. He would return to his partner soon. And if something prevented him, this one looked like a smart bird; she could find a life elsewhere. One thing Lorraine understood about doves was that their life was hazardous and, too often, brief. A hawk wasn't the worst way to go. One moment, one swallow and done. Life made a much crueler predator, chewing up and spitting back out to destroy again and again. And no mateless bird would have forty-six years to stand over a corpse and pluck their feathers away, that was for sure.

Lorraine adjusted her jacket and wiped away the mascara under her eyes. No need for Garrison to see she had been crying. The visit was over; there were other matters to attend to now. She needed to get flowers for Mr. and Mrs. Fitchett's graves, buy Garrison dinner somewhere, and be in bed early for their six o'clock flight out of Beaumont.

Tomorrow would be an even longer day. They wouldn't arrive back in Sitka until dinnertime. She'd stop at Pizza Express and pick up Spaghetti and Rigatoni, Alan's favorite. If he had questions, she'd answer them, but knowing her husband, he wouldn't. Not yet anyway. Then she would put a load in the laundry, make a grocery list, and wrap the gift for her granddaughter's ninth birthday on Tuesday. An American Girl Doll, wouldn't she be surprised?

Yes, she'd fly home, back to her life, with all her feathers intact. It was the way it had to be. But somehow, she knew this sadness tearing into her chest would never leave. What had been the burden of a ten-year-old Clancy was now hers...to be haunted by a caged bird.

EPILOGUE

Sitka, Alaska, One Year Later

Summer storms always made Garrison think of Molly. Most days he could forget her, but one whiff of rain, one flash of lightning, and he was back in that pool. Starting something he hadn't finished, something he could never finish. Some things just weren't meant to be.

The wind howled, and the dogs at his feet answered. "It's okay, boys," Garrison said. "It won't hurt us."

That wasn't completely true. Garrison knew the memories the rain stirred would hurt a little. They always did. But in spite of constant drizzle, he was glad to be here—home for the summer after one semester at LSU under his belt. He missed his weekend visits with Clancy, but he was glad for the time with Joel, Lorraine, and their family. *His* family. Some days it still felt too good to be true.

The wind blew harder, performing an overture on the row of wind chimes hanging from the porch soffit. They were so loud he might not have heard the car pull up had the wildly barking dogs not alerted him.

"Go inside, boys." Garrison opened the front door but kept his eyes on the figure approaching.

At first, he was sure he was hallucinating. It wasn't her. He'd been thinking about Molly, so he was imagining her face on this stranger walking toward him.

Yet, when she stepped closer and removed her hood, it was her.

"Molly? How?" He didn't wait for an answer nor an explanation. He took her in his arms the way he had imagined for the past year.

Her coat was drenched and her body tense in his embrace. "Pappy died," she whispered.

Garrison pulled back to look in her eyes. "I'm so sorry," he said. And he was, for her loss anyway.

Molly smoothed down her damp hair. She'd cut it shorter, and the new style accentuated her cheekbones. "Can we sit?"

Garrison wiped drops of water from the plastic chairs behind him. He had so much he wanted to say, but he knew he needed to let her lead the conversation.

"I was going through his things, and I found something strange," Molly's voice shook. "A business ledger that belonged to Dr. Fitchett."

Garrison's heart drummed with the rain.

"I couldn't figure it out. Not so much why he had it, but that in all the time we were looking, he never said anything about knowing them. Plus, the way you left. I know you said you wanted to get back to a normal life, but it was just so sudden."

"I know." Garrison looked into her eyes. "And I'm so sorry."

"Please, just let me finish." Molly rubbed her temples. "I've tried to put it behind me, but nothing added up. After a month of stewing over it all, I wrote Joel in prison."

Garrison's muscles stiffened. "You what?"

"I explained what I'd found, how you'd left. Long story short, he invited me to visit."

"And?"

"Well, I got my interview." Molly came the closest to a smile she had since arriving. "He told me everything."

"Everything, everything?"

"I can't imagine there being more."

Garrison stood. "He shouldn't have done that."

"He told me it's been hard for you too, living with how you left things." Molly lowered her eyes.

Garrison knelt in front of her. "It was one of the hardest things I've ever done, Molly. I racked my brain trying to find a way I could stay."

Molly lifted her head. "Clancy told me that you'd be angry with him, but he said he can't let you sacrifice what he did. That there was no reason to let our relationship be Crawl's last victim." Her eyes welled up. "Crawl. I still can't believe I'm talking about Pappy."

Garrison touched her knee. "I never wanted you to know, but I can't be angry with Clancy because you're here."

Molly opened her mouth and closed it again. For several minutes, neither spoke—neither moved.

The wind blew harder, knocking one of the wind chimes to the ground. Garrison was glad for a distraction and stood to retrieve it.

"That's a lot of wind chimes," Molly said. "And a lot of noise."

Garrison laughed. "Well, you know what they say. If your neighbor has wind chimes, you have wind chimes. I bet the whole street feels like they have them with all the clanging these do."

"Does Lorraine collect them?"

"Joel actually," Garrison said, leaving out the explanation as to why.

Molly stood. "We should probably take them down. They're getting all twisted together."

They worked quickly, fighting the wind and the rain. "I brought the ledger." Molly's voice was monotone. "Plus, some items I found that may tie him to other crimes. I don't know if it's enough to get Clancy out, but don't you think we've got to try?"

Garrison's hands froze on the string of seashell chimes he was unraveling. "I don't know." He pulled down a tangle of wind chimes. "Let's go inside. We can talk it out with Joel and Lorraine in the morning."

"Oh no, I've got a hotel."

Garrison smiled. "You're not going to a hotel. We've got lots of extra rooms."

"Will Joel and Lorraine mind?"

"Not at all," Garrison said. He knew they'd be glad to have Molly. What Joel *would* mind, however, is waking up to find his wind chimes removed. Without them, there would be nothing to scare away the birds. "Besides, I need help getting these untwisted and hung back up before morning."

Molly stared at the knot of wind chimes. "That's gonna require at least two pots of coffee."

"Done." Garrison smiled at Molly. There was no sparkle in her eyes for him like before, but she returned an actual smile. Garrison understood this would take time. They had so much to talk about, so much to unravel, but there was plenty of time for that.

Garrison thought about his grandpa as he went to retrieve Molly's bag. Maybe now that Crawl was gone, Clancy wouldn't be afraid of the truth coming out—the truth that would not just set him free, but Joel too. Garrison's time with Joel had taught him that prisons came in many forms. Some surrounded by immovable metal bars, some by hanging bits of clanging metal.

But maybe the day would come when they'd all be under this roof together. Then maybe Joel wouldn't mind taking the wind chimes down and learning to wake up to a different kind of song.

ACKNOWLEDGEMENTS

Thank you to my husband Josh for sharing life and the computer with me. Specifically, thanks for the following: working so hard so I could stay home with Asa and write this book, helping me block out my fight scenes (doing my stunts), giving me some of my best lines, and never questioning why I was googling the most lethal place to stab someone. Most of all, thanks for never letting me give up.

To my children, Jaleigh, Brandon, Aidan, and Asa for giving me so many reasons to put down the pencil or look up from the screen. Of all I could accomplish in life, nothing could ever make me prouder than being your mom.

To Sarah Anderson, my best friend, who gave me the idea for this book and has remained its biggest cheerleader. I'm glad you didn't have to open a publishing company in your garage to see this in print, but I know you would have. We're the best team since Oprah and Gayle.

To my parents, Shannon and Tammy McClain, for giving me everything and asking nothing in return. Thanks for reading books in front of me, reading stories to me, buying me books, and taking me to the library (and Hastings) weekly. Most of all, thank you for my happy childhood.

To my late grandfather, Glen McClain, for sharing Friday dinners and war stories with me.

To the rest of my family, my (better than fairy) godmother, aunts, uncles, cousins, in-laws, etc. Thanks for your support and love throughout my life. It would take an entire book to list all your names, but you know who you are, and I hope you know what you mean to me. Special thanks to the Smith/Fisher bunch. I'm sure you don't have to ask why this novel is set in Carthage. Thanks for the memories.

To my amazing group of friends, Bethany, Summer, Drew, Monica, Josh, Tausha, Lonnie, Trisha, and Greg to name a few. Life is so much more fun with you in it. Special thanks to my book club girls. There isn't much that good friends, a good book, a good laugh, and a good Margarita can't cure.

To Mandy Woolsey, thanks for putting a heart on all my author Facebook posts and sending a late night encouraging message when I needed it most. And to Mandy Taylor for all your enthusiasm about this book and the notebooks to start my next one. The world needs more Mandys. Heather Bean, you have also been a steadfast source of encouragement throughout this process and throughout every season of my life. Whitney Hernandez, thanks for being my number one Facebook fan in spite of the fact that I once stabbed you with a fork.

To the late JoAn Smith for telling me I was a writer and letting me share my stories. To Loretta Funk for teaching me almost everything I know about writing and entering me into that essay contest. To Danny Holmes (and his sweet wife Diane) for being a debate coach, life coach, and for believing in everything I ever did.

To my second family at Sanger Elementary for making my day job so much fun and for all your support. I work with the best people and get to share a love for reading with the sweetest students. I could not ask for more.

To Lourdes Venard, who greatly improved this book with her insightful edit. Anyone who is glad there is an epilogue should thank her.

To Sheri Williams, thanks for taking a chance on this book and making a lifelong dream come true. I'm grateful for the hard work put in by you and your staff. Special thanks to my amazingly talented and amazingly encouraging editor, Kimberly Coghlan, for meticulously polishing this book and giving such sound advice. And thank you Dimitar Stanchev for a truly remarkable cover.

I can't write a book set in 1991 and not thank my cousin, first friend, and childhood sidekick, Brandon Smith. Also, Jessica Lewis Gray and the late Stacy Allen because we were the girls of the '90s, and so much of my imagination is thanks to them.

Finally, I'm thankful to God for putting all the above mentioned in my path. If our lives are a book, I'm glad I found you all in various chapters of mine.

Made in United States
Orlando, FL
02 July 2023

34701767R00195